INSANITY

A Psychic Visions Novel

Dale Mayer

INSANITY
Beverly Dale Mayer
Valley Publishing Ltd.

ISBN-13: 978-1-778862-87-8
Print Edition

Books in This Series

Insanity

Soul Legacy

About This Book

Dr. Cresswell Simmons, a dream worker, is passionate about traumatized psychics and works in a psychiatric hospital to find those she can help. Six months ago, she barely survived a traumatic experience with a patient. Now on the cusp of returning to work and dreading every minute of it, she's asked to step back into the same case that almost destroyed her. She desperately wants to say no, but an eight-year-old boy's life is at stake.

Gray Burnett had worked on the original case, watching the devastation that had hurt Cressy. When asked to help her retrieve the information they need, he agrees—but more to protect her and the little boy than following orders. When her return to work is less than joyful, he wonders at the undercurrents in the hospital, as jealousy, admin disputes, even Board of Director members dominate the investigation and not in a good way.

Cressy is used to a world that doesn't understand her work, but she needs Gray to open up and to see what's going on around them. It's the only way they will survive, as the case takes a bizarre turn that shocks even her ...

Sign up to be notified of all Dale's releases here!
https://geni.us/DaleNews

CHAPTER 1

CRESSWELL SIMMONS BLINKED in the darkness, the drum of the phone beside her slow and insistent. She groaned as she reached out a hand. She checked the number on the caller ID and whispered, "Dr. Maddy?"

"Sorry Cressy," Dr. Maddy muttered. "I forgot what time it was."

"Or what time zone it was. Where are you?"

"I'm in England right now."

"Great, that's nice for you. I'm in Maine. Remember?"

"I know. I'm just …"

"You just what?"

"I'm in trouble."

At that, Cressy bolted upright.

"What kind of trouble? Do I need to call Drew? Grant? What's going on?"

Dr. Maddy's laughter rolled free through the phone. "No, not that kind of trouble. I need help, very specialized help."

"Oh no, not again." Cressy moaned.

"Unfortunately you're the only one I know who can do something about this."

"And you know how it hurts me to do it," she muttered.

"And yet you're getting better at it," Dr. Maddy added encouragingly.

"At least you hope I am."

"We've certainly saved a lot of people," Dr. Maddy noted, "so I don't really want to think of this as being something that we can't do more of."

"Because it's not you going into these crazy minds and trying to figure out how to straighten them up and decide who is sane and who is not."

"I know. This one's ..."

"Special?" Cressy asked. "You say that every time. You do know that, right?" She pushed herself up against the headboard and rubbed the sleep from her eyes. Looking around the room in the dim light, she checked the alarm clock. "It's five in the morning," she muttered.

"Yep, I know. I know, and I'm sorry."

"It's fine. Who am I going after, and what's going on?"

Dr. Maddy began, "It's a male."

"That's a change," she noted, with a yawn. "Won't make a damn bit of difference, you know? I still might not get in."

"You might not be able to, but Stefan has had some luck with him, and I've had just enough luck to realize that he's there."

"And, if he's there, why isn't he coming out?"

"Now this is the part that gets dicey."

"*Uh-oh*, don't tell me this is another dangerous one. You know I don't like those."

"I know you don't, but this is a boy. He's only twelve years old, and his mind is still at the point where we can do something with it."

"Where is he?"

"He's in Bishop's Sanatorium," Dr. Maddy stated.

Cressy hated that, absolutely hated it whenever it involved a sanatorium. Especially that one—her home away from home—when she'd been working at least. "And who'll get me out when I get locked in there?"

"I'm really hoping you will get in and get out without any trouble."

"You're hoping for that, but you're not sure that it'll happen, are you?"

"I can't be sure. You know that. It's dicey, but both Stefan and I think that the boy's in there and that he's hiding."

"And why is he hiding?" she asked. "You need to give me some background."

"His family was murdered. By a *family annihilator*, as the FBI profilers call it," Dr. Maddy explained, her voice low.

"Great, and I suppose you found this one through Grant."

"I heard about him from Grant, and Grant gave me all the background history on the boy. Which is already rough enough."

"Are you sure the child even wants to come back out?"

"I don't think he knows he has a choice. I think he's hiding because he believes the annihilator is still coming after him."

"Was the annihilator caught?"

"Yes," Dr. Maddy confirmed. "He's been locked up, and this little boy needs to know that it's safe to come back out to reality."

"*Great*. Well, you make it sound easy enough, but, if it were easy, you would have done it already."

At that, she sighed. "No, I ... It's never that easy, is it?"

"No, it sure isn't."

"The boy has had some testing done, and basically he's nonviolent, but he's withdrawn, disassociated from society. One of his doctors has been working with him and saw obvious signs of stressors, where slight noises make him jump. All kinds of stuff are going on in there."

"Right, of course there is," Cressy agreed. "And how is it you think I'll get him out?"

"I need you to go in there. I need you to go into his head and to tell him it's okay."

"Again, if it were that easy, you would have done it already. So what's the trick?"

"The trick is, he's not listening," Dr. Maddy shared. "As far as he's concerned, the wrong person was caught, and so he doesn't believe us. I haven't been able to convince him otherwise."

Cressy pondered that for a moment. "Okay. And you think it's all part of the boy's delusion?"

"Yes, I do. Grant does. Everybody does. We have a confession from the killer, so the boy should be free and clear. Yet he doesn't want to come out. I think he's just so caught up in his own psychopathy that he can't get out."

"Fine, I'll try," Cressy stated, "but, even if I can talk to him, that's no guarantee that he'll want to come out. You know it's safe in there."

"It is safe," Dr. Maddy acknowledged, "which is why he's there. I just need you to try."

"Is there something else that is special about this one?"

"There's always something special, but yes. He has a grandmother who's desperate to have him come back to her. The poor grandmother lost everybody, and now it's just this little boy and an aunt. We want to give him a chance at life."

"How long ago did this happen?"

"Four months."

Cressy winced at that. "Just enough time for him to settle in there."

"I know, and that's why it'll take somebody special, like you."

"Yeah, you know that the sympathy and flattery stuff really doesn't work on me."

At that, Dr. Maddy laughed. "I know, but will you try?"

"Yeah, I'll try. I also want the name of the FBI agent assigned to the case."

"Why is that?"

"Because I need to know what this boy went through and what he's built for a retreat, a shelter in his own head, so I can make him realize the world outside of that shelter is also safe. And Lord help us all if we're wrong ..."

"I can give you his name," Dr. Maddy replied, "but—"

"Oh, don't tell me. He's a nonbeliever, I suppose."

"Yeah, he is. He knows that Drew's married to me and that we have both worked with FBI Agent Grant Summers before, but, as far as this other agent is concerned, it's all BS."

"And is that because he's also very gifted and he's ignoring it or because he only sees black-and-white?"

"I've only met him one time, and I would tend to say he only sees black-and-white, but I don't really know," Dr. Dr. Maddy admitted. "That's up to you to sort out."

"You never make it easy, do you?"

"It's not me," she replied. "I'm a pushover for kids. ... Last time we talked, so were you."

"That's a low blow." Cressy growled into the phone.

"No, you're right. It is. I'm just ... I need you to go in after him."

"I told you that I would," Cressy repeated, "but I'm not going in unprepared. And you know what happens if I open up that line."

"I know. I do. Stefan will help. I'll be there, and, on this end, if you contact that FBI agent, we can make sure that nothing else happens."

"Yeah, but once we open the doors to crazy, crazy comes out," Cressy declared.

"And, when we open the doors to somebody who's hiding," Dr. Maddy added, "joy, laughter, and love can come out again. Let's give this little boy a chance."

"Fine," Cressy said, "but I'm calling the agent in the morning."

"You don't have to. He'll be there in an hour." And, with that, Dr. Maddy started to hang up.

"What's his name?" Cressy cried out.

Dr. Maddy's voice rang out loud and clear. "His name is Gray, and you met him last time. He was there." Then Dr. Maddy hung up, leaving Cressy to stare down at the phone in dismay.

She also hadn't asked for the name of the boy, but she knew the file would be coming. All the files would be. It's also why there would be an FBI agent attached, whether she asked for it or not. Obviously a whole lot more was going on in this case than Dr. Maddy had let on. Especially if the FBI would be at her door in an hour.

With that, she threw back the covers and headed for the shower. In spite of herself, she was intrigued. And a little scared. The last time she'd been caught up in one of Dr. Maddy's cases, Dr. Maddy had damn-near died. Cressy really wasn't about to sign up for another one of those again.

Yet, as she stepped into the bathroom and stared into the mirror, she shook her head. "Seems you did it anyway, fool." Then she got in and turned on the water.

CHAPTER 2

*K*NOCK-KNOCK. *KNOCK-KNOCK.*

Cressy stared at the door, her brows furrowing, as she studied the huge wooden piece. It had been a long time since she'd opened the door to strangers.

When a voice on the other side called out, "Dr. Cresswell Simmons? This is FBI Agent Gray Burnett."

She stared at the door with dread. She knew perfectly well that, once she opened it, *if* she opened it, there was no going back. But she still hadn't found a way to come to terms with what she was about to do. She got up and slowly walked toward the door, then opened up the little peephole and stared out, expecting to see a stranger on the other side, but this wasn't some stranger.

She opened the door to frown at him. "Don't I know you?"

He slowly nodded. "Yes, we've met."

She wasn't sure about where or when, but then she'd blocked out a lot of things in life that were unpleasant. The fact that she recognized him and yet didn't remember how she knew him meant that he belonged to an era that she did not want to recall. Slowly she opened the door wider and let him in.

He stepped inside, took a casual look around, and then turned to face her.

That's when it hit her. "You were part of the case," she murmured, staring at him, the fear rising deep inside her.

"I was. I was one of the FBI agents working that case back then."

She wrapped her arms around her chest, then closed the door and slowly walked back into her living room. "And you're here now. Why is that?" she asked, realizing her tone was hard.

He hesitated, then asked, "Did Dr. Maddy contact you?"

"Yes." Then she noted another connection. "You're the one who works with Grant."

He nodded. "I am. … Are you okay?"

She gave a bitter laugh. "How is anybody ever okay after something like that?"

"Look. I don't know why you even agreed to do this," he began. "I know what you went through last time, at least some of it, and it was pretty traumatizing."

"Yeah, it was," she confirmed, tossing him a look, "but I'm not some delicate flower."

He stared at her. "I never thought you were, but it was only a few months ago."

"Six months actually." She shook her head and stared out the window. "A pretty long six months."

He nodded in agreement.

"Why you?" she asked, turning to look at him.

"I honestly don't know. Grant just told me that I was connected."

Her eyebrows shot up at that. "Did he say in what way?"

"No, just that Dr. Maddy had insisted that it needed to be me. I don't know more than that." He hesitated and then raised both hands, as if frustrated in his own right. "I don't have much to do with this stuff, you know? I'm not a believer," he admitted, gentling his tone. "I'm not trying to insult you guys because I've seen some phenomenal work, especially from Dr. Maddy and Stefan."

"Yet you're still not a believer." She frowned. "Even though you just shared how you've seen some incredible things."

He studied her and then nodded again. "I know, and it sounds like a complete dichotomy. I get it."

"Because it is," she replied in exasperation. "You either believe what they've achieved, or you don't, in which case you're probably on the wrong side of the fence and definitely aren't the person I need with me for this battle."

"You say that as if you'll be at war," he noted cautiously.

She glared at him. "What do you think that last battle was?"

He winced at that. "From what I saw, it was some kind of a strange off-the-charts commotion, yes," he confirmed. "If you're thinking it'll be like that again, why would you even agree to do this?"

"Because apparently a twelve-year-old boy is at the heart of this."

"Yes, there is that." He let out a sigh.

"The question I'm struggling with is, why you agreed to go."

"Because a twelve-year-old boy is at the heart of this," he repeated.

At that, she realized he didn't want to be here, but he would do it just because of that boy. She blew out her breath. "That was the right answer." She gave him a weak smile.

His lips twitched. "I'm glad I passed one test, at least," he muttered. "But for somebody who doesn't deal with it all the time, this isn't very comfortable stuff."

"For somebody who *does* deal with it a lot, it's also not comfortable stuff, so don't kid yourself. What I do is already at the edge of normal in my world, and I take it way past *my* normal," she stated boldly. "I have a degree, and I work in a field where I have the respect of my colleagues for the results that I achieve, but they don't realize the kind of inside work I really do on the patients."

At that, a grimace slid across his face, and he gave a clipped nod. "Everything I've heard about what you do sounds like fantasy—or rather some horror movie."

"After the last time, absolutely," she agreed. "I had come up against something like that before, but never with that kind of power, that kind of strength," she whispered, wrapping her arms around herself. When she realized that they still stood in the front hallway, she motioned toward the living room. "Please, come in and sit down."

He hesitated, then kicked off his shoes and walked in, settling in the single armchair.

She looked over at him and smiled. "Obviously you're not at ease."

He shrugged. "Would you be?"

"I don't know," she replied. "I've never been in your situation."

"How did you get into this?" he asked curiously.

She snorted at that. "I'm not sure anybody *gets* into this. As you can imagine, I didn't have much choice."

"It would help me to understand if you could explain a little bit."

"Explain how I got into doing what I'm doing?" A bit of exasperation was evident in her voice. "An explanation will not help you at all. It won't make what we are facing any less challenging, and it sure as hell won't make it easier on me."

He stared off in a corner for a moment, then finally turned back to her. "Stefan told me that you wouldn't be easy."

She burst out laughing. "*Easy* isn't part of my domain."

"Dr. Maddy explained how it was a defense mechanism, kind of like a fear reflex."

She winced. "Yeah, see? That's the problem when working with people who understand what you're going through. There really is no privacy."

"Maybe not, yet we're here to accomplish one thing, and that's to see if there is a whole, sane boy on the inside, hiding from the world."

"Oh, he's there all right," she declared, "but apparently the family annihilator is right there with him."

Gray flattened his back against the chair and just stared at her. When his phone buzzed, he pulled it out and answered it automatically. "Hey, Grant. Yeah, I'm here," he answered calmly, but he knew his tone was off, and no way he would fool Grant, since they'd been close friends for well over a decade.

"Yeah, I know what you're going through," Grant said. "A bit of a shock, isn't it?"

"I'd seen her before, so some of it isn't a shock." And then he frowned at her, almost smiling inside when she gave him a frown right back.

"She's thinner than last time," Gray noted, narrowing his gaze as he eyed her. "Looks like she's had a hard time."

She snorted at that, then got up and walked into the kitchen.

He grinned and kept on talking. "Yeah, she just left the room." As soon as he thought she was out of earshot, he whispered into the phone, "What the hell?"

"I know. I know," Grant replied in a soothing tone. "It'll be bad. We get it. Or it could be bad anyway."

"Oh, no doubt about it. You missed what she just told me."

"What's that?"

"She said the annihilator is still in the boy's head—or something along that line," he clarified, yet still confused. "So, don't ask me any questions about it. That's something that needs to go back to Dr. Maddy and Stefan. Not sure Dr. Cresswell's totally sane."

"I'll talk to Dr. Maddy right away because that's not my understanding. I thought this would be a routine checkup, and all we needed was to confirm that the boy was really where he needed to be or that somebody there could help him," Grant stated, his voice sharp. "I'll get back to you." With that, Grant hung up.

As Gray sat here, trying to digest the little bit of information he had, … Cressy came back out into the living room, holding two cups of coffee. She held one out for him, which he gratefully accepted. "How did you know I like it black Dr. Cresswell?"

She snorted. "It wasn't hard, since that seems to be the way any 'real man' takes it," she declared, with an eye roll. "And call me Cressy. Everyone does."

He nodded in acknowledgement. "I'll admit that Grant and I both take it that way."

"Yep, and so do Rohan and Nick and a couple other FBI agents I've met over the years. A simple thing to remember."

He chuckled. "I appreciate it." She didn't respond and just sat back down again. "Look. Can I ask you what you mean when you said the annihilator is still there?"

"The boy saw something, and, when he saw something, he internalized it."

"Okay." When she didn't say anything else, he became restless. "I get that you don't want to share information, but it's kind of awkward, as if I'm trying to pull teeth here. I wasn't aware that the boy knew, saw, or had any information on the annihilator."

"I don't know that he has any info, nor did I say he had any," she corrected. "That's a different story."

He blinked. "Sorry?"

She sighed. "Just because the boy has experienced what he has, the information is in his memory banks, but that doesn't mean he knows it's there. Nor does it mean he can pull out that information."

"So he really can't help us solve the case?"

She frowned at him. "You haven't solved it?"

He frowned right back. "No."

"*Great*," she muttered under her breath. "I wasn't aware of that either." Just then her phone rang. "Yes, Stefan," she answered, with something akin to disgust in her tone. "He's here."

Gray immediately leaned forward and spoke. "Stefan, I'm here."

She put the phone down and announced, "Go ahead. You're on Speakerphone."

"I'm glad you two have met again," Stefan began calmly.

"You could have told me it would be him," Cressy noted.

"Would you have let him in the door?" Stefan asked.

She sighed. "I don't know. I didn't get a chance to decide that though, did I?"

He chuckled. "I think I know by now how you would

have reacted."

"So, in other words, I wasn't given a chance to react, and, once again, you were manipulating the situation. That seems to be a recurring thing."

Silence came on the other end, and even Gray was surprised, since very few people ever spoke to Stefan like that.

His tone was mild as he replied, "Get up on the wrong side of the bed this morning?"

"Yeah, ever since Dr. Maddy put in the request," Cressy muttered.

"It is a twelve-year-old boy, and I think he deserves a chance in life."

"Sure he does, but you do realize that—"

Before she could say anything more, Gray leaned forward and interrupted, before it got out of hand. This was not getting them anywhere. "Stefan, she mentioned something about the annihilator being there." When another round of silence came from the other end, Gray turned to see her frowning at him. "Unless she was just saying that to get rid of me."

She rolled her eyes. "I don't have time to spend saying crap just to get rid of you. The door is right there. I could just kick you out."

"I don't kick out that easily," Gray noted mildly.

"You just might in a case like this," she pointed out, her tone turning heavy.

Stefan, his voice hard, intervened. "Zip it, both of you. Are you sure about the annihilator, Cressy?"

"Of course I'm sure," she snapped. "I just don't know how much. I don't know whether it's just his memories, the little bit that he saw, or what. I don't know. But I also wasn't aware that this case hadn't been solved. You have to know that is a completely different story, as far as I'm concerned."

She heard voices in the background and realized Stefan was talking to somebody. "Grant says they have a lead on somebody, and he is nowhere near the boy."

She pinched the bridge of her nose.

Gray could tell that, whatever it was, it was upsetting her even more. "She doesn't appear to like that answer," he told Stefan. "Maybe it will help to know we did have a suspect charged and awaiting trial, but we're concerned it's the wrong suspect."

Stefan, his voice clipped, added, "I can take another look."

"Yeah, you need to," Cressy replied. Then she whispered, "I'm not sure I'm up for this."

Stefan's voice softened. "Look. If there was anyone else I could call, I would have, but you've had six months to get back out there."

"*Great*, thanks. *Hey, anybody else could have done this in that time, no problem. You've had your holiday, now get your act together and get out there.* That's it, right?"

"No," Stefan countered. "You know that's not what I meant."

"Maybe not, but I get it. You don't think I recognize that I'm taking a cowardly way out by not doing this work anymore?"

"It's not cowardly," Stefan declared. "Very few people have ever endured the kind of a scenario you had and survived. The fact that you *did* survive already makes you very special."

"*Great.* So, what do you want to bet that there isn't some sort of billboard to the spirits on the other side, saying, *Hey, look. She's the best of the best. Why don't you come give her another try? Anybody else? Any other takers? Let's put bets on it too.*" Her tone was irate by then. She got up and paced around the room, a small, lean fireball.

Watching her pace was giving Gray a headache. He leaned forward and whispered, "Stefan, is this dangerous for her?"

"Sure it's dangerous," Stefan replied, "and she knows that. We will do everything we can to minimize the danger. We underestimated just how dangerous her last case was. That blew up on us. We weren't prepared."

At that, she raced over to the coffee table, where her phone was, then leaned over it and stated, "We couldn't have done anything about it anyway."

"Do you think I don't consider that all the time too? You've been doing this work for a very long time. We've been helping a lot of people, but unfortunately there always seems to be more people to help. I do feel responsible for what you went through."

She groaned. "Look. You're not responsible, Stefan. I know that. I never held you responsible for it."

"You might not have, but that doesn't mean that I don't hold myself responsible," Stefan stated calmly. "We were working the case together, and neither of us had any idea it would blow up in our faces. Everything aside, we survived."

"Sure, we survived, but you went on to live a normal life, whereas I've been basically hiding in my apartment for six months."

"Isn't it time to come out then?" Gray asked her in a reasonable tone.

She turned and glared at him. "*Sure*, you handle the ghosties this time then, and we'll see how quickly you come out of your sanctuary afterward."

He pondered that. "I guess that's what it's all about though, isn't it? You're afraid."

She stared at him and, in dulcet tones, said, "Wow, give the man a prize."

He winced. "Look. I'm not trying to be thick over this, or difficult. I just mean that, if this is something you can't do, then I may as well go because we're just wasting time."

She groaned. "It wouldn't be so bad, but…"

"But what?" he asked, still bewildered.

"But what if it happens again?" she asked, glaring at him. "What if I'm walking right back into the same scenario I just got out of?"

He let out his breath slowly. "Is that even a possibility? I mean, surely the last time, when whatever happened, happened—and believe me. I haven't spent too much time thinking about it because it gives me the heebie-jeebies," he admitted, looking suspiciously around, "but is it really possible that something like that could ever happen a second time?"

"Yes," Stefan confirmed through the phone. "It is possible. Is it likely? No, but it is possible."

For the first time, Gray was starting to understand what was going on here. "So, are we seriously thinking this will be a repeat of that nightmare?" Her reluctance made some sense now. "I couldn't even come to grips with what happened last time. You know perfectly well that I'm not a great believer in any of this stuff, and, as she pointed out when I just told her that, it makes absolutely no sense, not when I've seen the remarkable things that you and Dr. Maddy have done."

"Which doesn't make me feel any better," Stefan admitted, "because she's right. Either you're a believer or you're not."

At that, Grant joined the conversation. "I don't know about that, Stefan," Grant added. "I can't do any of the stuff that you do, but I have seen enough that I no longer disbelieve. If you or Dr. Maddy tell me that I need to do something, and it's for the sake of saving lives, I do it and ask questions later. It took me a while to get there, but obviously Dr. Maddy has helped me on various FBI cases, and that has helped bring my belief system forward a little bit."

"Ya think?" Stefan quipped.

"Where is the boy staying?" Cressy asked shakily, but Gray could tell from the dread in her voice that she already knew.

Stefan replied, "You know where he is. He's being held at your local facility."

"Of course. My facility, right?"

"Yes," Stefan confirmed. "You still have an operating license, don't you?"

"If you mean, privileges at that hospital, yes, I do. So, was that the other reason you called me?"

"Yes, because you have privileges there," he admitted. "Though I could probably have gotten you in as a guest anyway. You're on a sabbatical. Is that correct?"

"Yes, but it's just about over. I've been getting questioned by my colleagues about whether or not I'm coming back. Up until now, the answer was an absolute yes," she muttered. "Or at least to ease back into it gently."

Gray watched her carefully, now that he understood more. He had been around some last time and had heard more about it afterward. Still he hadn't fully known what was going on, and maybe that was a problem now as well. "Look. I only came over to talk with her.," he admitted, staring at the phone. "Grant wanted me to come over."

"He wanted you here, so I could assess your energy and could confirm that I could work with you," she shared. "I just wasn't aware that this would all be happening right now."

"Yet you know that time is of the essence," Gray noted.

"Sure," she muttered. "Time is always of the essence."

Stefan, his voice warm, added, "Cressy, I know that this is something you've been holding off on, and I agree wholeheartedly that you should be getting back to work and all, but I certainly understand if you've been trying to tell yourself that you're not ready."

She snorted at that. "Trying to tell myself I'm not ready?" She shook her head. "I know I'm ready to a certain extent. I also know that this is not something I really want anything to do with, but, as agreed, I will go to the hospital and meet him."

"Good," Stefan replied, a note of satisfaction in his voice.

"But I'm not guaranteeing anything," she stated. "I might not even connect with the boy. As you probably know, I shut down everything for quite some time."

"I know you did," Stefan said. "That's part of the reason for the sabbatical. You burned out and, when you burn out, it can take a while to come back again."

"And that's only if I'm prepared to come back," she stated in a husky tone.

"Got it," Stefan replied. "I do appreciate the fact that you're willing to talk to the boy."

"Right," she muttered. "I was already booked to return to the office on Monday."

"You could go a little earlier, just to see where things are at the place, right?" Gray asked her.

Cressy sighed. "Yes, I could."

"What reason did you give for your absence?" Gray asked.

"I took a sabbatical for research."

"That works," Gray replied, "so nobody will question you too much."

"Except for asking questions about the research I was doing," she murmured. "I really don't want to give too many explanations."

"Don't give any if you don't have to," Gray suggested. "Sounds as if maybe keeping things quiet is more important."

"It's not always that easy," she noted. "Colleagues can be fairly persistent when they're looking to see what kind of work you're doing, since our jobs are only as safe as our results. The work is more of a life for us, and, if I've come back with new techniques, they'll want to know about it."

"Would you normally share?"

She gave him half a smile. "In my line of work I would normally share all kinds of things, but nobody—and I do mean *nobody* but the people on this phone call and Dr. Maddy—understand exactly what I do."

At that, Stefan laughed. "I don't even understand what you do. I understand the results, and I understand you're a miracle worker, but that's about it."

"Fine, I'll go in on Monday." When Stefan went silent, she groaned. "You want me to go in now, don't you? As in right now?"

"I don't know what's wrong with the boy at present," Stefan admitted apologetically, "but it seems something is changing, something is moving."

"And you can't sort it out?" she asked.

Stefan laughed. "No. Contrary to what everyone believes, I can't do everything all the time."

"Wow, that must have been an unfortunate surprise for you," Cressy quipped.

Stefan snorted. "You do know that you're the only person who ever talks to me like that?"

"The world would be better if more people did," she declared.

"You're just mad because I told Dr. Maddy to call you."

"You could have called me yourself, you know?"

"I could have, but I figured that the first contact after all this time would be better coming from her."

"You mean, the *request* would be better coming from her." Then Cressy let out a big heavy sigh. "You also knew I couldn't turn down anything to do with a twelve-year-old boy."

"I would like to know more about how that works," Gray said, from beside her.

She glanced at him and shrugged. "Part of the reason I got into this was, when my sister was eight, she had a psychotic episode and ended up in an institution herself. The only way I could stay in contact with her was … to do what I do."

"But what is it that you do?" Gray stared at her in frustration. "I have no idea what you were doing, but honestly all I saw last time was you going berserk. So, I wasn't at all sure what to think when I was asked to come help you now, and all I could think was, *Why me?*"

She studied him for a moment, then laughed and laughed. When she could finally speak again, she muttered, "Good God, you really have a death wish to show up now, if that's what you thought was going on last time."

"Nobody explained anything. At least not in any way that I could understand."

"That's the kicker," she noted. "Somebody may or may not have attempted to explain, but it's not the easiest thing to explain or to understand, so that's a whole different step."

"When and how did you contact your sister?" Gray asked, his tone mutinous.

She grinned. "I went into her mind to say hi."

He frowned at her. "Did she say hi back?"

"She absolutely did," Cressy confirmed. "I was the only one who could reach her, the only one who could talk to her, so I went dancing through her mind."

"Are you sure you were actually talking to her? I mean, you were just a kid yourself, right? How old were you?"

"I was ten," she replied. "As the older sister I felt responsible for her."

"Oh, I get that. I have a kid sister myself, but I don't go dancing through her mind. And that's ... a very strange way to put it."

"Not really," she corrected, with a heavy sigh. "All kinds of things are in people's minds that you don't want to touch on, and you don't really have any way of knowing how the filing system in each individual brain is set up. So, I open a door, ... check it out, and just choose to look further or to leave and try the next door. I call it *dancing through their mind* because I go from one aspect of their mind to another, until I get to wherever I need to be."

"And where you need to be is what?"

"In my sister's case, I needed to be where she was, the personality at her core. I knew that was the part of her I could talk to, so I could get her to come home."

"Come home?"

She studied him and shook her head. "You should tell Grant that you need to take on a different job and just refuse this one," she declared. "You'll sleep better at night."

"Probably, but I'm not the kind of person to walk away from a challenge."

"This isn't exactly a challenge," she argued, "but you might consider the fact that this will potentially be a very difficult scenario for you."

"You still aren't telling me anything."

"Nothing to tell," she replied in exasperation. "I go into people's minds, and I find out where they're at, what they're thinking, and how they're thinking. Then, based on my medical training, I diagnose them on whether they're actually psychotic or maybe just caught up in their own crazy world and don't know how to get out of it or many other different scenarios. Therefore, you might want to tell Grant you want to change jobs."

At that, Grant, who was still on the phone, along with Stefan, spoke up. "And, of course, I would tell him that he could walk away, except for the fact that Dr. Maddy says he's important."

"Stefan, why is he important?" Cressy asked.

"Because he was there the last time," he murmured. "Cressy, you pulled on Gray's energy as a ground."

Startled, she turned and stared at him. "I did?"

Gray just shrugged, having no idea what that meant.

"You did," Stefan declared. "So the fact that Gray functioned as a ground for you, seemingly unaware, while you used that to keep your own sanity, means that, if we run into problems in this case, Gray's the person I would want there with you to help you out."

"Even though I have no idea what you're talking about

and no idea how to do whatever it is that you think that I should do?" Gray asked, feeling more confused than ever.

"The thing is, you don't need to do anything, Gray," Stefan shared. "You have an energy that's compatible with hers. So what you would need to do is just give her permission to do what she needs to do."

At that, she burst out laughing. "If you guys could see the look on his face right now, it's priceless. He's trying to figure out how to run, and you really should let him." In between giggles, she was trying to keep her voice steady. "It's really not fair to him."

"Maybe not," Stefan admitted, "but the only reason you survived last time is because of him, so he stays."

CHAPTER 3

CRESSY WATCHED AS Gray left soon afterward. He hadn't said a whole lot more, and neither had she. He hadn't quit or asked for a transfer, but she was waiting for it. It was a bit scary for him and for her, particularly after what Stefan had shared. Gray didn't really feel as if he had any business being involved in this, and she understood that, but she also needed to assess what Stefan had revealed. Because, if she would do this, she would definitely stack the deck in her favor. Not to the extent of hurting somebody else because that would never work out karmically, but, if having Gray there would make a difference, then she would have him there.

As soon as he was gone, she phoned her office and checked in with her administrative assistant, who'd been assigned to help one of the other doctors in the meantime. Cressy told her admin that she would come in and do some work and just get a feel for the place again over the weekend. It was Friday, and her assistant was more than excited to know she was returning. They had always had a great working relationship but hadn't had contact while Cressy had been gone because she literally had come home to heal.

Cressy had managed her patient cases for a couple months, from a distance, in order to keep things moving through the system, but, after that, she had pretty well just crashed and burned, stepping away completely to heal, until she could actually start to think again. Now it was hard to know what to do, but the choices weren't terribly great either. She would do what she needed to do, and, if that meant helping this twelve-year-old boy, that's what she would do. Still, the whole scenario was difficult.

She knew Stefan didn't mean to put her on the spot, but he would do anything to help the people out there who were like them. Obviously this boy was gifted and didn't belong in a sanatorium. Normally she would have rushed in to help the boy, but, after enduring the firestorm she'd previously been involved in, she hesitated.

As she slowly rebuilt herself over these last six months, she'd been forced to face the fact that she wasn't as strong as she wanted to be. Not only that, but that her skills were lacking. It was a double blow. It was a bit like a loss of innocence, and, in that sense, it was devastating.

Devastating, yet, according to Stefan, also necessary to help Cressy come to terms with the type of work she did and to find peace with it. Of course, all of that sounded fine and dandy when it wasn't about her, but when it *was* about her, then it was a different story. Maybe she needed the rest anyway. She'd been pulling night shifts for what had seemed like an endless amount of time because it gave her easier access to the people in the way that she needed.

It was one thing to dance through their minds, but another thing completely to sit down and actually communicate with them, all to help them find their way home again. She had to do that in the privacy of her own office—or sometimes in their hospital rooms. However, since everything was recorded, she had to be careful that nothing she did in the *too-far-out-there* variety ended up on tape. So, *work and don't leave proof* was her mantra.

She did have a few people in her professional world who thought that Cressy shouldn't be allowed to do anything like this work, and a few had no idea what she even did. That made it even harder for Cressy to function, knowing that some people were out to get her.

Whether Cressy liked it or not, not everybody in the world wanted her to succeed.

BY SATURDAY MORNING, Cressy had had a good night's sleep, and that helped. She knew the fear was something she would just have to temper down. Plus, once she had done some of this work again, it would definitely be easier. Kinda like falling off a horse in that you had to force yourself to get back on in order to keep enjoying the sport. Still, it's not as if she enjoyed her gift as sport, but she knew she did good work, and people out there needed what she could do. That left her very little in the way of options, other than to just get back to work.

On the surface, it all sounded easy. Everything sounded fine, until it actually came time to do something like that, and then it wasn't quite so easy at all. However, she'd been doing this work for a lot of years, a lot of it as a professional, after she finally got her degrees. She'd worked on the side in a practicum as an assistant for many years as well.

So, getting back to work was just another step, another thing she needed to do in order to keep her professional status going. She had enjoyed her time off and had definitely needed it. She had been running herself into the ground long before that incident anyway, so a rest was good. She had done a lot of research and had taken the time to write up her notes into some sort of semi-coherent book.

As she got ready for her day, she pondered her options. If she were to officially meet this boy, she should probably take Gray with her, although it would look kind of odd to have him along—unless he'd already been assigned to the boy for a particular reason that only the FBI knew. Cressy had already told her admin to expect her there this weekend, so Cressy would go into the office early, by herself, just for an initial look-see, as she was slated to return to work full-time on Monday anyway.

As she considered that, she noted that solution felt much better regardless. She could go in before her coworkers all got in and could actually settle into being back in the space again. She could visit some of the patients, take a look at the client and the employee rosters, see who was new, who was different.

As she thought about it, she warmed to the idea even more. Not giving herself a chance to change her mind, she had breakfast, dressed for work, packed her bag, and headed to the center. As she walked in the front doors, the security guard looked at her, frowned for a moment, then his face cleared.

"Dr. Cresswell," he greeted her, with a beaming smile. "Are you back already?"

She laughed. "I am. It's been a long time."

"It has, and yet it hasn't," he replied, with a bashful grin. "It's nice to see you back here again, where you belong."

"Thank you, Jerome." She gave him a beaming smile. "I needed the rest though."

"Oh, that you did," he agreed. "You always worked yourself to the bone, but you're looking much better."

She grinned at him. "You always were a charmer."

"You're an easy one to charm." He waved at her and added, "Go on in. I don't think you'll find that much has changed at all."

"Oh, I think there'll be a few things," she replied. "At least I hope so."

He laughed at that. "Let's hope it's all good things."

And, with that, their banter concluded, and she headed inside, noting that her badge still worked on all the doors, which made her feel better. Nothing like having credentials that gave you control over where you went and what you went for, and, to a certain degree, that's what the key card gave her. She'd never really lost her access, the way she had lost what seemed like so much else in her life. Most of all was that sense of control, after the big blowup.

In this moment, it was just nice to know that some things were still functioning. Maybe in her heart of hearts, she was worried that somebody would have mentioned something—about what must have looked like a complete breakdown to many people. Maybe some thought Cressy wasn't fit to work anymore.

However, remembering that her own boss had contacted her not long ago—to verify that she was still coming back on time and appeared to be relieved when Cressy had confirmed that she was—she immediately discarded that idea and realized that she really was needed and wanted here. The fact that some people in her world didn't like to see her doing well wasn't her problem. It had always been and always would be their problem, not hers.

As she walked inside her office, she smiled as she noted how much was the same. Six months had seemed like a long time, yet it really didn't appear that much had changed at all. In a way, that was also kind of depressing as well. You would like to think that, over time, things would have shifted in some way, but there was a timeless look to the place, as if it were somehow above the ravages of time. She smiled at several of the receptionists. One was new, but another bounded to her feet in excitement, immediately running in her direction.

"Dr. Cressy," Mallory cried out, giving her a big hug. "It's so good to see you. I didn't think you were coming back until next week."

Cressy muttered, "I just wanted to get in, to see my office, to reorient myself with the grindstone, plus check out some files, all before I came in, ready to hit the ground running on Monday."

"Sure, that makes perfect sense. We're so glad to have you back," she declared. "The place has been a nuthouse ever since you left."

It was an old joke, and Cressy smiled to hear it again. "Considering we're actually in a nuthouse …" she whispered.

"Right? People don't believe that when I tell them where I work," she shared, with a chuckle.

"That's because, you know, respect for the patients and all."

Mallory smiled. "Yep, I hear you. It is what it is." She beamed at her and let her go. "If you need anything, just let me know."

"Yes, I will. Is any coffee on?"

"Coffee's *always* on. You know that," she teased. "It's the lifeblood of this place, at least for most of us."

And it was. Almost everybody would have agreed with that comment. Cressy smiled and nodded. "I'll grab some on my way through."

She headed over to her office and stepped inside, quickly

closing the door behind her. An eerie silence filled the place in a way that she hadn't really expected. Yet why wouldn't there be? It's not as if anybody had used her office in the meantime. This was a massive building, and, when Cressy had gone on her sabbatical, the place had been short-staffed as it was. She couldn't imagine it was any different now.

They were always looking for people to come and work for them. It was just one of the hardships in their world these days. There was always a shortage of help, and they struggled, desperately needing good doctors and good orderlies too. Cressy had no idea who was still here and who wasn't. She would get a staff list and figure it out as she went.

She would know a lot of people, and she probably wouldn't know an awful lot of others. It was just the way life would be for a while. She smiled as she sat down at her desk, then kicked back, put her feet up on the desk, and crossed her hands at the back of her head. It really was good to be back. She pondered all the reasons why she had held off. Most of it was out of fear, yet she could talk to almost nobody about that because nobody really understood everything she'd been through. No one but Stefan.

Since Stefan was the one pushing her to come back here, she wondered if he was doing it mostly because he realized she needed to get out of this six-month holiday-resort mentality she had been working under.

At that, he popped into her mind. *Feels good, doesn't it?*

"It does," she murmured, "but I'm not telling you that." He laughed at that, and she grinned. In her own office she could talk to him out loud, but she didn't dare do it when anybody else was around.

How are you feeling? he asked.

"Better, but worried. I'm okay though."

The worry is natural. However, you'll do just fine.

"The job is okay," she murmured. "I don't know how many of my patients are still here. I'll have to start at the beginning. That was the hardest thing, when I walked away. I had patients in need of treatment, some who were getting quite a bit better, and I just … I had to leave."

At some point in time, Stefan stated, *you must do what you need to do for yourself. We all do. You were burned out, and, as I recall, you were well on your way to that before our fiasco.*

"Was I?" she murmured. "Or was I just, I don't know, maybe I wasn't so much burned out as just needing more of a break."

Same diff, Stefan stated. *Burned out is burned out, no matter what you call it.*

She laughed. "Fine, I certainly needed more downtime, and I'll take more in the future, if and when I am done here."

I wonder, he murmured. *You're really not very good at taking time off before it's a necessity.*

She chuckled. "No, I'm not."

Did you give any more thought to having Gray around?

"Do I have a choice?" she asked. "I figured that would be something you guys insisted on."

We're trying not to insist on anything, he replied. *You know as well as I do that we have to work with the right energy, and, if we fall into that trap of insisting, then we don't have the right energy to work with …*

"Right, I know," she murmured. "I get it. I actually came in early so I could get the feel of the place again, and so I wouldn't worry about that all weekend. Plus I don't want that to happen on day one."

I'm glad you did. Plus it also gives us a chance to talk.

"Have you worked with anybody in here since?"

Nope, and that's actually been good too.

"I'm sure it has been," she said. "I do know that I left quite a few patients in the lurch, and that was hard for me. Hopefully now I can catch back up again."

You might find a bit more professional jealousy in the mix now.

"That will be a certainty," she agreed, with a laugh. "Not just because I took time off and actually got a sabbatical out of the deal but, aside from that, not everybody appreciated the way I went about it."

Of course not, Stefan noted. *All your time and effort? Everybody else wanted a piece of it.*

"Does anybody else really know what happened?" she asked cautiously.

No, I don't believe so.

"After we are done here, I'll get up and take a walk around and see who's here, who's not, and then get an update on the files," she murmured.

Good enough, and, if you sense anything at all, let me know.

"You mean, before I go see him?"

I highly suggest you take a covert visit first.

"Oh, I plan on it. Don't worry. I won't approach him without that. You're pretty sure he's in here, *huh?*"

I'm pretty sure he's in there, Stefan confirmed. *I'm just not sure what he's doing.*

And, with that, Stefan was gone.

Startled, she frowned, wishing Stefan had elaborated on that last point. Because *what he was doing* was one thing, but Stefan made it sound like the boy was doing something that startled Stefan, and that in itself was a whole different ball game.

With a few minutes to log in to her computer, she brought up several of the last notes on the meetings and went over a bunch. Then looked at the case files of the new patients who had arrived in the last six months. There was always somebody new, and she just didn't have any way of knowing who, not until she had a chance to log in and to check it out.

With that done, she noted that two hours had already gone by, and she still hadn't grabbed that coffee. That was kind of her life here. Always so much to do, so many patients, that Cressy found herself going from one thing to the next to the next. She got up and walked over to the luncheon area, where there was a coffee station, and thankfully found a fresh pot.

She quickly poured herself a cup, and, with her keys and her coffee, knowing it was late morning already, and various people were out and about, Cressy headed out and just wandered for a bit. She stopped to talk to several patients, some who knew her. Several others didn't know anybody. Many were on medication and were responding really well since she'd left, and that was good news. Also, as expected, several had deteriorated.

She understood why for a couple of them, and would work with them as soon as she got back into the groove again. But one of the things she had to watch out for was making sure she didn't do too much, too fast. Otherwise the patients would pull on her at a rate that she couldn't handle, and nobody would do well as a result. She didn't want to do that.

Continuing her walk, several security guards talked to her as she passed by. Most she had known for years and were happy to see her back. Nobody had shown any overt disgust that she was back, and the orderlies were all delighted. She had a great relationship with most of them too.

As a matter of fact, these people were her family, and, yet, for whatever reason, she'd been completely unable to handle being here after that last scenario. She wasn't sure that anybody knew exactly what had happened, but the bosses above had set it up so that she had applied for a break and was taking a research sabbatical. To a certain extent that was true, but there had also been a significant omission, but, hey, she was happy to just be going forward right now.

As she walked back down toward her office, Dr. Mendelsohn walked up in front of her, a big smile on his face. "There you are," he greeted her. "I heard you were coming back."

"I had never planned to be gone for so long," she said. "I just needed that long overdue break."

"Hey, I understand." He gave her an eye roll. "If I could get a cushy break like you got, I would."

She winced, knowing that would be something she heard from a lot of them. "You can always apply for a sabbatical, just like I did," she suggested.

"Yeah, that would be tempting, but, chances are, they won't give it to me. No way. I'm not their gifted child."

"I'm hardly a gifted child," she joked, trying to downplay it. She'd heard that comment from people quite a few times before as well, and it fell just as flat now as it had back then. "So, tell me about the patients. Anybody new? Anybody difficult? Any great breakthroughs? What have we got?" She quickly tried to put the conversation back on a more formal footing, and thankfully it worked.

He launched into a discussion on several of the patients

he'd been working with. "We've got one who's doing really, really well," he shared, with a big smile. "We're absolutely stunned at how well. It's almost like … magic. He's doing so great."

"Good, that's excellent," she agreed. "Tell me all about it."

And that set them off on a more professional discussion and away from the snide comments that really didn't help her at all. Particularly after she'd needed the sabbatical so badly and was feeling anything but gifted at that point.

Still, by the time he'd brought her up to date, he looked at his watch. "Now I've got an appointment." He gave her a bright smile and added, "So I've got to run." And, with that, he took off down the hallway.

She grinned at that because they all did just that on a regular basis. Everybody would do the best they could, but they would get caught up in their work, and then they would end up late and have to run to the next appointment. Feeling so much more at home than she'd really expected—also realizing just how much she'd missed this place—she slowly walked back to her office, intending to just pick up her purse and leave for the day.

Taking this extra time to visit had been her chance to get her footing and to begin to ease back into the world she'd left behind so abruptly.

At that moment, one of the board members—who shouldn't even have been here on a weekend—caught sight of her.

"Cressy?" Dr. Willoughby called out.

Cressy smiled and waited, as he walked over and gave her a firm hug.

"You're looking wonderful."

"Thank you," she said, with a smile. "I really did need a break."

He nodded. "I know, and we should never have pushed you so hard in the first place. Believe me. It's something we've all discussed since you left. You didn't take your holidays. You didn't take your breaks." He shook his head. "So now we've tried really hard to instill some mandatory downtime, with required holidays and breaks and keeping the overtime under control. I know that everybody likes the overtime and the money, but you're a prime example of what happens when it gets out of control."

"Yet I didn't do it for the money," she murmured.

"I know that and find it even more admirable, but the bottom line is, you needed time off, and you got it. Frankly I have to admit you're looking fabulous. So it must have done you some good."

She burst out laughing. "Still a cheerleader, I see."

"Absolutely. That's part of what I try to do here."

"That's true." Cressy chuckled. "I just popped in to check out the lay of the land, to confirm all my log-ins and whatnot still work, so I'll be at work bright and early Monday morning."

"Good," he said. "Now go home and get some rest."

She nodded. "I'm good now. While on sabbatical, I did a lot of research, collated all my notes, and managed to feel as if I was getting on top of things, instead of losing them," she shared, with an eye roll.

"Keeping on top of all those notes is huge," he murmured, as he stared around. "We've had a lot of changes, some in staff, some in patients. It'll take you a day or two to get caught up."

"That it will," she agreed, "but I'm looking forward to

it."

He beamed another smile in her direction, and then, just like that, he was gone.

For the most part, the staff Cressy spent any significant time with were quite busy and concerned with the patients. Some of them even came in after hours as she had, which, as far as Dr. Willoughby was concerned, was probably part of the burnout problem. And who knows? Maybe it was. Maybe Cressy had just taken on too much, tried to do too much, and, when it hit her, it just hit the wrong way.

Of course she couldn't tell him what had been the final straw. Just no way to explain any of that, which was okay too. She worked in the realm of mysteries, and, if her coworkers and colleagues didn't know everything, they didn't need to either.

At that, she headed back to her office. Sitting down, she opened up the file on the boy. She was supposed to go home, but she wouldn't until she checked in to see what was going on with this particular case. When she got to the files, she sat back with her coffee and started to read.

SHE WAS BACK, and the anticipation rolled through him. Wow, she really came back. He'd thought for sure that she would be gone for good.

He'd waited; he'd heard rumors. It would be one month, three months, and then even six months. He couldn't believe that she left for that length of time. It was so unlike her. She must have either burned out, gotten sick, or gotten pregnant. He had no idea because nobody was really talking, but maybe nobody was talking because nobody knew. Still, she was back now, and, for that, he was grateful. She was the best thing that had happened to him and had given him a whole new purpose, not to mention a whole new life. She was intuitive, smart, funny, and all of that was what he'd missed so terribly while she'd been gone.

But now something inside him blossomed all over again. He waited with anticipation for when she would come to him, hoping it would be today, but knowing that, chances were, it wouldn't be. He wouldn't be the first one she would sign up with, and that was too bad because he rather desperately wanted to work with her again.

But, hey, he wouldn't push it. People who drew attention to themselves at this place didn't do so well, and he wouldn't draw attention to himself. Not until he was ready. Not until they were ready. And then? All bets were off. He burst out laughing, the laughter a long cold echo down the hallway. He smiled as he heard it because, for everybody else, it would send chills down their spines. Yet, for him, it was absolutely perfect.

"Hey, Rocco. What are you laughing at?" a nearby patient asked.

He waved at him and said, "Nothing. Just nothing. Life is good. How're you doing, Junior?" Junior was six foot six and a former football player. He had taken one blow too many to the head, until he'd finally had some weird break that people were still trying to sort out.

Nodding, Junior replied, "Hey, life is good."

"Glad to hear that," Rocco replied, with a smile, an experienced smile—as he had been a practicing GP in his earlier life and still wore the white coat, as it kept him happy and calm. "You just keep smiling, man." Then he sauntered down the hallway, his white jacket flopping in the wind.

Everybody had nicknames for patients in here. Some of

the patients knew of these nicknames and were friendly and kosher, and then there was always that underbelly, with the sort of things no one mentioned. Whenever you got a group of people together, there were those who did well and those who did not.

Junior was of the group who always did well and always made sure he was on the successful side of life because being on the other side? ... That just sucked.

"YOU SURE YOU'RE up for it?" Grant asked over the phone.

Gray groaned. "Look. I said I would do it," he snapped.

"I know, but it clearly makes you uncomfortable."

"It makes me uncomfortable as shit, and, if you'd told me who it was in the first place, I probably wouldn't have shown up."

After a moment of silence, Grant laughed. "You keep telling yourself that," he teased. "Do you think I didn't recognize your reaction last time?"

Gray pinched the bridge of his nose. "Being the good friend that you are," he replied in a dry tone, "you won't bring it up, *right?*"

"Of course I won't bring it up," he quipped, his laughter choking his voice.

"Besides, she was damaged."

"She was, indeed," Grant agreed. "I didn't think she would even pull through, but Dr. Maddy and Stefan are beyond sure that she is strong enough to handle it now."

"I don't know how anybody could be," Gray muttered. "This is ... beyond anything known."

"That's exactly right," Grant stated. "It's some of the stuff they keep bringing me on a regular basis."

Gray burst out laughing at that. "Better you than me."

"Right? None of this is easy, but it's even more difficult when it's somebody you love and care about. You just want to help them. Look at Drew and Dr. Maddy."

"Hey, that works for Drew," Gray noted, "but it sure doesn't do anything for me."

"No, but I also know that what happened to Cressy was something that affected you as well."

"No, it didn't," he denied firmly. "I mean, obviously I was affected in the sense that somebody, anybody, was hurt from all that, but not in the way that you're thinking."

"*Sure*," Grant said. "When you open your heart a little bit, and somebody like that walks in, you can't just slam it shut and say, *Sorry, didn't mean it. I wanted an easy person instead*. Life's not like that."

"No, it isn't," he agreed cautiously, not sure where Grant was going with this. "What are you trying to say?"

"What I'm trying to say is that I saw your reaction, and I've been in this field for a very long time."

"Oh, no. Not some matchmaking nonsense," he muttered. "I'm not going for that."

"Good, that makes me feel better."

But the way he said it didn't make Gray feel any better at all. "What do you mean?"

"You have decided that you're not going in that direction. So I'm good with that."

"Yeah, but somehow that doesn't sound quite like what you are saying."

"Maybe not," Grant replied, the laughter in his voice deepening. "Just remember. I told you so."

And, with that, Gray tried to change the subject. "She went into the office today."

"Why?" he asked, his tone sharper than he intended.

"I think she wanted to get a feel for the place again, maybe without one million eyes staring at her."

"That does kind of make sense."

"It does, indeed," he agreed. "Does everybody else know what happened?"

"No, nobody does, and that's probably part of the problem. Since nobody really knows anything, there's always this mystery."

"A mystery that makes it harder on her."

"Of course it does," Grant concurred. "You know what mysteries are like. Everybody wants to solve them, and, because there aren't any clear-cut answers, rumors abound."

"But she was a workaholic beforehand?"

"Yes, she worked constantly. She had, as she would say, no life, and that became her life."

"*Great*," Gray muttered. "So have you heard how it went today?"

"Nope, but I do know that she'll be there Monday to resume work."

"How am I supposed to get in there and not have everybody ask a million questions? They'll think she's under some sort of special watch or something."

"She is, in a way," Grant noted. "I know this is your time off, and you wouldn't be doing this assignment without me pulling some strings."

"I appreciate the fact that you're keeping me on salary," Gray replied in a dry tone. "However, you know there's no way the FBI will be involved in this."

"I think you're wrong. That boy knows something, so you stay close and be there, just in case."

"Which also makes no sense," Gray added. "We don't

have funding to keep personnel on hold for hunches."

"That depends. The family annihilator has downed seven families across as many states. If having you befriend a boy who can give us answers, while somebody works on him, the Bureau is right there."

Gray winced at that. "Maybe, but it still sucks."

"Why? Because you don't want to just chill out and be around?"

"No, I'm happy to spend the time, and I'm happy to be there and to keep an eye on the doctor," he admitted. "However, I did see what happened last time, and no way you'll convince me that somebody can go through what she went through without being affected herself."

"Oh, she was affected, no doubt," Grant declared. "Yet I also trust Stefan. Plus Dr. Maddy says that Cressy is fine, that she can handle this, and that the whole thing has made her stronger, and I believe Dr. Maddy. I suggest you do too." And, with that, he hung up on him.

No way Grant didn't have some level of bias when it came to Stefan and Cressy. How could he not? Gray sat here in his chair, a drink of whiskey in his hand, while he contemplated the golden liquid in the glass. He kicked his feet off the footstool, then stood and walked over to the window, staring down at the wonderful nightlife spread out before him. It was a stunning display, and one that he absolutely adored, but he would leave in a heartbeat if he could find a place that wasn't full of madmen killing each other constantly, and people devouring kids, even inside a mental hospital.

This family annihilator was something else. Somebody who had to destroy families, who started off loving them, only to end up hating them and wiping them out in a heartbeat. It made no sense to him, but it was just one more in a long line of crazy. As long as he was still in the industry, he was in the industry to help. And, if that meant helping Cressy, he would do his part.

And, as Grant had so helpfully noted, the cataclysmic reaction she had caused in Gray's world was just something he would have to live with. How did you watch somebody go through what that woman had experienced and not feel for her? Then—when you realized what she was doing was something so far out of this world, so odd, and so beyond anything he'd ever experienced or had tried to understand— all that just made her even more special.

When he'd met her again, he saw no sign of that same woman. He'd been baffled at the idea that she could even be the same person from before that trauma and not just a shell on the inside, but she had changed. She almost looked like an elf, as if to say she wasn't even big enough to do this job. Yet there she was, and she'd already gone in today ahead of schedule to try and get her feet back on the ground again.

That couldn't have been easy. Not when the rest of the world had been told that she'd taken a research sabbatical, when only Stefan, Dr. Maddy, and Grant knew the better part of that truth. Cressy had battled one of the worst horrors and monsters of the world, and that monster had caught her, and, in that fight for survival and freedom, she'd almost died. When she'd come out and needed a chance to recuperate, Gray hadn't expected it to even be possible. But seeing her for himself, not only had she recuperated but she looked better than ever.

CHAPTER 4

W HEN MONDAY MORNING dawned bright and clear, Cressy stared around her bedroom through weary eyes. It was the day that she both wanted and dreaded at the same time. It's why she'd gone in already, hoping that would help make the transition a little bit easier on her. Maybe it did, but it didn't seem nearly enough yet. Still, she needed to go in today, with a bright, healthy attitude and show everybody that she was fine. Especially with the rumors that had run rampant in her absence.

For all she knew, they'd put it down to having some sort of cancer or other medical condition, where Cressy needed the time to do her own battling. But it didn't matter what anybody thought about her, Cressy had no intention of telling them the truth. It went way beyond anything that most people could handle. Dressed and ignoring the need to get her morning coffee at home, she headed for her car, knowing she could get a cup at work. She couldn't help wondering at what point in the day Gray would show up.

There had to be some sort of rules to keep him at bay. And yet, if he needed to be there because of anything that might be discussed with the boy, then that was part of the FBI's rightful jurisdiction. As much as she might want to control the situation, it wouldn't do any good. As she knew from previous bouts with law enforcement, when they wanted access and had the prerequisites required, not much she could do but emphasize the fact that her patient needed calm and quiet. Right now though, this was a whole different story and she understood as much as anybody how important it was to catch this serial killer before more families were annihilated, yet it still wasn't easy.

She'd fought long and hard for her patients in the past, and she would do no less this time.

The traffic was light, and, by the time she walked into the office, she was feeling better and grateful that she'd thought to come in over the weekend to get settled ever so slightly. The place was humming with the regular staff, and she received lots of greetings, as she smiled and waved, working her way to her office. There she sat down with a sigh of relief, the busy halls a hard reminder of what her life here was like.

It was a good life, but it was also a hardworking caring world, and she could expect to see a lot of people at her door, wondering how she was and what she had been doing. It was the latter part that was hard to explain. She had a cover story, and parts of it were actually true, which made it a whole lot easier, but it would still be awkward. She could expect a week or two of uneasy circumstances, where pitfalls awaited her if she mentioned the wrong thing, particularly considering she worked and, at times, practically lived in a psychiatric hospital.

It's as if everybody was always overanalyzing everything, and that included her coworkers. You would think that they all had enough to do, working on their own garbage. Yet the truth of the matter was, too often it wasn't that way at all, and everything you shared would be considered fair game. She had enough problems in her life without bringing on that kind of attention.

In her office, she quickly settled in and logged on to the computer system. Then she got up, took off her coat, dropped her purse in her bottom drawer, then walked out to the coffee station. With a cup of hot coffee in her hand, she headed back to her office and sat down, looking at the roster for the day. There would be inevitable meetings, and the first one would be the worst, as she tried to make her way through all those questions and inquiring looks.

As she checked her calendar, she realized that first meeting was actually at 8:30 a.m. sharp. She frowned at that. They hadn't used to do meetings quite so early, so there had obviously been a few changes she needed to get up to snuff on. As she walked into the meeting room, she was met with a chorus of greetings.

She laughed, smiled, hugged several people, and said, "Boy, it is good to be back."

At that came catcalls of derision, as people joked about other options she had in life, with coming back not being one of them. When Dr. Mendelsohn walked in, the catcalls immediately silenced. He pretended like he hadn't heard any of the comments, but no way you could work in a situation like this and not realize just how much people wanted to go home and stay there for a few days.

He looked over at her, smiled, and nodded. "Good to see you back." And, with that, he launched into the agenda for the meeting.

She was quick to catch up on notes, had lots of questions about a couple of the new patients she hadn't dealt with, took a look at the roster of who had been assigned to do what, and then realized she was on an easier duty.

When the meeting was over, she spoke to Dr. Mendelsohn. "You're going easy on me," she noted in a joking manner. "I'm fine, you know."

He looked over at her, then nodded. "Absolutely. I know you're fine. But I also know the FBI is coming this afternoon, and I wanted you to focus on that."

"Right. It's not as if I could ever forget about that, could I?"

"Nope, none of us can. And you know the score. The sooner they're out of our lives, the better it will be for all of us."

She nodded. "I agree with that," she muttered, with just enough feeling to make him laugh.

"It is good to have you back," he said once more. "We've had lots of staffing issues, while you've been gone."

"Anything I should know about?" she asked lightly, turning at the doorway to look back at him.

He pondered it for a moment, then shrugged. "A few people have lobbied for your job."

"Ah." She nodded. "I guess that's always a problem, when somebody takes time off. Nothing major I guess, and I expected it in a way."

"A sabbatical is just that. It's a sabbatical, and that means the job is there for you when you come back," he stated, "which is why not everybody has that option."

She smiled. "I really appreciate having that opportunity."

He gave her a big smile. "No way I would lose my star doctor. You get better results than anybody else, and, if I needed further proof of that, the last six months without you would definitely have provided all that I needed. Your results are still better, even after a sabbatical."

She stopped and looked at him in concern because she'd

been expecting that.

He stared back at her, and, when she remained silent, he added, "Yes, we've had several patients backslide a bit."

She had known that would likely happen.

"We've had more outbursts, more tantrums, more failed therapies, more people backsliding than I would have thought possible," he stated. "If you had some special mojo—and if I believed in that—I would have thought that, when you left on your sabbatical, it went with you. Now the value you offer is in keeping the profile up a bit. The proof will be whether we get six months of calm and peace again, now that you're back."

She smiled at him. "I'll do my best."

He nodded. "I know you do things here that you don't talk about, and I know they work because we see the proof of it. It's in the results. However, having you gone and not having that available to us, I sure hope you don't ask for another sabbatical for a very long time."

She burst out laughing. "I'm glad you noticed I was missing."

"Yeah, noticed it and felt the pain every day," he admitted, with a wry smile. "Dr. Maddy was in here several times, and she noticed as well."

At that, Cressy felt something inside her warming. "Thank you," she replied sincerely. "It's nice to know that, when you have a calling, it actually works."

"Your calling is here," he said, "and I sure hope you don't end up trying to become a writer, a researcher, or something else that would mean you leave the patients again because the effect you have on them is very obvious, and I, for one, appreciate whatever it is that you're doing here."

"Got it." She gave him a bright smile and headed back

to her office, humming on the inside. No matter what failures she'd had, it was nice to know that she was appreciated, even if people didn't understand what she did. Thankfully he didn't ask too many questions about that, again leaving the impression that he would rather not know.

Dr. Maddy knew what Cressy did because Dr. Maddy applied several of the same techniques when she had struggling patients as well. Some of the treatment methods they had developed together. Some of them Cressy had developed herself, then shared with Dr. Maddy, as a professional courtesy for patients everywhere. It was something that the two of them had no problem with.

Neither of them was competitive against each other, and that was more than Cressy could say for some of the doctors here. When your star was rising, there were always other people who looked on in disgust, certain you were doing something to cheat the hard-work and experience system—like sleeping your way to the top, particularly considering Cressy was female.

But Dr. Mendelsohn was right. Generally Cressy's patients did do much better than the norm. Of course she had tricks and techniques to help them that she couldn't even begin to explain to anybody else, and it wasn't something she could teach. This was the kind of stuff that you knew how to do or at least had the natural ability. You either had it or you didn't. And that was also Dr. Maddy's problem in finding people to help her out when things got dicey.

A couple new patients were here that Cressy wanted to go meet and observe for a little bit, and then there were some of her former patients she needed to say hello to.

They were no longer under her care, but, as the person who had been working with them before, Cressy did feel obligated to let them know that she was back again. What happened after that point in time would depend on how well they had done while she was away. Whether they would come back into her care or not was not something she was prepared to deal with right now, as there were a lot of other issues that needed her attention.

Pulling herself out of those thoughts, she had to get busy. She only had so much time before Gray showed up. With that realization, she got up and, with her notepad in tow, headed down the hallway to one of the new patients. She watched as the spirit of a young woman danced in the hallway, completely harmless, singing at the top of her lungs in joy. Cressy stopped and smiled.

The other woman looked at her, and her eyes lit up. "Hi," she cried out, almost in ecstasy.

"Hi, I'm Dr. Cressy," she said gently, with a smile.

The other woman beamed. "I know you," she replied in a childlike voice.

"Do you?" Cressy asked, with a note of humor. "I'm pleased to meet you because I'm not sure that I know you."

The other woman waved. "You know me. We've talked lots and lots."

"Have we?" Cressy asked, looking at her intently. "What have we talked about?"

"Life, death, and everything in between," she explained on a bright laugh. She suddenly stopped, frowning, looking around, as if to confirm that no one could overhear, then whispered, "Glad you're back."

"Me too," Cressy stated, with feeling. "Any particular reason that you're glad I'm back?"

The woman gave her a haunted look and then nodded slowly. "Bad things happened when you were gone." And, with that, the young woman disappeared in front of her.

Cressy slowly turned, but nobody was watching, which was a good thing. Also nobody was telling her off for speaking to the walls. Also a good thing. She wasn't usually so open to talk to spirits in public areas, but, when she'd seen the young soul, so obviously delighted to be out dancing, it had been hard not to. Chastising herself for a mistake that could get her in a lot of trouble, she quickly walked toward this young woman's hospital room.

As she walked into the room, she tapped on the open door and poked her head in. "Hey, Annalise. It's Dr. Cressy."

Annalise lay curled up in a ball on her bed. Completely immobile and no signs of the dancing soul who had been enjoying herself in the hallway a few moments earlier.

Cressy closed the door, fully aware of the cameras, then walked over and sat down gently across from her. "Hi. You're right, you know? We have spoken before, just not in a little while," she told her. "I've been gone, but I'm back now."

There was no movement from Annalise.

Cressy consulted the notes that she had made on Annalise before she left on sabbatical. At that time, this woman had been much more vocal, more animated, so this was not something Cressy liked to see. If this regression had been brought on by Cressy's absence, she would struggle to carry the guilt. While she'd definitely needed the break, it still hurt to see when other people suffered so. Cressy spent a few minutes assessing Annalise's energy but realized that she was back to hiding, not quite as bad as she had been before Cressy started working with her before, not even close to that.

Yet she was too stiff, lying still instead of relaxed, as if something were wrong.

Frowning, Cressy made a note and then left the young woman to her own thoughts.

Cressy carried on to the next patient and found a similar problem. These two patients, who had been verbal and animated before, now appeared to be more internalized than ever. She would have to check into their medications.

They weren't on her roster, which was another problem, and having left them because of the sabbatical, she might have trouble getting them in her care again. She meandered back toward her office, deep in thought as she studied the medications on the chart. For whatever reason the medications had been increased, and a couple of them had been changed out.

She looked down to see who had authorized this. Dr. Morgan Taylor's doing. Yes, he was a doctor, but generally he didn't have any say in the patient's medications. She paused, wondering what she should do about this, then decided she needed more time here to figure out what was going on.

As she went from patient to patient, she saw a disturbing pattern.

Where there had been slowly improving verbal patients, there was an abundance of immobile patients, lying in beds, almost catatonic. By the time lunchtime came around, she felt a surge of anger building inside her. She didn't know what the hell had happened here, but something had, and that needed to stop, so these patients could get back to where they were. She was angry, but she was mostly angry at herself because circumstances had forced her to leave, and it surely seemed as if she had abandoned these patients to whatever fate had befallen them.

Annalise had been almost ready to go home. She would need care, and she would need to be watched to ensure there wasn't any more backsliding, but she had been dealing with some of the issues that had brought her to the hospital in the first place. Which, in Annalise's case, were witnessing the murder of a young woman. She was raped and murdered in front of Annalise, who would apparently be the next victim. The two of them, best friends, had been kidnapped, but Annalise had been rescued, whereas her friend had not been so lucky.

Cressy and Annalise had been working through a lot of the guilt, working through a lot of the emotions all tied up in the trauma, and now here Annalise was, right back at the beginning. The simple case of survivor's guilt was enhanced by whatever had happened while Cressy had been away.

By the time she had reached the appointed hour for Gray to arrive, she felt even more confusion and sadness at the state of her former patients. Not to mention the fact that she hadn't even met the new patients yet. Knowing that Gray would be here in another ten, maybe fifteen minutes, she quickly went through her patient list to see who was new. As she went from one to the other, she realized how much work was waiting for her.

When she made her way back to her office and sat down again, a voice popped in from her open door.

"Depressing, isn't it?"

She raised her gaze to study Dr. Willoughby.

"Aren't you glad you came back?"

"What happened while I was gone?" she asked, her voice harsh.

He winced. "Honestly? Most of us aren't sure. It appeared as soon as you left. Within weeks or maybe a month, the place just started to fall apart."

She shook her head. "There was no reason for my patients, my former patients, to be in the state they're in now."

"We know. Believe me. And, when we heard that you were coming back, most of us cheered because we thought that maybe we could reverse whatever happened here. We can't have patients being so badly affected by the loss of one doctor that everybody goes into a major decline," he admitted. "However, no doubt about it. That's what's happened. I almost wondered if it was worth bringing you back because, if you ever decide you need to leave, … this could happen all over again."

She stared at him, wordless.

He winced. "I'm not trying to put pressure on you, but it's been very hard on all of us, trying to figure out what's happening."

She shook her head. "It makes no sense."

"Right."

"Did you have a new doctor in here? Any new orderly? Did you have anybody in or any major changes around here?"

"Are you thinking that they, … that someone traumatized the patients?" he asked.

She shrugged. "I don't know. I just can't justify it in my mind. I don't know what's going on, but six months?" she asked, almost on the verge of tears. "Six months later and some of my patients have reverted right back to where they started?"

He nodded. "I get that would send you looking for a cause," he began, "but none of us have any idea what's caused this, and it's happened right before our eyes."

"And nobody contacted me," she whispered.

"We were under strict orders not to," he stated, as he sat down in the chair beside her. "I don't know what happened to make you leave, and there was definitely a big part of me that was hoping you would stay away, but now that you're back, the pressure's on."

She blinked. "Pressure's on to do what?"

"To fix this," he replied. "Otherwise this place? ... We're all in trouble. Without results, the funding will be cut, and all these patients will be shipped elsewhere," he muttered.

GRAY WALKED INTO the hospital, showed his badge, and the woman just took one look at him and pointed. "She's in her office."

He nodded and headed toward Dr. Cressy's office, finding the door closed. He heard voices inside, animated, yet not in a good way. He knocked on the door, and a heavy silence came. Finally the door opened in front of him, and another doctor stepped out. He nodded at him, and mumbling a hello, quickly left.

Gray walked in to find Dr. Cressy sitting there, with an expression that suggested she was almost ready to pack it in. He sat down in the vacant chair and waited for her, giving her a little bit of time to adjust to his being here and the other doctor leaving. They had obviously been in the midst of a heated discussion. "You want to tell me what's going on?" he asked.

She just slowly shook her head. "I, ... I have to process some of this," she whispered. "I don't know what's happened, but this whole place ... has changed."

He titled his head, a grimace on his lips. "I gather you've

just now heard about what happened right after you left."

She stared at him. "Can you get me the files on that case?" she asked, with an urgency that surprised him. "I need to see." Her voice was muffled, as if coming from afar.

He opened his mouth, snapped it shut, and thought about it. "I guess, but can you tell me why?"

"Because I need to know what happened." She looked everywhere but at him. She hesitated, as if to collect herself. "Look." Then she got up, walked around him, and closed the door behind him. "What I do here, it's kind of special."

He nodded. "I don't know exactly what you do here, but believe me. I've certainly seen the effects of what places like Dr. Maddy's can do in terms of helping people."

"Right. Dr. Maddy works mostly with physically sick people. I work with mentally ill people. In the past, I would have said that we all have areas where our expertise comes in handy, and Dr. Maddy is doing what she does because she's very good at it."

Cressy was clearly drifting, and he needed to reel her in, but now was not the best time.

"By the same token, I'm very good at what I do. But what happened since I left," she said shakily, "I don't understand it. I don't like it, and I really don't know what's going on with this place."

"That I can understand. So, what do you need?"

"I need to know of any staff changes that have happened here over the last six months, any doctors, orderlies, right down to the kitchen staff," she explained but with a note of desperate urgency that had him sitting up and taking notice.

"You think something, someone in here is on a rampage? That a criminal is in here?"

She looked at him and shrugged. "Criminals blur that

line for me," she replied. "What I see as criminal and what you see as criminal can be very different," she murmured, almost trying to grasp an explanation that he would understand. "When you say *criminal,* you're also looking at something that's prosecutable. I'm looking at criminal as not being something that I care to prosecute, but something I want to fix, one way or another, because it's hurting people."

He stared at her. "So, are you doing something illegal?"

At that, half a smile twitched her lips, and she took a moment to let him hear her and hear her well. "How can it even be illegal ... when nobody can see, understand, or even comprehend what I do?"

He winced. "Now we're back to that Dr. Maddy kind of stuff."

She nodded. "And, if you trust her, please trust me as well."

"Okay. I'm willing to give it the benefit of the doubt," he stated, taking a moment to emphasize his point, "but it's still not that easy."

"Not only is it not that easy, it's damn-near impossible, and, if you haven't spent a lifetime doing this, the way I have, I wouldn't expect you to understand it at all."

"Okay, so that's not helpful either," he said, staring at her. "How am I supposed to help you if I can't see or understand?"

She replied, "Do you see or understand everything that Drew or Grant shares with you on cases that fall in Dr. Maddy's world?"

He winced. "No, obviously not, but you're asking me for information on patient files. Confidential patient files."

"I couldn't care less about privacy laws," she snapped, "not when it comes to this. I need to know what's going on, what has happened, and how it's happened." She was not having any of his excuses. "If that is something you can't get me, I'll phone your boss and get it that way."

He stared at her. "What? Just like that? You'll pick up the phone and call my boss because I'm asking questions?"

She looked at him with aplomb. "I have to because *this*, whatever *this* is, needs to stop, but, in order to stop it, I need to know what started it. Therefore, … I need absolutely everything we can get about the history on this place for the last six months. Any incidents, any criminal activity, any phone calls from this place to the police, any investigations opened over this time. Absolutely everything."

"Okay," he muttered. "Considering you're one of the doctors and the fact that we do have an open and active investigation into this place, I'll get that cleared."

"Please," she whispered.

"But that is completely separate from the boy I came to talk about."

"I haven't even made it to his room yet." She groaned, almost in disbelief.

He watched in alarm as he saw tears form in the corner of her eyes. "Hey, hey, hey," he said. "What is this?"

"I would call it an emotional return and a horrific sense of guilt. If I had never left, none of this would have happened. So many of my patients wouldn't have reverted to where I first met them."

"If you had never left," he retorted, "there's a darn-good chance that you wouldn't be in any shape to function at all. … You have to remember. Not just the patients are at risk here. If you hadn't left, chances are that you, yourself, would not be able to function, assuming you'd even survived. You cannot help anyone, if you're not at full strength."

She took a deep breath, slowly let it out, and nodded. "Thank you for that reminder."

Yet he could see it still wasn't enough. Whatever had happened or was happening would slam her with guilt until she found a way forward. "Can you fix this?" he asked, as he texted for the information that she needed.

She stared at him somberly. "I hope so, but in order to do that ..."

"Right, I get it," he said. "You need to know how it started. You haven't even told me what is going on."

She frowned and looked at the building around her. "I'm not sure I have an answer that will make any sense to you."

He frowned at her. "Seriously? Try me."

She nodded. "I don't know how you feel about things like ghosts, possessions, people on the other side who should have stayed there but didn't."

The hairs on the back of his neck rose. "You're serious, aren't you?"

"Oh, very serious," she stated flatly. "I think we've got a dark spirit here, but I don't know whose, and I don't know how, and you can bet that, once he got his hooks into this place, he won't let it go easily."

"And this dark spirit, we're back to the fact that nobody can see it, nobody can hear it."

"Oh, lots of people can see it, and lots of people can hear it," she corrected, "but there's a good chance you can't, and there's even a good chance that I might not be able to."

"Then how can you stop it?"

She gave him a hard glare. "There are times when I can do things that I really don't like to do, but I have to in order to save those around me."

It was cryptic, and it was even difficult to hear. He wanted to ask a million more questions, but just then his phone rang. He glanced down at his phone. "It's my boss."

"Tell him that I need this information or else," she snapped.

He looked at her curiously. "Or else what?"

"Or else that was just the start, and there'll be a whole string of deaths coming that you will not have any idea how to stop. The killer is here somewhere," she declared, as she again looked around the room. "The investigation has to start with those files."

OH, LOOK AT that, the fancy little doctor was back. Everywhere she went, people gave her well-wishes and big smiles. He chuckled inside.

If she only knew.

She was here under the illusion of having some power, but there was no power to be had. None and done. He'd snagged it all. Nobody knew or cared because they didn't want their perfect little lives to be impacted by anything around here.

The parents came by, made their dutiful little visits, smiled at Junior, then carried on with their lives outside of these walls. That's how they liked it; that's how they wanted it. They paid the bills, and everybody stayed quiet about Junior's problems relating to the world. It wasn't just Junior One or Junior Two. It was all of the Juniors in here. There were brothers, sisters, parents, … all locked up, and all with family at home, happy to have them locked away, so they didn't have to deal with them.

It was one of those facts of life that everybody came to some sort of raw conclusion about and ended up guiltily signing paperwork, Then, as soon as they stepped out of the building, they sighed with relief because that ordeal was over with.

He was here to make sure that wasn't true. The ordeal wasn't over with. The people here deserved to suffer, although some people here didn't. So they *would* suffer because he could make them.

If he couldn't live the life he wanted because of what somebody had done to him, then he would damn-sure confirm other people didn't get to live the life they wanted either. Not that most of them here cared. If he could find a way to get out into that big wide world, get out those front doors, that would be a huge boon for him.

Once again, he watched as the fancy little doctor walked rapidly down the hallway, her mind obviously occupied on something else, and he knew what that was. He knew the *something else* would be that boy. There had been a lot of attention on that boy.

He snorted at that.

He was sure that the kid was hiding, and, if he found a way to get in there, he would make sure that kid stayed in hiding forever. It's not that he wanted to torment kids, but he could only handle so much, and, knowing that the good little doctor would be focused on the kid the whole time, that was something he planned on changing. She needed to focus on him. He was pretty sure he could use her gift, … her talent, her ability, whatever that was, to his advantage. He wasn't sure about it, but she was definitely special.

She hadn't been here for six months, and he'd been here himself for a large part of that. Funny how he didn't remember his initial days here. Probably had had him all drugged up. Regardless, all that he'd heard about her had really tweaked his interest. Now that she was here, he sensed a shift in the power in the place, and that disturbed him. Not very much, yet she was someone to be wary of. It was as if, instead of the fear that walked the hallways, now there were these bursts of sunshine. It drove him batty. He wanted to shut it all down, make people suffer, and live in the dark, as he was forced to.

He would wait, give her time to see if these sunshine changes were her doing. And, if they were, well, he'd put a stop to it pretty fast. He would have to see how she would react to what he was doing. If she had any way to combat it, then that was easy to handle. He would shut her down too.

CHAPTER 5

CRESSY WALKED INTO the restricted area for the patients who needed constant care and found Adam's room. She scanned the brightly colored room, with a TV and cards and games and a bookcase. Everything here in this section appeared to be the same as when she'd left it. The energy was off, but then the energy in the entire place was off. She hadn't had a chance to figure out what made the light go out, or how to fix it yet, but everything felt wrong. She hated to even use that word, but that's how it felt, and that's what she would stick with using.

She smiled at the boy in front of her. "Hi, Adam," she greeted him cheerfully.

He just stared at the floor, his thin arms wrapped around him, as he rocked in place.

"Nice to meet you. I used to be here all the time," she shared, trying to get him to come out and say something. "Then I went away."

She kept speaking in a gentle voice, as she assessed his energy, his movements, his lack of eye contact. She recognized the symptoms easily. He had regressed. Somebody who had just decided life was too difficult, too complex, and it was much easier to go inside and to stay there. Not only had he pulled away from life, he had regressed in his psychological age too. While he may have been chronologically twelve years old, his mind was that of an eight-year-old, and that's where this boy was at.

Adam would eat when given food. Adam would drink when the need for water came up. Adam would sit in front of TV for hours and never request that the channel be changed. In many ways, these were the easiest of all patients, but they were definitely just hiding from life. And those were the ones whose minds she was skipping through, trying to help as much as she could. Definitely help was required for the others, but, if she could isolate the ones doing what this boy was doing, then she would maximize care for all of them.

Maybe that way she could reduce the number that they had to keep incarcerated. She sat down beside him, reached for a piece of paper, and drew a picture of Bugs Bunny. "Do you know who this is?" she asked in a conversational tone.

He didn't say anything, didn't look at her, didn't acknowledge her presence in any way. That was also normal. A part of him was assessing how much she would make him do and whether he could just ignore her. She wouldn't let him ignore her at all, but she wouldn't push it either. She knew that Gray was on the outside of the glass, listening, as was Dr. Mendelsohn. Somebody was always listening on these initial visits, as they tried to sort out what was going on inside the mind of their patient.

Having read Adam's patient file and what he'd been through, she understood his need, his fear. But what she didn't know exactly was whether Adam had given up, which was a very different state, or he was waiting for help. Oftentimes they got this idea because of the 9-1-1 calls that would go out in the world, and everybody knew about 9-1-1. So they were waiting for the police to come and rescue them. But this boy had gone inside so deep, so far, that nobody could rescue him. Except for possibly her.

She smiled, drew a couple more figures and asked, "What about this one?"

At no time did he acknowledge her in any way. She nodded, opened his file, and silently read a couple more paragraphs. He had an uncle apparently. An aunt and grandmother who loved him and had come to try and see him several times. Each time they came, Adam had thrown quite a fit.

"I see your uncle came to see you." She studied him for a reaction.

The rocking stopped and then slowly started again.

"He was hoping that you wanted to see him, but I can understand if it's too painful," she noted. "We can stop his visits if you want."

At that, the rocking stopped, and he looked at her—well, not quite *at* her, but the closest to actually looking at her as was possible without quite doing it.

Here was his reaction. She was glad to have Adam interacting with her.

Then in a voice that really surprised her, he gritted out, "Stop."

She turned toward Adam, then pried, "Stop the visit, or stop talking?"

He looked at her, blinked, and then collapsed in on himself, as if that was too much, as if he'd already said more than he could handle.

"Because I can do either," she told Adam. "Just tell me which one you want."

He frowned, but he spoke. "Visits." His voice was rusty as hell. He was barely audible.

"Good," she replied. "That's an easy one. We can stop

the visits. We'll talk later about why you want to stop those visits, but, for the moment, we absolutely do not want to stress you out any more than what you've already been through. I'm glad that you're settling in here."

In fact, he'd been here four months, and settling in the way he had was not what she would like to see. He had no contact with any of the other patients, ignored everybody as much as he could, and only dealt with anyone out of necessity. But Adam had answered her, so he was interested in finding out what was going on and how safe life was out of his cocoon.

She got up and asked, "Can I get you anything? Do you want any toys? Do you want anything to make you happy? Is there anything from home you would like to have that I could bring to you here?"

He stopped rocking again and then slowly shook his head.

Now that he was engaging with her, the restricted area was not the way to go with Adam. He would be placed in the main area, with more patient interactions. "Good enough," she replied in that same cheerful voice. "Do you want to stay here, or do you want me to take you back to your original room?"

At that, he got up, but whether it was because she had stood first or because he actually wanted to go back to his room, she didn't know. She watched as he headed toward the door. She opened the door and followed him. He went straight back down to where his first room assignment was, all on his own.

She noted, "You do that really well. Do you know how to get to the kitchen to get your lunch and how to go to the playroom?"

He immediately turned and headed toward the play-room.

"That's very good," she said. "What about your meals?"

He immediately turned and headed back to his room. "Do you eat your meals in here too?" she asked.

Socializing was important, so unless he was actually classed as a danger to other people, there was no reason for him to stay in his room. He didn't say anything to that, but she had worded it in such a way that he could respond without having to speak.

"I would like you to come to the main dining room for your lunch today. Would that be okay?"

He walked over to the bed, then sat down, as if that were his answer. No, as in hell no.

She was willing to give him some time to adjust but not when it came to something like that. "No?" she asked. "I can take you there." She looked down at her watch. "It's almost time. I'll come down and sit with you."

He stared at her, and she saw the fear lurking on the inside. She smiled at him encouragingly. "It's all right. I promise I'll stay there with you the whole time."

But, when she took a step toward him, he put his hands up over his head and started to shriek in an ungodly way. She knew it was basically a way to preserve his routine, an attempt to escape having to go to the dining room for food. She reached out gently with her hand and said, "No, enough of that."

But instead the caterwauling got louder and louder. She knew that the others were still behind her at the doorway, observing, but she was firmly adamant that this was one trial that Adam could not afford to win, not if she could get him back in any kind of shape and form quickly. She sat down beside him, put an arm around his shoulders, and just held him. When he realized that she wasn't leaving, he slowly stopped screaming and then curled up on his bed.

While he was there, she closed her eyes and gently sent energy to soothe his soul, to take off some of the rough edges that were bothering him, and to ease up the sensation of that fear riding his nerve endings. When the nerves were always alert and rubbed *edgy* like that, there was absolutely no peace, and things would set off the patient easily.

It was a problem with all people who had been through something as horrific as Adam had. Just no way for Cressy and the other medical staff here to acknowledge the stress that their systems were under. So keeping her head down, she just held him and mentally kept working on his energy. She worked and worked and worked, until he finally just sagged into her arms. She held him gently, pulling his hair off his forehead. "There, that's much better, isn't it?"

He didn't say anything. but his body had slumped into not a slumber but almost a passive state. Not a coma because an alertness was there. She would call it a meditative state. And, in this state, she could actually do some of her best work—but not with an audience, and definitely not when she didn't know what kind of reaction she would get from Adam.

It was far too soon to get the answers the FBI wanted, but, of course, she understood perfectly why they were here, just in case. The answers would come, she knew that now, but it would take time for Adam to learn to trust her, and she would have to do a fair bit of work to get his system back on track.

This boy had been traumatized, and it wouldn't take much to set him off again. The best thing she could do was work slowly and steadily to get that trust back.

She stood again and said, "Come on, Adam. Let's go get some food."

He looked up at her.

She held out a hand in anticipation, not forcing him, but reaching for him., "I'll stay with you. I promise."

He reached up slowly, taking her fingers in a death grip, but didn't move otherwise.

She smiled in assurance. "I'll have lunch too. I'm not even sure what's on the menu. Do you know?"

He just stared at her, unblinking.

"Let's go find out together."

And, with very little movement, she managed to tug him to his feet, then she led him calmly down to the kitchen. As she passed Dr. Mendelsohn, who looked at her in astonishment, she murmured, "Put out the word for silence in my corner, will you?"

He nodded and raced ahead of her. What that really meant was that there would be an orderly close enough by who could stop people from coming up and talking to her, while she was doing her mental dives into Adam. Sometimes she was just having lunch, and then it was as if all bets were off, and people would come visit with her, complain to her, whatever it was that they felt they needed to do. But today? Today it was all about Adam.

When she got to the cafeteria, she moved him slowly and carefully to a window seat, where they could both stare out the window. As soon as she had him in position, she sat down beside him and never moved. She kept her hand on him and just talked to him about what was outside the window and what a beautiful sunny day it was. Thankfully it was.

It was a stunningly gorgeous day, but that wouldn't make Adam feel any better, at least not yet. The outside world would be scary, but, in his case, the inside world was also scary. He needed to find a space where he could be himself and not be afraid of being attacked. That she'd got him down here revealed a lot, and she knew that her coworkers would be all over her for it—as if to put them in a bad light—but that wasn't her concern.

Her sole concern was this boy right now.

She sat here for the next half hour, until two plates came and were placed on the table. Adam jerked hard, his hand gripping hers tightly, when the plates landed a little too heavily in front of her. She frowned at that because movements around Adam and most patients had to be controlled and gentle, in order to not scare some of them here, but apparently that premise had been forgotten or ignored, a standard that had slid, or somebody new was handling it.

She looked up and frowned at the person delivering the food.

The man immediately winced and muttered, "Sorry about that."

She waved him away, saw Dr. Mendelsohn watching her, and she nudged him with a finger to come to her. He immediately stood just to the side, beyond the boy's vision.

She murmured, "We need cutlery, napkins, and something to drink. I don't know who that person is, but I don't want him back here."

He nodded and disappeared again. When he returned, he brought with him the items that she requested. She turned and gave Adam a fork and nudged his plate a little closer. "This looks good, doesn't it?" she asked in a comforting tone, yet in fact it looked terrible.

Not only had the food changed, it was as if the whole foundation of the place had changed, and, considering that, it wasn't so surprising that the food had deteriorated too. That fact alone just pissed her off even more. Filling these injured, damaged people with chemicals was never a good thing, but, when it was their only source of nutrients, and they couldn't heal with this crap, it was even more of a crime. This was something she would take care of very quickly.

She managed to get a little bit of food into Adam. He ate slowly, carefully, and on his own, as if every bite was very precious. And it was. It absolutely was precious. But it was the way he ate, with that caution, that fear that his world would explode at any moment that made her heart break. She kept her hand on his and sat beside him, forcing herself to eat a few bites too. It was terrible food, absolutely terrible, and she knew that her job here would end up exploding in fury if she didn't get this place under proper control, focused on the health of these patients. She didn't know what had happened, but, wow, they had really let this place slide.

She felt a presence beside her, and she looked up to see Gray. Surprised, but realizing that he didn't know the etiquette at a place like this, she smiled and pointed to a chair beside her. She had a lot of things coming her way, and so much had changed here that she even wondered if the sanatorium would be okay with her way anymore. Regardless Cressy did recognize her uncertainty about being back again.

"Adam, this is Gray," she told the boy.

Adam made no move toward her, but he kept eating willingly enough, getting another couple bites down.

She noted Gray had a cup of coffee. "What's the matter, no food?"

He looked at her, and she caught the glimmer of a wince. She nodded. "Yeah, a few things need to change," she muttered.

He looked over at Adam. "How're you doing, Adam?"

Adam made no sound or movement, either for or against showing any willingness to converse.

Cressy smiled at Gray. "Adam's doing just fine," she replied cheerfully, as she patted his hand again.

His grip on her fingers tightened, and she nodded.

"It's all right. I'm not leaving you. We'll finish here, and then we'll return to your room, so you can lie down and relax."

Almost immediately he shoved his plate back, as if to say he wanted to go lie down now.

She assessed the amount of food he'd eaten and then nodded. "That's fine. We can go back now if you want to."

He immediately stood, and she laughed at his eagerness. "At least that was a response of some kind."

He just stared at her, his face quivering, his shoulders and his hands tightening. She looked around in concern to see what the trigger was, but she didn't see anything obvious. Again she had to fight off the frustration because, having just returned to work, she didn't know what undercurrents were going on around here.

She turned to Gray. "You can either walk back with us, or you can stay here, and I'll see you in a bit."

He immediately stood, his coffee in his hand, and replied, "I'll walk with you."

He stepped in behind them a few paces, as if to keep an eye on her. An eye on her and probably an eye on Adam. By the time she got Adam into the hallway, he was walking faster and faster, as if he couldn't get away fast enough.

"I get it, Adam," she told him. "I can sense the nervousness, and that's all right. We'll get there just fine. Slow your steps. Let's take everything slow and controlled."

But her words weren't helping. By the time they made it to his room, he was almost in a panic. As soon as he got in, he slammed the door hard, and, whether it was on purpose or not, nearly hit Gray in the face. Then Adam ran to his bed and curled up under the covers.

She grabbed another blanket, put it over his shoulders, then sat down beside him. "Take it easy. You did really well."

He rocked himself back and forth, back and forth.

It was a comfort motion that reminded him of better times. "You're doing fine. Nobody'll get you here. You'll be fine." But she knew words were empty sometimes, particularly when the patients were caught up in their own mental anguish, and this was one of those times. Looking back over at Gray, she held up a finger, asking for a minute, then she slowly, methodically soothed Adam's energy, easing back some of the fear and letting his body breathe again.

When he took a deep slow breath, she smiled. "Now I want you to have a little nap. Okay?"

And, for the first time, he nodded and gave her half a smile. And, with that, she got up to leave, but he immediately reached for her.

She shook her head. "You're fine, and now I want you to sleep. I want you to feel better, to wake up rested, and I'll be here pretty soon again. In fact, I'll be here every day now, so you'll be fine. Just take it one step at a time. Can you do that for me?"

He kind of sank into his own mental space again, but he curled up under the covers and closed his eyes. Moving, she gently let herself out into the hallway and stood there looking in the window, watching him.

Gray sighed at her side. "Did you get anywhere?"

"I'm actually not at all upset with how far I got with him today," she shared, "but there have been enough changes here at the center that I need to get a lot of things clarified and figure out what's been going on."

At that, Dr. Mendelsohn raced toward her. "How is he?"

"I've got him napping now." She motioned at the window.

"But that's the first time he's come out for food," he declared, staring at her. He shook his head. "I forgot how good you were with souls like that."

"In his case, Adam just needed reassurance that he was okay," she murmured. "And that he would be okay."

"Yet you know that's one of the things we work hard on," he stated, his tone serious. "Trying to help them all feel that way."

"Exactly." She hesitated but had to ask, "What the hell happened to this place since I've been gone?"

Dr. Mendelsohn winced at that. "I wondered if you would even notice."

Gray frowned but remained silent, as he took in this conversation with interest.

"Oh yeah, I've noticed," she confirmed. "The food is shit. The kitchen staff seem to be either rough or uncaring, or I'm not exactly sure what that was at lunch today. That little slip by the server was not supposed to be happening and couldn't have come at a worst time. I almost had Adam calm, and then all that noise and mess happened."

Dr. Mendelsohn nodded. "That was unfortunate, and that particular staff member has been chastised a couple times for being a little loud. He's trying to be fast, and being fast has also made him noisy."

She stared at her colleague. "Maybe, but it also seems to be that we need more of one and less of the other."

He nodded. "I can't tell you how much I'm glad that you're back," he repeated, with relief in his voice. "I mean, it's … We've needed change for a long time. The last six months have been pretty rough, but, once people started talking budget cuts and all that stuff, believe me. Not everybody had any kind of power to go up against them."

"Was it the board?" she asked. "Because I never had any problems with them before."

"Yeah, and then you left, and it's as if they were waiting for you to leave, just so they could jump in and change things," he suggested. "The food's gone way down, and, although most of us have complained, we haven't had any effective method of getting them to change. So we're really hoping that you do."

"You and I both know how much food quality matters, especially here," she stated. "People are paying an exorbitant price to be here and to get the treatment that they need, and we can't even give the patients good basic nutrition? That's ridiculous."

"I know." He raised both hands, shaking his head. "I know that, but good luck trying to tell them."

"Have there been changes on the board level too?"

He nodded. "Yes, there has been, and you know we don't have much say in any of that. All of a sudden, there's another change, and it just becomes a fact of life."

She stared at him for a long moment. "Maybe, but it will certainly be part of my decision-making as to whether I stay, if that's the kind of crap I have to deal with now," she murmured, more to herself than to Dr. Mendelsohn.

He stared at her in horror. "Please don't tell me that you're looking at leaving. We've all been waiting for you to return."

"If I can't function up to my usual level or at least close to it, no point in my being here."

"I know. I know," he admitted. "Everybody was afraid of your level of success in patient care and advocating for the patients. They didn't know what would happen to the center and to them if you were to leave. But then you were gone, and they took advantage of it."

"Sure, but, if they want me back, I must have a certain amount of control over what is going on here. To start with, the food is a big one."

He winced. "We've all stopped eating here because it's so bad."

She shook her head. "That is not something that should ever happen. Yeah, sure, we the colleagues and coworkers don't need to eat it. We can bring our own food. We can go out to eat," she noted. "But the patients? ... They can't leave. They don't have options. They're stuck here. They're depending on us to fulfill their needs—mentally, emotionally, and physically," she snapped.

He held up a hand beseechingly. "Don't tell me. Tell the board of directors. It was not my decision to make these cuts."

She groaned. "I feel as if I've come back to fight on every angle," she muttered. "This isn't the way therapy is supposed to be."

He laughed. "You and I both know that. However, if the board can get away with it, this is exactly how therapy will go—because they are fixated on the bottom line."

"Yeah," she muttered. "Just one more battle I'll have to face." She shrugged, then rubbed her face with both hands. "I can't say I'm looking forward to it."

"No, but you're not alone. We've all been fighting it while you've been gone, and we were honestly hoping that, once you got back, you would pick up the slack again and help us."

"Picking up the slack is one thing, but I'm not doing it alone. So, if you guys will help, that's one thing, but it can get ugly."

"Oh, I know," he muttered. "We did lose a couple people, as things did get ugly awhile back."

She nodded. "There could be more firings over all this as well. For me, if that's what happens, then I'm good with it because I won't work here if I'm not allowed to function. And, if they're trying to hamstring me with things like this? That's … That's just garbage, and believe me. If they cannot get their heads out of their asses, I will walk."

"I know," he admitted, "particularly after coming back from all that time away. You know what it's like to have that break, and, if you want to take another, you'll take it." He looked around the room from Cressy to Gray, then back at her. "However, I'm also hoping that you'll recognize and see how much people suffered while you were away."

"Thank you for that," she snapped, glaring at him. "You and I both know how much these patients mean to me. I had to leave last time. I had no choice. Now I'm back, and the last thing I want to do is leave, but, if it comes down to compromising my work, you know I will."

He nodded soberly. "So, we need a plan, a plan to ensure that this doesn't happen anymore."

"Yeah, well, have you got a way to do that?" she asked,

staring at him. "Because, so far, it seems that whatever the board wants, they're getting, at the expense of our patients, and that just pisses me off."

He chuckled. "You pissed off is way better than anybody not pissed off. So get pissed off," he encouraged. "About that plan part? … That would be a solid no for me. I've tried everything I know to do and failed. I suggest you take it in, then come up with a plan, and let's figure out how to get this place back the way it was. And I have to tell you, we're all damn glad to have you home."

GRAY COULDN'T BELIEVE what he was hearing. But it seemed as if everybody was anxious to have her back at work, fighting the battles that they hadn't managed to fight while she was gone. He could see the frustration and the anger in her demeanor, as she realized just how much certain people had taken advantage of her absence.

Not being able to clearly explain why she had left had also caused some distress and further tied her hands, but Gray understood that as well. There really were no easy answers when it came to something like this, but she would have to push forward and find a way to make it work. Otherwise she would have to back off and walk away.

He didn't think backing off and walking away was something she was very good at doing. It was very obvious that she cared about the patients, even this boy she'd barely met. He waited until she was alone in her office, before he stepped back in and asked her when she would be ready to leave.

She looked at him and replied, "I won't be leaving for quite a while." She was staring his way but not really seeing him. "You go on." When he frowned at her, she smiled reassuringly. "Honestly, I've got tons of things to do here, so leaving? … Just not happening for quite a while."

He motioned toward the man who had just left. "Sounds as if things haven't been very good in your absence."

"It's so typical when you get a couple people on the board, who are more concerned about the bottom line and shareholder payouts than anything even slightly related to patient care. So budget cuts were made, and the service suffers."

Gray frowned. "But surely they don't want to risk the facility's getting a bad reputation and losing all these well-heeled patients and families."

"They think it won't happen," she stated. "Unfortunately it happens way too often and never when they're ready."

"I don't think you're ever ready to see your bottom line drop," he noted, with a smile. "So I can understand that part."

"Maybe, but anytime they put the bottom line over basic patient care, they'll always get a fight from me." She stared out at the hallway and groaned. "And, of course, with me gone, nobody bothered to fight them, so things have slipped pretty badly."

"Do you have any leverage?"

"Not really, not since I left anyway. If I had stayed, I would have plenty, … no doubt. I hate to say it, but Dr. Mendelsohn was right when he noted that some people were kind of scared of me." She dragged out the word *scared* a bit. When Gray's eyebrows shot up, she gave a deprecating smile. "I had a very good reputation, … until I had to walk," she shared. "I knew at the time that walking would hurt my career, but I firmly believed that everybody here would have looked after these patients, but that clearly didn't happen."

"So … what did happen?"

"I'm not completely certain, but it appears the board moved in and made all kinds of changes, supposedly without anybody really knowing what it was they were doing, and now, after six months, the changes are pretty well entrenched, so they're figuring that it'll stay that way."

"Will it?"

She looked at him and nodded slowly. "Maybe, … but I won't be here if they do."

"Would you really walk?"

"Absolutely. If they won't listen to what is best for the patients, then I don't want to be here anymore. I won't contribute to a facility that cares so little for their patients. Of course I haven't had a chance to look into the details of the changes yet, but providing a nutritious and satisfying meal in a safe and calming environment is pretty basic and easy to measure. If they've gone that far wrong, who knows what else has happened. If they won't fix it, I can't be here."

"The thing is, you have to convince them of that, don't you?"

"Not only convince them of that but also make them realize that what they're doing is not only fundamentally wrong but not that far from criminal. I don't think I have anybody on my side to help do that."

"Are you sure?" he asked, with a wry look. "Seems like you have a lot of people on your side."

"Stefan and Dr. Maddy, yes. But inside this institution? No. I have a lot of people who are glad that I'm back to spearhead change," she clarified. "I'm not sure that means I can count them as on my side. I'm on the side of every patient, and, if I can make the change happen, then the staff will be all for it. They may want change, but they may not stand beside me to get it. So, if you're expecting them to actually go to bat in a case like this, it won't happen. If they had the spines to do that, it would have already happened."

He let out a slow breath. "So, you're just back and already in fighting form, *huh?*"

"Apparently." She snorted, sending a wry look in his direction. "But whether I like it or not is a whole fucking different story."

He nodded. "So, when you say you're not leaving for a while tonight …"

"I really mean I'm not leaving," she stated clearly.

"At all?"

She shook her head. "I'll probably just stay here tonight."

"Oh, no. No, no, no," he said. "Remember how burned out you got before?"

"And you know very well why I'm here," she stated, with a hard look in his direction.

He flushed at that. "Actually I don't get any of that. It's all a little too far-fetched for my brain to even want to understand, so I'm not sure that's an excuse you can use with me."

"I'm not using it as an excuse with you. I don't have to, and I have no plans to do so."

He winced. "Oh, now you're trying to put me in my place again, aren't you?"

She laughed. "I don't know exactly what place you're even talking about, so I don't think that's something I can even do."

"I'm not against that," he murmured.

"Good, but whatever is going on *here* is not a good deal."

"But can you actually stop it?"

"I don't know," she admitted. "That will remain to be seen."

He nodded. "You can't really expect me to be happy that you're planning on staying here … and overnight at that."

She frowned at him. "Do you have any idea how many times Dr. Maddy has had to stay overnight?"

"I think she actually works from home more than not these days."

"She could, and, maybe if I had a better understanding of what was going on here, I could do that too. But I'm much better off staying here, particularly right now, while I'm trying to figure out what's going on and what it'll take to try and stop it."

He didn't know what to say to that, and he was clearly out of arguments.

She smiled. "Go on home. This isn't your battle." His eyebrows shot up, and she just sighed. "Seriously it's not. If anything happens with the boy, or if he starts talking, I'll call you. Other than that, nothing you can do here. I told Dr. Maddy that as well."

"Dr. Maddy isn't the one who sent me here. It was Drew, her partner, through Grant, who's my boss. I don't get the option of being able to say, *Oh, that's nice. Okay, I think I'll go on home then*," he explained. "That just isn't something I can do."

She stared at him and then nodded. "Fine. If that's not something you can do, I'm sorry, but I'm not sure what I can do about it."

He laughed at that. "You really don't pull your punches, do you?"

"Not sure what punches I'm supposed to pull because

none of this is making any sense."

And again he didn't know how to handle her; she was different from most people. Most people respected the badge and, when he said to do something, they did it. In her case, she not only seemed unimpressed by the badge, she had her own ideas of what his orders should be, and, if they weren't the orders that she wanted them to be, he got the distinct impression she would just ignore them. His phone rang just then, and he sighed when he saw it was Grant. "I'm putting you on Speakerphone, Grant."

"Good." He called out, "Cressy, you there?"

"Yeah, I'm here," she confirmed. "What's up?"

"Nothing, so far. I'm hoping you have something."

"Not yet, and there won't likely be much for a while."

"Why is that?"

"Because this place has gone to pot while I've been gone," she snapped, her voice hard. "I have some things to fix, and some of is an absolute must. It's all required in order to make the patients improve that much faster."

Silence came from the other end. "Okay, so do you want to explain that a little bit more?"

"Not really. Just so you know, a whole mess of changes were made, related directly to the quality of patient care while I was gone, and it's showing in the status of the actual patients."

Grant appeared to understand how business worked in these parts. "As in budget cuts and the board of directors?"

"Yeah, it's almost as if you've paid attention to Dr. Maddy, when she goes on a rant."

"Yeah, well, I didn't always pay attention, but you don't make that mistake more than once."

She burst out laughing. "Glad she's got you so well

trained," she said, with feeling. "But I've been gone for quite a few months, and, while I was absent, people who didn't like some of the things that I fought against managed to get several issues slid through, and now I'll have a fight to get it back again."

"You know you can always count on Dr. Maddy and Stefan to back you up."

"Yeah, I can, but, in a case like this, I don't even know if Dr. Maddy is aware that the changes were made. She's more of a consultant than a board member when it comes to this kind of stuff, and I was the one who brought her in. Therefore, I'm guessing nobody bothered to consult her on anything. I'll talk to her later and see where that goes."

"You do that, but it still doesn't change the fact that we need to talk to this boy."

"You can't talk to him now. I just finally got a bit of a connection with him."

"You say *finally*, but you've only been there today, so what do you mean by *finally*?"

"It took a bit to figure out how to get him on board. I'm not saying that he is. I'm just saying we're working on it."

"Is there anything we can do to help?"

"Yeah, get my board back on track. They've changed the food, changed the medicines, changed the rules. I don't even know whether they have the same security or not."

"Do you think that part's important?"

"Yes, it's critical," she declared. "The minute it doesn't feel safe, … then nobody relaxes. I get that being safe is really almost a misnomer or a deceptiveness here in the facility, but the patients must feel some level of safety in order to start moving forward in life, and that boy is a perfect example. From what I saw today, … I don't think he feels safe at all."

"First, you speak of a little boy, a boy. Adam is twelve, right?"

"Yes, and he's regressed psychologically and emotionally. I feel he's back to an eight-year-old. Hence my usage of the term *boy*."

"And yet he still feels unsafe—"

"I'm not saying that he's scared of the staff or that he's scared of anything that could happen to him here, but that sense of safety is what's keeping him locked up and hidden inside, along with his memories and any information you could possibly want from him. As long as he feels that he can't relax or can't be safe, all that information will stay exactly where it is. Locked up in his brain."

"You know I don't want to hear that," he muttered.

"No, you probably don't," she agreed. "But, Grant, the atmosphere here is different. The energy is different," she explained, trying to grasp wording that he would under-stand. "It's kind of a package deal. We can only do so much, based on how people handle what's going on around them. Thus, if Adam is not happy, safe, content, I can't make a move forward. Those are just basic elements that every person deserves in life, and somehow I have to give them to him, before we can start prying through his consciousness to get him to come back out."

"You make it sound so easy," Grant teased, almost in chuckles.

"Not at all, but some shit is going down with the board of directors. Therefore, I need to know how much of this is on the edge of actual criminality and whether I could at least threaten to get a criminal investigation going in order to scare some of these people into getting their asses back in line again, back to caring about what they should be caring about. Otherwise, if we can do absolutely nothing in that regard, I'll have to find another avenue to make this work."

Shocked silence came from Grant on the other end, before Gray jumped in. "I don't think there's any criminal investigation we can open on something like this. If people haven't been doing something illegal and are just making board decisions about running and maintain the facility, I would say that doesn't involve the FBI."

At that, Grant laughed. "You'd be surprised at what people do when it comes to board members. However, as you said, I don't have any reason to open an investigation. At least, not right now."

"So, do you want some reason to open an investigation?" she asked curiously.

"Is that something you want?"

"Absolutely I do," she snapped, "and the sooner, the better."

"Then you'll need to provide me a legit reason," Grant stated, "and not just supposition or malevolence on your part."

"Yeah, that's not my style, so I'll forgive you for even implying such a thing."

"I am not implying anything," Grant replied, "but I can't have you jerking around law enforcement because you want better patient care."

"I think that should actually be the law because I don't understand how that can be optional."

"It's not supposed to be. A place like that is supposed to be looking after their patients as a priority. Yet there is a fair amount of room for interpretation, and these things tend to be subjective."

"All I can tell you is that, in the six months I've been gone, they've apparently made as many changes as they wanted, and none of it is for the good of the patients."

CHAPTER 6

W HEN CRESSY WAS finally alone that night, she sat in her office and just listened to the silence. The center itself was down to its evening crew, and, around this time, dinner was being served. For the most part, things had calmed down. Not the fury inside her, mind you. That was something that she was trying to figure out how to manage, in advance of the meeting with the board that would be coming.

She had a pretty good idea that they were preparing for a fight against her too, and they had the advantage of sufficient time to plan for it. That was fine. If that's what it would take, then she was up for it. It just frustrated her to no end that the minute she turned her back, somebody stepped in, took advantage, and managed to slash the patient care budget.

As she worked through a bunch of her emails, she answered notes from a few of her colleagues and got herself ready for an evening session, something she hadn't done in a while. Some of her former patients here were doing okay, but many were doing much less than okay, and she needed to figure out why they had regressed significantly.

It was easy to place blame, but since she hadn't been here to actually be part of the fight, it wasn't as if she had any right to judge. The others may or may not have cared enough to fight, and many probably felt quite powerless when it came to the board of directors. Not everybody was up for that kind of argument and exposure. Cressy wasn't either, but she didn't feel that she had a choice, and it just came with the territory.

Dr. Alice poked her head in, then smiled warmly. "It's good to have you back."

Cressy grinned. "It's good to be back, and I was thrilled, until I saw how things are going. Is all this change due to budget cuts? What is the story with that anyway?"

At that, Dr. Alice's smile fell away, and she nodded. "Yeah, we knew you would be livid about it all, when you got in, and honestly we didn't know what to do about it. Anytime we tried to protest, we were told flat-out that our jobs were on the line. Most of us need these jobs, and some of us, like me, absolutely love working here. So it's almost as if we're held over a barrel about it."

"Oh, absolutely," Cressy agreed. "Still, it's not good to see things go down the drain this way."

"No, it sure isn't, and, if you're up for the fight, we're right there with you," she offered, "but you know what it's like when the board gets going."

"I do, indeed." Cressy shook her head. "It seems the minute I was gone, they moved in and started doing whatever they wanted with the changes."

She nodded. "They have, and I don't even know for sure that all of them are bad, but, as I'm sure you noticed, the food has definitely gone downhill."

"I noticed that at lunch," she confirmed. "And food is huge. Do these people not know that good food is far more than calories to keep someone alive? It's literally nutrition for the brains and bodies of our patients."

"It's a no-brainer, but it's a budget thing," Dr. Alice stated, "and good food costs more."

"Yet why should patient care be sabotaged by budget?" She rolled her head slowly, knowing that the argument was an age-old discussion.

"If you've got any pull with the board of directors now, we'd love to see the changes reversed."

Cressy wondered about that and wondered whether anybody gave enough of a crap to even worry about it, but again Cressy was prepared to only fight certain battles. Obviously the same was true for the others as well. She didn't say anything more about it, and, when Dr. Alice finally left, Cressy needed to destress and prep for a night session.

She walked over to the corner of her office, behind her desk so nobody would catch a glimpse of her. Then, just like Dr. Maddy had shown her many years ago, she sat down cross-legged and slowly pulled away from the stress churning through her system, trying to pull some of the harmony and the joy of what she did back into her field. It was hard because she wanted everything to work smoothly, and, while she was away from here, it was actually easier to remember the good parts than the bad.

Now that she was back in it again, the bad parts had all the makings of one hell of a headache. She'd often wondered about having her own place, like an investor-money setup, creating her own center. It was something that crossed her mind on a regular basis. She'd been offered some money to do it at one point but just hadn't thought she was really ready for that kind of responsibility. Yet the more she thought about it now, the more she had to wonder. Just enough was going on in this place to drive her batty, so maybe she would be better off on her own. Just before she started to drift a little further, Stefan's voice popped into her head.

Anytime you're ready to do it, you know we're there for you.

She smiled at that. "It would take an awful lot of money, a lot of know-how, and would create a hell of a lot of headaches," she murmured.

That doesn't mean it would be wrong, he added. *And you wouldn't have to do it alone.*

"Maybe not. I'm not sure I'm up for that just yet."

Got it, but anytime you decide you are up for it, let us know. I'm sure we could roust up the money for a center.

"One of Dr. Maddy's centers?" she asked, with a smile.

No, we'll make it a Dr. Cressy center, he clarified, with a note of humor. *The work you do is just as important as the work she does, just in a different field.*

"I know, and honestly I do think about it sometimes, and then I get scared off due to all the bureaucracy."

But if you were on the board, he noted, *you would have much less to worry about, where bureaucracy is concerned.*

She thought about that and slowly nodded. "I guess that's what it comes down to. It depends on whether I would have a board of directors I would have to kowtow to. If I didn't, then fine. I could run it the way I need to, but, if I do, it's a different story, since one board of directors is the same as the rest."

Unless you have people on the board who actually care about the place.

"How do you get that? ... Ah, I know how you get that," she declared, with a knowing smile. "You have people on the board of directors who remember what it was like when their own family member was part of the system that didn't give a crap."

Exactly, he agreed. *It's not that difficult to find people like that to serve.*

"No, it sure isn't. I can think of plenty of people I've helped, now that you mention it."

Exactly. I don't know what kind of money it would cost even just to buy the center that you're working for now, he mentioned, *but that's always another option.*

She laughed. "I do not have that kind of money, and I'm not sure other people have that kind of money either."

Oh, you would be surprised, and people definitely do, but we would need to find the right kind of funding.

"Yeah, we're talking millions upon millions," she noted.

Millions upon millions are out there, he told her. *Don't kid yourself about any scarcity of money.*

"Then put out the word, Stefan. And, if need be, if changes here are not successful, maybe that's what we'll end up doing."

You still have to get control of the board there though, if that's the route you go to set up shop, and that means buying up shares.

"I don't have that kind of money or know-how," she admitted, "so that'll take somebody else with a different expertise."

I do have a couple people I could mention it to.

"Fly at it then because I'm heading for the mother of all fights," she murmured. "What pisses me off is that what I've been fighting for is the most basic of health care in terms of good nutrition. You should see how they cut the budget for food and what they're serving now. God, there's absolutely nothing here that'll help rebuild brains, bodies, and damaged souls."

Food won't help damaged souls, Stefan added, *but it's all part of the same package, and it's certainly a red flag. If they are willing to skimp on that, it's cause for concern on what other corners they are cutting.*

"Exactly," she murmured. "Anyway, if you know anybody, go ahead and talk to them. I would run it—or at least co-run it." She groaned. "I mean, I have too much aversion to the paperwork to be fully involved, plus all the meetings and crap like that. Yet ... I'm in them all the time anyway, so I'm not sure it would be any different."

And, with that, he just laughed and disconnected in her head.

She smiled, and, after the conversation with him, found it much easier to slip out of her body and to roam freely. She felt her body start to stretch, feeling the freedom take over her soul, as she was released from her physical form. She felt sorry for anybody who didn't know how to do this, yet the bulk of the world never enjoyed the experience. She was sorry for them because it was such a unique feeling to fly free, and, of course, she wasn't alone.

She flew free here because so many of her patients were here on this mental plane, and, as she headed out into the hallway, she saw various individuals and their energy flowing around the building easily, most of them not sure what they were doing. Likely they thought they were in a dream state.

Yet some of them knew exactly what they were doing because she'd met them on this plane before. As she walked toward Annalise, the woman looked up and cried out in delight, racing toward her. Cressy braced as the flow of energy shot right into her and passed on through. Cressy laughed. "You always did love to do that."

"I'm so happy you're here," Annalise cried out, happy and bouncing all over the place. "Oh my, do we get to play again?"

"To a certain extent," Cressy replied. "This is my first time back here in a long while."

"I know. I know," she cried out. "I didn't want you to leave. It's been terrible with you gone."

Annalise cried out with the overdramatization of the young woman that she was inside. Really Annalise was a forty-year-old woman, but, when she was in this spiritual plane, she was a young woman, one who enjoyed life, had fun, and raced around the center, laughing as if she had not a care in the world.

She didn't have those cares, until she returned to her body and the world that had hurt her so badly that she preferred to not actually live but more to just exist by the means other people demanded of her. If Annalise had a choice, she probably would have danced out of her body and stayed here forever, but it was hard on bodies if you did that.

It was important for souls to come back and connect to life, if they could. Unfortunately not all of them could, and some wouldn't even try. Other things were on their minds, and, as far as they were concerned, better things, things that didn't hurt as much as reality did, and Dr. Cressy certainly understood. Who was she to judge anybody else's experience, when Cressy's own sister had been in the exact same position? Pain was pain. It didn't matter what form or shape it took. It was all about the interpretation and how it affected you.

Spending a few minutes with Annalise, Cressy left her doing cartwheels up and down the hallway, hoping that one of the other residents would come out and play with her. Occasionally they did have a resident who could come and play, and then Annalise was absolutely in her element.

Cressy didn't know whether any such patient was here now or not. She watched and waited, but she noted no sign of anybody coming to join Annalise. Cressy wondered if Annalise realized just what was happening but figured she probably didn't at this stage. Regardless, as long as she was happy, Cressy wouldn't bother Annalise too much at the moment. There would be time for more questions down the road.

Right now Cressy needed to see who was here, who wasn't here, and whether those she expected to see were actually here or not. She could do an awful lot of work on patients and for them in this realm, but finding those who could step into this realm was a whole different story. She moved on down the hallway, checking on the patients she knew, going from room to room.

She still had the high-security ward to check out, but she was avoiding that at the moment, while she started out with the easier patients. She laughed and smiled as she saw several of them. She was sad when she realized that one of the young men she had really enjoyed spending time with had apparently passed on. She made a note to check his file and see what had happened.

He'd shown so much progress, and she really hoped it had nothing to do with her leaving. She already had enough guilt going on in her system without that. But just because she felt guilty didn't mean that she was to blame, and she had to keep reminding herself of that. At times you could and should take on the blame of knowing you'd done something wrong, and then other times you realized you just had nothing more to give. She'd also been physically affected by the last blowup that had happened and was not too willing to jump right back into something similar.

By the time she'd gotten through all the regular hallways that she had planned on checking out, she felt much better, knowing that several of the patients were waiting for her, these patients noting that Cressy was back on that plane. She spent a few minutes just being with them, catching up and checking on how they were doing, what they were up to, anything that had happened in the meantime. Progress on all levels, as far as Cressy was concerned.

Then she headed down the hallway toward the room of the man she'd been trying to help back then, when the blowup had happened. He was no longer here, and it was the first time she'd been in that hallway since the attack happened. She'd tried to force herself to go there earlier and had somehow managed to evade the entire concept all day. Not that it was unexpected because just enough memories remained in the back of her mind to keep her away from it, yet she couldn't allow fear to have control over her.

It was one thing to have a problem and to acknowledge it, but quite another not to acknowledge it, thus giving it that kind of power over you all the time. As she headed toward that corner, she took a right and slowly drifted down the hallway, looking for any energy, looking for any emotions of her own that were locked up in her body or mind and unwilling to be open. Happily, she found her system was functioning fully as she moved swiftly through the area. She smiled when she came to the end of the hallway because she found nothing, no reaction, no negativity, absolutely nothing.

Feeling much better and feeling some of the stress in her system drift off, she slowly headed back down this hallway, deciding that she would take a quick gander over in the high-security area, before going back to her office and writing down notes.

She needed to sort out who she would help and how, plus what kind of help she could actually give at this point. As she moved toward the high-security area, she checked out the sheet to see how many rooms were full. Unfortunately she realized that every one of them was taken, and one was assigned to the man that she'd been trying to help when everything had blown up six months ago.

She shook her head. She couldn't believe it. Maybe the list was out of date. So she headed to the room assigned to Rodney.

She froze when she saw his name on the door, and, when a hard slam came against the inside of the door, she drifted backward to get away. Yet getting away was the last thing she needed to do. She took a deep breath and slowly, with all the protection enabled around her, her spirit slipped into his room to find some man standing against the door, his head banging against it constantly. This was not Rodney. This man's forehead was bruised, and his arms were wrapped around him, but he just stood there in place.

Bang. Bang. Bang.

Her heart went out to him, but she also knew that she had to be careful. She wasn't sure what was going on, and she could never take a chance of going in and dealing with another patient like Rodney, not until she knew his full history. Since his correct name was not on the room, she didn't have a way to pull his medical history. She would have to resolve that problem, then check his history, see about this kind of behavior. Watching the stranger harm himself was painful. She immediately pulled back into her body and then headed to her office.

Once she was there, she sat in place for a long moment,

settling her spirit back into her body. Then she got up and walked right back down to that unit. Outside of his room, she checked what medication the misnamed patient was on and whose care he was currently under. Dr. Weatherby, which was fine and dandy.

As she stood here, one of the orderlies came up and asked her, "Everything okay, Doc?"

She smiled at him. "He appears to be struggling."

"He does this every night," he told her, with a shrug. "They've changed his medication time and time again, but nothing ever stops it."

She nodded. "Anybody ever talked to him about it?"

"He's nonverbal," the orderly said.

She didn't know who this orderly was. He wasn't one of her regulars, so she asked him, "How long have you been here?"

He looked at her and then shrugged. "I guess four months now, maybe." He looked at her intently for a moment and then asked, "You're new too?"

"No, not so much new as returned. I'm just back from a sabbatical."

"Ah, right, Dr. Cresswell," he said reading her name tag. "Pleased to meet you."

She smiled. "What's your name?"

"Simon, and I really do appreciate the chance at the job here."

Of course, at four months he'd just passed his probationary period and was hoping there wouldn't be any issues. She had no issues with him, at least not yet. It remained to be seen just what was going on at this place and who survived the shake-up. But it seemed that the board hadn't skimped on security. She smiled at him. "I'm glad you're happy to be here. This work is definitely not for everybody."

"I feel sorry for them," Simon replied, staring around at the sealed doors. "It's not much of a life."

"No, it sure isn't," she agreed. "We're trying to make it easier on them."

"I hear you, but I'm not sure how much good it's doing though," he stated doubtfully.

She smiled. "And that is one of our constant challenges."

"Agreed." And, with that, he stepped back.

She took note of the medication this patient was on and then headed back to her office. When she got there, she quickly sent a text to Dr. Weatherby, asking about the meds for that patient.

Instead she got a phone call. "You're back five minutes," he noted wearily. "And you pick up on the problem patient right off the bat?"

She chuckled. "I don't know that I picked up on the problem patient, but I was down in that area and heard the steady banging of his forehead on the wall."

"No, you're right. I keep mixing up his medication, hoping to find something that'll work. I hate to say it, but he's been way worse. If you want to take him under your care, feel free," he offered in a very low tone. "I've tried everything, and I don't have anything else to offer."

She winced at that. "Let me take a look at his file and see what you've tried. Then I'll consider it. Also I need his correct name. The wrong name is on his door."

"Really? I can't imagine. I'll double-check. But don't take on a new patient just for me," Dr. Weatherby added. "I don't want to stress you out and send you off on another sabbatical, So forget I asked for help with him. I'll keep him."

She laughed. "Everybody seems concerned that I'll take off again."

"Hey, … you left so fast that we weren't sure exactly what happened."

"Yeah, when you hit that wall," she said lightly, "you just hit the wall, and there doesn't seem to be any rhyme or reason."

"If that's what it was, good enough."

Of course that meant he didn't believe her but was willing to accept her reasons, just as everybody else was. She appreciated it. Only so much she could actually tell anyone. None of it would be believed to some degree, and she would wind up in this place as a patient herself.

The last thing she wanted to do was to end up with people running through her head. Even if she got into that kind of trouble, only so much help somebody like Stefan could give her. When she got off the phone, she updated her notes and then decided that, rather than sleep here, she would be better off going home, and she would need the comfort of that now, more than ever.

She'd done what she could for tonight, but that was about it. As she walked to her vehicle, she went through the long main hallway toward the double front doors, the big entranceway. She should have gone around to the doctor's entrance. It would have been quicker. As she reached the front doors, she heard an odd sound. She turned and frowned at the security guard at the front desk.

He looked at her. "Got a problem?"

She shrugged. "Just thought I heard something."

He snorted. "In this place, you hear all kinds of stuff."

She nodded. "I guess. I had forgotten what it sounds like."

He laughed. "That's all right. I'm sure you'll be back into the swing of things in no time."

She nodded agreeably and stepped out of the front doors. As soon as she got outside, she headed to her car, wondering what she had heard because it was odd, and it didn't make a whole lot of sense. It was like that pounding, that banging that her problem patient had been doing inside, yet amplified ten times worse outside. She stood in the parking lot, listening for it again, but there was nothing. Then, just as she got into the car, she heard it once more, this time louder and louder and louder, as if somebody were running toward her, yet was on the other plane.

She knew it wasn't physical running, but it was definitely somebody out there on the ethers, and then she heard this scream that made her blood curdle. She bolted back out of her vehicle and looked around, not sure whether she was facing somebody in reality or just an unruly spirit.

When nothing materialized, she took several slow deep breaths and then realized that the security guard was standing in the front of the building, watching her. Not sure what she'd seen or heard but knowing perfectly well that her behavior would be watched, she gave the security guard a wave, got into her vehicle again, and forced herself to drive away.

As soon as she got home, she phoned Stefan.

"What's the matter?" he asked immediately.

"I'm not exactly sure," she muttered. "I'm not certain that whatever happened last time is actually over with."

"Explain," he demanded, his tone sharp.

She quickly told him about the vehicle scenario.

"It could have been anything," he muttered.

"It could have been, yes, but I suspect it was quite a bit

more than that. I'm pretty sure it was that same energy again. It had that … that same signature."

"Did you see it?"

She hesitated, then replied, "No, I didn't. I heard it."

A long silence came on the other end. "Are you telling me that you can now *hear* energy? And it's the same person?"

"I don't know what I'm telling you," she admitted. "I'm just trying to explain what I heard. I'm not saying for sure it's the same signature, but I feels like it. It *sounds like it.*"

"It is possible," Stefan noted cautiously, "but we've never really had anybody who could *hear* it."

"Believe me. I don't want to be the first one," she stated, with a wry note to her voice.

He chuckled. "Maybe not, but you and I both know that, when shit happens, it tends to happen in great big piles, never nice little dumps."

"Yeah, especially for me. And, by the way, Stefan, that's not helping," she muttered.

"No, but right now you need to get a hold of yourself, ensure you're protected at all times, and, when you go back tomorrow, see if anything has changed."

SHE HAS NO *idea.*

That was always the fun part, but it was also sad because he'd expected more of a challenge when she returned. Unless he'd burned her out. That was an interesting possibility, but one that he didn't really want to consider. He knew that she would be back. He'd counted on it, but he didn't want her to come back damaged. That wouldn't be any fun. She was really the only one he could communicate with, the only one who had some idea of what he could do. Even then, what he really wanted from her was help to get away. He needed her for that.

She had thought that this was over, that the last time was a one-off, that she had won, but she hadn't. Just as she'd been burned out, so had he, but he'd just gone into sleep mode. In her case, she'd managed to walk away and had done something very different for a time, and now she was back. He wondered at that, wondered what drove her to come back to something like this.

The people here were crazy, absolutely nuts. Why would you want anything to do with them, especially after what she'd been through? There had been quite a stink over it all, and, even then, there were no answers in many ways, certainly not for him or from him.

Nobody had answers, and it was answers everybody always wanted, even when none were to be found. That was the part that always got to him. It was the clueless ones who fascinated him the most. How could you go through life completely dulled to what was going on around you? Desensitized to the whole world, locked into just your tiny part of it, and be expected carry on? Except that they were just a shell. Of course he might have had something to do with that too, trying to get them all to forget.

Still, now what?

She was back, so that was something. What would she change? He had already heard that she was pissed off about some things. That made him laugh, like anybody gave a crap about the food here. Nobody did. It was all about budgets.

She'd always had friends in high places, friends who other people didn't have access to, and she always made things happen, and nobody really understood how. Even him. He didn't understand that, and it worried him.

In many ways her return worried him, when really it shouldn't. He should be all-powerful, yet she'd had the power to actually ruin everything he had set up, and that terrified him too. Nobody should have that kind of power over him. He didn't like anything about it, but what was he supposed to do, except follow along and see where she was headed? He'd ruined her plans once before, and he was sure he could do it again.

And that boy? The one who she was here for? That was just too damn bad. He liked the young ones, and there was no way in hell he would let Adam go. If they were to go, it would mean that they were fine, healthy, and moving on to the next stage of their recovery, and that was a joke. Nobody was leaving that he didn't say could leave. His decree was law, and he would be damned if he'd let her overrule him on that.

CHAPTER 7

CRESSY WOKE BRIGHT and early, and, when she opened the door to step out and head to work, Gray stood there, waiting for her. She frowned at him, and he just smiled back. She sighed. "You again."

"Yep, me again," he replied cheerfully.

"I'm sure the FBI has more cases for you to work on than this."

"Yes, they do, but I have faith that you'll find something."

She stared at him, uncomprehending. "You do realize that it can take days, months, even years for progress in a case like Adam's, right?"

He nodded. "Yes, but, if that were the case, I don't think Grant would be all over this in quite the same way."

She winced at that. "Okay, that's a low blow."

He chuckled. "You have a reputation, Doc."

"Reputations can get you in a hell of a lot of trouble," she warned. "Besides, simply having a reputation doesn't mean that it's actually warranted."

"I find reputations are often warranted," he murmured. "In your case, you just might not like it."

"No, I sure don't. Yet it is what it is."

He chuckled at that too. "You didn't eat breakfast."

"How do you know?" she asked in exasperation.

"I can tell. You also didn't grab any coffee."

She just glared at him, as she walked to her car. "Not everything is quite so cut-and-dried."

"No, probably not," he agreed, "but, if I go pick up something, will you eat it?"

She stared at him and asked, "What are you now, my nursemaid?"

"If that's what the job requires, then, yes, absolutely." He gave her a look.

"Fine," she muttered. "Coffee is at the office. I'll see you there in a few minutes."

And, with that, he got into his vehicle and took off.

She got into hers, and, at a much slower pace, she headed to work. She walked in and waved at the staff, heading directly for her office. She stashed her purse, logged onto her computer, and, while everything was booting up, she headed off to the coffee station. Thankfully she found a fairly full pot. She poured two cups and headed back to her office.

As she walked down the hallway, one of the doctors looked at the cups in her hand and said, "Wow, you haven't even been here two days yet, and you're already double-fisting it."

She rolled her eyes at his crude joke and replied, "Hardly that."

He laughed. "Still, it's good to have you back."

"Glad to hear that," she murmured, "because I feel like I'm about to raise Cain." He looked at her in question. She shrugged. "Some of these changes made while I was away are unacceptable."

He winced. "Yeah, not exactly fun, are they? But it was made very clear that, if we complain, it would be our jobs," he muttered.

"Yeah, in that case, it'll be my job."

He stared at her astonishment. "Seriously?"

"Oh, hell yeah," she declared. "I refuse to accept these changes."

When she got back to her office, her cell phone was buzzing. She quickly picked up the phone, surprised to hear a man identify himself, someone from her past but not connected to her work, someone who was now located in New Orleans. After his introduction, she was still a bit confused. "Okay, so Stefan contacted you. I understand that, but I'm not sure what that has to do with me."

"I'm looking for a business to invest in," he replied. Still, she frowned at that, not following. He continued. "I know the kind of work you do, at least Stefan has let me in on some of it."

"Okay, so to be very specific, you realize that I work at an institution for psychiatric patients." She had to step lightly, not sure how much this man knew of her real line of work.

"Yes, and my partner also works in a similar energy field of work."

Ah, he used the magic word—*energy*. Then she put two and two together. "Now I know who you are," she said out loud, a bit too cheerfully, then cringed right away. "So, how much money do you have to invest?" she asked bluntly. "I would very much like to purchase this place and take it away from the shareholders, if it came to that."

He laughed at her blunt approach. "I can look into what you've got going on there and do some investigating into the shareholders and what's happening, but it's likely to be fairly hidden information."

"That's fine," she replied. "While I was gone on a six-month sabbatical, they cut the food budget and are now serving these already fragile unhealthy people this overly processed garbage for food. They've cut the staff significantly, and they've even cut the hygiene supplies. They've cut wellness hours and all kinds of programs that require extra staff. It's basically become a program of more drugs to keep everybody sedated, so the patients are just quiet," she explained. "But a drug-induced state of calm does not allow for healing or for getting healthier."

"Understood," he agreed. "Stefan mentioned the sabbatical."

"Yeah."

"If you care that much, why the sabbatical?"

She hesitated and then asked, "Is your partner a ferryman?"

"Yes, wow. How did you guess that?" he asked. "What's that got to do with it?"

"I assume you understand what happens when things go wrong in her corner, with the kind of specialized work she does?"

"Yes," he said cautiously.

"Something like that went wrong while I was working with a patient," she murmured. "I survived it, but there was definitely a price tag."

"Ah," he muttered. "Okay, got it. What about the people you work with?"

"The entire staff doesn't know what I fully do, just that I get results the other doctors don't. However, the board took advantage of my absence to make a lot of changes," she shared. "Changes that I'm sure are much better for the immediate budget but won't be that good for the long-term bottom line. Patient health and recovery is what I am worried about here, and that is what keeps new patients coming here. Anyone can sedate the patients and house them until they die. I want to help them get better."

"You do know that these places are supposed to operate at least somewhat at a profit."

"No, they're supposed to operate," she argued, with finality. "The profit part is optional."

"So, in other words, you're looking for someone to invest but don't plan to give anybody their money back?" he asked. "That will be a much harder thing to understand."

"I have some money to invest," she admitted, "but I don't have *that* kind of money."

"Can you give me some idea of what kind of money you mean?"

She immediately shared a figure.

"That's actually very respectable, but do you want to put it all into something like this?"

"If I had control, that would be fine by me. However, if other people will be yanking my chain, then no." She took a deep breath. "I'll have to do something else."

"Interesting," he murmured. "I don't know any of the patients you worked with. I would need a roster of some of perhaps some of your more affluent clients who would be willing to talk with me."

"Yeah, I've got a bunch of those," she replied, "and I've called on them in the past. I just need to confirm that they are okay with my sharing their names first."

"Good. Do that, and let me talk to a few of them, and we'll see what we might do."

"Good enough." She hung up, and, as she did, Gray walked in.

He motioned at the phone. "I just caught the tail end of

that," he said, as she pointed at the door. He quickly closed it and asked, "What is that all about?"

"I would appreciate it if you don't say anything to anybody, but I'm considering my options here."

"Is it that bad?"

She shrugged. "A lot of things here need to be fixed, and I'll get a lot of guff from the board about it," she explained. "If I don't get any guff, it will really surprise me. Still, while I would obviously prefer it that way, I still have to—"

"You could take it to the board and see what kind of response you get before calling in the big guns, if I may say so."

"Yeah, that's the plan," she stated, with a smirk. "However, if you've ever dealt with a board of directors, they're all about keeping their shareholders happy, and that is directly related to the payout at the end of the day. That's what everyone on the board cares about, and we both know it."

"You don't agree with that?"

"I don't agree with these hospitals turning into profit machines," she declared. "Break even? Yes. Profit enough to support expansion or updating infrastructure? Yes. But profit for the sake of profit for the shareholders? No, that's a bit hard for me to understand. Especially when the tradeoff is substandard care."

"Oh, that's clear enough." He sat down and happily picked up the coffee she had brought in for him. "Have you had a chance to assess any of the patients yet?"

"Nope," she said cheerfully. "I just got off the phone."

"I'm surprised that was your first call."

"He called me." When Gray stared at her, she shrugged. "Somebody from Stefan's corner of the world, his partner at least." Cressy smiled. "Now *she* is somebody you really should meet."

"Why?" he asked, already frowning in apprehension.

"Because she does work that would actually send your nightmares into overdrive. Maybe then you would stop looking at me like I am some sort of alien." His eyes widened, and she nodded. "She would be called a ferryman."

"I don't understand the term."

"She helps people cross over to the other side. However, in her case, she specializes in mass disasters."

He blinked and then swallowed hard. "Yeah, you got that right."

Then she grinned. "She's also incredibly gifted. Her partner just contacted me. He's some kind of financial whiz." She gave a wave of her hand. "So, I was pretty crystal clear about what I wanted and what I didn't want."

"And that is?" he asked, fascinated.

She lowered her voice. "I want control of the board. I want to get this place back to where it is supposed to be, and I want to start seeing people heal and get out of here to live a normal life. At the rate this is going here, these patients will become permanent residents, drugged to the hilt, providing lovely monthly checks for the board and their precious shareholders."

He contemplated his coffee for a long moment. "I guess in that sense, it is better for the board if they're more of a sanatorium and long-term care facility."

"True, and there is a place for that, but these people aren't supposed to need that. These patients are to be assessed and treated here, if appropriate, or otherwise moved on to long-term facilities," she pointed out, "unless that too has been changed while I was gone, although I wouldn't be at all surprised if that isn't in the works."

"Do you think that is possible?"

"It's certainly outside of the system we were all hired into, and I think plenty of people here we could help. I don't want to lose track of that."

"Got it," he noted. "It's not great when you go away, then come back, only to find that everything is different, *huh?*"

"No, it's not great at all," she muttered. "It really sucks."

He laughed. "I kind of meant it as a joke, you know."

She gave him a weak grin. "I got it, but there are things at play here that I really don't understand. As I get some of these things off my plate, at least to that extent, I can relax and get to work."

He frowned. "That doesn't seem to be all just finances."

"Sure isn't," she murmured.

"And when you say something is going on, what do you mean?"

"Remember that part about you not believing and understanding any of this stuff? You're probably better off just not asking questions at this point." When he glared at her, she shrugged. "Some of this stuff is pretty freaky. I don't have any proof."

"You actually deal in proof?" he asked, his eyebrows raising.

She glared at him. "No, I don't, not for people like you."

His tone mild, he repeated, "People like me?"

She sighed. "Look. I'm not trying to get into a spitting contest with you right now, but some of what I saw and heard yesterday doesn't make me happy, and then I got a definite feeling that something was off when I got into my car last night."

"You want to explain that?" He sat taller, leaned closed

and frowned.

She laughed. "Sure, if you insist." She told him about the sound of somebody running toward her and nobody being there, then the screaming. His eyebrows slowly rose. "As I told you, not the kind of stuff that you can really do anything about."

"Yet you believe it?"

"Oh, I absolutely believe it. I just don't know where it's coming from. But I can tell that trouble is out there, and it's connected to this place. I don't know if it has anything to do with the nightmare that sent me into the sabbatical in the first place." At that, he bolted to his feet in alarm, and she held up a hand. "Don't worry about it."

"Don't worry?" he cried out. "It's bad enough that you were burned out for six months, but now you think it's happening again?"

She gave him a feral smile. "Yes." Meanwhile she sent him some calm energy. "But you know something? I think I came back bigger, … faster, … stronger." At the look on his face, she burst out laughing. "Yes, I'm serious." Then she lowered her voice and added, "I hate to say it, but then …" She hesitated.

"What?"

She grabbed a notepad, picked up a pen, and quickly wrote something down, then tilted it toward him.

He looked at it, then slowly nodded. "I can see to that too."

"Good," she murmured. "Sooner than later, please."

"Got it." He frowned and opened his mouth, then caught himself just in time. Sitting down now, he pulled up his phone and quickly texted her. She read the text as he sat across from her. He was asking if she thought she was being watched. She nodded immediately and quickly sent another text. **Watched, listened to, and I don't want to actually say stalked, but it feels that way.**

His frown was instant, and he hopped to his feet again. "Look. I've got an errand to run. I'll be back in an hour or so."

"An hour is good," she said. "It's not as if I'll have any shortage of work between now and then."

"Right. Did you contact the boy?"

"Not this morning, but I can wait until you get back."

At that, he gave her a bright smile and nodded. "Appreciate it." Then he quickly left.

He might appreciate it, she knew, but she appreciated what he was doing first and foremost. Only as she sat here, with that weird buzz going on behind her, did she realize something else was off. When he got back, hopefully with bug detectors, he could tell her if her office had been bugged.

Considering it was a perfect opportunity for anybody who might have been interested in what she was up to when she got back, it wouldn't be that surprising. What she didn't know was whether her phone call this morning had been overheard or not.

When Dr. Mendelsohn walked in a little bit later, his tone was a little too genial and patronizing. "Hey, how're you doing?"

"I'm doing fine. How about you?"

"Good. So, we talked about some of this, and I gather you've already gotten wind of even more of the changes." She looked up at him and didn't say a whole lot. "Now, we need to be sure we don't go too far and have you getting on your high horse about it."

"No? If you actually expect me to work under the kinds

of changes you've implemented while I was away, that is BS, and it's not happening."

She rarely swore, and appropriately his eyebrows shot up at her vehemence. "You know we have to keep everybody happy."

"You have to keep *some* people happy, and you've done without me for all this time, so doing without me won't be that much of an issue again, now will it?"

"Now hold on. We have some very specialized people here, and the only reason they're here is because you would be their primary physician."

"Yeah, and then I had to leave on a sabbatical," she pointed out. "Do you still have those people?"

"Yes, we do," he confirmed, staring at her, "only because we kept promising them that you were coming back."

She sat back. "Give me a list of names, so I'll know who I'm supposed to give special VIP treatment to."

He winced at that. "You know that's not how we operate."

"No, but it sure sounds like you want me to keep that in mind, when I'm out there looking at what's going on here."

"The food isn't that bad," he offered.

"The food is disgusting," she declared. "More important, it's completely dead food with no nutrition, and these patients not only need to keep up their basic nutrition, they also need supplements. Yet I've noticed that all supplementations have been cut as well."

"We were trying to get a new dietician on board." She gave him a flat look at that, and he flushed. "Look. Give yourself a few days to get used to being back here," he suggested, "and then, when you come up with some recommendations for changes that you feel need to be made, I will do all I can. Give them to me, and I'll take them to the board myself."

Her look was as calm as she could manage, yet it still made him jump to his feet and walk to the door. "Now, Dr. Cressy. I know you're upset right now," he said, fumbling with the door knob, "but it changed once, so it can certainly change again."

"It should never have been changed in the first place," she snapped. "You haven't seen any progress since I've been gone, have you?"

He flushed at that. "There's been some progress."

"BS," she declared. "There's been no progress at all. There are a couple of reasons for that, but one of them is the fact that you really downgraded nutrition by serving that terrible food, and you cut all the supplements. I realize a lot of people aren't big fans of supplements, but, when it comes to what these people actually need and what they're actually lacking in, it's important. And not only did you get rid of all supplements, you also cut all the testing for them. That is just ridiculous."

"If we weren't going to supplement anyway, no point in doing the testing."

"Those two things you need to get back online for every single patient, and you need to do it fast. Then you need to get the food situation fixed. Now, what is this about minimal security at nighttime?"

"We haven't had any problems since that last bout, so there was no need for extra security."

She glared at him.

"I don't even know all the details of that incident, and I was kind of hoping that one of these days you and I could sit down and I could hear them." She snorted at that. "But I also understand that, from your perspective, security is important. What I can tell you is that there hasn't been any further events while you've been gone, so the security was deemed not necessary. It was also costing an extra $75,000 for God's sake, and that was money we needed for other things."

"Yeah, *what* other things?" she asked, looking at him with blatant disbelief. "I get that you think the extra security was just a one-off event," she spat, almost gritting her teeth, "but that particular *one-off event* resulted in my not coming back for six months. I chose not to file any lawsuits over it, and you should know that fortune smiled on you there, but you can't be sure that another person wouldn't sue the center."

At the term *lawsuit*, he paled.

"Let's not forget that you guys had cut all that security *prior* to this *event*," she reminded him. "So I suggest you talk to the board about getting these things fixed and fast."

"Nice to have you back," he stated in a dry tone, as he turned and walked out of her office.

She was under no illusions that the board would change everything, but she needed them to change a lot of things, and one out of three wasn't a bad start. The fact that they had put everything on the back burner that she had spent months getting approved was more than depressing. The realization that it would take months to get all the patients back up to where they had been before she left was disheartening at best.

She only had herself to blame for that, but she didn't dare take any more chances with anybody else's safety, especially not hers. Fool her once was one thing; fool her again, that was on her.

"I KNOW, GRANT, but she wrote me a message, while I was in her office, asking to have the room swept on the sly so nobody knows."

"Good God, what kind of an outfit is she working for? And this is definitely not within our purview."

"It might not be in our purview, but if we want her to trust us—"

"I know. I know, and Dr. Maddy would say that, if Cressy needs it, then we need to get it because Cressy's got better instincts than the rest of us put together."

"Ouch, that's insulting."

"It might be insulting, but Dr. Maddy is pretty adamant about Cressy's abilities."

"Fine. So, I'm two minutes away from the office."

"Good, stop in there, pick up what you need, and get back to me."

It took Gray a good thirty minutes to sign out the equipment that he wanted, then he stopped and picked up a couple tools that he might need. She had asked for one thing, but he'd gone a little beyond that, not sure what was going on and not wanting to come back for more, which would look suspicious as hell. With everything finally collected and loaded in the car, he headed toward the center. As he got closer, while stopped at a red traffic light, he sent her a text. **On my way back. Be there in a few minutes.**

There was no response, but he didn't worry about it because she could be with a patient or in a meeting. He consolidated everything into his bag, so it didn't look quite so obvious that he was bringing tools into the center, but no security guard even talked to him as he walked in.

Of course he had to sign the visitor's log, but he expected that. As he walked to her office, the receptionist looked at him and smiled. "She's not in there."

"Where is she?" he asked.

"She's with a patient right now."

"Okay, how much longer?"

She looked at her watch. "She should be back in her office in about twenty minutes, and then she has a meeting."

"Good enough. I'll wait in her office." Not giving the woman a chance to argue, he stepped into Cressy's office and closed the door behind him.

With that, he got right to work. Not a whole lot of area to search in her office, which, once done, made him feel better, and he sent a quick message to Grant. **Found zilch in her office, but I brought video cameras. I'll set that up too.**

At that, Grant called him. "Everything should already be set up for cameras."

"Except I'm not sure about her office, what with privacy issues and whatnot. She also has a little back room there, where she sleeps."

"Did you check in there for anything?"

"No, I haven't yet, and I was wondering if I even should. It seems kind of intrusive to put cameras in there."

"But, if you tell her, at least she'll be aware of it."

"That's true enough. I'll do that."

Hanging up the phone, he walked into the little alcove that she generally slept in when she stayed overnight, something that he really didn't approve of, but could also understand the need for, at times. With that, he turned his bug detector back on and stared at the flashing green light. "Shit," he muttered, under his breath.

It didn't take him very long to find it because this room

was very small. There was a small overhead light, and the bug was planted there. With that discovery, he took several photos, which he sent to Grant, and then he left that room and went back into her office. Then he called Grant. Still Gray spoke quietly, just to be sure his words didn't carry to that back room. "You were right. It was in her sleeping area."

"Why would they do that? I mean, there's got to be other places."

"No, but that's where she'll let down her guard, and that's where she's likely to *contact* people," he noted.

"She needs to know about that."

"Right, and I'm all for telling her, but she won't be a happy camper."

"No, she won't, but it'll also confirm her suspicion that something is off. We'll just have to make sure she knows what's going on."

"So, who do we suspect put this in here? I highly doubt that it was mandated by the center."

"Oh, I'm not so sure about that," Grant argued. "This hospital is sounding dodgier by the day."

"Yeah, ya think?" Gray swore. "She really needs another job, doesn't she?"

"She needs something," he agreed, with a laugh, "but I don't know where she'll end up."

"She's very talented, and I bet Dr. Maddy would take her on in a heartbeat."

"Yeah, Drew has mentioned that to me, even in context of other gifted people who work with Dr. Maddy. It's not the same kind of work though, which is probably why Dr. Maddy and Cressy have hesitated to go in that direction. Though that doesn't mean that Dr. Maddy isn't willing to open up something where the two of them could work together."

"*Hmm*, I hadn't considered that, but I suppose it's possible. Now, whether Dr. Maddy actually has funding to open up another center, would be another question," Gray added, remembering the tail end of the conversation he'd heard yesterday.

"That is a constant," Grant stated, with a laugh. "But Drew tells me that the more Dr. Maddy gets incredible results, the more the money pours in."

"Yeah, but what happens one day when it dries up, and you're left to wonder what happened?"

"That day hasn't happened, and we're not going there yet," Grant stated. "We need Drew's and Dr. Maddy's help, along with Stefan's and Cressy's. Thankfully they are there for us."

"Got it." After he hung up, Gray quickly set up two video cameras with sound and a recording device in her office. Just as he finished and put away his tools, she walked in and stopped at the doorway.

"I wasn't expecting to see you here."

He motioned for her to come in and to close the door.

With one eyebrow raised, she stepped in, closed the door behind her, and told him, "I have a meeting with the family of a patient here in about twenty minutes."

He nodded slowly. "Okay. Remember what you asked me?" She stared at him, dread in her gaze, and he nodded. "Not here but in there."

Then he pointed to the small room that she used to crash in. She stared at the room, then turned and looked at him in horror.

He nodded. "I didn't dismantle it," he whispered, "because this will give us a chance to see who's after you." She just shook her head, wordless. "I know it's a bit of a shock, but you were right to be worried. Listen. I've installed video cameras here and our own trackers," he added in a low tone. "So, if somebody comes to check on this, we'll find them fast."

"Why would they check it though?" she asked. "Apparently they can get whatever they want from that bug."

"Yes, but I've added some static to it, so hopefully they'll be coming soon to see why it's not functioning very well."

"Ah, well, aren't you the sly one," she murmured. "Will you see them when they come?"

"Absolutely." He smiled. "That was the whole point."

She nodded. "I'm glad to hear that. Why the cameras in here?"

"Because I want to see if anybody else is coming in and doing anything else in your office. I've checked for other bugs here and didn't find any, but that doesn't mean somebody doesn't have some kind of keylogger set up on your computer."

"I just brought my laptop from home," she admitted in protest.

"Did they ask you to let IT gain access to it?"

"No," she said slowly, "but it's pretty standard to have IT do that."

"It might be standard, but I'd like to see your laptop after IT's been here."

"Sure," she agreed, "particularly if you think something funky is going on."

"Now that we have proof that something *is* going on, it's even more important. So, it's better to be sure than to keep guessing."

She gave him a clipped nod.

A discreet tap on her door had her receptionist opening it and announcing, "Your next meeting is here, Doctor."

She gave her a smile and replied, "I'll just be a few minutes." She turned to Gray and asked, "How about having lunch out of here after a bit?"

"Perfect. I could suggest something."

She nodded. "Give me forty-five minutes." Then she checked her watch, hesitated, and added, "Though it could be a little longer."

"Bad meeting?"

"No, but it's the family of somebody I had to leave while I was working with them. I'm sure now it'll be a case of their wondering why I had to leave, since their son is doing so much worse. What I plan to do about it is the main topic on the agenda." She brushed her hair off her face, gave him a gentle smile, and admitted, "The thing is, I completely understand their concern and share it. So we'll have a long talk, and I'll see what I can do."

"But you can't help everybody. Just remember that."

"That message became very clear to me when I had to walk away six months ago."

Gray stepped out, smiled at the receptionist, and headed to his car. There, he opened his laptop, quickly updated his notes, and sent the update to Grant.

When Grant called him a few minutes later, Grant stated, "I told Dr. Maddy."

"What did she say?"

"She's really concerned about the situation."

"Any particular reason?"

"Cressy's instincts obviously proved correct about something being off. The fact that she didn't have the location quite right isn't a concern."

In Gray's world, that wasn't anything to be concerned about at all because, Jesus, the woman had sensed that something was wrong and had requested help for it. "She was quite upset when I told her."

Grant added, "But I'm not sure she really understands the severity of it all."

"Right," Gray replied, "but I think she was more concerned that somebody would have heard her conversations up until now. Though, when we did have a couple frank conversations, that inner door was actually shut."

"That's good," Grant noted, "but she needs to watch it from here on out."

"Yeah, I know. I disturbed the transmission a little, yet not enough to actually impede it. Just enough to give them lots of static, so they'll want to come fix it."

"Good, and I presume you set up video cameras in there?"

"Yep, I sure did, and I also put a bug in for her, in case people are going into her back room without her knowing."

"Okay, let's keep after it, and watch it pretty closely."

"Did you send me the case files on what happened to her six months ago?"

"No, I will though," he replied, and his voice was distracted for a moment there. "Okay, I just sent them to you."

"How bad was it?"

"You saw it at the time."

"I know, but I didn't get any follow-up."

"Didn't you?" Grant asked.

"No. Remember? I got shot and ended up in the hospital, while she went to convalesce."

Grant groaned. "Right. One of the guards shot you by mistake. What a mess."

"Good thing he was a lousy shot and missed all the vital organs. So, the patient who attacked Cressy six months ago died, did he not?"

"I don't think the patient died, but I believe he is comatose and nonfunctioning."

"We need to know for sure. So has anybody checked on that in a while?"

"Are you thinking it's all related?"

"I don't know, but that was a pretty scary, uncertain, and strange event for me, so I would just prefer to determine if he's still in that condition."

"Good point. However, you do understand that these patients with energy skills can still operate while in a coma, right?"

"I hate to actually hear that, yet keeping myself in the dark over it is even worse."

"It absolutely is," Grant agreed. "The more you do in this field, the more you'll be exposed to. So keep an open mind and try not to get bogged down by the semantics."

"Yeah, I'm not terribly thrilled about any of that," Gray shared, with a note of humor. "But after finding that bug in her room, something very earthly is going on here, so her troubles are not all coming from the other side."

"Agreed, so stick close to her."

"What? To her or to the boy?"

After a moment of exasperation, Grant said, "I can tell you that the boy is our legal position, but Cressy is right in the middle of it. Also something's going on with her. Better be safe than sorry."

"No, I hear you, and I'm not happy about any of it, but I'll stay as close as I can."

"Gray, I need to apologize for asking you to use your

holiday time for something like this. I know that you had plans to visit your family, but I had no idea it would wind up this way."

"Yeah, I know," he replied, "but I won't leave Cressy in the lurch like this either. Until we sort out what's going on here, we need to confirm she's safe."

"Glad to hear you say that, and really hope you don't regret it in the future."

"I saw her work last time—or at least I saw some of her work. I didn't understand it then, and I don't understand what's happening now, but I definitely got a weird feeling when I walked the hallways today. I'm not so keen on being there, that's for sure."

There was silence for a moment, then Grant asked in an odd tone, "When you say a *weird feeling*, what do you mean?"

"Like I am being watched, like, I don't know, the hair on the back of my neck is rising. There's just a really strange vibe in that place."

"Remember. Your instincts are pretty good too. Do you think there's some criminal element to it?"

"Do I have full license to check out what I need to check out?"

"Sure, particularly if you tell me what area you're thinking of."

"I want to check out some of the doctors. Some of them appear to be really friendly and happy that she's back, but I'm not so sure it's genuine."

"She was quite a force to be contended with before," Grant noted, "so keep that in mind. There's bound to be some professional rivalry now that she's back. Some people may not be so happy to see the golden girl back to reclaim her space."

"You know, it doesn't seem that she even needs to worry about reclaiming it. She's clearly at the top of the food chain. You and I just don't have a clue about the predators she's keeping us safe from."

"A rather unique position, I would say," Grant stated seriously. "On the inside, there's more going on than you would expect, but you also know there's an awful lot here that you cannot help or even understand."

"No, but I can work at keeping her safe."

"Did that work last time?" Grant asked, with a note of humor.

"According to you, Stefan, and Dr. Maddy, I was some-how instrumental in doing that. If only I had a clue what I'd done."

"Dr. Maddy would say that innocence or that absolute lack of knowing is also the reason you were an able assistant."

"That doesn't help me either because, if I helped once, I want to help again, especially if there's a need. However, when I don't know what I did, it doesn't help."

"No, I get it," Grant stated. "Just stick close, and, if things go bump in the night, remember that you agreed to stay on for this assignment."

And, with that, Grant hung up.

CHAPTER 8

C RESSY SLIPPED OUT of her office, without even saying anything to her receptionist, who was on the phone, then stepped out the front doors and kept on walking. She knew that Gray would be watching out for her. She was still unnerved from what he'd found and, on the heels of that, had had a very difficult conversation with family members of a former patient. They had asked her, pleaded with her, to take their son back into her care again and to not leave him. The *not leaving* part was hard. She couldn't guarantee what was happening in her life down the road either. She understood the panic everybody felt, but it also weighed on her that she couldn't do everything. Particularly since she also had to battle so many other fronts. When she got to the sidewalk, a car door opened beside her, and she stopped, startled. It was Gray.

"Hop in."

She rolled her eyes at his peremptory tone. "What if I don't want to?" But she was already seated at that point.

He just grinned at her. "A little late for that."

She nodded. "Yeah, a little late for everything," she muttered.

"Tough day?"

She shrugged. "Some of them are just absolutely insane. Sometimes you think you can manage, and then shit happens, and you realize you're not managing anything at all," she muttered.

"Food then?" he asked comfortably.

She laughed. "That seems to be your answer to everything."

"Not everything, but to a lot of things, yes."

"It's not quite that simple. You know that, right?"

"I know that it's not that simple to you, but, to me, it looks much simpler than you make it."

She didn't know what to say to that, so she just stayed quiet.

He noted her silence and smiled.

"You won't get your way all the time," she muttered.

"Maybe not, and maybe I don't need it all the time," he shared, "but, when you're as down and struggling as you are now, somebody needs to look after you."

She burst out laughing at that. "You do realize I'm paid the big bucks to look after other people, right?"

"I do, and then unfortunately you look after everybody but yourself. Hence what happened, happened."

"That actually had nothing to do with it," she muttered, as she stared out the windshield. "Where are we going?"

"To a nice little family restaurant around the corner," he replied.

"Ah, Jojo's."

"Yep, Jojo's," he said, with a chuckle. "I gather you know it."

"Most of us know it," she stated, smiling. "And they know me, although I haven't been there for a bit."

"That's okay. It'll be a great time for you to renew their acquaintance."

"They're a lovely couple," she added warmly. And, indeed, when she walked in, the proprietor raced over and gave her a big hug.

"I haven't seen you in forever," she cried out. "I thought you were gone."

"I'm back now." Cressy beamed at the other woman. "And I'm starving."

At that, Jojo's expression immediately changed. "Come, come, come," she said courteously. "You want your same table or something different?"

Cressy glanced at Gray, but still she smiled. "The same table will be fine." It was so easy to slip back into that routine, where somebody was looking after her for a change. She smiled as she took her seat. "Coffee please." At that, Jojo frowned at her. "Yes, I know. I drink too much coffee, but right now I could really use it," Cressy added.

Jojo immediately nodded and disappeared.

"Sounds more like a mother hen's den than a restaurant," Gray noted, as he sat down across from her.

"I came here a lot, and I even used to work at the table here a fair bit. They didn't really like me doing it, though it wasn't so much that I was taking up a table but because they felt it was bad for me."

He grinned. "I knew I liked them."

She laughed. "Not everybody sees me as incapable of looking after myself. You know that, right?"

"Maybe not, but not everybody sees you the way I have these last few days either. So, that seems fair enough to me."

"These last few days have been an anomaly." She added a dismissive hand wave, as if that would make him feel better. It was obvious from the look in his eye that he didn't believe her. She sighed. "Okay, so I worked a lot when I was here before, but I had a lot of cases to deal with."

"Of course, and you'll always give 110 percent to every damn thing."

"I'd give a lot more than that if I could," she added cheerfully. "These patients deserve it."

"You do know that so many people don't agree with you on that."

Her smile fell away, and she nodded. "That is one of the great sources of sadness in my field. ... A lot of doctors don't know what to do with their patients and don't even *want* to deal with them. So, locking them up sounds like the best idea to them. For me, that's not even a viable answer. It's not even something to contemplate."

"I guess you make a lot of enemies then, don't you?"

She stared at him and frowned. "I wouldn't have thought so," she murmured. "I worked hard for the benefit of my patients, and I thought that was appreciated. But then I come back and see all the changes that everybody made in the meantime, based on the budget of all things, and I realize that maybe I was kind of an irritant that was in their way. So, once I was gone, things could flow much more easily, and they could implement what they'd wanted to do all along. I'm certainly reassessing my life choices right now." He stared at her, and she shrugged. "That doesn't mean I'm prepared to make any major life changes immediately, but I'm certainly taking a good look."

"Taking a look is always good," he told her. "I understand that the type of work you do is something that very few people can do, so to lose you would be significant."

She smiled. "I don't know about that. You sound as if you've been talking to Dr. Maddy or something. She's a huge fan."

"As are Stefan and Grant and Drew."

"They're all connected." She gave another wave of her hand, as if negating their individual opinions. "And they all love Dr. Maddy, so, if she says something, it becomes law right there."

"You know, having met the woman, I kind of believe that myself, and it seems she's never known to be wrong."

"We're all wrong some time," Cressy admitted, studying him. The moment was interrupted when Jojo brought the coffee. Cressy was quiet for a moment and thanked the woman, who quickly put down the coffee and left.

Cressy leaned forward and added, "Now, back to the elephant in the room. What the hell is going on that somebody would put a bug in the back room of my office?"

"I don't know." He leaned forward too, his voice just as low as hers. "You tell me. ... What do you do in that back room?" She paled and he nodded. "See? That's the thing. Most people would think that you sleep in there, but there's absolutely no reason for somebody to bug that room specifically, if all you're doing is sleeping. So, is there anything you need to tell me?"

She snorted. "If you mean, am I having a hot and heavy romance with somebody I shouldn't be, like a patient or another doctor or a board member, maybe to get my budgets passed, the answer is no, no, and oh hell no. But ..." Then she stopped.

"Yeah, so it's that 'but' I need to know about."

She glared at him. "You don't need to know everything in my world."

"Yes, I do. Right now I really do. This is the problem, and you need to come out with it. I would have liked to know all that when I first came on, so I had a better way to assess things," he explained. "So, now I'm in my head, going back over every conversation that I heard and saw in this place, since I've been here."

"You've hardly even been here," she stated, staring at him.

"Exactly, but you almost become invisible, and people talk around you and about you and behind you," he replied. "Believe me. My ears are incredibly sharp, and I've heard all kinds of stuff."

"You mean, the stuff where they're saying that they're not really happy I'm back?"

He hesitated, then slowly nodded.

"Yeah, I'm getting that impression too," she muttered. She pressed on her temples a couple times. "What I don't know is what I'm supposed to do about it and why. I mean, if they're decent with the patients, whatever, but if they're backing the budget cuts because comatose patients are easier to deal with and because they want to work less, then they shouldn't be in this field."

"Are there really doctors who would rather drug these patients than try to help them?"

"In the profession in general, a whole group of people know the difference, but there's also a large group who truly believe that keeping them drugged is actually helping them, and, when they have that conviction, it's so much harder to change because they don't see that we are doing any good." She sighed heavily, then picked up her cup of coffee, took a sip of the hot brew, winced, and added cream.

"I've never seen you add cream before."

She rolled her eyes at him. "You really don't know me all that well."

"I'm getting there." Then he added, "Listen. I've asked for the files from the previous case, plus all updates."

She froze for a moment, then looked over at him. "Why?"

"I don't know. Instincts, I guess. I need another look to confirm I haven't missed anything."

At that, her hand shook, and she quickly put down her coffee.

He nodded. "And apparently that bothers you."

She stared at him. "Did you think it wouldn't bother me?" she murmured. "Just the reminder of that period of my life is pretty rough."

"I get that, and I'm not doing this to deliberately throw you off your game, but, if there is any connection, we need to know. We have to."

"I think … I think I would know if there was a connection."

"But you're not really sure, are you?"

She shook her head. "No, I'm not, but I would like to think I would know."

"I get that, and I hope, for your sake, that you would, but what if you're wrong? What if there isn't any knowing beforehand? What if whatever happened set something else in motion?"

She stared at him. "Have you been talking to Stefan?" She picked up her coffee and tried for another sip, hating the thought of all this being brought back up again. Yet she really had no choice. If it had to be brought up, it did, but she wanted it dealt with and gone forever. Better to face it now. "Read through the files, but remember. I lived the details, so I don't want to go over them again."

He nodded. "And you're pretty sure there's absolutely no chance that this connects to anything right now?"

"Like what? What would it be? I'm not in danger." He

just gave her a flat stare. She shrugged. "Well, yeah, obviously somebody's up to no good, bugging my office, but I
would presume that has more to do with my position there
than anything else."

"So, it's really a problem, *huh*?"

"Apparently, though I can't say it's anything I thought
was a problem before. But seeing all that's gone on in my
absence, apparently loyalties shifted at some point, and some
of them may have moved in a direction I never expected."

"Ya think?" He shook his head. "We just need to ensure
you stay safe."

"I'm all for that, but I thought you were here to keep
this boy safe," she noted. "I'm only here to see if I can help
him. It's up to you to protect Adam in the meantime."

"He's under heavy lock and key, right? So, is that not
safe?"

She looked out the window behind his head. "I don't
know. I'm not sure anywhere is safe right now. Not like
this."

He leaned forward. "What's going on, Cressy?"

She shrugged. "As I told you, everything has changed.
The atmosphere is different."

"You keep saying that, but think about it. How much of
that is just that you haven't been there? Or maybe it seems
new and different since you've come back."

"Maybe I've changed." She frowned at him, startled.
"You know what? That's probably what it is. It's not so
much that anything or anyone there has changed as much as
I have. Wow, I, … I considered that I had changed, but I
wasn't really seeing that. Maybe that's what this is all about."

Just then their meals arrived. She stared down at the
food, then smiled and thanked the other woman. After Jojo

left, Cressy picked up her fork and muttered, "I'm not hungry at all now."

"Maybe, but I also know that you've got to eat."

Such an inflexible tone filled his voice that she looked up and smirked. "Back to that *taking care of me* thing, *huh?*"

"Or maybe it's back to making sure you take care of yourself."

She winced at that. "I don't have a death wish, you know? I just care about my patients."

"I get that, and I know that you truly care and want to do right by them, but you also need all your senses alert, until we figure out what's going on right now."

"Now that"—she picked up her fork and stabbed the air in his direction—"is quite true." Then she dug into her meal.

There wasn't anything good about what he was saying, but, as long as things were happening that she didn't like, maybe she did need to leave, maybe that was what this was all about. Maybe her tone and time had shifted here, and maybe it was time for a change. When she was almost finished eating, she murmured, "Maybe it is time to leave."

"What would you do?" he asked.

She contemplated that and shrugged. "Probably find another center."

He didn't say anything at first. "So, you would stay in this kind of work?"

"Absolutely. It's what I do. As long as I can help people—and I do feel that I need to—I'll do whatever I can."

He just nodded.

She was grateful for that. At least there was no condemnation or any *run and save yourself* type mentality. "Most people don't really understand, but, when you have a calling for something, it's really not a choice."

"I'm sure Dr. Maddy would agree with you."

She laughed. "Absolutely. Maybe I should start to think about working with Dr. Maddy," she muttered.

"Would you like to?"

"I would still need to be working in my own field, so I don't know if there's enough call for that in her world. I mean, she does whatever she can, and she already sends those she can't help any further over to me."

"I would really like to ask more about what you do," he began, with a wry look, "but I'm not sure I would even understand it."

"No, probably not. I like to say that I dance into people's minds and play with them in their own playgrounds. I talk to them and help them sort through their feelings and beliefs about what's gone on in their lives. In short, I help them be right in their own minds. In this case, with the boy, he has his fears."

"Dance in their minds?" he repeated.

She smiled. "Right? I knew you'd pick up on that, and I'm sure that's not something you want to hear."

"Maybe I don't want to hear it," he admitted, as he pushed his own empty plate off to the side. "Yet the way you say it, it doesn't sound bad at all."

"It's not bad." She stared at him. "Why would you think that?"

He shrugged. "I guess because I'm thinking that they don't have a choice and that you're inside messing around with their thought processes."

She smiled. "No, that's definitely not what I'm doing, though I can see why you would get that impression. That's because you haven't worked with me, and I haven't worked with you, not energetically."

"No, and I'm not sure I want you in there either," he muttered, with a little more force than intended. She burst out laughing, and he smiled at her. "Now that makes me feel better. Although that sounded a little rusty."

"What?" she asked, looking at him curiously.

"Laughter. It doesn't sound as if you've done very much for a while."

"Not for the last six months anyway," she admitted. "There hasn't been a whole lot to laugh about."

At that, he smiled. "Times are changing."

"They're changing, indeed, but I'm back to wondering what it is I want to do with my life."

"You don't have to make a decision right now anyway. Even if they did manage to squeeze you out of there—which doesn't make sense when you're the one who brings in the big paying customers—but, even if they did, you would still have plenty of options."

"I did think about some of those options a bit, but I was more focused on getting back to my patients. Even now it would be very hard for me to leave them again because I *know* what I would be leaving them to. Last time I had the benefit of a doubt and assumed my colleagues would have my back and the decency to put patient care above all."

"So, are they all like that?"

"No, absolutely not, and that's the problem. I don't know who is and who isn't. They all tell me how they're absolutely delighted to have me back, but clearly that's not true."

"And you don't know whether you can believe them or not?"

"No, not now. Especially not now that I know what you

found in my office. And in that back room particularly."

"Why that room?"

She winced. "Because I do some of my night sessions there." At his off look, she added, "And, no, my night sessions are not what you would think of as nighttime sessions."

His grin flashed. "Dang, and I was just going to say, *Tell me more.*"

She rolled her eyes at that. "No, it's definitely not that kind of a thing, but I can't really explain it here. It would have to be someplace where I don't have to worry about being overheard."

"Let's go for a walk. It'll help us digest some of that food."

"I need to get back to the office," she muttered.

"Yeah, I know, but you also need to take care of yourself, so, if you could help me understand some of this, that would be good."

When they got up, he paid both bills. She looked at him when he did so. He shrugged. "Hey, I'll just expense it."

"Oh, *great*, so my taxes pay for it. How very generous of you."

He grinned. "Does that bother you?"

"Maybe it's okay in this instance." She shrugged. "I really don't know what to say. I presume if they don't like the expense chit, they'll kick it back to you anyway."

"Absolutely."

"Then tell me if they won't cover it because it's not as if I'm destitute."

She had said it in such a dry tone that he had to laugh.

She shook her head. "I'm sure your background research on me has already provided you with that information."

"I know that you're fairly wealthy and that you live a very modest lifestyle, basically living for your patients," he shared, with a smile.

"Yeah, I do, and, until recently, never really found that to be a problem."

"Maybe not, but that doesn't mean that other people aren't holding grudges against you."

"Good God, but why? Why would anybody bother? I just don't get it. There are people way wealthier than I am."

"Maybe, but that doesn't mean anything. As a matter of fact, in some cases, it makes things way worse. Can you think of any reason for people to dislike you?"

Outside, she stopped and stared at him. "Most people don't even know that I have money, and I sure wouldn't mind if we left it that way."

"Got it, and I'm okay with that. I'm just not sure that it would be an option before this is all said and done."

She hated to hear that too. "I've been there a long time. I did get paid while I was on sabbatical, at least for quite a bit of it. I got medical leave for whatever the insurance covered. Then that was the end of it."

"Yet you were totally okay to not work for six months?"

"Honestly I don't have to work for a living at all, and I'm sure you know that too."

He gave her a big smile and a nod. "Yeah, so I understand."

"Is that a crime now too?"

"No, only for people who are looking for a reason to hate you."

"Yeah, but people looking to hate me don't really need a reason."

GRAY MADE IT back to his apartment, where he immediately set up the monitoring equipment and hooked into the system he had set up in her office. He heard her talking.

"That's fine. I'm on my way down now."

She hung up the phone, and he heard her footsteps.

He adjusted the tone, making sure it was as crisp and as clear as he needed it to be, and then he checked in on the other equipment in the back room that she wouldn't talk about. He figured it was where she did whatever she and Dr. Maddy apparently did so well that nobody else understood. Voodoo stuff, as he would most likely call it.

Checking that everything was all working, he sat back and tried to figure out what he was supposed to do next. The boy wasn't even on her roster today, and yet Gray needed to push Cressy in order to get any information she could from Adam.

Meanwhile, no way Gray would allow himself to sit here and do nothing. He pulled up the case files from the prior incident, wishing he had the follow-ups, but they were coming later. He went over the event again and again. The first couple times hadn't gotten him anywhere, and he kept thinking that maybe, just maybe, if he read one more section again, he would come up with something that made sense, but, so far, there just wasn't anything.

She'd been working on a patient, when the patient had gone off the rails and had attacked her. The attack had been prolonged, since the security cameras weren't working, and she'd had nobody outside the room waiting for her. After a good twenty minutes, she was found unconscious in the room, with the patient basically sitting on her, hitting her face over and over and over again.

When he'd been hauled off, and she'd been rushed to

emergency, there had been a lot of talk about what had happened and why, but nobody seemed to understand it. It brought up an ugly debate regarding the lack of security and the safety risks to the doctors and staff, all with good reason.

That wasn't something that should ever have been allowed, but they'd gotten lax because the center had had no problems before with doctors around a violent patient. With Dr. Cressy being one of the biggest proponents of not having everybody doped up and locked up and in chains, it had been simple to just write it off as a one-time incident that nobody needed to worry about, and, for a while, everybody had agreed. Still, a big push remained to increase adherence to the usual safety protocols and to ensure the procedural systems in place were followed.

The orderly who had been there with Cressy had left her, after receiving notice of a disturbance out front, and it took a good twenty minutes for that to be calmed down. By the time he'd made it back, right when Gray had returned too, they'd found her unconscious on the floor. She'd been comatose for ten days afterward.

The patient had been subdued and then put into the high-security area. He hadn't had any reason to attack her, and, up until that point, their relationship had been incredibly strong, with the patient showing great strides of improvement. He'd been out in the common room areas multiple times, where he'd been slowly socializing and a model patient.

Until this incident.

Nobody knew what had set it off. The other patients all heard about what had happened, several of them saying they had heard Cressy crying for help, but no one had paid any attention. That was not easy to keep under wraps. Although only a few patients had heard her cries, that notation made Gray suspicious all over again.

Had the orderly deliberately left on his own, or had somebody pulled some strings to have a disturbance out in the front so they could attack her?

But why attack her? And, if they would attack her, why hadn't they done a decent job of it? They could have killed her. She was right there, incapable of defending herself at that point.

Certainly a lot of people wondered at the time if the perpetrator or perpetrators just didn't have the means or the wherewithal to kill her because no weapons were available. The report of her being in a coma for as long as she was had been according to Grant. And, all thanks of Dr. Maddy and Stefan, who'd fought long and hard to keep her alive, Cressy was returned to the land of the living and fully sane.

When she'd finally regained consciousness, her recovery had been slow and deliberate. Slow because she had made it slow, needing time to assimilate what had happened and to sort it out. Whether she ever had, Gray didn't know.

He wasn't privy to that personal information, and that was frustrating. He didn't know exactly what had happened, so he didn't know if it could happen again. And now that he saw how security was running in the sanatorium, he realized that things had gotten even more lax.

He pondered that and then started a deep dive into the other doctors at the center. They had to be thoroughly vetted before they were hired, but that didn't mean that some people hadn't slipped in who weren't so carefully vetted. If they were making other changes that lowered the formerly higher standards, maybe that was a change they made at some point as well. The real question was, who was behind it

INSANITY

all?

Whoever it was had to be pretty powerful. Gray had no idea if a single person was behind all this, and that was a big question. In reality, he wasn't even supposed to be looking at her life as part of this case; he was only trying to get information from a twelve-year-old boy who had been traumatized. Yet, in order to do that, it appeared that he had to do a deep dive into Cressy's life at this center.

What he found wasn't making him happy. Not that anything was terribly wrong, but a lot of things just weren't right. Something about Cressy had become a problem. He hadn't heard very much in the way of coworkers who were unhappy with her return, but he definitely found some jealousy, a couple people calling her Queen Bee and things like that. But that kind of thing was a far cry from putting recording devices in her rooms, or was that somebody looking to see just what her methodology was, knowing she did *something* in that tiny room of her own?

But who would know that?

He picked up the phone, and, knowing it was a long shot, he called Dr. Maddy. She answered right away.

"Gray," she greeted him, her voice calm. "I presume you have a reason for calling me directly."

"Yes. Cressy's busy with people, and I'm back at my apartment, monitoring the equipment. I don't know if Grant told you, but we found a listening device. However, it was *where* we found it that is most disturbing."

"Where did you find it?"

"She has another room here, behind her office, where she sleeps."

"Yes. I do too."

"Do you only sleep in that room?"

147

She hesitated and then asked, "What do you mean?"

"That's where the listening device was. If she was only sleeping there, that would not be a great place to set up a listening device." Hesitating, he added, "Look. I don't know really understand what you guys actually do, although she's tried to explain it. However, I'm wondering if she would do something in that room that someone would potentially be trying to figure out. To listen in on. Even if I can't know or I don't need to know, I still need some inkling here. I don't even know how to explain it, but it's a very odd choice of location."

Silence came first on the other end. "Have you asked her about that?" she asked curiously.

"Yes, not that I got a full answer. I will be asking her again though. But, as I'm running through all the doctors and doing a full check on the place right now, that is something I could really use help with."

"I would suspect that she does a lot of her healing work there. Call it her playground, as she would call it, or more like a work area."

"She did say something about dancing in playgrounds with her patients in their minds."

"Yes, that's a good way to look at it. She brings out the part of their psyche that's healthy and works to heal the parts that aren't healthy, once she's made a connection with the healthy part."

"Is that really possible?" he asked curiously.

"Absolutely," Dr. Maddy confirmed. "I do a variation of that myself, depending on what my patients have for issues, but not if I'm just dealing with physical issues. That's a whole different story. In her case, she's dealing with psychological issues—in most cases trauma that has affected people at the absolute core of who they are. So that's a whole lot harder to treat. She is very gifted, but nobody can help everybody all the time. What she has been doing a lot of is checking patients for us to see whether they're actually having episodic breaks or are mentally in need of healing or medication because of trauma or various other health concerns. In particular, we are interested if they're actually psychics, like Stefan and I are, and have been locked up because of the things that they see, feel, and hear," she shared. "Cressy's role in that aspect is absolutely invaluable."

He sat back. "So, she's kind of like a psychic detector?"

Dr. Maddy laughed. "I won't say yes or no to that, and I'm sure she would be quite offended by the term, so I wouldn't use it, if I were you. Yet she has the ability to see whether people are incarcerated, rightly or not, and what type of work needs to be done."

"Which is why there have been some seemingly miraculous healings," he stated in understanding.

"Yes, in some cases those *miraculous* healings are actually occurring where she's identified somebody who really only needs to accept and to understand their psychic gifts, and yet to be quiet about the aspects of their gifts that the world can't handle," she explained, with a note of amusement. "Once identified, we have a special program where we work with those people to help keep them on the straight and narrow."

"So, she finds them, gets them into your program, and you work at getting them to help establish and to control their abilities. God, it's no wonder the world wouldn't understand that."

"Exactly," she replied, "and no way we can help the world understand because the world isn't ready to understand. They want to believe that everything they see and hear is real. They don't want to know that people are out there who can do things that would cause you, and sometimes even me, to cringe in our sleep."

"Jesus, I don't want to know about that."

"Nope, you sure don't. However, just because they're in these centers or in a hospital, psychiatric hospital, under care, and off the grid, doesn't mean that they're any less dangerous. Much better that we identify who is where and then help them. Help them control their energy, control their abilities, and go on to lead fulfilling lives, and, in many cases, helping others like them."

"But that's not what she's doing now, right?"

"Not necessarily, but I thought you were supposed to be helping her with the boy. Things like that can go sideways very quickly, and she's there to help control it. A lot of the patients there don't want to deal with the realities of their lives. They're happy to be in the situation they're in, where they can play in their playgrounds and be that child, not dealing with any of the realities of their life," she murmured. "Still a tremendous number of patients don't know how to control their gifts and are seeing things that are well past what they were ever taught was real. So the world has assessed them as being lost in imaginary worlds, incapable of dealing with day-to-day events, and they're quite wrong. By identifying those people, who are strong enough to move from the situation they're in, and teaching them to control their abilities, how they can come out and live in this world, is all important and frees up resources for others, who need more help. But the longer they're in a situation like that, the harder it is for them. So catching them as fast and as young as possible is important."

"I can see that," Gray noted, feeling shaken. "So, all in all, that isn't a primary part of her job, but one of the many things that she does as a sideline?"

"She assesses every patient in that building and everyone who comes in for care, and I bring her into a couple of my locations on a regular basis."

"You only have one in town, don't you?"

She chuckled. "Yes, but we are not bound by our physical location. I've had Cressy consult on special cases in England, Germany, Switzerland, Australia, and I could go on and on, but I think you get my drift."

"Are you telling me that she doesn't actually need to be there to do that?"

"No, she doesn't, and sometimes neither do I." Then her tone turned brisk. "Now, I hope you have a better handle on things. I guess that's quite a bit of information for you to assimilate, and I need to get back to work myself. So, if you need me, and I'm not available, just leave a message, and I'll get back to you when I can." And, with that, she disconnected.

He stared down at the phone in disbelief, wondering if her husband, Drew, much less Gray's boss, Grant, had really accepted and had come to terms with all this. Hating it, but not really having much choice, Gray phoned Grant, told him a little about his question for Dr. Maddy and her response, then explained his dilemma. "I really have to ask you, man, is all this for real?"

"It is for real," Grant agreed. "For Dr. Maddy to explain that much to you, … it means that she trusts you."

"I don't know," he muttered. "That kind of trust is scary too."

Grant laughed. "It's very scary on her part as well. Imagine if you shared that with just anybody."

"Yeah, you know what would happen …" Gray replied in disbelief. "I would be put right into that center where Cressy works."

"You would," Grant noted, with a note of humor. "Why do you think it's important to have somebody like Cressy at these places, trying to help those who have been incarcerated wrongly?"

"Are there really that many?"

"Yeah, she saves probably ten to twelve a year, just from that center. At least I think that's the last figure I got from Dr. Maddy. More than that, Cressy can also really help a lot more people because of the kind of work she does."

"Yet nobody can really tell me what work she does."

"Nope. I sure can't. However, I've worked a lot of cases with Dr. Maddy and Stefan and their other gifted energy workers. So I've been exposed to more of it than you have. It takes time to get to the point where you accept them at their word. So understanding what Cressy does isn't really needed. Just trust her to do her magic. And her work seems to vary, depending on the problem she finds," he explained. "Some people are traumatized because of something that has happened in their world, and they need somebody, like Dr. Maddy or Cressy or Stefan, to connect with to let them know that they're safe and that it's okay to come back out again."

"And that sounds like the boy."

"To a certain extent, yes. What he actually saw happen to his family is something he may or may never recover from. Yet the fact that he is only twelve means it's possible that they can help him get past it."

"What do they do, block it out?" he asked in disbelief.

"How else would you ever face the world, knowing that monsters like that are out there?"

"The problem is, once you're touched by a monster, they would say that it gives you a certain ... sensitivity, I don't even know what I mean by this, but, once touched, you're never really free."

"When I think of all the victims in the world who have been touched by such monsters, that just makes my skin crawl."

"Exactly."

"If that is so for the boy, ... does that also mean it's true for Cressy? I mean, considering that she's not only been touched by monsters—"

"I would think so, but you can bet that nobody's talking about it. Those gifted people seem to accept a certain amount of hazard inherent in their work, for which they don't get paid extra. We get hazard pay for hazardous duty, but, for them, it's very different. They get hazard pay in the sense of karma or energy, but they get no actual compensation when things go bad, and things can go really bad."

"Which is what happened to Cressy."

"Yes. Apparently when she went in there, the patient who attacked her wasn't actually himself, or so the theory goes. Dr. Maddy and Stefan are still trying to figure it out. They've bandied about possession or maybe how the patient was a weak-willed medium and had been channeled by somebody else. They spoke of *MPD* and *hooks* and *blocks* and admitted that they still don't know all that can be found on the spirit plane. Scary to think of, knowing what we *do* know about it."

"Right," Gray muttered, taking a deep breath. "Jesus. So, you're talking possession now, or even multiple personality disorder?"

"To a certain extent, yes. Believe me. It took me a long time to *not* sit there and stare at Dr. Maddy and Stefan and the others who worked as consultants with us on these *special* cases, wondering just what the hell was going on. Yet, after enough time goes by, enough of *these* cases come to you, then you realize woo-woo things are out there that you do *not* want to argue with. So, if it takes people like Dr. Maddy and Cressy and Stefan to make this world a safer place for the rest of us, I'm totally okay to be on their side and to keep them safe, so they can do whatever they need to do," he declared calmly. "And I know most people wouldn't agree with me, but Drew will tell you, as Dr. Maddy's husband, that, once you fall in love, and you see just what that person can do—that nobody else in the world can do—it changes you. So, even if the monsters can touch us and can leave us changed, we also have the good guys who can touch us and can leave us changed as well."

"I can't even imagine," Gray muttered.

"Ah, but you actually can," Grant argued, laughter in his voice, "because you're there. You're already to that point, dealing with Cressy. You just don't know all of what she can do yet."

"If she can do even a tiny fraction of what you're talking about, obviously her job is important. I just wonder, who looks after her, who protects her when things go bad?"

"I think that's one of the reasons it took her a long time to come back—because nobody was there for her."

"Yet everybody keeps saying I was some kind of... what? Was it a *ground*?"

"You were in the building at the time, correct?"

"Yes, but more toward the end. This patient was trying

to contact somebody, like some one-person séance was going on. I thought the whole thing was malarkey."

"Yeah, so did I. Yet Dr. Maddy and Stefan warned me that it wasn't malarkey, that she couldn't see the evil but felt it, and that it was bad news."

"Yeah, ya think? Too bad Cressy or the others didn't know that ahead of time."

"You were there," Grant pointed out. "And you know how quickly things can go from okay to not okay."

"I was actually being relieved at the time, so I missed some of it."

"Then you came back."

"I was driving away, yet heard the alarm blaring at the facility. So I raced back, so mad that I was that far away from her, but thankful I still heard the warning alarm. By the time I pounded on the front doors and convinced the guard to let me in—the facility was on full lockdown by then—I entered the room and hauled this other person off Cressy."

"So when were you shot?" Grant asked.

"One of the guards shot me in the hallway, midway to Cressy."

"Wow. The power of adrenaline kept you going, I presume."

Gray shook his head. "Yet the thing that really got to me was the absolutely insane strength that her patient had."

"Yeah. Rodney's body didn't have that physical strength. That strength you speak of came from the other side, the spirit world. So the worst part is that Rodney has gifts that he uses to hurt, not heal."

"Yeah, and I had nightmares for months."

"Yep, and those nightmares will never go away," he shared, "because the next time there's something, there will be another guy just like that."

"Why is it that people decided that contacting the other side would be a good idea, particularly in a hospital space like that?"

"I'm not sure that the patient even knew what went on during the attack. There is some question about that. Then the staff sedated him afterward for days. He was in a drug-induced coma, so he may have no memory of all this. The sanatorium had another doctor who thought this séance idea would allow the patient to bring his alternate personality out. Unfortunately that alternate personality, along with these unknown energy skills, weren't coming out. So, when Cressy was working on Rodney, he apparently chose that time and place to use his skills to attack her.

"Don't quote me on this because I don't have any recent updates, but what I remember happening right after the attack was this. That patient was under heavy security. As far as they're concerned, whenever he is conscious, the doctors confirm that his alternate personality is still the one in control. During Cressy's absence, the other doctors talked to Rodney. They tried to calm him down and to bring out any other personalities he might have, but that one is staying dominant. And could very well still be connected to the spirit world."

"She says there's a different energy to the place, that it feels not … wrong, but off in some way."

"If you think about what she'd been through, it kind of makes sense."

"That was another thing she did admit, that maybe it was she who had changed, how maybe she was the one who wasn't the same anymore."

"I can't imagine anybody being the same after what she

went through," Grant said. "So keep that in mind, when you're looking at going down this pathway."

Gray startled. "What pathway?"

"With Cressy. And, if you don't realize you're already halfway in love with her, I think you need your head examined."

"Whoa, whoa, whoa, I didn't say anything about that."

"You don't have to. The fact that you were used as a ground means a lot. Dr. Maddy would say that you still had free will, but then comes the point where you're back here again, and that means even more attachment is here between you two. You have a connection with her."

"No, *you* asked me to be here."

"Yep, because Stefan and Dr. Maddy stressed how it was important, and still you could have said no. Just think about it. I asked, and you jumped at the first chance you got. You could have walked away, but instead you jumped at it. And I know you probably aren't ready to even make that kind of acknowledgment. Still, you need to because, if anything else goes wrong, you can bet she'll reach out and will need your help again."

"And I'm expected to help her somehow?" he asked in disbelief. "I don't even know what I did in the first place."

Grant burst out laughing. "Dr. Maddy would say you didn't have to do anything. You just had to be there, and Cressy would do the rest herself."

CHAPTER 9

I T WAS A long day, a hard day, and, by the time Cressy was done, she was once again questioning her decision to come back. She looked up to see Gray in the doorway. "Hey." She was amazed at how much fatigue could fill that one word—more than she meant to let on, for sure. No matter, from the look on his face, he was almost as tired. "You don't look so good."

"I'm fine." He gave a wave of his hand. "I presume you didn't get to the boy at all."

She winced. "No, I did not."

"You're avoiding him," he accused.

Her back stiffened, and she glared at him. "Not that it's any of your business, but that boy is traumatized, and I have to make progress slowly."

"I get that," he replied, staring at her, "but other people are waiting for answers."

"I know," she snapped, then her shoulders slumped. "It's just not that easy."

"It's never easy," he admitted, "but we don't need any more dead families."

She swallowed hard and nodded. "Fine, I'll work on him again tomorrow." He let out a sound of exasperation, and she glared at him. "Take it or leave it."

"I'll have to take it because you won't give me any

choice, will you?"

"I have to do what's right for him."

"And for yourself," he corrected.

"Sure," she agreed. "Those two things don't have to be exclusive of each other."

"Maybe not, but it would be nice to know that you'll also be looking after yourself. I think you need to help this boy, even if it's only for your own self-confidence."

At that, she stared at him, stunned, and then her gaze narrowed. "You don't know anything about it." Her voice was tight, as she hated that this conversation was even brought up. "It's taken me a while to get back into this. I will do some more work when I get home tonight, but knowing that somebody has bugged the back room where I tend to do a lot of my work," she whispered, "that's something else again. It's … it's tough, and it's left me feeling that I can't do what I need to do."

"So what do you need so you can do that?" he asked instantly.

"I don't know. I just don't know." She raised her hands, glaring at him. "Peace and quiet would help."

He grinned at her. "If you want me to quit bugging you, that won't happen."

"It has to happen. I need a certain environment to do this work."

"You mean, a safe environment?"

She waved her hands at that. "Don't go putting words in my mouth. I know you think you know what I'm talking about, but I can guarantee you that you don't."

"I *don't* know what you're talking about, and I'm not sure I can actually understand anything without more explanation. Obviously this is relatively new for me, but I am trying."

She nodded. "You're trying, but it's five o'clock, and you're probably here to make sure that I leave, more than anything else."

He smiled at her. "News flash."

"What?" she growled, glaring at him.

"It's seven."

She blinked. "What?"

"Yeah, it's 7:00 p.m. So, yeah, to a certain extent, I *am* here to ensure you leave, partly because I can see that you have no clue how much time has even gone by."

She pulled up her phone, took a look, then shook her head. "I wasn't expecting that." She let out a slow breath.

"I gather you can't come back too fast to the work you were doing."

"No, I can't," she agreed. "There's an adjustment period. There's an energy shift I have to make," she muttered. She scrubbed her face. "But I am getting there. I've spoken with Adam several times, but not enough to get to the point of being able to question him. The cops questioned him, and that traumatized him just as much as anything else in his life."

"I get that, and believe me. I'm acutely aware that he's a victim too, and that he desperately needs help. But I'm also aware that it's only a matter of time before we have another whole family of victims. If we can't get a handle on this, it'll just keep on happening."

"Presumably you're doing something other than just waiting for this boy because, if that's your only pathway to getting answers, … it's not a good one." He knew that. Of course he did. It's just that this kid was one of the FBI's best pathways. "I can't even believe that the FBI is letting you spend all this time here."

"I have other cases that I'm working on, and I've got reports to write up, but this is a very important case."

She stared at him, her gaze narrowing, as she intensely studied his face.

He sighed. "You don't have to analyze me, you know?"

"Don't *have* to. It's pretty easy. You're still recovering."

He laughed at her. "No," he corrected. "*Recovered.* I was cleared for partial duty last week."

"You were shot," she reminded him, and, at that comment, he stiffened and glared at her. She shrugged. "*Right.* You don't like other people interfering in your business, *huh?* Imagine that? Neither do I."

"Okay, great, so we could work on a truce."

"We could, but I wonder if you even know what that means." She groaned and raised both hands. "Look. I'm not getting anything done here right now anyway, so, yes, I'm packing up to go home."

"Good." Then he just crossed his arms and leaned against the doorway.

She sighed. "Don't tell me. You'll wait until I leave."

"I absolutely will."

"What if I wanted to stop and talk to somebody on my way?"

"That's nice. I'll stop with you."

Since obviously nothing else in his demeanor was interested in being anything but agreeable, she started packing up her stuff. He watched as she locked her desk and filing cabinet and shut off her computer.

"Do you log off?"

She sighed. "Since I've come back, yes. I didn't use to."

"Are your computer files encrypted?"

"I've always kept my files encrypted, yes," she replied, taking her time to answer this one. "I don't know that anybody ever found them."

"Were they here when you got back?"

She nodded. "They were, and it didn't appear that anybody had been here. But I did wonder if that's why people would be putting listening devices in my office—except for the part about it being in *that* room."

He nodded. "I didn't find another device here in the office, but that didn't mean that there wasn't one installed after the sweep."

She winced at that. "Great, I was hoping that would mean I was free and clear in here."

"No, but remember. I have cameras now." And then he repeated where they both were.

"So, not only is there a bug in my most private space, now you can actually see when I log in?" she asked in horror.

He frowned. "You do know that's got nothing to do with why I'm here, right?"

"I don't care," she declared, sitting back down again, looking at her computer and then up at him. "That is a huge invasion of privacy and security."

"I don't think I can see your keystrokes," he told her. "Go ahead and try it now, and I'll bring it up on my phone." He quickly brought up the cameras on his phone and watched as she inputted various codes into her computer, and he shook his head. "If you're sitting like that, no chance it gets out." He came around and showed her. Then he watched as she sagged visibly with relief.

"That makes me feel better," she muttered. "I really can't have you getting into my files."

Such an uneasiness filled her tone that he wanted to reassure her, but what he'd set up was pretty basic, pretty simple, and a lot of other people could easily set up something like this as well. "I'm not trying to freak you out, but you do know this isn't a difficult thing to acquire or to set up, right?"

"So what are my options to keep this clear?" she murmured.

He hesitated. "I can set up a different kind of security, but then nobody else in the department would see your work either."

"Good," she muttered. "Until I know who's actually on my side, I would just as soon keep it that way."

"Do you really think people are going against you?"

"It's not so much *going against me*. I think they just got comfortable. I was gone. They got comfortable taking an easier path. And, as I told you earlier, their jobs are easier if the patients are sedated, and I don't know whether it's everybody or if it's just a couple."

"But even if it's just a couple—"

"It's too many," she replied instantly. "I need to know that everything I put in this computer is safe, until we sort this all out."

"Patient files?"

She nodded and then added, "Research as well."

"Your own kind?"

And again she nodded.

"So that could very well be something that would cause you a lot of trouble if it were found out?"

She winced. "Only in the sense that people would have more of an idea of what I do and how I do it. That, of course, would be difficult in itself. No way that people would comprehend this."

CHAPTER 10

CRESSY WOKE IN the middle of the night to a buzz. She reached for her phone—1:45 a.m. The phone call was for her, at least presumably, as her phone ringing. She answered it in a sleepy voice, only to hear panic on the other end.

"Doctor, it's Andrea on the night shift. The boy, Adam, he's awake and screaming. He won't stop."

She bolted upright. "What is he screaming? Can you make out the words?"

"Something about *They're coming for me. They're coming for me.*"

"So, a nightmare maybe?" she asked cautiously, even as she hopped out of bed, throwing on clothes.

"It's possible, but it's nothing normal sounding," Andrea added. "We've given him something to try and calm him down, but we've given him as much as we can for his size, and it's not working. He's starting to convulse and change all kinds of colors," she told Cressy. "The other doctor told us to knock him out, but I don't know. I'm really uncertain about what to do."

"I'm on my way," Cressy stated. "Does it help to have anybody in there with him?"

"I don't think anything's helping. The screams? God, they're like from another world."

"I'm dressed, grabbing my keys and my purse," she muttered, and she was. She headed to the front door, locked up, and raced down to her car. She was at the center twelve minutes later.

As she rushed inside, Andrea looked at her and cried out, "Oh, thank God. He's calmed down a little bit but not much."

She nodded, and, with Andrea leading the way, they raced to Adam's room. As soon as she got into the same hallway, she heard him.

The screams were interjected with major sobs. Andrea quickly unlocked the door, and two orderlies stood to the side, as Cressy raced in. As soon as the boy saw her, his screams stopped, and the tears started. He opened his arms, and she dropped beside him and just hugged him close.

"Easy," she muttered, "take it easy." She looked over at Andrea and motioned for her to leave.

Andrea asked, "Are you sure?"

Cressy nodded. "I'll call for help if I need anything." With one orderly standing guard outside the room, she just sat here and held the boy.

When his sobs slowly calmed, she noted his complete exhaustion had just wasted him away. His color was pale to the point of white. His eyes, when he opened them, were almost blank and staring at nothing.

"You want to tell me what just happened?"

He looked up at her and slowly shook his head.

She wasn't sure if the drugs were kicking in or something else. "Nightmares?"

He paused and then slowly nodded.

"And you've had them before, right?" she guessed.

He nodded again.

"Are they always the same?"

He looked at her and started to shake.

"Okay. Not always the same, and this time was worse, right?"

At that, he started to cry again, but he was nodding his head and clutching at her.

"It's okay. I'm here. It's all right now."

He whispered, "They'll get me."

"They?"

He paused and then nodded. "They. They. I think there were … two of them."

"Were they chasing you down the hallway?" she asked.

He looked up at her and then nodded.

"Got it. You're afraid they'll find you here, aren't you, Adam?"

"They *will* find me," he declared, his voice serious. "It's only a matter of time."

"I'm not so sure about that," she noted in a calm voice.

"They shouldn't have found me here," he said pointedly, "but they did." He looked over at the door, shuddered, and buried his face against her hair.

She held him close, most of his body in her lap, as she just sat here, rocking back and forth. When she heard the door open, she turned to frown at Andrea, only to see Gray standing there, looking disheveled and worried. She smiled up at Gray. "Adam just had a nightmare."

Gray looked at her steadily, but she saw the disbelief in his eyes. She shrugged. "No need to worry. It was just a bad one."

"I'll get coffee." And, with that, he disappeared out the door.

Adam looked up at her and asked, "Who is he?"

"He's one of the good guys," she murmured.

"He didn't look like he believed you."

She smiled. "Just like I'm a guardian angel, so is he."

At that, Adam relaxed ever so slightly. "If you're a guardian angel, you needed to get here earlier."

She winced at that. "You could be right about that, but I still don't think they'll find you here."

"Not that they will, but they have," he stated quite clearly.

"Can you describe them?"

He looked at her, unwavering, his eyes turning almost black. "Hard, ... hard to say. They're in doctor's scrubs."

"Both of them?"

"Yes, but one"—he frowned—"one is paler, harder to see."

"Okay, and what about the other one?"

"White, dark hair." And then he shrugged. "Adult."

She nodded because how did a twelve-year-old give her any specifics, when to him they were just an adult male with dark hair? "That's fine," she said.

He sighed and yawned, and she slowly laid him back down again on the bed. He reached up and clutched at her again. "That's all right. I'll just sit here beside you."

"Promise?" he asked, his voice thick.

"Promise," she murmured.

She knew he was heading into a drugged state from the thickness of his tone and his tongue. By the time he took several deep breaths and drifted off again, she straightened and rose and wandered around his room, trying to sort out what just happened. When the door opened again, Gray walked in, with two mugs of coffee. She walked over and appreciatively accepted one.

"How is he?" Gray whispered.

"He's asleep now, but that is due to drugs. They sedated him before they called, and the dosage is finally kicking in. Unfortunately they didn't contact me in time to stop the administration of the drugs. And I think they gave him an extra heavy dose. I'll have to check his file to see what they did."

"Why was it given? Do you know what set him off?"

"According to Adam, the bad guys found him in this place and chased him down the hallway to his room."

Gray stepped back out, looked down the hallway, and stepped back in again. "This hallway?" he whispered harshly.

Her face sobered, as she nodded. "Yes, which means a certain amount of clarity as to his location, his room, which is home base, and then he gave me a fair description but not much detail."

"Such as?" he demanded.

"Adult male, white, dark hair, but in doctor's scrubs."

At that, Gray groaned. "You know that could be 50 percent of the population here, right?"

"It's probably closer to about 65 percent," she corrected absent-mindedly, as her mind drifted through all the adult males that she knew. "It could even be a patient."

"Aren't they locked up at night?"

"Not all are locked up, no," she replied. "The main doors in and out of the areas are locked, but not all of the patients' rooms are locked."

"But Adam said *they* and only described one?" Gray asked cautiously.

"He told me that the second one was paler and faint."

At that, Gray nodded. "Probably farther behind."

She didn't say anything to that but turned to look back

at Adam. "He's asleep now, and, from the depth of that breathing, I would say it's more drugs than natural." Walking out of Adam's room, she smiled at the orderly and whispered, "He's calm and should be good for the night now."

She closed the door and locked it, so that Adam couldn't go down the hallway on her, and so nobody else could go in.

As Cressy and Gray went to her office, she asked him, "Who called you?"

He hesitated, then said, "You."

"No." She frowned, turning to look at him. "I didn't call you. I didn't have a chance to call you."

He nodded. "Yeah, I know. I don't really have much of an explanation for it, but I woke up out of a deep sleep, with you screaming in my head."

She stood still, stared at him, took a sip of coffee as she contemplated that, then slowly carried on to her office. "For one, I don't scream often. Two, I wasn't screaming tonight. And, three, even if I was, you shouldn't have been able to hear me."

"I'll say that something very weird is going on, and I don't like it."

She snorted at that. "Welcome to my world."

"Yeah, but it sucks. All this shit that goes on, and you don't have any rhyme or reason for it?"

"Nope, and sometimes we never get any rhyme or reason for it."

"How did you know to come?" he asked her.

"Andrea from the night shift phoned me to say that Adam was out of control."

"Even though a doctor was on hand?"

"Yes, she knew I didn't want Adam overly doped up,

and, of course, the other doctor on call was all for knocking Adam out for the night."

"Ouch," Gray muttered.

"Yeah, there's knocking him out for the night, and then there's knocking him out until he's, you know, well past the night's milestone," Cressy said sadly. "And we're back to that. Some people would like to see more medication and less actual improvements."

"You'll have fun here, won't you?"

"No, I can't say I will," she muttered. "It feels very much as if I'm going against this whole establishment again, and it's not a very comfortable feeling."

"I'm sorry to hear that," Gray said gently.

She unlocked her office, walked in, dropped her purse on her desk, carefully set down her coffee, and then slumped into her big leather chair.

He sat down in the visitor's chair.

"What time is it?" she asked him.

"Probably about four o'clock in the morning," he guessed, with a note of humor. "Isn't that the time we all love to be out?"

She shook her head. "The trouble is, it's not likely we'll get back to sleep now."

"No, God no," he agreed, with a groan. "That's really not one of the options, is it? Will you sleep here?"

"If I have to, yes," she murmured. "I can sleep here, providing I can actually get the chance."

His lips quirked. "Is that a hint for me to leave?"

"No," she stated. "I appreciate the fact that you came. I'm not sure why you came or how you got the message, but you did. So I guess I will attempt to avoid that next time—or maybe even use it."

"*Great.*" Frowning, he asked. "When you say *use it*, meaning what?"

"Meaning that, if I ever need you, I can call you that way."

"What? By screaming in my head?" he asked, with a shake of his head. "I haven't even heard Grant mention things like that before, but I would prefer a phone call than this."

"Well, Dr. Maddy's husband Drew has heard things like that before. He's very attuned to Dr. Maddy, and, when Dr. Maddy is distressed, he gets all kinds of messages. She sends out a network distress call, if she can't get a hold of Stefan very clearly."

"Get hold of Stefan very clearly?"

She shrugged. "If Dr. Maddy's in trouble, and she needs somebody, she will reach out to whoever she needs. Stefan comes first because that's the work he does, and then comes Drew, as he is her partner. I know for a fact that he has had her reach out and shake him by the throat to get his attention."

At that, Gray's eyes widened, and she gave him a lazy smile. "Yeah, it's not all fun and games."

"I don't think *any* of this is fun and games," he declared, staring at her. "It all sounds very improbable and quite horrific in many ways."

"In many ways, it is," she agreed. "Yet we're doing an awful lot of good, when we get a chance to." She gave him an eye roll. "It doesn't always work out that way."

"No, it appears that you're up against a lot of politics here."

"Too much of it." Cressy frowned. "It's one of the things I dislike the most about this type of a thing. Working for a board of directors really sucks."

"It would be the same thing though if you went to work for Dr. Maddy, wouldn't it?"

"Possibly, I don't know. That would be one of the things I would discuss with her, before I ever came on board."

"Would you seriously do it?"

"I don't know, but, when shit like this happens, it makes me all the more inclined to do so."

"Inclined, yes," he replied gently, "but you do have a fair bit of autonomy here."

"I *did*," she clarified, with an eye roll. "However, my sabbatical apparently changed all that. A lot of power plays happened while I was gone. Changes were implemented, and a lot of staff are just fine with the new way and don't see why I would be rocking the boat."

"Ah." Gray nodded. "That's another trick, isn't it? Change out all the staff, so nobody knows what it was like before, so nobody can complain, so it looks like you're the one who's off your rocker."

"And, in this case, that's a little too close to the truth."

He winced at that. "Sorry, I didn't really mean it that way."

"No, but you know, when you're the one making a fuss over *nothing*, in many ways it means that they've won."

"So ... No, that would be crazy, I guess."

"What's crazy?"

"Setting up your own institute."

"Now you sound like Stefan. I certainly could, but it would also take a tremendous amount of money, time, and energy that I don't have."

"So you partner with somebody who does."

"Yes, and that is actually something I'm contemplating,

but it's still a huge commitment on my part, and I'm not sure I'm up for it. You know there's a reason I went and took this sabbatical, and it's not a reason I need to take lightly at this point."

"No, of course not," he muttered. "Would they all really be happy to see you leave?"

"A lot of them would be happy to see me leave, and a lot of them probably wouldn't really notice either way. And those who supposedly say they're really happy that I'm back" I don't know if I trust them."

He stared at her. "Wow," he murmured. "That really sounds like an awful way to live."

She smiled. "I'm not sure that's even a fair statement either," she murmured. "Yet, when you think about it, and you have all these power plays going on behind your back, you don't know who can be trusted and who can't, so you get kind of paranoid. And, if that's the way I'm living, it's not how I would choose to live. That's not why am I here."

"You've only been back a couple days," he pointed out. "Maybe give it a bit of a rest yet."

"Oh, I will, but don't kid yourself. I know perfectly well that what's going on isn't a good thing."

"Maybe, but that doesn't mean it's a bad thing either," he warned.

She smiled. "It does make you wonder."

"It does. And, if you're really unhappy, then you do need to leave. However, if this is your field, this is where your heart is."

"I know," she agreed, "but I don't need the anguish and the frustration of dealing with the board for something as simple as feeding our patients good healthy food."

"Then either change out the board, change out the institute, or … I don't know. Maybe go work with Dr. Maddy. From what you say and her knowledge about all your techniques, I would think that at least the group of people she's already been working with must already be on board with this type of stuff.

"That's very true, and one of the reasons why I would consider it."

"Yet, you're in a different field."

"Yep, I am," she confirmed, with a nod. She finished her coffee, looked down at the mug, and muttered, "Thanks for bringing this, by the way."

"Not a problem." He stared at her and asked, 'So, if I leave you here, you will sleep, right?"

"That's the hope," she murmured. "Will it happen? I don't know." She looked back at her little room and sighed. "I haven't slept in there or even spent any time in there since you found the bug."

"I understand that, but, as long as you're not talking on the phone or doing anything secretive, you should be fine. Just remember. We want to keep it live." He lowered his voice for the last bit.

She nodded. "As much as I don't like the idea, I probably will have to." She yawned just then.

"Then do," he agreed. "If you want, I can stay here."

Immediately she shook her head. "No, no, go on home," she said. "You should get some sleep tonight too. I hadn't intended that you come here at all," she muttered. She got up and waved at the door. "If you go, I can lock the door."

"Would you normally?"

She hesitated, then shook her head. "No, I probably wouldn't have, but now I feel that I need to."

"Any particular reason why?"

"As I told you before, the place feels off, so I would say, *Better safe than sorry.*"

"So, either you need to do something to make it feel better," he replied briskly, "or you need to leave."

"Not easy choices, either way."

But he stood, headed to the door, looked back at her, and nodded. "Lock up behind me."

She smiled and approached the door. "I will."

"Call me if you need me," he said, but still he hesitated.

She patted his cheek gently. "I'm fine, you know." He frowned at her, and she shook her head. "I really am fine."

"No, you're really not fine, but, if you say it enough, you might actually convince yourself." And, with that, he was gone.

She slowly locked up her office door and headed to the room that she used to crash. There was just a single cot, but she was grateful to lie down and to close her eyes. What surprised her though was that the last thought on her mind wasn't about her patient but of Gray. The man was dynamite, particularly when he was in hero mode.

The fact that she even noticed confirmed how tired she was and how much she needed his help.

GRAY HEADED HOME and quickly crashed himself. When he woke up a few hours later, he still felt groggy, but his phone was ringing. The ringing woke him up. He answered it to find Grant on the other end.

"I hear you were at the center last night?" he asked.

"Yes, I'm not exactly sure what the hell happened," he replied, "but I woke up because I could feel that Cressy was screaming at me to get there, and, sure enough, when I got there, she was there, had been called in to deal with the boy, who was apparently out of control. By the time she got there, he was medicated more than she would have liked, and he did crash when he saw her and calmed down quite a bit."

"Did he say anything?"

"Something about being chased through the halls by somebody in doctor's scrubs, and he could only give the description of a white dark-haired male with a second fainter person. He swears there were two of them, more distinct in his nightmares."

"So, one dominant and one not so dominant. Interesting," Grant noted. "Did she have any explanation for it?"

"Not when I talked to her last night," Gray said, yawning. "I only got to bed at a little after 4:00 a.m."

"Interesting. Did she go home?"

"She did not. She chose instead to stay at the center in the back room of her office, where the bug is."

"Again, interesting."

"I assured her that it was safe, as long as she wasn't talking on the phone."

"Or talking in her sleep," Grant pointed out.

Gray hesitated at that. "Do you really think that's something we have to be worried about?"

"I don't know," Grant admitted.

"I also put surveillance in there, so we can see if anyone goes in there ourselves. I can give that a quick run through, while I have some coffee."

"Good, let me know soon." And, with that, he hung up.

Gray stared down at his phone, shaking his head at the concept. He quickly got set up and hooked on to the audio equipment. Instantly, as he played it back, he heard her soft breathing. It was almost an intimate sound, and it made him feel bad, as if he was eavesdropping. A few whimpers came, as she struggled with sleep herself and her own demons, but nothing else. He fast forwarded it, put it on Play at super-high speeds so he could get through it faster, and there was nothing else.

Relieved at that, he had a second cup of coffee and tried to discern where to focus his actions for the day. He phoned Grant back. "Nothing on the tape."

"Good. Probably go give it another bug sweep though."

"Any particular reason why?"

"Because I don't like anything about this."

"No, I don't either," Gray agreed. "That boy was legitimately traumatized last night. I saw him at the very end of it."

"Sure, but is it anything more than nightmares? You and I would have nightmares too, if we'd been through and seen what he had."

"I know, and that is a very valid point. He's a traumatized little boy, so I don't know why anybody's expecting him to produce anything out of this."

"Honestly? Because Dr. Maddy says so," he noted, with a wry sigh. "I have learned to listen to Stefan and Dr. Maddy and the others in that group. So when Dr. Maddy says something needs to be watched, I watch. But it's hard to get budget money when I have absolutely nothing to give our superiors."

"No, I understand that too, but if you trust her that much then …"

"I do," Grant declared. "We don't listen to our own detriment."

"Fine. It does feel strange."

"Technically you're not actually on the clock anyway,

so …"

"I know."

"That makes me feel worse for taking up your time."

"Not at all," Gray replied. "You know how I feel about what happened to her in the first place. She really doesn't get a good feeling being there at work though."

"No, but how much of that is about her own demons?" Grant pointed out.

"That's something that I told her. Either she needs to find a way to make this not so traumatizing, or she needs to find another place to work."

"What did she say to that?"

"She understood. She just didn't know which pathway to travel at the moment."

"She's only been back a few days, so no reason why she would have answers to something like that so quickly," Grant pointed out. "If you think about it, it would be a mistake to make quick decisions that affect our career, especially not in a situation like this."

"I know, but there's an awful lot of strife there too."

"She told me about some of it," Grant shared. "I don't know how much of it is brought on by who she is, what she was trying to do, or the fact that the center just might not be ready for her methods."

"They don't even know really, do they?"

He laughed. "No, but her methods work, and, while she was gone, their ratings and reputation went way the hell down," he noted. "So they're keeping her on the roster, hoping that will boost them, but I wouldn't be at all surprised if there won't be an awful lot more people trying to figure out what she's doing, so that they can mimic it and then get rid of her."

"Hell, if it's not that easy, I can't see that going well."

"Nope, it isn't," Grant stated, "and part of the problem is, people won't believe you because, in their mind, it is that easy because they don't know what's going on. And because it's that easy in their head, they think they can just copy her methods."

"Right. Well, I think she would be better off either taking over the place and booting out the board, which probably isn't all that easy to do, I suppose. Me? I would just go in there with a sledgehammer. So I guess I'm really not board material," he muttered. "Or she could always take the job Dr. Maddy has offered many times, I hear."

"That's because Cressy's incredibly gifted, and she does some of the same work that Dr. Maddy does. People like that are in a very short supply. Drew tells me how Dr. Maddy would love to have Cressy, but it's a complementary system, not the same type, so it's not ideal for Cressy either. Dr. Maddy knows it but doesn't want to see Cressy in a lesser scenario because … her skills are not something that can be duplicated."

"In a way that's actually reassuring." Gray gave a half laugh. "I can't imagine having people like her running all over the place."

"You mean, like Stefan and Dr. Maddy," he clarified, with a wry smile. "And you're right. We don't want people like that running all over the place. I just happen to know that people like that are worth their weight in gold, and we just never seem to have enough of them. I mean, Drew tells me how Dr. Maddy could do absolutely nothing but individual clients and make millions, but she also knows that she can benefit many more people than that, which is why she managed to get her clinic set up, which did not come without a cost of colleagues and other personnel. A lot of people don't like what she does, and some consider it very much in the woo-woo category. And those people no longer work there because, as Dr. Maddy would say, she can't have that kind of negativity around the patients."

"And you know something? I'm pretty sure Cressy would say the same thing," Gray muttered. "How do we find her a place like Dr. Maddy's but for the purpose of emotional or psychological health or whatever you want to call it? Because this is almost like psychic help."

"Exactly." Grant laughed. "Believe me. I've no idea. It's hard enough to keep Cressy under lock and key now, without her expanding into so much else in life, but I do know it's important that she has her own platform, ... one that complements Dr. Maddy and Stefan. Because the sheer number of people they help is astronomical. And while they still can't help everybody, they're helping hundreds if not thousands a year, and that is worth everything," he stated. "I've asked Drew how he handles it, being married to Dr. Maddy. He told me that he would never try to take her away from it, so I get it."

"I don't know what it's like to take over a board like that. You would have to buy out shares, I guess. There'd be all kinds of hell to pay. If you happen to know anybody who's got money to invest, let me know, and I can share that with Cressy. ... Or maybe another center entirely," Gray added calmly. "And then she can talk to some of the best patients and families she's got and move them."

At that, Grant laughed. "That would be kind of a dirty move. But you know something? It's probably about the only way it'll work."

At that the two men ended the call.

Gray pondered his choices and then decided he really wanted to go back to the center to see if everything was okay and to check on Adam. After he had a couple pieces of toast, he drove to the clinic and walked into the hospital. The receptionist just nodded at his presence. He signed in and carried on to Cressy's office. He didn't know whether people accepted why he was here, ... didn't care why he was here, were curious, or were so done with their jobs ...in a place like this that nobody really gave a crap. He knew it was possible to be for all those reasons.

He headed straight to Cressy's office, and, when he tried the door, it was still locked. He stood outside and phoned her. Just as he was about to disconnect, the door opened.

There she stood, still sleepy. She yawned in his face and then apologized, stumbling backward. "Hey, I gather it's morning."

"It is definitely morning." He smiled at her. "Looks like you got some sleep though."

She nodded. "I didn't expect to, but, hey, I'll take it."

"Sounds like a good idea."

She looked up at him, peered into his eyes, and asked, "What about you?"

"I got some—a couple hours anyway."

"But that's all?"

He nodded. "Yeah, I got home and settled, and then I woke up about seven, with a phone call from Grant."

"I didn't turn off my phone, of course, but I did leave it out on my desk."

He laughed at that. "That's a good way to do it. When you need sleep, you need sleep."

She walked over to her desk, and, pushing her hair back off her face, she pulled a hair clip out of her desk drawer, quickly tamed the wild curls, and shoved in the clip, so it actually looked demure and professional.

"I don't know how you did that, but you went from delightfully mussed to professional, with just a few strokes."

She grinned at him. "Lots of practice."

"It would be nice to keep you the other way," he muttered.

She stared at him, a flush rising on her cheeks.

"You're beautiful," he admitted. "And, hey, I'm a guy. It's hardly a surprise to think I would find you attractive."

The flush deepened down her cheeks, and she shook her head. "I'm not even going there."

"Why not?" he asked in a teasing voice. "Chicken?" She frowned at him, and he burst out laughing. "I shouldn't tease you, but you are awfully cute when you blush." She gave him a repressing frown, and he just laughed again. "Frowns don't work on me," he told her cheerfully.

"Why not?" she asked, with a groan. "It would be much easier if they did."

"They don't. Too bad for you." He chuckled.

She sighed. "Whatever. Did you get breakfast?"

"I did, a couple pieces of toast anyway."

She nodded. "I'll have to go get coffee down at the cafeteria and maybe a muffin, if there is anything edible."

"Do you get to eat here?"

"I always have. Of course that perk may have changed over the time I've been gone. If it has, nobody's told me about it, so I won't worry about it today."

"You want coffee?"

"Absolutely."

"Good, let's walk down and get something then."

Together they walked to the cafeteria, where she quickly

grabbed a coffee and a muffin and then decided on a second one for later. With their mugs and her small plate, they headed back to her office.

He felt people watching them, the voices stopping in the cafeteria, some whispers here and there, and some watching as they walked out.

"So, are people watching us just because you're back, because I'm here, or simply because we're together?" he asked.

She didn't answer for a long moment. When they had almost reached her office, she replied, "It's probably all three."

"*Great*," he muttered. "Any idea how many staff members you've got here?"

"A couple hundred. Well, there *were* a couple hundred. With the budget cuts, I guess they are focusing on profits. ... They've probably cut down the staff by half."

At that heavy note of bitterness in her tone, he looked over at her.

She shrugged. "I don't know any of that for certain. I'm just assuming that, once the directors got their way, everything probably got cut."

He nodded. "If you were to move to another center, do you have any patients who would move with you?"

"Yep, several. I had contacted patients and families of patients before I took the sabbatical, and they were willing to stay as long as I was coming back. I guess most of them stayed, though some were looking for other places within a few months, once I was gone." She shook her head. "That's partly how I know things have changed so much because there was an awful lot of complaining going on."

He nodded. "How much of it do you think was sour

grapes. just because you weren't here, versus actual changes going on?"

"Oh, I have no idea." She looked at him quizzically. "I guess that's possible. Nobody likes change, and they really don't like it when it comes to their family, so that could have happened as well," she noted. "But I would have thought most people would have waited until I got back, before they complained. So, when the complaints started, I heard how somebody changed the food, how they don't like the new staff, and things like that. ... And staff? Well, that comes and goes, but they did tell me that the beds weren't being changed as often, the floors weren't being cleaned as often, that sort of thing. That is a sign of staffing cuts for sure, and that's not good because cleanliness in a place like this is huge. We get so many sick people, with their immune systems already compromised because their bodies are constantly in a fight, so that's just one more reason to go to the board."

"Do you have a board meeting set?"

She winced at that. "No, I've held off on it, while I tried to get enough ammunition together to make my case."

"But you're not expecting to make too much in the way of a case, are you?"

"Have you ever been to a board meeting, where you fight the whole board?" she asked. "It's not pretty, and I have to fight everybody from the position of having just come back from a sabbatical. And now, with all these changes in place—well and truly under their belts—that is one of the ugliest fights there is. They know I'm at a disadvantage, and I know their dirty laundry. I'm not sure what I'm supposed to do about it, but I will go to bat because it's the right thing to do for my patients. When all is said and done, if I'm not okay with how it is, then I'll need to make a change."

"Right, and I guess that's one of the questions I'm asking. Is there any other place you could go?"

"Probably. I … I was sought after at one point, but then I took the sabbatical."

"Do you really think that's affected people?"

"It was quite a burnout, and I'm sure that information passed through the community. If somebody wanted to, I suppose they could make it look like I couldn't handle it, then got stressed and bent out of shape. Anyone can make it sound more detrimental than it was, making me out to have had a nervous breakdown or whatever. I need to find out what kind of rumors really are circulating in the community, and if I'm actually changing places, I would need to do it, whether temporarily or permanently."

He stared at her. "After all you've done for this place, do you really expect these people to sabotage you?"

She quirked her lips at him. "If they want to keep me here, and I really don't know that they do, though certainly a lot of my older patients aren't very happy, then it's quite possible they would do all kinds of shit."

He nodded. "Wow, I expect something like that in the corporate world. That happens all the time, but here? In a place like this? I wouldn't have guessed."

"It's the same issue though. It comes down to the profitability and the bottom line. The medical world isn't always very nice either," she pointed out. "Competition for patients is fierce, and, since I brought a lot of them in, it is possible that some would leave with me if I went to another center. And the fact is, if I could guarantee that I would be bringing a bunch of clients with me, then sure, a lot of doors would open. But, if I'm looking for a new job, it would be far better if I was headhunted first, so I could make certain demands.

Otherwise, it's just me, going hat in hand, looking for a job, having no leverage to negotiate with. So, there is that to consider."

"In this situation it would be more a case of you seeking a location with a more amiable, energetic system," Gray pointed out. "I'm pretty sure that any headhunter would cheerfully make discreet inquiries on your behalf to get you into the best position possible."

She laughed. "Maybe. Honestly, job-seeking is not really something I would care to go back into, but, if I can't make the changes that I need to make here, then that's exactly what will happen."

He nodded.

She quickly checked her email, while she sat here, and he watched her answering a couple, while he sipped his coffee.

Then she frowned. "Oh, that's interesting."

"What's that?"

"An email from the family of one of my patients, saying they want to move him," she shared.

"What?" He stared at her. "Why is that?"

"Unhappy with the level of care is what I'm seeing here." She frowned at that. "I need to make a phone call and see what their complaint really is," she murmured. "Let me see if I can fix it."

"You won't fix all the complaints. You do know that."

"I do, hence the need for a board meeting."

"Do you know when the next one is?"

"In a couple days," she said. "I wanted an extra one for this purpose, but I don't want to give them too much time to fortify their positions. The trouble is, their position, the implementation of all these changes, is already in place, which means I'm the one who has to fight to overturn their established policies or decisions."

"You need something clearly down on paper, document-ing the detrimental effects, complete with the budget impacts, and you haven't really been here long enough to that."

"I know. That's why I've not gotten to that point yet."

"Got it." Gray nodded. "If you're looking for somebody to help you organize some of that information, I could do it."

She looked at him. "I don't see you as a pencil pusher."

"I'm not," he admitted, with a wry look. "Yet I do know how to share and organize information, and I've got the time, as I'm not doing a whole lot at the moment."

"You could go off and do other FBI work."

"I could, but, since I'm technically still on leave from an injury, I don't really have other current case assignments. And honestly it feels weird not to be doing more."

She pondered that, staring at him intently. "But you're not that badly hurt."

He laughed. "I'm not, but I'm not quite cleared yet for full duty."

"So, you're essentially in between. This is now becoming perfectly clear. Grant asked you to do this as a favor, didn't he?" Her statement was crystal clear, and she gave him a smile.

He smiled back. "Maybe, but it's also very valuable in-formation that we need from Adam."

"And yet the annihilator hasn't killed anybody else, has he?"

"No, not as far as we can tell."

When he hesitated, she studied him carefully. "What?" she asked "What is it you're trying not to ask?"

He winced. "I'm not even sure that's what I'm doing, but I guess what I'm wondering is …" Then he stopped.

"If you don't ask, I can't answer," she reminded him.

"Yeah, but it sounds stupid."

"Yeah, in my world, more often than not, it's not stupid as much as unbelievable."

"Fine," he said, with a headshake. "Is there any chance the annihilator is connected to the boy?"

"Absolutely," she stated flat-out. "It's one of the things that I'm trying to see."

He stared. "What? I was expecting you to laugh it off."

"No, that's not out of the realm of possibility. There are too many things that this annihilator could be doing, and one of them is that he could potentially be sitting in Adam's psyche, waiting for an opportunity to come after him again."

"Would that not mean that both the annihilator and Adam had psychic abilities?"

"Yes and no," she replied. "A lot of people do a lot of shit to others, and it's not always psychic abilities. They're just assholes," she stated bluntly.

After a moment, he hopped up and announced, "Okay, I'll head down to the office. I need to check in on the tapes that we've got. I'll be back in a little bit." He was out the door, when he stopped and looked back at her. "How about lunch?"

She laughed. "You want to go out for lunch?"

"It would probably be good if you did get out for a while."

She pondered that and then shrugged. "If you want to pick me up at noon, that should work." She consulted her calendar and nodded. "I think we can do that."

"Fine, I'll be back then." He gave her a smile and left,

heading to his car. Instincts had him walking past his car and over to hers. As he got closer, he noticed. He stopped and stared, stunned.

All four of her tires had been slashed.

CHAPTER 11

"**S**LASHED? WHAT DO you mean?" Cressy still had her phone to her ear, as she walked rapidly toward Gray in the parking lot. "All of them, are you serious?" He pointed to her car. She stared in shock. "*Great*," she muttered, disconnecting their phone call. "Is that a warning? Does someone really not want me to be here?"

"That would make sense to me. I've already phoned for a tow truck."

"I need new tires now obviously." She stared in dismay. "That's not exactly an expense I was expecting. Not that I can't afford it, but what the hell? Who does that?"

"I'll take care of it. When the tow gets here, I'll have them take it to town, put new tires on your rims, and bring it back. I also want a look at the hospital's security cameras. I'll need to assess everybody who came and went today."

She looked up, surprised, and then nodded. "Go ahead and talk to security. They'll get it for you." And, with that, Cressy dashed back inside.

Sonia, who was on the front desk, looked up and asked, "Problems, Doctor?"

"Yeah, somebody slashed my tires."

Sonia gasped. "Seriously?"

The security guard passing by overheard and hurried over. "What was that about your tires?"

"All have been slashed. Can you go talk to Gray, the FBI guy? He's out by my car in my regular spot. He'll want access to the cameras and whatnot."

He bolted outside to take a look, as Cressy crossed her arms, trying to calm her nerves. She then detoured back to the cafeteria, picked up another cup of coffee, then headed back into her office to pick up her notepads and the files she had set out.

She needed to put it past her and to start her day with her patients, but first she checked in on Adam. She unlocked the door and stepped inside, to see him sitting up groggily. "Hey, Adam. How are you doing?" she asked, smiling as she sat down at the end of his bed.

He stared at her, both hands rubbing his eyes. "I don't know. Weird dreams. Really weird."

She nodded. "I get that, and I'm sorry."

He shrugged. "I'm hungry."

"Good. Do you want to get dressed and come down to the cafeteria with me?"

He looked at her, looked at the door, and shook his head.

"Ah. You want me to get you some breakfast?"

He immediately smiled. "Can you stay and eat with me?"

"That I can do." She smiled, thrilled that he was talking to her. "What is your choice for breakfast? Meanwhile, get up, brush your teeth, and get dressed while I'm gone."

"Cereal," he told her.

When she frowned at that, Adam just glared. "I like cereal." His voice was still soft, yet heavy from all the screaming last night.

"Maybe, but how about sausage and eggs or some bacon

and toast?"

His shoulders slumped.

"I'll check and see what's there."

With him agreeing to that, she headed to the cafeteria, picked up a tray, and grabbed a muffin, a small bowl of cereal, a plate with a little bit of scrambled eggs, some bacon, and a couple pieces of toast. She then added little packets of peanut butter and jam on the side.

Getting cutlery, a carton of milk and a carton of juice, she headed back to his room. When she unlocked the door and stepped inside, he was sitting at his little table, staring out the window. She walked over, smiled, and put the tray on the table.

His face lit up when he saw the cereal.

She laughed. "I thought maybe we could compromise."

He nodded. "They don't like it when I eat cereal."

"Yeah? Who is they?"

He gave her a sideways look.

She didn't say any more, just pulled up the only other chair in the room and sat down beside him with her coffee. "Why don't you tell me about them."

"Nobody believes me."

She nodded. "I believe you, Adam."

He looked up, his gaze searching and then shrugged. "Won't make any difference. Nobody ever talks to them. Nobody tells them to leave me alone." Then he paused in the act of putting a spoon of cereal in his mouth. "I don't think they would stop anyway."

"That's not necessarily true," she replied. "I can do all kinds of things." He looked up at her. She shrugged. "Maybe I can talk to these two."

He looked her up and down, frowning at her size.

"They're big."

She flashed a wicked grin at him. "That's okay. I have skills you don't know about."

He just shrugged and went back to eating. With the bowl of cereal gone, he absentmindedly picked up a piece of bacon, and, before he realized it, he'd finished it all off. She nudged the jam toward him, but he picked up the peanut butter and slathered it on a piece of toast, ate that, and then put jam on the other one.

"You're not doing too badly," Cressy said cheerfully.

He frowned. "I'm not usually this hungry." He reached for the carton of milk, which he downed all at once. Then he opened up the orange juice too.

She watched him carefully because this was the kind of thing that happened after a hard energy burn. If he had been in the ethers during the night, seriously running from predators, then this level of burnout was reasonable. This is exactly the kind of side effects she would expect.

When he reached for the muffin, he ate half of it and then sat back, but just a few minutes later, he picked up his fork and ate a couple bites of the eggs here and there, a few moments at a time. Now all that was left was a little bit of egg and half a muffin. He stared down at the tray, looked up at her, and frowned. "I ate a lot," he announced.

"Yeah. Do you want me to leave you the rest of that muffin?"

He nodded.

"So, these guys, do they tell you anything?"

"Only to behave myself and, if I'm good, they'll leave me alone."

He had said it in such a nonchalant way that she knew he believed it. "Do you know if these guys have hurt anybody else before?"

He gave her a haunted look and then slowly nodded.

"Your family?"

He nodded again. "That's how I know they're bad," he said softly. Tears collected in the corner of his eyes. "They hurt people."

"I get it," she murmured. "How do you think they found you here?"

"I don't know," he whispered. Looking around, he started to sink in on himself, his arms wrapped around him, with his knees up against his chest.

"If they found you, I'll set up a guard to keep them away from you."

He twisted his head, resting against his knees, so he could look over at her. "A guard? I don't think one guard will stop two men."

"This is a different kind of a guard, a magic guard."

His gaze lit up with interest. "Like magic-magic or like magic tricks?" he asked, frowning.

"Magic-magic," she replied, with a smile, knowing that's exactly what she would do. "I'll do it tonight before you go to bed. Have they ever come to talk to you during the day?"

He nodded vehemently.

She stopped and stared. "Really?"

He nodded again. "It's usually just a whisper outside the door though."

"What do they say?"

"They just say my name, like a warning."

"You mean like, 'Adam, watch out?' or what?"

"*Adam, remember us. Behave yourself. Be a good boy.* They say all kind of things."

"Ah, I see. Okay, and is it always the same voice?"

He shook his head at that. "In the daytime, ... it sounds, I don't know, just different."

"But then again, sometimes nighttime versus daytime sounds appear different anyway, don't they?"

"A little more echoey at nighttime, I guess," he muttered. He got up, walked over to his bed, and threw himself down.

"Do you want to go back to sleep?"

He shook his head. "No."

"Do you want to go visit with the others, watch some TV, and do some of your schoolwork?"

He shook his head, then curled up on the bed, pulled the pillow tighter up against his head, and just laid there.

She got up, grabbed a blanket, threw it around his shoulders, and tucked him in. "If you want to sleep some more, go ahead."

He didn't say anything.

She grabbed the tray and headed to the door.

When she was almost out, he called her, "Dr. Cressy!"

"Yes, honey. What's the matter?" She took a few steps back toward him.

"C-could you put that magical guard around now?"

She looked at him, then smiled. "Absolutely I can," she declared, putting down the tray, "You'll know it's me when I come because I'll give you a magic knock before I come in."

"Can you keep everybody else out?"

"I can for a little while, but the staff will need to check on you," she replied seriously. "They're here to help. They have to know that you're okay."

"Can't you just do it?"

"I can today, I guess. Do you want me to?"

"Yes."

"Okay, I'll do that. Give me a few minutes to set up the magical guard."

And, with that, she stepped outside, placed his tray on one of the big trolleys in the hall for that purpose, and then walked back to his door. Using the keypad, she quickly locked the door, then left a note not to be disturbed and that nobody was to enter but Dr. Cresswell. Then she immediately pulled out her phone and casually leaned up against the wall, as if she were reading or sending texts. In the meantime, she closed her eyes and put up a full-on guard around his door. Then, as an afterthought, she set it around the window too. Also she sent a text message to Stefan. **I just set up a guard around Adam's room at his request.**

Stefan popped into her head. *His request?*

She quickly explained.

His voice dark, Stefan murmured, *I'll put a trigger on it too, just to make sure I'm notified if anything comes up against it.*

If you could, that would help, thank you. I'm beginning to wonder if somebody here is actively working against his care.

To see you fail?

I hadn't considered that motive, not until you brought it up, she muttered. *But there's definitely a lot of shit going on that I hadn't expected.*

Maybe it's time to leave? he asked.

Maybe. I've been hearing that a lot lately, but a lot of these patients need my help.

He hesitated to say anything.

I know I have an option of moving them, but that's an expensive process.

No, I hear you, Stefan replied. *Did you ever talk to my New Orleans connection?*

I did, and he was looking at options.

He's very good with money, so, if there's any way to make it happen, he would be the one to know how.

Yeah, but to change the board, we need other people to buy shares, she noted. *That's the whole point of taking over a board like this. Still, if they have a ruling amount of shares, nothing I can do.*

Do you have any shares?

I do, but only 10 percent.

So, somebody would still have to collect 41 percent to make it a ruling majority.

Yeah, and then they would be the one I'm dealing with, she muttered. *And that won't necessarily be easy either.*

Depends on who it is though, Stefan pointed out. *We can probably free up some money.*

I thought you were focused on helping Dr. Maddy's clinic.

Yet your work is just as important, he muttered, *if not more so because people like us are incarcerated against their will, with nobody out there to understand their problems. By the way, since you've been back, have you had a chance to check out any of the people admitted while you were gone? To see if anyone there doesn't need to be?*

Not yet, but it's on my to-do list for the day. I have a couple meetings to get through first, and then it's all about patients for the day.

Okay, let me know. With that, he was gone.

She looked up and started down the hallway. She hadn't gotten very far when one of the orderlies called out to her. She turned and smiled. "Hey, Keith."

He gave her a big beaming smile. "It's sure good to see you back. Things haven't been the same since you left."

"I noticed," she murmured. She hesitated and then asked

in a low tone, "Did your hours get cut?"

He nodded. "Yeah, no overtime. Plus ten of us were laid off completely. Another ten were dropped to part-time, and maybe another ... dozen, I guess, took early retirement."

She nodded. "I had some complaints while I was off, about the meal quality and housekeeping going down. Of course I saw for myself the minute I got back. Orderlies are few and far between, and security is way down, and, my God, there's not an ounce of nutrition in that food."

"They pulled the security almost immediately after you left, saying it was too expensive," he muttered. He glanced around and added, "I sure hope you don't leave."

"Is there talk of me leaving?"

"The talk of you leaving started long before you ever came back," he shared. "Lots of people muttering about how you shouldn't be back, and others saying they hoped you came back, and others hoping but didn't think you would stay because of all the changes."

She nodded. "I worked really hard to improve the care here," she explained. "Then I'm gone for six months, and everything is out the window. I don't know that I'll get it back up again. I'll have to go up against the board, and they're probably pretty entrenched in how they want to run the place now."

"Yeah, that's because they're trying to run it at a profit."

"Yeah, and I was just trying to run it a hair over profit, so we could break even and save for capital investments. However, once you get a board of directors looking for dividends, it's pretty tough," she muttered. "So, that's what I'm up against now, and, in fact, the changes have already happened, so I don't really have much in the way of options."

He nodded. "If you do leave, maybe you can go to another center and give me a good word?" he asked, looking at her, his tone hopeful. "I would be happy to move with you."

She sent him a beaming smile. "I'll take that under consideration, but don't tell anybody, okay?"

He nodded. "I do know at least a dozen of us who would like to leave," he shared. "A lot of patients would like to leave as well."

She pondered that. "You want to give me a list?"

He nodded. "Can I email it to you?"

"Absolutely." Then she stopped and corrected, "Just in case somebody is checking on my email, you might want to send it in a text instead?"

"I can do that."

With that done, she headed to the first of her meetings for the day. As she walked toward the meeting room, she passed through one of the minimum-security areas and noted the patients in there for assessment. She opened up her senses as she walked through the door, and she noted twelve different energies. Several of them were quite confused, scrambled even, and a couple were dealing with a lot of black, a lot of deep dark red.

She winced at that because they needed to be treated immediately. Medication changes were crucial, and they potentially needed to go into the high-security area, but a couple really concerned her. She stopped, knowing that she had only ten minutes until her meeting but headed toward one of them. The energy was light, almost a silvery pale, which was feeble and groggy.

She stopped outside the woman's room and smiled at her. "Hey, I'm Dr. Cressy. I just wanted to introduce myself."

The fragile-looking female looked up at her and shrugged. "That's nice."

She studied her, seeing the slashes on her wrist and the puncture marks on the arms. "Did you try again?"

The woman startled, looked up at her, and then nodded slowly.

"Nothing really worth living for?" Cressy asked gently.

She slowly shook her head.

"What about a different home life? Would that help?"

"I don't think so," she whispered, her voice faint. "It's been changed a couple times."

"Are you in foster care?"

She nodded. "I'm seventeen. I can leave now."

"And you left, didn't you?"

"I did." She smiled. "That turned out to be a bad decision too."

"I'm sorry," Cressy murmured. "Sometimes when we're in a rough position, it's the only thing that we're really comfortable with, so we tend to think another rough position is normal because it feels comfortable, because it's what we're used to."

"That's just sick," the patient declared, glaring at her. "I didn't choose to go into another shitty situation because it's what I'm used to."

"Consciously, no," Cressy agreed immediately. "However, subconsciously you were looking for something that would feel right."

At that, the young woman stared at her in shock, before sagging back against her headboard. "Jesus, that's messed up."

"It is messed up. Yet, if you can understand the changes that you need for yourself, then you can potentially avoid that same situation again."

The young woman stared off at the wall.

"Just think about it," Cressy suggested. "And, if you want to talk, you can just give me a shout."

"Okay," she muttered, and Cressy stepped out and carried on.

Now it was past the meeting time to start, and she had to get there fast. As she raced toward the meeting room, she noted purple and pink lines dancing up and down the hallway. She stopped in her tracks and turned to look at the adjacent room's occupant—a fifty-year-old woman sitting on the bed, a vacant look on her face. Cressy pulled up her chart, took a quick look, and realized she had just been admitted, having been found at home on her own after a wellness check. "Sadie," Cressy whispered.

There was no response. She immediately opened up her senses, danced into the hallway herself and asked, "Sadie?"

The purple and pink lines instantly formed into a facsimile of the woman on the bed, and she looked at her. "Hey, you know my name," she whispered, and then she danced with joy. "Are you supposed to be here?" she asked Cressy.

"I'm supposed to be here," Cressy replied, as she studied the older woman. "Why are you here?"

"Because I got off my meds," she muttered. "They made me feel weird."

"Right. When you're not taking your meds, what do you do?"

"Generally I like to be on this plane," she muttered, "but they don't like it when I'm over here. Then they increase my meds, so I can't come over here. So … I get off my meds so I can."

At that slightly convoluted explanation, Cressy nodded slowly. "Can I come back and talk to you later?" she asked Sadie. "I have a meeting to go to."

"Yeah, absolutely. I would really like it. Maybe we could have tea?" she asked hopefully.

Cressy smiled and whispered to the other spirit form, "Tea would be lovely. Give me an hour or so." And, with that, she raced off to her meeting.

She knew perfectly well that Sadie was one who Stefan needed to talk to. Somehow they had to find a way to make the woman understand that the spirit world had a lot to offer, but the real world had more options for her.

She needed to spend more time on the other side and maybe even use the spirit world as a reward or a nighttime activity, to be free of all the stresses of this world. And, with her mind contemplating all of it, she quickly sent Stefan a message about Sadie, then raced into the meeting, apologizing instinctively because she already knew she was late.

HE WATCHED HER walk up and down the hallway.

She was acting … He didn't want to say *crazy*, but definitely an element of crazy was in her actions right now. He understood what she was doing, but he didn't think she knew that he knew. And that secret he kept close to his heart. It put a smile on his face. It was always fascinating to see how people acted when they thought nobody knew what you were doing. He looked around at the young woman, then stopped and realized that it wasn't a young woman at all. She had to be close to fifty. He wasn't sure what her name was, Sybil or something like that. He wandered closer, but she ignored him.

Frowning, he stared at her a little more intently, but she wasn't even seeing him. He shrugged at that. Maybe that was okay too. Sometimes life was better off when nobody saw you. He headed down the hallway toward the meeting room and stood at the doorway to watch everybody jockeying around for their seats. The look on Cressy's face was pretty funny. She thought it was a general management meeting, but several board members were here, so she quickly realized she had been set up.

She wasn't prepared to meet with the board, and they hadn't given her a chance to prepare either. Instead of letting her request the meeting, they had made it very clear, by doing it this way, that they were in charge and that she was nobody.

He could almost see the moment she realized it, and she accepted it right away—in a fatalistic way. He really wished he could stay and be a fly on the wall, but this was a meeting he didn't have time to attend; he had other things to see to. Issues that he definitely couldn't wait around to act upon. With one final look at the general meeting goers, he turned and walked out. He quickly disappeared down the hallway. He passed Sybil or Sadie again, and he called out once more to her, and, when she didn't respond, he shrugged and wished her a good day.

But he felt something off, as he walked past her, something that didn't feel quite right. He turned suddenly, hoping to catch her at something, but she was just sitting there, with a vacant look on her face. Frowning, he carried on, wondering why anybody would work in a place like this. The people here gave him the creeps.

GRAY SAT AT his desk in the FBI office. With something crazy going on at the center, he knew there was only so much he could do to help Cressy. What he was good at was what was in front of him, tracking down real people, real killers, real messed-up monsters.

He didn't know anything about the monsters that she dealt with, and he had no way to even join her in the fight, except to do what he knew how to do best. Since slashed tires were no ghostly event, that meant his world. That's why he was looking at the files of every doctor and nurse and orderly and cook and employee in the place. Yet nothing here was really popping.

As he carefully went through file after file, several things made him sit up and wonder. For example, one doctor had a drunk-driving charge tossed, yet he had blown quite a bit over the limit, almost two times over in fact. Another vehicle has been involved, and a woman had been badly injured. So the question really was, *How the hell had that gotten tossed?*

It made no sense, unless this doctor had connections that nobody was willing to talk about, and that was unfortunately all too possible. He set that folder off to the side for further investigation and then continued to work on others. It didn't take long to find a couple other anomalies.

Dr. Ada, who was one of the early scientists involved in the project to create this hospital, had a drug problem. Apparently she had gone to rehab several times, but was always welcomed back to the center, and that was a bit disconcerting too. How did you let somebody like that back into a center where she not only had access to the drugs but was also supposedly helping to guide other people with similar problems?

Gray also put her folder off to the side.

Several here concerned him, but, on the whole, considering a little over one hundred people worked there, most appeared to be who they said they were. A few orderlies caught his attention. One had a juvie record but had been clean ever since, and that was over sixteen years ago. Another had several misdemeanors, and another had been charged for shoplifting.

All in all, there was just enough here that Gray wondered how the HR department at Cressy's hospital functioned and what their criteria was for some of these hires.

It was interesting to see just how many people he wouldn't have thought appropriate to be on the staff there, yet were doing either just fine or somehow staying under the radar. Maybe it was that ability to keep under the radar that Gray was questioning because otherwise it made no sense to him. How did somebody get to work at this kind of a facility without being thoroughly vetted? At that, he picked up the phone and called Dr. Maddy.

Her voice was slightly harried when she answered, but, as soon as she connected to who it was, he could almost feel her pausing, taking a deep breath, and saying, "Hey, what's going on?"

"That's one thing I would like to know," he stated. "There are some issues here in terms of hiring, and I was wondering what kind of policy you guys implemented at your place and how that would compare to Cressy's center?"

"Such as?"

He explained about the juvie records, the misdemeanors, the two doctors. It was the doctors she was surprised at more than anything else really.

"I won't say that it's unusual," she began. "A lot of people have records, you know, that don't really involve anything to do with patient care. So a lot of times people are willing to look the other way, particularly if they're a big name or somebody who comes highly respected. They won't let one blot on their record destroy a career."

Gray knew the drill.

"As far as that drunk driving incident, that concerns me, but that would be more your department, not mine."

"So, it is possible that you could have people with similar things on their records at your center?"

"I would hope not, but I won't say no because it's quite possible Would I want to see something like that in my place? No. But short of me doing all the hiring myself, it's not impossible."

"Yet you're pretty involved in the hiring, aren't you?"

"I am, but what I do is the final check, you know? Better safe than sorry, but I would be looking at their energy. I'm not looking at their recommendations, at their histories, or whether they have a criminal record. They should have already been through a criminal background check and had their references verified. I am the final answer, and the one who says yes or no at the end of the day, and that has absolutely nothing to do with what's on paper."

He paused, as he thought about that. "Do you think Cressy's doing that here?"

"She certainly hasn't been for the last six months," Dr. Maddy noted. "I'm not sure how long any of these people have been there. Before that, I'm not sure she was involved in the hiring at all. She might have been able to vote or to give input, but I can't imagine she had any more involvement than that."

"Interesting."

"You're thinking it's somebody who works there?"

"I don't know whether it's somebody who works there or somebody who comes as a regular visitor," he suggested. "Hundreds and hundreds of people go through a check like that in order to work there. Who knows? There are orderlies, families of patients, families of staff members, the workers, vendors, contractors. It's endless really. I mean, how hard would it be to get into a center like that, when literally hundreds of people are coming and going, particularly if the person is well-known to the staff."

"It wouldn't take much really," Dr. Maddy suggested. "They would sign in. They would sign out."

"Right, and I do have copies of the sign-in books in front of me, but I can't say that that's making anything clear."

At that, Dr. Maddy laughed. "No, I wouldn't be at all surprised. They tend to be more unclear than anything."

"Why is that?"

"Because there are just so many names, some of which are easy to read and some that aren't." She hesitated and added, "I have abilities to do things that other people don't necessarily have, so my place is run a little bit differently."

"You want to explain that?" he asked, with a note of humor.

Dr. Maddy replied, "I have all kinds of safeguards on my floors, energy safeguards. If I see something or feel something off, that would mean at that point that my safeguards aren't working."

"Whoa, whoa, whoa, what do you mean?" he asked in astonishment. "Wouldn't it mean that they *are* working?"

"No, because, if I'm feeling it, it means that it's already gone past the point of breaking through the barriers I have set up," she explained. "There should never be a point in time that somebody has the ability to set off my energy guard, except for a patient who is showing some kind of, you know, odd symptom that I wasn't expecting or something." She paused. "But, in terms of visitors, in terms of danger to my patients from outside, I now keep quite a secure setting. So, if somebody gets through all that, then my own internal alarms would go off. In the meantime, I have alarms set up that do trigger my alarms, but in a very different way, so I know who needs to get it."

"So you're saying nobody could get onto your floor with like a weapon or something, intent on killing somebody."

"I won't say they can't because we have found people can do all kinds of things, and I'm always playing catch-up as to what they can and cannot do. However, the chances of it happening are slim."

"And in a place like Cressy's?"

"In a place like that, where she has no autonomy, where she doesn't have much in the way of rights or rules at this point in time, I would imagine it's quite possible. They have a security setup, but if it's not the right kind of security, it's next to useless in a sense."

"*Right kind,*" he repeated. "I'm afraid to hear about that *right* kind."

She chuckled. "That's because the right kind for me would be *my* kind."

"But that doesn't mean they have that here."

"Not only might they not have it there," Dr. Maddy pointed out, "it takes somebody like me to set it up."

"Do you monitor everything?"

"At this point, I have trained several other people to help monitor my floor, in case I'm working with a patient or out of town. We can't have just one person being the only one doing this," she noted. "That's always been one of my problems. I try to keep it compartmentalized and make ways to delegate. That is how you help as many people as you can, and, when you work one-on-one, you can't help one thousand."

"So what do you do?"

"I've been working on training people to do a triage, so that we know which patient needs more help, which ones can help themselves, which ones just need a little bit of help to push the healing process in the right direction, and then they just need monitoring. We're working with all kinds of stuff," Dr. Maddy noted, "but I'm not sure that any of it is as good as being on the spot."

"No, I don't imagine it is," he admitted. "I can't imagine the choices you have to make on a daily basis as to whether to help someone or not, just to keep it all on the up-and-up."

"Choosing is one horrific part of it. I do try to do everything with everyone I come across, or who calls out to me, because I believe there is a universal standard that you do the best you can. If you can't do it, you can't, but, once the request has gone out, the last thing you want to do is turn it down."

He found it hard to deal with a judicial system that was energetic in form.

She chuckled. "Some people would say the spirit around us was law, just a case of right and wrong. And, if you do right, all's good. If you do wrong, well then, there's karmic payback."

"I don't think I'm ready to hear that," he muttered.

"No, probably not." Dr. Maddy chuckled. "Still that doesn't mean it's not there, and it's not real. And some people don't understand that, by doing the best that you can, you are on the right side of the law. However, if you deliberately go out to hurt people, ... there are consequences for that, and people like that don't heal very well. Now even though they're working at changing who they were and who they've been all their life, it can take way longer to heal because of it.

"Therefore, those people have to start with a different kind of medical training. It's actually one of the reasons that I absolutely love working with children. They don't have a long history of being ugly to others, and, if they do, it's a short span, and we can work with them very quickly to understand what they've been doing is wrong, and they can throw off those shackles very quickly," she murmured. "Adults? That's a different story. The older we get, the more entrenched we are into being right and into hurting others that we think have hurt us. The deeper the trauma goes, the harder it is for a body to heal."

Long after that phone call, Gray sat back, thinking about what Dr. Maddy had just shared. He'd just been given a lesson in Energy 101 with Dr. Maddy. He realized just how fascinating it was to talk to her and to get her view on how some of this stuff worked. It didn't make a whole lot of sense, not until she put it in that kind of context, but to think that healing could happen rapidly once one had dealt with their issues was absolutely fascinating. And, of course, for a lot of people, it was more than fascinating; it was lifesaving.

And those people who weren't ready to heal, who didn't want to improve because the cost was too high for them or because they didn't care about the cost or because they wanted the power to do what they could to hurt others? He had to wonder if something like that wasn't going on at Cressy's place. It was even hard to understand that he was sitting here contemplating some of these issues at all.

He'd seen a lot of what had happened to Cressy last time, but he hadn't understood any of it. It had been easier to block it out than to try and explain the weird energy that had been flowing around them, the almost tumultuous storm that he'd been hard-pressed to find any explanation for. And yet Dr. Maddy had no problem with it, and she could explain it very simply.

That was all fine, and he needed that, but, at the moment, he needed to start with making a list and checking it twice. He almost smiled at the Christmas rhyme in his head, only to realize no pretty gifts would be at the end of this one. This would just, if he were lucky, stop another chaotic nightmare for a boy. The fact that any of this was even connected to that boy terrified Gray because, if they had an annihilator who had psychic abilities, it was more than awful, and Gray had no power to put a stop to it.

What would happen if that were true? Gray couldn't bear thinking about this.

CHAPTER 12

CRESSY ADDRESSED THE panel in front of her. "You called this meeting, and I didn't even get a chance to prepare for it? That's interesting."

At that, one of the men looked at her and gave her a benevolent smile. "What's to prepare for?" he asked. "Apparently you're back in good health and good spirits. Although a few of us suggested that maybe you needed a psych eval done."

She gave him a slow smile of the sort that made him sink back against his chair, almost quivering in place. "I would be interested to know who made that suggestion. And, just for the record, if a psych eval was a requirement, it would have to include *all* staff and board members of course. In that case, I would be happy to line up for mine."

He pulled himself together, straightened his tie and shoulders, and glared at her. "What's that supposed to mean?"

"Anything short of such an equitable standard would be considered intimidation," she murmured. "Members of the Board, let me be clear. If you didn't want me to come back, that's all you had to say. I would have been perfectly capable of making a decision at that point, fair and square. Yet, at the moment, it sounds to me as if you're just afraid I'm coming back."

The spokesman sniffed. A hard, irritating sound that made her laugh.

"It sure sounds that way, doesn't it?" she proposed, looking from one to the other. "That makes me very intrigued as to what it is that you're hiding."

One of the other men looked at her in alarm. "Whoa, whoa, whoa. We're not trying to hide anything."

"Since I've been gone," she began, "you've cut the cleaning staff. You've cut the orderlies. You've decimated the food bill and terminated the chef that was doing a great job. I haven't even begun to document the true impacts and costs of those changes yet, not to mention the others. I've had nothing but complaints from patients and families that I brought into this place. In fairness, some of that is due to the fact that I wasn't here, but it is the decline in patient care and service standards that has really pissed them off."

At that, the members looked at each other uneasily.

Cressy gave them the same benevolent smile she had given their spokesman before. "So, now I guess there are a few decisions to be made."

"What do you mean?" Dr. Mendelsohn asked in alarm at her side. "We are all very delighted to have you back."

"No, you're not," she argued, shaking her head. "You can't even begin to convince me of that now." She waved a hand at the four board members here. "And just how many shares do you all collectively own in this place?"

At that, they all stiffened and glared at her.

She nodded, looking at Mendelsohn and the others, all sitting, staring. "So, together I would presume you account for 51 percent at least—the four of you anyway—and, therefore, all these changes have been made exactly as you wanted, despite the consequences."

"It's better for the shareholders and for the board," said the one man, still struggling with his tie, which was obviously too tight.

"It has nothing to do with budgets then?" She laughed. "Wow, color me impressed. You even said that with a straight face."

He glared at her. "Look. This is no laughing matter. We were hemorrhaging money, and a lot of that was due to the changes that you insisted upon."

"Yes, patient care. It's what we're supposed to do here, and, yes, it's kind of important to me."

He shook his head at that. "No, it was a lot more than that. They didn't need a chef on board. *These* people don't need gourmet food."

"If that's what you think was happening, you, sir, have been sold a bill of goods. In a facility such as this, a chef is far less expensive than multiple cooks," she shared. "A well-trained chef can manage the kitchen, and he didn't just cook. He managed things so the food budgets were a lot less, waste was limited or nearly nonexistent, and the food was healthy and nutritious, instead of the way it is now. What you are serving now is low-quality overprocessed crap that is constantly being wasted."

"That chef cost us a bundle!"

"A drop in the bucket compared to what these private fees are costing the families," she murmured, giving him one more of those flat stares she knew he couldn't endure.

He swallowed several times and shook his head. "These changes have been made, and they won't be undone," he declared defiantly.

"I see," she replied. "In that case, not a whole lot to say about it in this *meeting*, is there?" She got up and collected her notepad.

"What does that mean? And, if you're thinking about quitting, that's just fine. I'm sure the world will have a great time understanding just how unstable you are right now."

At that, several audible gasps came from other people in this meeting.

That was a low blow, too low, even for an ambush meeting such as this.

Cressy turned slowly, stared at him, and asked, "Could you repeat that please?"

Maintaining his puffed-up stance, he repeated, "It's obvious that you needed time off because of mental distress," he stated, with a flat smile. "Most facilities won't be too eager to take you on after that."

"Oh my. Once again, you really are under a misapprehension, aren't you?"

"What do you mean?" he asked.

"No, never mind, that's … that's totally okay," she said. "It's best to let you find out all on your own." And, with that, her head held high, she gave a bland smile to everyone else in the room. "Thank you so much for this meeting, gentlemen."

She turned and walked out and immediately heard the buzz behind her. Dr. Mendelsohn raced up behind her.

"Cressy, please give them a chance. They're just really scared that you would start trying to make changes as soon as you got back."

"I was, and, bluntness aside, they had a right to be scared. But if you think that is now done and over, and they all can feel quite comfortable, you're wrong," she stated.

He stopped and looked at her. "Why?" he asked cautiously.

She laughed. "Oh, don't worry about it," she murmured. "Life has a way of throwing us curveballs. I guess I've just been thrown one. I will adjust, and maybe even kick it back."

He looked relieved. "So, you won't leave, right?"

"What do you guys care if I leave or not?" she asked calmly, with a smile on her face. "You've made it very clear that I'm not needed here and that the board doesn't want me here. Now that I'm back from my sabbatical, you've officially given me a chance to return, as is required, so now they're looking for a way to get rid of me," she explained. "I get it. Whatever you do, let's not insult my intelligence. Do *not* tell me that's *not* on their agenda."

He flushed and then admitted, "Yes, it's been discussed. They don't know how to get rid of you now, but the fact that you are back means that they can now move to the next step."

"Of course," she quipped, with a mocking smile. "Don't mind me. I'll just go deal with, you know, what we're supposed to deal with here, which, I'll remind you, … is patient care."

And, with that, she turned and walked away, heading straight for her office. She very quickly closed the door, locked it behind her, and then sat down in the corner, closed her eyes, and started deep breathing. She was stunned and didn't know how she had let this happen. She'd been so concerned about all the patients and so gung-ho to get things back to the way it had been—when their patient care standards were actually something she could be proud of— that she'd played right into their hands. She was working for the patients, while the board was figuring out how to get rid of her, even going so far as threatening to poison the well by not-so-subtly putting out the word about her being unstable.

She took ten minutes to calm down and to refocus, while she heard her phone ringing off the hook. She finally looked to see that Gray was calling. She hesitated, not wanting to answer, but realized he would just come charging into her office if she didn't. She answered it.

"Are you okay?" he asked.

"I've been better."

He hesitated. "Did you have a board meeting or something?"

"Or something. It felt more like a lynching though."

His breath caught.

"Yeah, that's about how I felt when I walked in to what was supposed to be a general staff meeting, only to see four of the board members, not coincidentally the members who probably have, though nobody confirmed it, 51 percent of the shares. They quickly made it very clear they were the ones in charge, and they were the ones making decisions, and they would run the place, just as they had been doing since I had been gone. One even went so far as to say that, should I decide to leave, he would ensure others in the field knew that I was unstable and had an unfortunate history of mental breakdown."

After a moment of silence, Gray exploded, "What?"

"Yeah, so at the moment, I'm adjusting to a new reality."

"No, that's not what you're doing at all," he argued. "I can feel it from here."

She paused. "Feel what?"

"I don't know," he admitted briskly, "but I would like to come up."

"You certainly can," she said. "I'm not sure what I'm doing right now."

"Are you quitting?"

"I can't just quit on some of these patients. I must have a plan in place for their care."

"What kind of plan could you possibly have?" he asked in confusion.

"I'm not sure yet," she told him. "Again I don't have one in place, so that needs to be next."

"You know, Dr. Maddy will never listen to any of those lies."

She laughed. "No, Dr. Maddy's always been my fallback," she agreed lightly, "but again it's not the ideal situation."

"But it could be," he argued.

"It sounds like you actually want me to go there."

"I'm certainly not against it, and I think it would be a hell of a lot better for you than spending another minute around those assholes you work with right now."

"What about the patients?" she asked.

"I don't know what to say about that, but, if the families and patients are happy to be with you, then maybe they'll move too. Rumors or not, they do know you."

"It's all very distressing for the patients," she noted.

"Maybe, but it seems it would be less stress to move versus staying in a place like that, where obviously nobody cares."

"Yeah, I don't know," she murmured. "That's something I'm still struggling with."

"I hate to ask right now, but how's the boy?"

"He's doing better." She quickly explained about the energy guard that she had told Adam about earlier.

"Will that work?"

"To make him feel better? Absolutely."

"No, no. Would it ... I can't even believe I'm asking

this."

She burst out laughing. "You mean, will it work-work, as in, will it keep away the boogeyman? I don't know about keeping him away, but it will certainly send out alarms to me if somebody goes in there and tries to attack Adam."

"Jesus."

"You knew that though," she stated curiously. "I mean, at least I thought you knew that."

"I'm not sure I know anything at this point," he muttered. "It seems that everything I ever thought I knew has to be reevaluated now."

"Oh, well, that is something you'll get used to." She chuckled. "Only so much of this can anyone make any sense of at any given time."

"Says you," he muttered. "This is ... this is beyond anything I've ever considered."

"Maybe, yet we don't really have a whole lot of choice. Some of this is pretty stupid stuff."

"Yeah, you're not kidding," he muttered. "Look. I know that you shouldn't be making any decisions right now," he stated, "so maybe just talk to Dr. Maddy and toss some ideas around."

"Maybe, but I think at the moment I'll go have a cup of tea."

He hesitated. "Tea?"

She laughed. "Yes, with a patient. I was invited."

"Good," he replied, a bit of relief in his voice. "Please stay in touch."

"What's the matter, Mr. Big FBI Agent?" she asked in a teasing voice. "Are you worried about me? Or is it just my patient?"

He hesitated and then replied, "It was never just about

your patient. I was there six months ago. Remember?"

At that, her laughter fell away. "I suppose you want me to go for a psych eval too then."

"What? Did they actually suggest that?" he asked.

"Yes, but don't worry, I told them that I would be happy to join them in the line, since, if they require that of me, they would also have to include the staff and the board. Otherwise it was clearly an attempt at intimidation. Believe me. Nobody liked that idea much either."

He burst out laughing. "But, as a volley goes, it wasn't a bad one to fire."

"Won't do me any good though," she said. "At this very moment, I'm sure they probably actively trying to figure out how to get rid of me."

"What will you do then?"

"One of the things I need to do … You any good with computers?"

"Sure I am. Why?"

"Can you log on to my system remotely?"

"If you give me access. What are you thinking?"

"I better download my patient files, not to mention my own research, just in case I get walked out of this place very quickly." Even as she voiced that thought, she felt an urgency rising within her. "I mean, as of right now."

She quickly gave him access to her computer, and she went to her file cabinets and started pulling everything out. She had left a lot of it behind last time because she hadn't had a chance to do otherwise. But now she had this feeling that everybody here would have something to say, one way or another, about her staying or not staying.

She highly suspected she wouldn't have the option and may get moved out by security very quickly, even within a matter of hours. The rising, bubbling feeling put her idea of tea with Sadie on hold. By the time Cressy had packed everything up into boxes, she sent Gray a text, asking if he could come collect the files she had in her office, just in case.

When he asked when, she wrote **Now, please.**

He immediately sent a text back. **Be there in five.**

With that, she kept her door locked and made sure that, aside from the boxes, absolutely everything in her office was okay to stay, if she were forced to walk out. She had no idea what the hell was going on, but something had been brewing, and obviously her return had kicked it into high gear. She had all her files in boxes, topped off with her laptop. Now her desk was emptied too, just as she heard people outside, knocking on the door, only to have them go away after a few minutes.

What she didn't want was security to come in and unlock the door to remove her. That would have been one step too far. She had really hoped they would give her time to collect herself and evaluate her position, especially after that obviously disruptive meeting.

She couldn't even believe that she was at this point. But she was, and that's all there was to it. Then she thought about little Adam and frowned. This wouldn't be good for him, but what was she supposed to do about it? She immediately phoned Stefan.

He answered with "Not sure what's going on, but it sounds big."

"I think I'm being maneuvered out of my job right now," she replied. "I had an unpleasant ambush-style meeting with several of the board members this morning. I'm actually getting Gray to collect all my files online, and he's coming to help me with my physical files that I've packed up in boxes here. But I'm really worried about little Adam and several of the other patients." She reminded him about Sadie. "She is definitely a candidate for you. There is a young woman here who is suicidal, who desperately needs help before she succeeds in her next attempt."

"Any idea what's happened to her?"

"Yes. Trauma of the criminal kind, but, even though her stepfather has been arrested and is doing jail time, he only got a few years, and a couple have already passed, so she's sliding every day because she knows he'll get out."

"*Great*," Stefan muttered. "And you think he'll come after her?"

"I don't think he can live without her. A very weird obsessive energy is around her."

"Names please," he said immediately.

She gave them to him and then added, "I have a few more, but, on the whole, some of these patients will be fine here, and then there are those who I need to be sure get out of here relatively quickly."

"You're talking about Adam, I presume?"

"Adam is just one of them but yes. He's a ward of the state, and I am not certain how to ensure he can come with me, wherever it is that I go. Right now he trusts me, and we've gained some ground, but—"

"Got it," Stefan interrupted. "Let me contact Grant, and we'll see what we can pull together."

Just as quickly, she said, "I've got to go."

She hung up, looked at the doorway, and frowned. Whatever was coming toward her had an energy she did not like. Not sure she was up for any other confrontations, she walked to the window, wondering how long it would be before they brought in security. At the window, she opened it wide, seeing Gray racing toward the front door.

Just then she heard keys in the door.

She quickly grabbed her bag and her purse and stepped out the window, closing it partially in the hopes that they wouldn't see it right away. Then she booked it out of sight.

GRAY WALKED IN and headed straight for her office, just in time to see several people in her office, men in business suits, staring around in confusion. He stepped in and growled, "What's going on here?"

All of them jumped, as if he were the last person they expected to see. A look of chagrin crossed Dr. Mendelsohn's face. "We thought she was in here. Honestly we were concerned she might harm herself."

At that, Gray faced the doctor directly. "Hogwash. So, you are part of the conspiracy too, are you?" Gray turned, took a note of all her boxes, and immediately made a phone call. "I need a team here to collect Dr. Cresswell's files," he ordered, stepping forward.

At that, someone protested. "Hey, what are you talking about?"

Gray gave him a flat stare. "As of right now, I am putting this institution under federal investigation," he stated, low and clear, his tone calm.

"No, no, no, nothing is wrong here at all," one of the men replied in a soothing tone.

He turned, stared at the man, and asked, "And your name?"

The man frowned.

"I asked you a question," Gray snapped. "Do I need to remind you who I am?"

At that, the other man flushed in anger. "You can't throw your weight around here. We only allowed you here as a courtesy."

At that, one of the other men gasped. "No, no, no, no, that's not true. Obviously we're here to cooperate as best we can."

Gray nodded, his eyebrows raised. "Really? Is that what that meeting was all about this morning?"

"Did she contact you?" One of the men gasped.

He faced him. "She expected this and saw it coming. She is on record regarding some criminal activity here that is making her very uneasy. She predicted there would be a move to get rid of her very quickly, and here you all are, forcing yourself into her space, with no regard for her privacy or that of her patients, for that matter."

At that, one of the men paled.

"Believe me. I will be looking into it," Gray declared, his voice hard. "Not to mention, I have already found all kinds of irregularities in your staffing files." Some of the men took several steps back, and he nodded. "That has been noted."

One of them shook their heads. "I don't know what you're talking about. Scare tactics don't work here. We have rights, and we know it."

"You do, indeed, and not a one of you is leaving here until I know the exact whereabouts of Dr. Cresswell, as well as who each of you are and your involvement in this mess that you've just created."

At that, Dr. Mendelsohn spoke up. "You already know who I am. I came here to try and stop them."

"Stop them from what?" When the doctor hesitated, Gray took one look at him and just knew. "You people really would walk her out of the building today, wouldn't you?"

Dr. Mendelsohn flushed. "Look. She was seeing things, acting strange in the hallways."

He snorted at that. "Are you suggesting she was doing anything different than before?"

He frowned at that. "No, I'm not. It's probably just that we haven't seen that behavior for a while, so maybe it appeared a little more unusual," he clarified, with half a smile.

"So now because she's back, and you're all concerned about potential changes in your pocketbooks, you set out to get her fired, is that it?" Gray asked.

Dr. Mendelsohn swallowed. "No, no, that's not it. She's one of the most gifted doctors I know, and her results are nothing short of phenomenal."

"So, help me understand why you are part of this movement to get rid of her?" Gray asked, his eyebrows raising.

"I'm not," he argued. "I'm one of the ones who protested against it. I'm also very aware that we're quite likely to lose patients because of this."

"And that's fine," one of the other men snapped. "We'll get other patients."

With that, Gray turned to look him. "Only if I don't shut you down," he added smoothly, "because all I'm seeing so far is a lynch mob."

At that came a commotion at the door, as several of Gray's coworkers entered. He looked at them, smiled, and nodded. "I need statements from everybody here. I need names, full positions, and involvements." He turned to look at Mendelsohn and stated, "I also need the full minutes from the meeting that you had earlier today."

"This has nothing to do with you," one of the men

snapped. "You're only here because of the one patient."

"I'm also here because we're opening an investigation into whoever installed a listening device in Dr. Cresswell's office," Gray stated. "You do understand it's against the law to bug somebody's office? Not to mention potential violations of patient privacy, which is also quite serious."

At that, Dr. Mendelsohn cried out, "What?"

Gray nodded. "So, don't go telling me what I can and cannot do, sir. Also, you have yet to produce Dr. Cresswell, which worries me beyond everything else."

At that, Dr. Mendelsohn looked around. "She's not with you?" he asked.

"No, I just arrived. You want to explain to me where she is?"

"That's why we came in because the door was locked. We thought she was in here."

Gray just gave him a flat stare again, and he flushed.

Mendelsohn added, "Honestly it was easier to come in and try to deal with it, than to let them run wild."

"Really? You have quite an interesting system for staffing here."

At that, Dr. Mendelsohn hesitated and then asked, "What did you mean about staffing irregularities?"

Gray began, "As if you don't know, several of your staff members here have juvenile records, histories of drug abuse, drunk driving and DUI records, domestic violence, petty theft, and a half-dozen other infractions that should never have been cleared on a criminal background check for a facility of this nature."

The color left his face. He shook his head. "What? None of that should have happened."

"Maybe not, but it did. So now I'll find out how this

place is running. You are charged with caring for some of the most vulnerable patients in society and are potentially exposing them to criminally negligent danger through your staffing process." Gray repeated, "Now, if you don't tell me right now where Dr. Cresswell is, there'll be even more hell to pay."

"I don't know where she is," Dr. Mendelsohn repeated. "I thought she was here. We unlocked her door."

"Her private office? You unlocked her private office?"

"We do have that right," he protested.

"Sure you do, as long as you had justification. What was your justification today?"

At that, one of the men replied, "She was upset, so we thought maybe she was too delicate for the news that she got this morning."

He stared at him. "You thought what?"

At that, every one of the men paled as they heard the tone in Gray's voice.

"Look. We were just trying to do what was right."

Gray turned to the FBI agents in the room. "As you can see, a huge mess is going on here, so let's not get sucked into it. Go ahead and get to work on statements."

Ignoring their protests, each of the men were separated, as Gray turned to Dr. Mendelsohn. In a dangerous tone he stated, "Now, you tell me what the hell's going on here, how long it's been going on, and how does this affect Dr. Cresswell. But first, tell me where Dr. Cressy is, and I mean *now*."

It was all about finding Dr. Cressy.

With everybody lined up for interviews, and the FBI taking care of the boxes she had asked him to grab, he headed out to do a full search of the facility. Twenty minutes later, when he stood by her car in the parking lot, he realized something was seriously wrong. He called Grant. "She disappeared," he said in a panic.

"Who disappeared?" Grant asked, clearly still distracted by whatever work he was doing.

"Cressy!" Gray quickly gave him a short version of the events.

"What?'

"Yeah, exactly." Gray rubbed his free hand over his face in frustration. "I don't know where she's gone. Her vehicle's here, but there's no sign of her, in the hospital or out. I've got the rest of the team here doing a full search room to room, but she didn't have time to get anywhere."

"What are you thinking happened?"

"I don't know, and I don't have any proof either way. All I can tell you is that, … she's missing."

"Put the place on full lockdown," Grant ordered. "I'll be there in five. She's got to be there somewhere."

CHAPTER 13

CRESSY MOANED SOFTLY, her hand reaching up to her aching head, only to find that her hands were tied and something covered her head. She shuddered in place, as pain racked through her. Yet all she could think of was that something was seriously wrong, and somehow somebody had attacked her. She called out into the ethers to Stefan and to Dr. Maddy. Not only did she get both of them answering her cry for help but several other voices replied as well.

Immediately Stefan stepped in. *Take it easy. Do you know where you are?*

"No," she gasped. "I can't see anything. My eyes are covered, and my hands are bound."

Tell us what led up to this.

She quickly gave him as much as she remembered, finishing with, "The last thing I remember was going through the window."

But why? Were you trying to get away from Gray for some reason? Dr. Maddy asked.

"No, not at all," Cressy explained. "I thought I could buy some time for him to get in there and to secure my files. I assumed the board was coming in to escort me out for good, so I thought that, if Gray came in, and I wasn't there, he might do something. When I heard the sound of keys, I knew they were trying to get through the door to me, so I wanted to escape quickly. The last thing I wanted was to get walked out and locked out. Then I wouldn't have any access to what I needed to sort things out. I need to know what the hell is going on."

So you went out the window and then what?

"I was headed toward my car, and ... that's the last thing I remember."

According to Gray, Dr. Maddy said, her voice calm, *your car is still there, and the FBI assumes either you've been taken off the grounds by another vehicle or you're still on the grounds.*

She groaned. "I honestly don't know where I am." She shifted and then gasped. "I'm in some sort of container, confinement unit, or something of the sort," she whispered. 'There's not much room here at all."

Can you hear anything? Stefan asked urgently.

She opened up her senses a bit wider. "No, it's silent. Wait. There's a weird hum in the background. Like machinery."

Like a furnace? Dishwasher? Laundry? Vacuum? What kind of a hum?

She contemplated for a moment, wishing that the pounding in her head would stop. "Maybe a washing machine, but I can't really tell."

No, but it gives me a place to send them to search for you, Stefan noted.

She hesitated. "Do you think somebody stuffed me into a washer?" she cried out in horror.

Let's hope not, he muttered, *since that would mean somebody could turn it on at any moment.*

She started to struggle, only to find herself held with golden bonds.

Easy, Dr. Maddy told her. *That's me stopping you from*

struggling because we don't know where you are.

She gasped and relaxed back. "God, this is not how I thought my day would go."

No, I'm sure it's not, Stefan agreed. *On the other hand, you had some inkling, didn't you?*

"Yes, that's why I started collecting files and information, but I thought I had a few days. I didn't think they would move in on me quite so fast."

Any idea why they're moving so quickly?

She hesitated, but then said, "In the past, I've always been able to rally the troops to make change happen. I presume they're afraid I would do that again."

At that, with a note of humor in Dr. Maddy's voice, she added, *You know how these people like to operate. They don't like change. Once they get something the way they want it, they aren't willing to give it up, particularly if it comes to dollars. That's probably what this is about.*

"Yeah, their own personal profit dollars. They cut staff. They cut orderlies. They cut shift hours. They cut overtime. They cut the budget. They cut security. What they really cut was quality of life for the patients," Cressy snapped.

That's okay, Stefan replied. *This will just provide proof, and then a full investigation will be needed.*

"*Great,*" she muttered, followed by a groan. "I was really hoping to stay out of the public eye."

I hear you, Stefan noted. *Have you thought any more about leaving?*

She laughed. Or would have if she could have. "Great time to ask," she muttered.

I know, but you've got nothing else to do, so you might as well think about it.

"That's really not what I want to hear right now."

Maybe not, Stefan agreed cheerfully, *but obviously something is afoot there.*

"There is, but I'd rather try to fix it than start all over someplace else, especially where people don't understand what I do."

Do you think they understand there? Dr. Maddy asked.

Cressy hesitated and sighed. "No, they don't. I'm not sure anybody there understands what I do, outside of you guys."

Right, Stefan agreed. *Keep your mind open, as we work our way through this. You need to be vigilant for any sounds, any change, anything at all.*

"Have you sent people this way?" Cressy asked.

Absolutely, Stefan confirmed. *They're checking out all the utility areas, the basement, and every place there is to check on the premises.*

"What about Gray? Is he here?"

He's leading the charge, Stefan declared, with a smile. *You appear to have made an impression on him.*

"Unfortunately I made the impression last time, when I really wasn't at my best."

Are you kidding? That was totally your best. You fought off a monster, and you won, Stefan murmured. *It doesn't get any better than that for abilities.*

"You think so? Right now I'm not so certain I won."

He hesitated, then asked, *What do you mean by that?*

"It occurred to me that the monster might be … I don't want to say *connected* to the family annihilator but it's something. I'm wondering if he has his hooks into my business. I've got Adam here being tormented by some energy predator, and, from what he told me, I'm wondering if it isn't the same person. The poor little guy is terrified in there. Did you check his energy guard?"

Yes, it hasn't been touched, Stefan stated immediately. *Adam is safe.*

"Thank God for that. This is why I can't just leave," she cried out. "His progress will be completely held back. A kid like that could spend his life in an institution like this, simply because nobody can help him."

First, let's get you dealt with, Dr. Maddy stated firmly. *I can always arrange to get Adam moved here.*

"Not exactly your forte," Cressy pointed out.

But that doesn't mean it's not a good place for him. He would be safe, and you can always come here and work. I'll need a couple more floors though, she said, with a note of laughter. *Particularly if we'll do more than just him.*

"And you know a million other people we need to help are out there," Cressy stated. "Adam's just one of many. And now that I've connected with them …"

I know, Dr. Maddy agreed, her voice quiet. *It's even harder to let go.*

"Exactly," Cressy muttered.

Let's deal with one thing at a time, Stefan reminded them. *Let's work on getting you collected from wherever the hell you've been stashed.*

"That's another thing that makes no sense," Cressy admitted. "Do they really expect to keep me hidden down here? How long could that go on?"

That would be one of the questions I would love to ask them, Stefan replied, *but first we have to find you.*

"Wait," she said, "I think I hear voices." At that, she heard a murmur somewhere close by.

Stay quiet. We don't yet know whether it's friend or foe.

"*Great*," Cressy whispered. "No, that is definitely somebody. Definitely someone is out there."

Stop. You need to focus on listening.

She subsided at the force of Dr. Maddy's tone. Cressy waited anxiously, realizing they were afraid it was her kidnapper returning. Just then her container was shifted and moved. She heard an *oomph*, as somebody realized how heavy it was. Then suddenly she heard an exclamation, and her head covering was removed, and gentle hands were on her face.

Feeling the tears beginning, she opened her eyes to see Gray staring down at her.

He reached out and swooped her up into his arms and held her close. "Good God," he whispered. "I was five minutes away. What happened?"

She shrugged.

When he turned, she took a look at the men who had come in with him, seeing the look of relief on their faces. She smiled up at them, teary-eyed, and whispered, "Thank you."

Her voice was hoarse, but she wasn't even sure why. She frowned, then tried to speak again, but it was … it was almost as if some pressure was put against her vocal cords. She looked up at Gray and made a funny sound.

"What?" he asked. "Easy now. Don't try to talk. We don't know what kind of injuries you may have sustained."

She tried hard to talk, confused, since she'd been talking earlier. Just then she realized she'd been talking to Stefan and Dr. Maddy in her mind.

She sent out one last warning and looked up at Gray.

Then her eyes rolled back in her head, and, with that, she lost consciousness.

GRAY DIDN'T KNOW he could move that fast, but, in no time, he had Cressy upstairs, on the main floor, his team calling for an ambulance on the way. He met a group of doctors from the center, some he had seen before, others were new.

As soon as they saw Cressy in his arms, they cried out and raced forward.

Gray froze and glared at them.

Dr. Mendelsohn said, "Remember. We are doctors."

Gray shook his head. "Maybe, but, for all I know, one of you assholes did this to her," he snapped. "I can't trust any of you right now." He watched the shock reverberate through them, and he nodded. "She was kidnapped, tied up, and stashed in one of your commercial washing machines in the laundry downstairs," he stated, his voice harsh. "This place stays under lockdown, until we've ascertained who we have here. Also I'll need access to schedules and exactly where everybody was at the time Cressy went missing."

"Are you serious?" Mendelsohn asked, his voice quavering. "We just saw her this morning."

"And, since you last saw her, you decided to go after her job. Then guess what? Somebody went after her in a far more personal way." Gray shifted, hearing the ambulance coming, and declared, "She'll be in a proper hospital for a full exam."

"Do you know what happened?" Dr. Mendelsohn asked.

Gray shook his head. "No, I don't, but I know that she was having trouble speaking. She was awake when I first found her, then she crashed."

Among the sea of worried faces, he realized just how many of them probably really cared about her. Still he just didn't know who could be trusted and who could not.

Talking to the FBI team behind him, he left instructions, just in time to see Grant racing through the front door.

Seeing Cressy in Gray's arms, a look of relief washed over his buddy's face. "Thank God for that," Grant said. "Is that ambulance for her?"

"It is. She could hardly talk, and then she crashed. She's unconscious, so I need her to get checked out and fast."

"You go," Grant told him. "I'll handle this."

"Yeah, good luck with that," Gray murmured. "All kinds of things are wrong in this place."

"You go. I'll get to the bottom of it," he promised. "It's no longer a simple case involving Adam. Obviously something much bigger is here."

At that, Gray headed outside. When Grant called back to him, he turned.

"Do you know anything about how Adam is?"

He shook his head. "I didn't get a chance to ask her. Check in with Stefan first."

At that, Grant's eyebrows popped up. "First?"

"Yeah. I'm pretty sure he's got a hand in this too. At least with Adam's care and safety."

"Good to know. Get going." Grant pointed, as the ambulance pulled up in front of them and quickly opened their back doors. "I'll take care of this."

And, with that, Gray laid Cressy down on a gurney, and the first responders quickly loaded her up. As they checked her vitals, Gray hopped into the back and stayed with her the whole way. He just held her hand, feeling some connection had been made between them. Maybe he just wanted any connection at all. Maybe he just wanted to know she was safe and couldn't escape his arms again.

He didn't know what the hell was going on here, but,

when it came to finding something rotten, he'd found the motherlode. By the time she was taken into emergency, he was escorted to a chair off to the side, where he sat and texted Grant, who phoned him a few minutes later.

"We're still going through statements, and a full search has been done. We have absolutely no way of knowing who did this."

"Cameras?"

"Everything's down," Grant muttered.

"So, that's an inside job."

He hesitated and then replied, "It's possible."

"You're not convinced?" Gray asked him.

"Not yet, just way too much public-and-vendor access and way too little security."

"That was one of her concerns when she got back," Gray noted in frustration. "She told me that the security team had been cut back, as if they believed she had made too much of the previous attack on her and had invented the notion that the facility needed security in the first place."

"Idiots," Grant declared. "Stay where you are. I'll pop in, as soon as we've got this place under control." And, with that, he hung up.

Gray looked up to see a doctor walking toward him. He sat down in the chair beside Gray, who immediately pulled out his ID.

"I understood the FBI was involved. This is the same woman I treated six months ago," the doctor murmured, studying Gray. "And I don't even know what to say this time."

At that, Gray's heart froze. "What do you mean?"

"Nothing necessarily is wrong with her. Yet we expected to find a constriction of her throat. We've taken a scope down there, looking for damage or a potential blockage, and found nothing. She's breathing on her own, so I don't know what the problem is." He sighed. "I want to keep her here for observation."

"You said she's breathing on her own."

"Yes, but I'm not sure she'll talk right away."

"That's fine, as long as she's not in danger of dying."

"No, she's not in danger of dying." Yet he hesitated. "The trouble is, all our tests show there is no constriction."

"So how do you know there is one?"

"It explains her failure to speak. Plus that's what she is telling us. She's awake. She's conscious, and she's motioning in a way to show us how she can't talk because her throat is seized."

He stared at the doctor, and the doctor stared back. "*Great*," Gray muttered.

"Look. I saw this young woman last time, and I know she took time off after that horrific attack. All I can think is that this could be PTSD or something. Maybe she is reliving her worst memory, stuck in a reoccurring event."

Gray shook his head at that. "I know you mean well, but it has nothing to do with that."

The doctor stared at him steadily.

"I don't suppose you know Stefan Kronos, do you?"

"Yes, I'm familiar with the name," he replied cautiously.

"Dr. Maddy?"

At that, the doctor nodded. "Yes, absolutely."

"Why don't you talk to them," Gray suggested, "because they're her friends, and they're the ones who were talking to her earlier today."

At that, the doctor frowned at him. "If it's got to do with them, it's something I really don't even know how to begin to treat," the doc admitted. "They stepped in last time too."

"Unfortunately it seems the world that we know is only the world we know *so far*, and some people have experiences that cross into areas we have no exposure to."

"Yeah, you're not kidding." The doctor stood and pulled out his phone. "I'll talk to Stefan, and that will determine treatment."

"Got it," Gray said. "I'll wait here."

The doctor paused, then said, "She's asking for you, so you can go in, but don't try to get her to talk yet."

"No, I won't," Gray agreed, "at least not until we know what the hell is stopping it."

The doc pointed to a nurse nearby and said, "Take him to her room." And, with that, the doctor walked away, already making the call to Stefan.

Gray headed to Cressy's room, thanking the nurse. He pulled back the curtain and stepped into the small area. She was lying there, the stark contrast of the huge hospital bed emphasizing just how small she really was. When he stepped up to her side and reached for her hand, she opened her eyes. He saw her tears welling up, and, feeling like a heel, he sat down beside her. "I'm so sorry. If only I'd gotten there a little earlier."

She immediately placed a finger against his lips to stop him.

He sighed. "I really wish you could tell me what the hell happened."

She gave him a quirk of a smile, and he saw a notepad in front on her. She picked it up and started to write. Moments later, she turned it around. *I saw you arrive at the center.*

He stared at her. "You actually saw that I was there, and

you left anyway?"

She nodded and continued to write. *The board was about to come through the door, and I wanted to buy some time to get my files secured. I went out the window, then headed for my car. After that, I don't know what happened.*

He stared at her in shock. "Your car is still at the hospital. It was just returned with new tires."

She nodded. *I think I was hit over the head,* she wrote, her other hand going up to her hairline. *Don't know.*

He nodded at that. "The doctor confirmed that you have an injury on the back of your head, as if somebody came up and hit you from behind."

She pondered that and nodded. *That fits,* she wrote.

"About your throat?"

She shrugged. *No clue,* she wrote.

"Damn." He stared at the pad of paper in her hand. "Any chance it's metaphysical somehow?"

She looked up at him, an awareness coming into her gaze, and then she slowly nodded. As her hand moved across the notepad, she quickly wrote. *Someone doesn't want me to talk.*

"What is it that somebody is afraid you will say?"

CHAPTER 14

CRESSY WOKE A few hours later, disoriented and more tired than she'd expected. She yawned and then winced at her throat cramping.

Almost immediately a nurse walked in and beamed at her. "You're awake. That's great."

"Have I slept long?" she whispered.

"It's lovely to hear your voice. You've been asleep all afternoon, off and on." She gave Cressy a gentle smile. "But then, after the trauma you went through, that's the best thing for you."

Cressy didn't say anything to that, knowing it was quite true. She looked around, but nobody else was here. "Have you seen Gray?" she asked, her voice a hoarse whisper.

The nurse nodded. "Yes, he's been back and forth the whole day."

She smiled at that. Rather than trying to say anything else, she just nodded.

"Would you like a cup of coffee or a cup of tea?" the nurse asked. "It might help ease the soreness."

Cressy nodded immediately, a big smile breaking across her face.

"That's obviously a yes. Let me go see what I can find for you." And, with that, she quickly disappeared down the hallway. Cressy sat back and pulled the covers up against her chest, trying to ward off a chill, but it was a chill that she didn't really understand. It was more a chill of circumstance than actual cold.

She'd felt these kinds of chills before, but they were almost always psychic chills. And most hospitals were not great places for her. But right now that was where she was, and there wasn't much hope of getting out of here anytime soon.

At that, Dr. Maddy's voice whispered through her head. *No, not for a while.*

Cressy smiled at that. *Have you been working on me?* she asked.

Yep, Stefan too. You've got a block around your throat, but we're not sure if you put it there or if somebody else did.

That's not good, she muttered.

No, it's loosened up quite a bit, and we think that it should be something you can probably get rid of now, but you need to do what you can to figure out who it is who did this and see if you can recognize the energy that put it there.

I'll need some peace and quiet for that.

Once the nurse returns with your tea, you should have that, Dr. Maddy murmured. *I have to get back to my other patients now. Let me know if you need anything.*

Thanks. Cressy felt her friend disappear from her mind.

It was a very different relationship, knowing you had access to each other's deepest souls, the way the two of them did. They hadn't even known about each other until Cressy had started working in this field and had bumped up against Dr. Maddy. Cressy had been so focused on her own world that she hadn't even heard very much about Dr. Maddy's reputation. Although she'd learned very quickly.

Now they were fast friends, bonded by a skill and a dedication of service that Cressy had never experienced with anybody else. She was also very aware that Dr. Maddy was hooked into a whole network of talented people. Cressy had never had such an advantage, and it made a difference. It really helped to know that she wasn't alone in this and that people were out there who were ready and able to help her, if need be.

After the attack on her six months earlier, she'd certainly had that truth proven out time and time again. Now here she was again, wondering what the hell was going on in her world and whether this latest attack and this loss of her voice was something psychic all over again.

At that, Stefan popped in. *That's a question I wanted to ask you. Do you have any ideas? Did you have any feelings at the time?*

It felt like I was blocked, like I was frozen in time. I didn't really understand where I was, who I was, or what had happened for a very brief time, she murmured.

Silence came from Stefan at first. *Now that's an interesting way to describe it,* he noted in a conversational tone.

Not a good way though, I'm sure.

Not necessarily a bad way either though, he noted, ever cheerful. *The thing is, you're alive, and now we just have to ensure something like that doesn't happen again.*

True. I was so stressed over the meeting I'd just had with the board, my own reactions were well and truly stunted. That's the part that upsets me the most. I had my guard down.

Of course, Stefan agreed in understanding. *Whenever we lose control, and something bad happens, it reminds us just how little margin of error we have in our lives.*

Isn't that the truth, she muttered. *And it's sad because I thought I was welcome there. I thought I was doing well.*

But maybe the welcome wasn't so much from the board and

the staff as much as it was from the actual patients.

Right now it makes me question everything, she murmured. Then she brightened. *Has the FBI actually begun an investigation?*

They're all over it, Stefan confirmed cheerfully. *They were looking for an excuse to go in anyway, especially after all the things that you had shared. Plus it gave them a chance to move Adam.*

But move him where? she asked cautiously. *He's very fragile right now, and I had just begun to see a breakthrough with him, and now this had to happen.*

I've been talking with him. Adam's doing much better than I would have expected. Stefan smiled. *He's a bright boy.*

He sure is, Cressy agreed, *and he's been through an awful lot already.*

He has, but he's also strong. We can't ever forget that.

She nodded and sank back against the bed again, staring out the window. *What do I do from here? I won't go back to work. I'm sure they've already revoked everything in terms of my access, and I won't get to help the patients I was working with,* she said in a disappointed tone.

Can't you go in and work with them from where you are?

She pondered that. *A couple I could, like Sadie, who was dancing down the hallway.* Cressy smiled.

I could check on her too, Stefan offered.

I'd planned to see her for tea. She had invited me earlier, but the board railroaded me before I had a chance to take her up on the offer. You will check on her?

Yeah.

Why is that? Cressy teased. *Can't the great Stefan split off his energy to others, do some delegation to handle everything all at once?*

He gave a guffaw of laughter, making her smile.

It's good to hear your laughter, Cressy noted.

It's good to hear you making jokes, he said equally calmly. *We both know that our fields are tough, and, at times, a little breath of humor can make all the difference for getting from one moment to the next.*

Very true, she murmured.

The nurse returned just then.

Cressy gave her a smile of appreciation as a thank-you, hating to even try to use her voice again.

When she'd used it accidentally earlier, it had been a harsh shock. A part of her should have realized what losing her voice was all about; yet another part was desperately trying to let herself off the hook, knowing she wasn't in full form. She didn't let herself off the hook very often, and that pressure had increased, particularly after the attack from six months ago. Now it felt that she was sliding back into that same problem again, with this most recent incident.

Regardless, for some reason, she was under attack.

She didn't know who, where, or why, but this time it was physical and emotional and psychic, making it that much harder on her. She didn't know what she'd done to deserve any of this, but all she could think of was that somebody didn't want her back at the hospital. But, if that was the case, why?

What was it that her presence would influence?

Who had the ability to do this?

Who would benefit from it?

As soon as the nurse was gone, Cressy sipped her tea and pondered everything she had heard and had assimilated, while she'd been a prisoner in that washing machine. There hadn't been any noise, no one speaking, no sounds she could discern from an attacker. Even at the very time she'd been attacked, there was so little warning. She had no chance to even get any impressions.

That was the thing. It had been so fast that she'd had no time to even move—as if she was there one minute, and the next she was under somebody else's control. The speed in which it had happened was one of the things that bothered her the most. How did she reconcile becoming a victim so very quickly? You thought you were doing so great, yet somebody could turn around and do that to you. Meanwhile, you didn't even have a chance to react.

The world was full of little shits, as she'd come to realize over time, but she'd had a little security in knowing she had extra abilities that, if nothing else, would give her a warning—just as she had been able to ask for help from Stefan and Dr. Maddy. Let's face it. Without them, Cressy could still be a victim. She could still be locked up for whatever purpose this guy had in his mind. The fact that he was still out there was terrifying, and it made no sense, considering everything she'd been through so far, yet there it was.

Now she looked at everybody sideways, wondering who was responsible and who wasn't. She finished her tea, and then feeling the same weariness creep over her again, she closed her eyes and drifted off to sleep. When a sudden noise sounded in her room, she bolted awake and stared around in a panic, but nothing was here. Frozen, her breath slamming against her chest, she slowly sank against the headboard, wondering if this would ever be over, when a voice in her head whispered, *Never!*

It was gone as quickly as it had come. She lay here, feeling a creepy iciness take over her body.

She knew that voice.

That voice belonged to someone she should never have to hear from again. Inside, she was quaking with fear. That should never have happened. That voice should never have called out to her again. She felt her panic rising higher and higher, faster and stronger.

Stefan stepped into her mind and ordered her to stop it.

She calmed ever so slightly, taking a shuddering breath and closing her eyes, trying desperately to stem the tide of panic.

What the hell was that? Stefan asked sharply.

She couldn't even tell him. How could she? It was a voice from the dead. A voice that should never have been allowed to come back. But Stefan seemed to know. He always seemed to know.

In her mind, he whispered, *Dear God.*

She gave a broken laugh. *Yeah, if there's a God out there, I feel like He's forsaken us about now.*

No, Cressy, Stefan snapped. *You have to stay in control.*

I haven't been in control for a very long time apparently. And then I heard that voice.

Tell me exactly what you heard. When she told him as clearly as she could, he asked, *Is there any chance that you made a mistake?*

Her laugh was broken, bordering on hysteria. *How could I be mistaken? He's been in my nightmares for the past six months.*

Are you sure he's just been in your nightmares?

She paused at that. *Meaning?*

Is there any chance that he's actually been tormenting you all this time? I mean, is there a chance that he's here. You may have thought it was nightmares, but maybe he's been with you all along.

I don't know, she admitted. *You know how hard it's been for me to even deal with his reality for the last six months.*

And now, for your first couple days back, he's there.

Is it him? Is he there? Is he the one who's doing this? If so, why now? Or is it something else altogether?

I don't know. I was hoping you could tell me that.

I was hoping I could tell you that too, Cressy replied, *but right now I can't. I don't think I can tell you anything at all.* She burst into tears.

TIRED AND WORN out, Gray headed to the hospital. They had done interviews all day, checked over security cameras, and everything possible, and there was no sign of anything related to Cressy's attack and capture and transport to the utility room at the center. Nothing about her tires all being slashed as well. The fact that there was nothing on tape, no witnesses and no clues at all for both of these violent events at the center, made him even more suspicious, as he told the security guys watching the cameras.

"If there had been even a glitch in the security system, I would have felt better. But absolutely nothing? No way. That's not the way this will go down."

The security guys had looked at him, both of them holding up their hands. "Look. We didn't have anything to do with this. You can check out all this."

"Oh, I see what I can check. Blind spots everywhere, frozen cameras, security that should have been up and running smoothly, that's not running at all."

The two security guards shared a look and then nodded. "Look, man. We've both been here for years, but they really cut back on security. Dr. Cresswell had increased it before, but the powers that be decided that nothing bad would ever happen again. I hate to say it, but they implied that she was basically responsible for it, and, if she hadn't done what she'd done, then the issue would have never come up."

Gray stared at the two men, both of them backing up in response to Gray's body language.

"Look. We're just telling you what we were told," said one guard apologetically. "We both really like Dr. Cressy. She's good. She's really good with the patients, and she even treats us like human beings, which is way more than I can say for a lot of people around here. Sorry, but we just didn't see anything."

How could the security guys and all of those cameras see nothing, even with the board's cuts? The trouble was, a good share of those cameras weren't functional and were up for appearances only. The number of operational cameras, security doors and windows, and staff had all been itemized; and they had cut corners at every turn.

When Gray really looked at it, he realized what the center had kept was the *appearance* of security, but very little true security was had at all.

He left abruptly and drove off. He got out of his car in the hospital parking lot and stretched. He was still really angry, and he didn't want to go in there and upset her. He also didn't want to do anything to reinforce the guilt she undoubtedly felt. This whole nightmare was not her fault, but he knew she would feel responsible for it, and that was something he couldn't let happen.

When his phone rang, as he started toward the front doors, he quickly answered. "Hey, Grant. I'm at the hospital back to check on Cressy. I'm heading in now."

"Any news?"

"You mean, anything positive? No, not a damn thing. I had a long talk with a couple security guys in the control room. According to them, over the last six months the board has steadily cut security, just like everything else. They've cut the staff, removed equipment, not made repairs, reduced the number of alarms, anything they could to cut the budget. If it saved them ten bucks, they did it."

"Jesus," Grant muttered, "in a place like that?"

"Right? Some of the most vulnerable of all. But get this. To the casual eye, security is a priority, and you see everything you would expect. But it's all a facade, The board removed the bulk of any security system but left the shell. How did you fare with the hospital staff?"

"I talked to several of the other doctors. Some said they were supportive of the changes, and some were not in favor at all but didn't feel that anyone would listen to them, so they went along. Most of them were horrified at what had happened to Dr. Cresswell again, particularly since this was the second time."

"And being the second time, any reaction to that?"

Grant sighed. "I might as well tell you. A few thought she deserved it."

He froze in the act of opening the hospital front door. "What?"

"Yeah, I know." Grant's tone was grim. "They figured that she'd already brought it on once, so she must have bad practices that put her in danger."

"What is it they thought she did?"

"In this case nobody really knows, but she did avoid them by going out her window," Grant noted.

"She did because they were trying to force their way into her office, and she wanted to get away from them to buy me some time. She believed they would confiscate her files and her access to everything, then march her right out the front door."

"Technically speaking, she wasn't fired at the meeting," Grant said cautiously.

"No, she wasn't, but I gather things got very heated, and it was evident that it was headed that way, particularly after she stood up to them and called them out. She contacted me right away after the meeting and asked me to log in remotely and to save her work, since there was no way to track what was going on without that, and then she told me to come get her paper files."

"Did you actually end up getting them?"

"I did. She had them boxed up by the time this all happened, and I had the team secure them, before we even figured out that she was missing."

"The hospital is likely to put in a court order, looking for them."

"That's fine, and, once I have a chance to scan through and to confirm nothing implicates anybody, and I copy anything she needs, they can have them. A lot of it is her research materials as well."

"Why would there be anything that implicates anyone?" Grant asked. "These are files from when she was there before, right?"

"Yes. But also something crazy is going on, and I wasn't willing to let it all go, not until we had a chance to discuss it."

"So you think somebody at the hospital is playing games?"

"Definitely something is going on," Gray admitted. "It's not as if we had to look very far. She's just been kidnapped and stuffed into a commercial washing machine, after all."

"That's the thing, and it's better you know now. I mean, … already some people doubt her story on that, as well."

"Doubting what story?" Gray asked, getting further enraged. "I'm the one who found her in the damn washer."

"Some people are intimating your relationship is closer than it should be, and you were just protecting her."

He stared blindly out at the world around him. "Jesus! What kind of people are they? They're already trying to completely nullify the fact that she was knocked over the head and kidnapped."

"That's what it sounds like, yes," Grant replied.

"I know, but you and I both know it's not true. Not to mention Dr. Maddy and Stefan, who helped us to find her," Gray stated, his voice harsh.

"Of course I do," Grant said, "but the scenario isn't great for her right now, especially with the nonbelievers, with most people not knowing what all Cressy can do. The unknown brings up people's fears."

"These other assholes are trying to make her life miserable, and they are the problem."

"I won't argue that," Grant noted. "I know Dr. Maddy is always trying to figure out how to get Cressy to come on board, as her skills are pretty impressive. And nobody wants to see anybody—Cressy, Dr. Maddy, or Stefan—treated like this because, once it starts, it's pretty damn hard to stop."

Gray didn't even know what to say to that. "I think somebody at that center set her up."

"That doesn't mean it's criminal, and it definitely doesn't mean it's an FBI matter."

"Don't worry. I have vacation time on the books," he

said immediately.

Grant laughed. "I figured you would say that. I've got a meeting with the director tomorrow. I'll talk to him about what's going on at this place. I know it's a long shot, but, considering that a doctor was attacked, and everybody is trying to browbeat her into leaving, when she's only just returned after an earlier attack," Grant spelled out, "I'm hoping I can get some traction."

"Either way," Gray declared, "I'm not leaving her."

There was a moment of silence on the other end. Then Grant asked, "How bad is it for you?"

Gray gave a broken laugh. "If you'd asked how *good* was it, I might feel better, but the fact that you actually said it the way you did, means it's probably pretty bad."

Grant chuckled. "I told you it would happen sometime."

"Yeah. You also told me that it would likely be her, and I told you that it wouldn't happen."

"Sure, but there's something very special about her, and you already know how affected you were last time."

"I know, and it was deadly. I don't want to go through anything like that again."

"Yet here you are."

"Whether I like it or not, yes, here I am. She's in trouble. Somebody is after her. She's been attacked, and those assholes, who are supposed to be her colleagues and looking after the patients, are throwing her to the wolves. For all we know, somebody is hauling drugs in and out of that place."

"You find me even the slightest bit of proof on something like that," Grant stated, "and I'll have that place torn apart brick by brick, and their bank accounts will be frozen and under forensic analysis. You know that. And believe me. I would make sure that they pay."

"Yeah. I'm pretty sure I found something. I just haven't had a chance to go back and take a look."

"At the center?"

"Yes. I saw one of the doctors coming out of one of the locker rooms with something in his arms, and he quickly booked it out the front door. I saw it on the security camera when I was there."

"Any idea what time it was?"

He gave him the details and added, "You should see it yourself."

"Good, I'll go take a look at that," Grant stated, "because, if I've got a reason to shut it down, believe me. We'll have it shut down in no time."

"Find it then, because, if nothing else, I'm pretty sure that whoever attacked her will attack her again. As far as I'm concerned, whoever it is has something to do with that clinic. It's the only thing that makes sense, … particularly since it's happened twice."

"You also have to consider that somebody else might be trying to make it look like she's unstable, trying to make it look like the hospital itself is to blame, and making the opportunity to push her in a direction that she had no intention of going. Or pushing somebody else to do something ahead of schedule."

"So she slashed her own tires? So she hit herself on the back of her head? No way. None of those scenarios sound decent, so I'll ignore what you just said."

Grant laughed. "If holding your head in the clouds works for you, fly at it."

"No, it doesn't, but I'm heading to her hospital room right now. I'm hoping she's got something more to say about what happened, but, even if she doesn't, she needs somebody to keep an eye on her."

"Do you think she'll be at risk there?" Grant asked, his voice hard. "Because that's a completely different story too."

"I don't know," Gray admitted. "I'll check it out and let you know in a few minutes."

"How close are you right now?"

"I'm just coming up on her room." He knocked on the door and pushed it open, and, stepping inside, he froze. "I don't know where the hell she is, but she sure as hell isn't here." He did one rapid but thorough search of the room, then cried out, "Grant, she's gone. She's not here anymore."

With that, he hung up. And raced out of the hospital.

CHAPTER 15

I T WAS HARD to explain the sense of urgency that had Cressy bolting from bed, snagging her clothes from the closet, sliding out into the hallway, all of that on a mere whim. She had to keep checking to confirm nobody was close by. Then she ran down to the opposite end of the hall, where, opening a door, she found a broom closet. Locking the door behind her, she felt some relief.

Quickly she dressed in her clothes, even as she searched the linen closet for something that would help to hide her presence. A doctor's white coat was here, which she quickly put on. Then, with a quick glance outside, she stepped out into the hallway and proceeded to the exit as fast as she could, without raising any alarms. Nobody said anything or tried to stop her from leaving the building.

She stood outside of the back entrance, shaky yet with that sense that she'd made it just in the nick of time, but she had made it. She had absolutely no idea what it was that she had escaped from, where she was going, or what was after her, but she knew, without a doubt, she couldn't stay here.

Now, as she stood in the back parking lot of the hospital, without a cell phone or any means to contact anyone, even asking for help at this point would make her look like an idiot. She closed her eyes, then gathering up the last of her waning strength, she called out to Stefan. *Any chance I can ask you to contact Gray?*

In progress, Stefan said, his voice calm. *Where are you?*

In the rear parking lot.

He hesitated, then asked, *Why?*

Yeah, if I knew that, I would have answers to solve this headache. I suddenly got that instinctive feeling that I needed to run. I didn't question the urge, I just got up and bolted.

His breath exhaled noisily in her mind.

She smiled at that. *Sorry to be a bother. Apparently I'm quite a trial at the moment.*

No, not at all, but if you felt that strongly about it—

I did.

Then of course you had to leave. I do believe Gray is at the hospital or at least nearby, Stefan told her. *I'm calling him now.*

And, with that, he exited her mind, and she realized just how nice it was to have an emergency system such as this. It wasn't fair to call in her friends like that all the time, but considering the headache she had right now, it was actually one of the best answers she could hope for. Knowing that Dr. Maddy would be listening in on the ethers to a certain extent, Cressy sent a message, saying she was fine but had bolted from her room because something was off.

Dr. Maddy came in through her mind and asked, *Off in what way?*

Yeah, I don't know, Cressy replied, with a heavy groan. *I'm pretty sure that will be the question everybody wants me to answer.*

Dr. Maddy laughed. *And you'll do the best you can to answer it. Don't ever feel guilty because you did what you had to do for survival.*

That's the thing I can't understand. What if I'm just being paranoid?

Then we will all understand it, she replied calmly. *Remember who you're talking to here. You must know that we've all been through something similar, and not one of us would do anything other than run when our instincts say to run. Now, make sure you're staying in a very public area so you can be found, yet not so public that you're in everybody's view.*

Yeah, you make that sound as if it's an easy thing to separate, she muttered. *I'm just in the parking lot, walking back and forth, hoping that Gray is nearby.*

I believe he is, I just don't know exactly where and what he's doing there.

If he's at the hospital, he probably just arrived, which means he's probably in my room and about to raise Cain.

At that, Dr. Maddy sucked in her breath. *Yeah, that's exactly what's happening right now,* she confirmed, with a note of humor in her voice. *It would be nice if he could modulate that though.*

He doesn't believe he can do anything along those lines, Cressy relayed. *Will you tell him?* Cressy asked.

No, I sure won't, Dr. Maddy stated, with a half a laugh. *You know perfectly well that's not an easy thing to understand.*

It might not be easy to understand, but, after everything he's been through, I think he might appreciate some explanation.

Maybe. We'll see how far along this pathway he gets before I feel the need to try and explain how much of it is him.

You know he won't accept it.

Maybe not, but he might surprise you. Drew doesn't like to have anything to do with this, but there's no doubt that he's my ground, and, with him, I can do so much more.

And he's okay with that?

Certainly, she declared. *That's what love is all about.*

I'm not there yet, Cressy murmured. *Anytime I get close to anyone, they usually end up running like hell or go screaming into the night.*

Maybe you should dance in their mind to confirm every-thing is okay in there, before *you go out with someone new,* Dr. Maddy suggested in a mockingly scolding tone.

It's not even that I'm trying to do it, she said. *It's just that, when people are having nightmares, I think I can help, so I go in and soothe them. Sometimes they don't appear to take that in a very good way.*

Most people are very upset to find out that you can go through their mind. Period.

Yeah, I was a little slow to come to that kind of realization. Unfortunately.

At that, Dr. Maddy laughed. *Hold tight. Gray's on his way to you.*

Great, she said, then disconnected from Dr. Maddy so she could go off and do her own thing. It was one thing to connect, but another to take too much of anybody's time. Cressy watched the exit, until suddenly it burst open, and Gray raced out.

He turned, looking around, even as he kept going in a forward motion. He spun in such a smooth, controlled way that she was in awe. He spun all the way around, his gaze sliding past her, only to come back around and land on her. He raced toward her.

"Are you all right?" He grabbed her by the shoulders, then pulled her close and hung on tight. A moment later he stopped, held her by the shoulders, and stared intently at her.

"I'm fine," she said.

He frowned. "If you were fine, you wouldn't be out here."

She grabbed his hands and said, "Don't shake me."

Immediately he winced and stopped the unconscious motion. "Sorry." He took a deep breath. "I really didn't handle it well when I hit your room and realized you were gone."

"And, once again, it's as if we're just passing in the night. I just left a couple minutes ago."

"You want to tell me why?"

She pondered that and nodded. "I don't really have a great explanation, except my instincts told me to run."

His breath sucked back, and he stared at her in shock.

She nodded. "As I said, I don't really have a great explanation."

"So, this instinct of yours, ... it didn't tell you why?"

"No, it didn't. Just to run."

He frowned. "Are you keeping something from me?"

She shook her head. "I'm not trying to. At the moment, I haven't even had a chance to discern just what's going on," she told him. "All I can tell you is, when that happened, I bolted and grabbed my clothes, then raced down the hallway. I actually got dressed in a closet. I grabbed a doctor's jacket and headed out," she explained. "I must have just missed you."

He scrubbed his face, before running his hands through his hair, all the while staring at her wildly. "Just missed me *again*? It's as if you're sliding out just ahead of me."

She glared at him. "I didn't do it on purpose."

"Actually you did leave on purpose. Both times."

"Sure, and, if you'd been given the nudge I was, you would have left too."

His breath let out slowly, and he nodded. "Fine, I'll give you that. I don't know what that nudge felt like, but I've been in situations where my instincts had me flat-out taking off in the opposite direction, even though everybody told me to stop," he muttered.

"Was it the best choice?"

"Absolutely," he confirmed. "The spot where I'd been standing just blew up. I think a rocket landed just seconds afterward." Her jaw dropped, and she stared at him. "Hey, not everything is sunshine and roses in my world either."

"Is that why you're off on medical leave?" He gave her a look. She shrugged. "I mean, obviously something happened."

"Yes, something happened, but this time it wasn't a rocket so much as bullets."

"*This* time?" She continued staring at him in shock.

"So, yes, I understand. When instincts tell you to run, it's time to run," he agreed. "It would have been nice if you would have told me though."

"I would have," she admitted, giving him a hard smile, "if I hadn't been knocked out *and* had my phone."

"Ah, shit. You lost it when they got you?"

"Unless it's been found. It could very well be somewhere at the clinic."

He shook his head. "I haven't heard from anybody that it was found."

"Of course not, which means I need another phone, and I need it fast."

Then he frowned and asked, "You called Stefan, didn't you?"

She grinned. "Yeah, sometimes it helps to have somebody on the ethers, somebody who's always there, always available. I know it's not how he wants to be looked at, but there are times when calling out to him is all I can do."

Gray nodded. "You are very blessed. You know that, right?"

"I do know that," she said in all seriousness. "I also spoke to Dr. Maddy already."

"Good, so I presume there's no long-term damage from that latest attack?"

"I don't think so, but I really would like to go home." He shook his head, and she glared at that. "What's wrong with going home?"

"If somebody is after you, where would they go?"

She winced. "They'd go to my home of course. Damn. Can we at least go get some clothes and my backup tablet, then maybe find a hotel? Unless you can give me my laptop from my case files boxes?"

He pondered it for a moment, then nodded. "I can do that. I'll have one of the agents meet us and drop it off for you. And a hotel's probably the best idea."

"Unless you have a safe house or something I can go to," she said bitterly. "I don't want to go to any friends and bring something like this onto their shoulders."

"No, of course not," he agreed, as he made a sudden decision, while she watched determination dawn on his expression. "Come on. Let's go."

And, with him walking at a rapid clip, she came up behind him as fast as she could go, but, even then, he was moving so fast that her legs were already starting to tire. He must have sensed something because he came to a stop, then turned and looked at her. "Jesus, I'm sorry. I didn't mean to make you run."

She shrugged. "Normally, it wouldn't be a problem, but today I'm still playing catch-up."

"I could carry you."

"No, no, no." She backed up, her hands out in front of her. "Not needed. I can walk, just don't race maybe, not for the rest of today."

He smiled, wrapped an arm around her shoulders, tucked her up close, and suggested, "We'll walk together."

"I'm not sure whether that'll be a good idea or bad. I mean, there's a good chance that you'll be targeted because of me."

"In that case, good," he declared. "If that's the way these guys want to play, then that's the way we'll play."

She frowned at him. "Haven't you been shot and targeted enough in your life?" He just ignored her question and didn't answer. She smiled, trying to ease all the tension. "Have to be a tough guy, *huh*?" Again he didn't say anything, he just kept on walking, and she shrugged. "Fine, but it's your choice."

"It usually is, but at least I know the score."

She winced at that. "No, that's true. I'm sorry. I'm also very grateful that you're here helping me."

"Yet I wasn't here at the time," he repeated. "So what I'm wondering is, does somebody know that? Could somebody be setting this up, so that I'm coming in just at the last second and don't have any way to get to you?"

"I don't know," she admitted. "I wouldn't have thought that was possible, but, in my world, everything is possible, especially the things that you haven't had a chance to even ask about. The more that we do in this field, the more we realize that so much more has yet to be explored, with the potential to do even better. More and more, we come up against people, finding things that shouldn't be possible, yet somehow are. So we can't really know for sure."

He just nodded, couldn't say much about all that, as

they got to his vehicle. He quickly unlocked and opened the door for her. When he came around to the other side, she looked at him.

"Can we also get a cell phone?"

He leaned forward, opened the glove box, and pulled out a brand-new cell, still in its original packaging, and handed it to her.

"What's that?"

"A burner phone. It can't be traced. Probably the best answer right now. You can make the calls you need to, and nobody will know."

She stared at it, as if it were a lifeline. "That would be lovely."

His lips quirked. "I do understand what it's like to be cut off from all communication," he said. "Okay, so, it'll be a quick trip to your home, and then I want you out of there."

"Do we really think somebody will try and get me there?" she asked.

"You tell me. What do you think is likely to happen at this point?"

She thought about it, pondering long and hard. "If they're seriously after me to silence me, whether by locking me up in a sanatorium as a patient or … otherwise, that would make the most sense."

"Yeah, that would be my take on it," he agreed, with a sigh. "I get that it's not something you want to consider, but that doesn't mean we shouldn't."

"In which case, we're back to that whole scenario of what happened in the hospital."

He pulled up outside her apartment. "Now, we'll go in there fast, you hear me? Just focus on what you need for at least a few days."

She nodded slowly. "And this will go away after that, right?"

"No, it won't," he declared. "I'm not sure what's going on, but you can expect this to be something that we have to deal with for several more days potentially. You've been attacked at your place of work, and you left the hospital because you were afraid of another attack or some quack deeming you insane, and now you are again in a position where we don't know what's going on, but we don't want a repeat."

He watched as she shuddered at the thought.

"No, I definitely do not," she agreed, her voice getting stronger. "I rebuilt my life after that mess last year, and I thought I was coming back to a supportive and healthy environment," she explained, trying to keep the bitterness out of her tone. "Instead it appears as if everybody just wants me gone."

"You can't say everybody," he noted. "I get that it seems that everybody right now, but I don't think the patients wanted you gone. I don't think the families of the patients wanted you gone. I think the board and at least some of your colleagues did, but it remains to be seen who did what in this deal. It could be that some were being intimidated and pressured."

"Right, and we still don't know even that any of them had anything to do with the attack at all."

"Nope, we sure don't," he replied, as he continued to check their surroundings.

"It could be that I'm just doubly screwed."

He chuckled at that, then got out, came around to her side, and reminded her, "Stay with me at all times, please."

She looked up him, startled. "What are you expecting?"

"Nothing, but you keep disappearing on me, and I don't like it."

She smirked. "I suppose you thought you were better at keeping track of people than that, *huh?*"

"I would be if they were on my side and cooperating," he said, his tone quiet, as he looked over at her. "You have a phone now, so, if you decide to run again, could you please give me a call?"

"I will. … And, just in case this needs to be said, I didn't do this to get away from you."

He searched her face and asked, "Are you sure?"

"Absolutely I'm sure. Nothing like that was in my mind," she told him. "Literally I could just feel everything closing in on me, and a voice telling me to run."

He nodded. As they walked up to the elevator—deeming it easier for Cressy than the stairs right now—he asked, "Just because I'm not really sure about how all this works in your world, did it ever occur to you that the voice, telling you to run, could have been the wrong voice?"

Her eyes widened, and then she slowly nodded. "It's possible. I mean, particularly if somebody is capable of throwing their voice or making it sound like somebody else's." She frowned at that. "That would … Oh, hell. That would not be a good thing at all."

"In what way?"

"It would mean that I could hear Stefan's voice, for example. If he told me to get up and to run, I wouldn't even think about it. I would be up out of my seat and booking it regardless."

"Is that something these people can do?" he asked in horror.

"Not that we know of," she replied. "So far, from what

I've seen, all of us who can communicate telepathically have a unique signature. But again … who really knows?"

"Right, we don't really know what we don't really know, do we?"

"No, and every year it seems like people are coming out of the woodwork with more abilities, doing more things than we would really like to see."

"Yet the ones who *can* do things, end up in hospitals, like where you work."

She nodded slowly. "Like boys, such as Adam. He's been traumatized, and he needs help and support. He'll end up fairly gifted, but, if we don't get a handle on his abilities and have him understand them, chances are he'll wind up in a hospital like that for a long time."

"Meaning that, as soon as he starts talking about it to the wrong person, he'll—"

"Exactly. Then he won't know anything more than to shut up, to stay quiet, and to hopefully survive, but that staying quiet will also lock him down into life in the hospital," she noted. "All kinds of names and labels will be attributed to him, and it will be even harder to break free from that stigma. Once the medical society gets locked into thinking that he or any patient has a particular issue, it's very hard to get them to change their minds, unless the patient is doing therapy, and the doctors can actually see improvements. But then you have to convince every other agency who helped put away the person, and it gets to be one big headache. It's not impossible, and, with the right kind of support, he would do just fine."

"Are you the right kind of support?"

"I'm certainly one part of the team, yes," she confirmed. "Yet that's only if I'm able to work with him, and, if I can't, then I don't know what to say."

He didn't either. He let her walk ahead of him into the elevator. Then, as soon as they got off on her floor, he took her elbow and whispered, "I'll go in first."

She took a deep breath, nodded, then frowned. "You're really expecting trouble, aren't you?"

"I'm not expecting trouble, but, so far, nothing has gone the way we've anticipated, so why would it change now?"

She hated to hear that, but he had a point. He had been doing enough of this the lone ranger way, and, if he was here at her side, she might have a chance of getting out of this alive, with her mind still intact. After that attack on her six months ago, she wasn't sure that she would ever be strong enough to do this again. Yet here she was, facing monsters. Yet how many of these were in her mind or just in her nightmares?

THE SENSE OF foreboding was building in Gray, the closer they got to Cressy's apartment.

He wasn't sure what was going on, but everything, so far, had indicated a major attack happening. He pulled out his weapon, and, with her tucked up behind him, he approached the door. Of course he found it wasn't even closed.

He heard her suck in a breath, then looked over at her with a reassuring smile, knowing she still wasn't convinced. He whispered, "Stay out here."

She winced at that but nodded. He gave her a narrow-eyed gaze, but she replied with a thumbs-up sign, indicating that she understood and, at least on the surface, planned on listening. It was hard for him to even describe how he'd felt upon finding that she had booked it from that hospital and, for the second time, not being where she was supposed to be, having bailed just in front of him. It was that part that got to him. Was that deliberate? Was she trying to get away from him? Was she trying to confuse the issues? Or was is simply the physical world reactions versus the psychic world reactions?

He didn't know, but it made for a very bewildering time right now, and he hated that. He wanted clarity in all things, yet that appeared to be the one thing he wouldn't get. Pushing open the door, he stepped in, his gun out, as he searched the living room. He shook his head because the place had been tossed, yet it looked more like impotent rage than anything else.

He studied the layout and listened, but there was nothing. It was silent. It felt like whoever had been here had come and gone. The silence was deafening, and whoever it was had left right away. That was interesting, because the intruder must have known that she wasn't here, had to know that she was on her way back, didn't give a damn, or hoped she would be here, and they could take care of her at the same time.

Not something he wanted to consider.

He walked through to the bathroom. nudging open that door, but seeing no signs of anyone, he headed into the bedroom. A similar story. The bedding was tossed, the clothing from the closet was dragged out, drawers were dumped. And yet nothing was taken, from what he could see. It just looked like somebody had come in, then, in a fit of rage and more to upset her than anything, trashed the place. Gray walked back to the front door, nudged her inside, and shut it quickly behind them. He took several photographs of the damage and sent it to Grant.

Moments later, his phone rang.

"Are you serious? Her place has been tossed?" Grant asked him.

"Yeah, it's been tossed all right, but what for?"

Grant added, "Stay with me on the phone, until I know that you both have left the building."

"Sure thing. Putting you on Speaker." Gray turned and looked at Cressy, who stood in the middle of the living room, her arms wrapped around her chest, and she nodded.

"It definitely doesn't look like a normal robbery. Not that I'm any kind of an expert on *normal*," she quipped, with a half laugh and a hint of hysteria.

He walked over, wrapped his arms around her, and suggested, "Let's get you a few outfits, if anything can be salvaged, and then we better get out of here."

She nodded and headed to the bedroom, where she stopped in the doorway and gasped. He came up behind her. "It's the same thing, just shock value, trying to upset you."

"They did a good job," she snapped. "This bedroom was my sanctuary, the place where I could destress. Now look at it."

It was a mess, yet the intruder could have done far worse. "I think this was done just to upset you," he said, looking at it. "It's not destruction—no fires set, no dismantling the furniture, no cutting up the clothes. I have to wonder if they took something, though it may be hard to tell in this mess."

"I know, but I'll take a quick look though."

"Okay, grab a bag. Get some clothes, if you want anything here. Otherwise we can stop and get you whatever you need."

"I think I can probably grab something here, but I want to get it all washed first, after somebody has been pawing through my underwear and everything else. No way in hell I would wear any of this until we know it's okay."

"Or, if you want, we can just leave it for now, and we'll go get what you need somewhere else."

She turned and looked at him hopefully. "Can we?"

"Sure. It's probably best if we don't touch any of this anyway."

"I've already got a team on the way," Grant spoke up. "So avoid touching anything as much as you can. You know the drill."

"Yeah, got it." Gray stared at her bedroom. "I'm not sure she can grab anything here anyway."

"Then don't," Grant said. "If she wants any electronics there, then that's a different story."

"I have a tablet here in my bedroom." When she found it, she grumbled, "Except somebody stepped on it, dammit."

"That's all right. We'll fix you up." Then he took Grant off Speakerphone, speaking to him directly. "As soon as you guys get here, we'll be leaving."

"They're only ten minutes out. If you want to leave now, go ahead."

"We'll stay to pass off the scene to the team, if we can."

"Fine. We also need a list of people who hate her to this extent," Grant told him. "You know that, right?"

"Yeah. I'll talk to her when we get to a hotel. I just don't like anything about this right now."

"Nothing to like," Grant noted. "The good news is the anger. Someone is getting pissed off, and they either want her to stop or they want something that she has. I just don't know which. This much anger will make them forget to be cautious, and that will help."

"Considering she stirred up quite a bit of trouble on her first day back, it may be hard to narrow down that list."

"I know, but talk to her, and we'll see."

"I'll get back to you once we get settled." With that, he hung up, then turned and looked at her. "Only take something if you really want it," he said, "and do it now, before forensics gets here. They'll tear this place apart."

She winced and stepped back. "There's really nothing here I care about. It's just … *stuff.*"

"Good, let's go. We'll buy you some clothes and whatever else you need somewhere else." She nodded. "Do you have any treasures here, family mementos or things like that?"

She slowly shook her head. "No, that kind of thing is all at the house. This is my sanctuary and fairly close to the clinic, so it's a great place to unwind after working all day. I'm not one to have a lot of stuff anyway."

"Another house?" he repeated, startled.

She looked at him and then nodded. "Yes, I have a house. It's about an hour away from here."

"Do you want to go there?"

She shook her head. "No, it's actually rented."

"Okay," he said, still thrown by that.

"What's the matter?" she asked.

"I guess that threw me. I didn't realize you had another property."

She shrugged. "It's family property, and I haven't ever used it for myself, though I do have some things stored there."

"Okay, so is there any reason the person who ransacked your apartment would know about the family home?"

"I don't know how. It only became mine a couple years

back, and it's been rented ever since," she shared, with a shrug. "I don't really do anything with it. I boxed up some family things and have them stored there."

"So, if they pay on time, they don't really have anything to do with you?"

She nodded. "Exactly, and they were local anyway. They approached me not long ago to see if I was interested in selling it to them."

"Would you?"

"Probably. I just didn't know what to do with it at the time, so I kept up the status quo. Yet I can see selling it at some point. It's not a property I'm attached to or anything." She looked around and raised both hands. "I'm far more connected to this apartment, and, when I'm working, it becomes a secondary place anyway."

"You mentioned it was more of a sanctuary."

"It is, and, when I needed to get away from work and when things were tough, this was the one place I could go to and be alone and destress."

"I wonder if that's the reason they upended it because it doesn't appear that they took anything, nor does it seem that anything needs repair or replacing. So how much of this is just for appearances and to take away something you had that mattered?"

"My sanctuary?" she asked, looking at him. He nodded slowly, staring at her. "That's a little disconcerting," she muttered, "because that would imply that somebody actually knew how much I needed this place, and they did it out of spite."

"It doesn't look like as if they did that great of a job at it either, since everything is pretty much just tossed. I mean, they could have done a more damaging job. They could have ripped things up. They could have opened shampoo bottles and tossed them onto everything. They could have poured mustard everywhere, could have destroyed the furniture, and that sort of thing. They could have done actual destruction here, but instead they just stuck their fingers into every corner, as if knowing that would disturb whatever balance you had here."

She swallowed and then nodded. "You could be right." On that note she turned and headed to the front door.

"Where are you going?" he asked.

"Your friends are here," she muttered, just as the doorbell rang.

As she went to open it, he said, "Wait."

She turned to him, frowning.

Waving a hand at her, he motioned for her to get away from the door. "Let me check." She stepped back, as he looked through the peephole, and, sure enough, a valid FBI badge stared him in the face. He opened the door to find two of his coworkers. They came in, took one look, raised an eyebrow, and Gray nodded. "I'm taking her out of here. I'll let Grant know where we end up, after we get her settled somewhere."

"Actually Grant's got a couple places for you as options," replied one agent. "Contact him, if you don't have another spot in mind."

"Got it." Gray took one last look around and asked her, "Ready?"

"Absolutely." She shook her head, then determinedly strode from the room.

The guys asked him, "How is she?"

He shrugged. "I'm not exactly sure right now. An awful lot is going on."

"She checked herself out of the hospital, I heard."

"She did."

On that grim note, he turned and followed her.

GRAY THOUGHT CRESSY was a little too calm for his liking. They just did some shopping for her and picked up food for them. Met up with one of his coworkers to reclaim her work laptop. Considering what she'd already been through, it was amazing that she was even functioning. She was exhausted, that was obvious, and, as soon as they checked in to a nondescript hotel, he led the way up to the second-story room, keeping a close eye on her.

"I'm fine, you know," she murmured.

"Fine, exhausted, injured, been through a number of shocks, yet you're still holding something back." At that, he got a sharp look from her but no explanation. He nodded. "And that just proves my point."

"And your point is?"

"You're keeping something from me."

"I'm not sure I'm keeping anything from you," she argued. "I just haven't figured it out yet."

"Ah, I guess that's a fine distinction, isn't it?"

"For me it is," she stated flatly. "I'm under attack. I don't know why. Yet some of it is all too familiar. Still, I don't know for sure that it's actually familiar, and that's what's got me stumped."

"Meaning that you're afraid somebody is capable of imitating someone's voice?"

"Ventriloquists are everywhere," she stated. "I mean, it's a good old circus act, right?"

"Sure." He walked into the room and set down the few

bags of clothing they had picked up on the way. Just quick stops, where she hadn't even given much thought to what she was doing. She had grabbed some leggings, T-shirts, underwear, and a sweater. He'd watched in amazement because she was the fastest shopper he'd ever seen.

He'd been prepared for a full hour or two, but she'd been in and out in minutes with the clothes, then grabbed a few essentials from the personal hygiene and skin care section. He figured it had more to do with the scenario than her ability to actually curtail shopping, though he could be wrong. She was also far too exhausted to handle much more.

He brought the food they'd picked up over to the table, then set it down and opened the bags. "Come on. You need to eat."

She nodded. "I'm not hungry at all."

"You should know that doesn't matter."

"Right, I'm burning through energy at an elevated level and need to replenish it."

"That's not quite the way I would put it," he muttered, with a note of humor.

She gave him a lopsided smile. "Hang around us very much longer, and you will."

"I gathered as much," he admitted. "So tell me. When did you figure out what you could do?"

She shrugged. "When I was a child. I just didn't realize what I was doing. Once I did, I made the mistake of telling people."

"Ouch, so they sent you for therapy?"

"Oh, yeah, psych eval, therapy, and whatnot. The teachers got involved, and I got the whole nine yards. Then I learned to shut my mouth. Generally, once I did, it stayed shut, and things were easier." She shot him a grim look.

"Gradually the heat died down, and the backlash was more manageable."

"Until somebody like me comes along and tries to get you to open up again."

"Even the way you say that makes it sound wrong," she noted, yet her face was cracking into the first smile he'd seen in the last hour.

"Yeah, it does, especially when I put it that way, doesn't it? Sorry about that. I'm sure there are more delicate or sensitive ways to put this stuff, but I'm just not in the know."

"It doesn't matter," she said. "Enough is going on right now that I won't worry about semantics."

"I appreciate that," he replied humbly.

She snorted. "That really doesn't suit you."

"And here I was trying so hard," he protested, with a smirk.

"Maybe too hard, so give it a rest."

"Wow, now you're hurting my feelings."

She shook her head, opened up the to-go bag and stared down at the fast-food burger morosely.

"*Uh-oh*, you don't like fast food either, *huh*?"

"Not usually. It doesn't feed the soul," she murmured. "It takes energy to digest it, instead of giving me energy from it."

"All food takes energy to digest," he protested.

"Yeah, and then some takes even more, but, hey, I need the fuel, so I will shut up and eat what you provided."

"You could have said something, you know."

"Too tired," she mumbled, her mouth already wrapped around the burger.

"I guess there is something to be said for that." He

picked up one of the two burgers he'd bought for himself and polished off the first in a few bites.

She watched him in amazement, as a second one quickly went by the wayside as well. "You see? That's part of the problem. You inhaled that so quickly that your body will burn through it just as fast."

He shrugged. "Mine wasn't intended to keep me up for long. I just need fuel for when I need it."

"Meaning that, if we come under attack, you're prepped and ready to go."

He gave her a long knowing look and then slowly nodded. "That's one way to look at it."

"*Great*," she muttered. "I guess there's really no getting away from the fact that something is seriously wrong in my world."

"If it were just the board members trying to ditch you, I wouldn't be anywhere near as concerned," he admitted. "However, it seems to be more than that. Even you have to admit now that whatever is going on could all be related— but might not be related at all."

"I don't know what it is at this point. Not a clue. Where did you take my files to? Or maybe I should ask, were you able to get any of my physical files out?"

He nodded. "I got your files, and I cleaned off your hard drive."

"Oh good," she replied.

"I don't suppose anything in there is what somebody was after, right?"

She frowned at him. "How long ago do you think my place was broken into?"

He stared at her. "That's a good question, and maybe we should find that out first. You're thinking that somebody saw that my guys put the contents of your office in my car, so went to your apartment, thinking they would find it there?"

"That would make sense, wouldn't it?"

"As much sense as any of this does," he admitted. "And believe me. Not a lot of it makes any sense at all."

She smiled. "Yeah, I hear you there," she murmured, "but, if we're sensible about this, it stands to reason that, if they were looking for something in my office, they were expecting to find it there. So the next logical spot would be my apartment."

"That brings me back to whoever put the bug in your office."

"Yeah, I'm still a little disturbed about that," she admitted. "I wish I knew if it was there beforehand."

"That would be nice and would definitely help give us a time frame. If it was beforehand, what would that mean to you?"

"It would mean that somebody associated with the clinic—board members, doctors, coworkers, whoever," she began, searching for the right words, "was involved in trying to do something, or to find something, even back then. But if it happened after I came back, it could be someone trying to figure out what I might be up to, what I might care to do, now that I am back. It could have all kinds of implications, but it would be more about getting rid of me now, I would think."

"Then the question would be, do you think the fact that we found the bug made any difference at all?"

"We left it in place though, right?"

"We did, but that doesn't mean somebody didn't realize that we might have found it."

"They know that now, at least whoever you told, but maybe someone else placed it there." She pondered that and then shrugged. "I suppose anything is possible at this point." She yawned just then and stared down at the fries in front of her. "I don't think I can eat any of those."

He looked at her in astonishment. "They're fries, an American staple."

"Yep, they sure are, unless you use energy in healing," she noted. "And then it's just—how shall I say it delicately? What goes in is what comes out."

"Meaning?" His tone was ominous, as he watched her carefully.

"Meaning that when you want good things out of your body, you have to put good things into your body," she muttered. She got up slowly, then walked over to the corner in the hotel room. "A coffeepot is here though."

"No way. How does coffee fit into the *good stuff in, good stuff out* formula?" he asked in a half-teasing voice. "Because I sure don't see you slowing down on the coffee."

"I would inject it, if I could," she admitted, with no smile in sight. "Some things are just needed in order to keep functioning."

"That's called a crutch."

"Maybe, but it's one I could really use right now."

He decided to take pity on her. "Then make some coffee. I don't mind in the least."

She stared at the contraption in front of her. "I've never used one of these successfully before."

He joined her, took a look at it, and noted, "It's one of those pod units."

"Yeah, last time I used one of these, I was traveling and kept breaking the pods without actually getting my fill."

He nodded. "There is a trick to it." He quickly showed her how it worked and then handed her a hot cup of coffee. "Try that."

She took a sip, nodded, then sat down on the couch.

"If you won't eat this, you haven't had anywhere near-enough food, you know."

"I'm fine. I'm too tired right now anyway." He frowned at her. "Don't bother, really," she protested. "I can't eat any more right now. If I was that hungry, I would have eaten it because food is food in the end." Still she eyed the fries with distaste.

He groaned. "I suppose you're one of those *green smoothies in the morning* people, aren't you?"

"No, not necessarily, but, if I can't get all my greens and veggies any other way, it's a good way to do it," she noted. "I really would prefer steak and eggs though." When he stared at her in astonishment, she shrugged. "What can I say? I'm a carnivorous rabbit."

"Is that even a thing?"

"I eat a lot of meat, and I eat a lot of vegetables, but the rest? ... Not so much."

"Interesting," he murmured. "Does that help you in your work?"

"Yes. However, if I have a big job to do, I actually fast ahead of time."

"Like for how long? A couple hours?"

"A couple days if it's massive," she shared. "It all depends on what I'm doing. If it's a regular working day where I'm doing a lot of energy work, fasting helps. If I don't, then it's pretty hard to get clarity on what I need to do while I'm under."

He shook his head. "I have so many questions on all

INSANITY

that."

"Don't bother," she murmured. "I'm too tired to answer any more questions right now anyway." She leaned back against the armrest, holding her coffee delicately, as she closed her eyes.

"You want to tell me what's going on?"

"*You* want to tell me what's going on?" she replied, without opening her eyes.

He glared at her. "Funny."

"Not really," she muttered, opening her eyes again to face him. "I'm too damn tired. I need some time to digest. I need to figure out what's going on, who could be behind this, and I honestly haven't got a clue. And that's what everybody wants to know. *Hey, how come you don't know who's attacking you? How come you don't know who planted a bug in your office? How come you don't know who trashed your apartment?*"

At that, he noted with alarm that her eyes were overly shiny, and he realized just how exhausted she was. "Hey, hey, hey, take it easy now." The tears were literally at the corner of her eyes. She sniffled several times, trying to hold them back. Immediately he got up, walked over and sat down on the couch beside her, tugging her into his arms. "I'm sorry."

She shook her head and sniffled again.

He sighed, pulled her back a little bit, and gently stroked her shoulders. "Listen. It's been a pretty rough time, so why don't you just go to bed."

"I would like to, but I'm not sure I can sleep yet. My head is still churning."

He winced at that. "I understand that feeling too," he muttered. "It's hard to get past some of this stuff."

"It's terrible," she said, "absolutely terrible. You close

285

your eyes, and all this boils right back up again."

"No, I hear you."

They sat for a while, as she sipped her coffee, leaning against his chest and making no move to leave.

"How come you're so nice, considering the industry that you work in?" she asked suddenly.

He laughed at that. "I don't know too many people who would consider me nice. Plus you don't have to be an asshole just to work for the FBI—although, having said that, the job changes you. I think making an effort to be nice when you're not arresting people or hunting down monsters is even more important, so you get some balance in your life."

"Back to that whole nice guy syndrome. Grant too."

"Which most guys would not appreciate being called, by the way." She snickered at that, and he grinned, loving the laughter in her tone. "You can joke, but I'm telling you. Drew wouldn't take it nicely either."

"Yeah, he would," she agreed, shifting more onto the couch. He lifted the empty coffee cup out of her hand. "He's got Dr. Maddy though, so he doesn't care what anybody else thinks."

"That's a good point," Gray admitted. "The two of them seem very happy."

"Yeah, I never understood how that could work though. Anybody I know would get kind of freaked out if they found out what I do."

"Because you're a shrink?"

"That and then the other stuff."

"So, do you want to tell me about that other stuff, since it sounds like something I should know," he mentioned, with a note of humor.

"It depends on if you plan on sticking around," she said.

"I have this … kind of test that I do to see if guys will hang around, once they figure it out."

"Seriously?" He twisted slightly to look at her face, but her eyes were closed, and the corner of her lips were twitching. "Right, I guess I already failed it."

She burst out laughing and then sank back against him, yawning again.

"Just sleep."

"I can't sleep here," she muttered.

"Just close your eyes for a minute, and you might be surprised," he suggested.

"It's not fair to sleep on you. That'll hardly give you a decent night's sleep."

"I don't think you'll sleep that long anyway," he murmured.

He watched as she gently slept in his arms. Even against all her protestations, she dropped off almost immediately and stayed that way. When his phone rang, he immediately answered it, hoping it wouldn't wake her.

Grant was on the other end.

"According to her, you're a nice guy," Gray greeted his boss, speaking softly but with a note of laughter in his tone.

"What are you talking about?" Grant asked, a bit confused.

"Cressy says that you're a nice guy."

"Wow, of course I am," Grant stated. "What's your problem?"

"I told her that most guys wouldn't like being called nice. Then she told me that you, me, and Drew were some of the nice ones. She said Drew already had Dr. Maddy, so he wouldn't care if people called him nice."

"You guys are having some interesting conversations,"

Grant noted. "Did you even consider discussing the issue at hand?"

"You mean, the fact that she has no idea who's after her, who would have tossed her apartment or attacked her or anything along that line?"

"Yeah."

"Yeah, that came up. I tried to push for more, but she keeps telling me how she's too exhausted to think about it."

"Where is she now?"

"She's sleeping on my lap."

At that came a soft gasp and then a low chuckle. "Of course she is. How could I expect anything else?" he teased.

"Don't even go there," Gray warned.

"I don't have to. You already did." Grant laughed. "Just treat her right."

"I wasn't planning on doing anything other than that. She's like a wounded bird," he murmured.

"Yeah, but this one's got all kinds of skills and so much more. She may seem to be a wounded bird, but you better believe … that she's part raptor too." With that, Grant rang off.

Gray stared down at the tiny woman in his arms. Raptor? No way, hummingbird maybe, sparrow, but raptor? *Uh-uh*, not possible. He closed his eyes, thinking he would rest them for a few minutes. Once she was in a deep-enough sleep, he would carry her to the bedroom.

Then she shifted in his arms, murmuring, fighting against something out on the ethers.

Even the fact that there were ethers was enough to make his skin crawl, especially as he thought about what could be out there and what could be happening. As he watched her intently, it seemed she was shaking off something or certainly trying to fight off something. He reached out a hand and gently shook her shoulders, but, as quick as a wink, she turned on him, and this tiny sparrow of a woman was suddenly the size of the whole room. He stared in shock as she just seemed to expand and expand and expand.

"Jesus," he cried out. "Wake up!" Just like that, she snapped and was suddenly in his arms again.

She pushed off his chest and stared at him, bleary-eyed. "Did you just wake me up?" she asked in an accusing tone.

He looked down at her in shock, nodded immediately. She studied him for a moment, and he watched as a door came down over her face, making her expression completely bland.

"I see." She turned away and stood and headed to the bedroom. "In that case I'll head off to bed." Then she closed the door on him.

"Whoa, whoa, whoa," he cried out. "A little explanation would be nice."

"Not getting it," she snapped. "Next time don't try to hold me while I sleep."

"Yeah, thank you, you're welcome. For all you know I saved you."

"You mean, *I* saved *you*," she replied with a snort, and then came silence.

CHAPTER 16

CRESSY WOKE UP the next morning, achy, sore, tired, and depressed, more so than she had been in a very long time. But then nothing quite like realizing her energy had gone into overdrive, while she'd been sleeping on Gray's lap. According to his reaction, something happened that she didn't even want to ask him about. Just so many things could have happened, and she really had no way of knowing what it was because she didn't want to talk about it.

She stepped into the shower and soaked under the hot water as long as she felt she could, then quickly dressed in her brand-new clothes, snapping off the tags as she went. Finally dressed, with a towel still wrapped around her head, she went out to see if she could make one of those coffees. As she moved into the living room, she looked around to see if Gray was here but saw no sign of him. Then found he was sprawled out on the floor under the window. She stared at that and walked closer. When he opened his eyes, she jumped back.

"I'm fine," he said.

"Do you always sleep on floors, when couches are available?"

"When the couches are half my size, yes," he said. "I'd rather sleep on a hard surface than wake up as a pretzel."

She eyed his length and looked back at the couch, then

shrugged. "Good point." She then headed over to check out the coffee machine.

"Did you get any sleep?"

"I did, thanks."

"It doesn't sound like it," he noted.

"I actually didn't do too badly, when I think about it," she replied.

"You mean, considering."

"Yes, considering," she agreed, "but then that's my life right now."

"I'm sorry."

She made the coffee and then slowly turned and looked at him. "For what?"

"For reacting like any normal person. If you had warned me, I wouldn't have been quite so surprised."

"Since it can change from time to time, I can't really warn anybody, can I?"

"When you say *change*, what does that mean?" he asked cautiously.

"*Change*, that's what I mean. It changes. Sometimes it's this way. Sometimes it's that way."

"This way and that way," he repeated, "and yet you're doing a good job of avoiding saying exactly what it is."

"It's hard to explain."

"But it's not that hard to explain," he stated flatly, staring at her.

"Fine. I get into nightmare mode, and I go on the defensive."

"Yeah, so that …"

"That *thing*?" she asked.

"Yeah, that's one word for it," he muttered, "though not quite the right one."

"You'd be surprised," she said in a surprisingly cheerful voice. "That *thing* is an animation from my own psyche. So, you could say, it was me."

He stopped and stared. "So that was you, *huh*?"

She pondered that. "Yeah, I guess that's me."

"Okay, hang on a minute," he began. "I'm really not trying to be a jerk. I would like a straight answer and not something you're beating around the bush on."

"That's nice," she muttered. "We would all like answers, but we don't always get them."

He wasn't even sure what to say that. "So, what you're trying to tell me is that *form*, that *projection*, ... changes."

"It changes, depending on my nightmares, yes," she confirmed.

"Isn't that a little insane?" he asked pointedly.

"Absolutely, and, for the longest time, I used to call the energetic side of myself *Insanity*. With a capital *I*, like a noun, as in a name."

"So ..." He pondered that. "It's determined by your nightmares?"

"Yes, also determined by my dreams."

"Okay, so this form that you come out as, is created as a byproduct of what your subconscious is thinking at the time."

"Very good," she said in a mocking tone.

He flushed and glared at her. "Look. I'm just trying to navigate this, and you possibly remember," he replied, glaring at her, "that I don't have the same experience with all of this that you do."

"No, and you sure don't want it either," she declared, giving him a bright smile, "because it sucks."

"I don't know. After my initial shock, that was a kind of

cool thing, person, impression, holographic image, whatever." He raised both hands in frustration. "Whatever you want to call it, I've certainly never seen anything like it."

"Sure, because I was overly exhausted. If I hadn't been quite so tired, I would have realized that sleeping in your arms was the worst thing I could have done because these hallucinations, these energetic forms, are always worse when I'm really exhausted."

"That makes sense. I mean, if you think about it, everything about us—our control, our attitude, our judgment—everything is worse when we're overtired."

She nodded. "Are you getting coffee or just lying on the floor?"

He laughed. "I'll go to the bathroom, then take a quick shower. When I come out, we'll talk some more."

"Oh, *yippee*, unless I find something else to do."

"If you find something else to do, please find a list of people, possible suspects, we can investigate."

She slowly raised her gaze and stared at him. "Is that you or Grant asking?"

"Both of us," Gray confirmed. "Why?"

"Because I don't want to investigate people just because they might not like me. That's hardly the way to make friends in life."

"I'm not too bothered about you making friends right now," he said coolly, as he hopped to his feet and walked to the bathroom. "I'm much more concerned about keeping you safe. If they have nothing to hide, then it doesn't matter. However, if they do have something to hide, that's a different story." He called from the bathroom door, "I want a list, and I want it when I come back out." And, with that, he stalked into the bathroom and slammed the door.

She studied that door for a moment. She knew he was pissed off because he'd figured out that she was deliberately avoiding giving him names. One problem was how did she explain to him that she had no real friends. At least not many, and the ones she did have were Dr. Maddy and Stefan and a few others like them.

Cressy had colleagues she considered good acquaintances, but none that she would have seen outside of the hospital. She had patients that she would have loved to be friends with, and was, but only in the spirit world, where they could interact normally.

As she stared down at the pad of paper he'd left on the coffee table, she picked up the pen on top but didn't even know where to start. How could she? Basically some of the doctors and a few of the orderlies she was friendly with, but the rest? Well, she wasn't so sure. At that, she wondered about Keith. He would have texted her that list they had discussed, yet not necessarily to her. She had a new phone after all. She hadn't even thought about that. So, wherever her phone was, there would have been a list from him. She winced at that. She quickly phoned the hospital and got Keith on the other end of the line.

"Doc, are you okay?"

"I am. Did you send me that list of people who might want to stay with me?"

"I did," he confirmed.

"Unfortunately my phone's gone missing, and I'm wondering if that had something to do with my latest attack."

"Oh, jeez," Keith muttered in horror. "That wouldn't be good."

"No, but I have a burner phone now, so can you resend it to that?"

"Sure." Then he lowered his voice. "All kinds of shit are going on around here right now. I guess you're not coming back, *huh?*"

"I'm not sure whether I'm coming back or not," she murmured. "Until we find out who attacked me, it's not safe for me or anyone else, for me to come back."

"No, I would say *not*," he agreed. "Damn. If you find another job, remember that I'm quite happy to move too."

"Got it. I'll keep it in mind."

CHAPTER 17

W ITH THAT, AND a warning for Keith to be careful and to watch his own back, since it had been his phone that had sent the list to hers, Cressy hung up. She sat here for a long moment, waiting for the list to come through. When it did, she sent it to her laptop, and, from that point on, she opened up Keith's list into a much larger screen and took a closer look.

The names of those people who wanted to stay with her weren't necessarily a surprise. They were all orderlies that she got along well with and some kitchen staff who were really good to work with. As a matter of fact, it was a great foundational start.

Of course that just brought back to mind everything she still had ahead of her to deal with, though she now had the time and energy to deal with the advanced thought processes required to critically weigh the alternatives. With the list off to one side, she opened up a blank page and stared down at it, trying to figure out what she was supposed to give Gray as her list. She had a hard time describing anyone as enemies or potential suspects.

Finally she started by putting down a couple of her colleagues who she knew would be totally okay if she didn't return. It was to be expected that there would always be a certain amount of discord or professional jealousy in a place like that, so it wasn't really a surprise.

A few other names she could put down that she didn't think would cause trouble, but she couldn't really be sure. Of course, if trouble was to be had, one never really knew who was involved in it anyway. Sometimes people made it seem as if they were completely innocent or on your side, but then, when you actually heard about it later, they had participated in the process that acted against you.

She really didn't want to do this right now—or ever— but she knew Gray wouldn't give her a chance to walk away from it. As far as he was concerned, it was mandatory to sort out who was on her side and who wasn't. She got it, but it just wasn't a nice thing to consider.

The shower turned off in the bathroom, and she realized that her time was up. Gray would come out and would expect her to have something written down. She glared at the paper in frustration. Putting something down was possible, but putting down the right names? Now that was a whole different story. She didn't want to put down the wrong ones and have their lives upended indiscriminately because she happened to think they didn't like her or wouldn't want to be around her very much.

She wasn't sure very many people would, since apparently she had issues. She almost smiled at that. In her world, everybody had issues, and it's not as if she should be held responsible for them, but some people would not be that generous. Still, things needed to be dealt with, and this was just one of them.

With that clarification, she got to work. She listed all the doctors who had argued against her changes at the clinic and some who had almost feigned surprise to see her. That wasn't a big list, but it was a good start. With a few names down, it was something at least, and maybe Gray could start with that, without making her feel too bad, as she got to work on the rest. She'd had to correct some orderlies and report them because they weren't doing their jobs, and she could understand they might hold that against her. It would certainly make them an easy pawn for anybody else's shenanigans, not that she wanted to consider that either, but it was hard not to.

A few kitchen staff she'd chastised in some way came to mind. Then she remembered a couple nurses she'd had arguments with, nurses who didn't agree with her treatments, some of whom had gone on to report her.

Frowning at that, she pondered the names on her list, then had to go to her email to see who all had probably put her on a shit list. With that done, she actually felt better because she had a few on her list. At that, she stopped and frowned. How could something like that even begin to make her feel better?

She hadn't even realized just how many enemies she might have accrued. As she considered the names, she wondered if any of them were serious contenders for this mess. Some of them still had access to the clinic and could have knocked her unconscious, but would they have carried her to the basement and dumped her in the washing machine? That would have taken some serious muscle. Except, as she thought about it, she had actually been standing fairly close to where the laundry chute would have been anyway. Therefore, if a laundry cart had been nearby, she could have been just tossed into that and pushed right back inside the center. That was the point that got her.

Why take her back into the hospital?

Why not just take her to their vehicle? She really didn't

understand that. Not that she had to understand it, she got that, but it would certainly make some of this easier if she could make sense of it. Of course anybody under threat would probably say the same thing. She pondered it for another moment, then went back to her list, knowing Gray would be out at any time. She worked hard on it, and, by the time he stepped out and looked over to see her writing away, she had twenty-four names. She looked up and gave him a sad look.

"What's the matter?" he asked, walking closer.

"This isn't a fun process at all," she stated. "I didn't realize I had accumulated so many potential enemies."

"Remember. Just because they might be enemies in your mind, doesn't mean they have anything to do with this," he said.

"No, I get that, and that's a good thing because I ended up with quite a few names here."

He walked forward, and she lifted the notepad and handed it to him. He looked at it with a smile. "At least you're being honest," he noted. "In a case like this, we need some idea of who, and then we can start knocking people off the list."

"I sure hope you can write off most of these people," she said. "I would hate to think that anybody wanted something like this to happen to me."

"Get over that because somebody already did," he declared, raising an eyebrow. "Otherwise you wouldn't have ended up in this situation."

She glared at him but didn't say anything because she knew he was right.

"Not to pry, but did I hear you on the phone?" he asked.

She nodded. "Keith, one of the orderlies from work, had

sent me a list of people who he knew would like to move with me. You know, staff who might want to apply somewhere else, if I moved on."

His eyebrows shot up at that. "Wow, that was pretty fast."

"No, I think a lot of them have been pretty unhappy for a while, and this was just the tip of the iceberg. He'd already heard rumors that I was leaving, and he wanted me to know that, if I would land at a good place, he would like to come too."

"That's kind of nice." Gray sat down beside her.

She could smell his aftershave wafting through the room, though she didn't even know where he'd gotten it from. Maybe he'd bought it while she was grabbing a few of her things, and she hadn't even noticed, but she wasn't the most observant person as of late. "I don't know about *nice*," she replied. "I hadn't seriously considered it, but, when he mentioned that there was quite a group of them willing to relocate, I asked him to put the names down on a list."

"Good, you're being proactive about your future."

"Is it though? But sitting here, working on this list, I realized that, if he'd sent his list, if someone had my phone, he could be in trouble now. What are the chances that somebody could go after him?"

He stared at her. "So, that brings up a completely different issue. What are the chances that other people are upset that you could actually be leaving?"

"But that wouldn't make sense," she argued. "I mean, I just got back, so why would I be leaving?"

"How many waves did you make on the first day?"

She winced. "Obviously I wasn't very happy. They'd made an awful lot of changes, horrid changes, putting profits over patients," she murmured. "Changes that had begun almost immediately after I left. Things I would never be okay with. I hadn't realized they were setting me up to not come back, but then realized I had to actually come back because of the way it all went down. So I guess they were planning that, as soon as I got back, I would be moved on again."

"Potentially." Gray nodded. "Still, all kinds of things can come out of something like this. Did you ever sign a waiver, relieving them of dereliction of duty over the lack of security when you were attacked the first time?"

She stared at him. "I don't think so, ... although they were asking me to sign some waivers."

"Did you?"

She pondered that and then shook her head. "No, I don't think so. I remember being in very bad shape, and my legal advice was to not sign anything, but I just forgot about it."

He didn't say anything, just nodded.

"Why?" she asked. "Do you think they're trying to back-track?"

"No, I think they're hoping that you won't backtrack. It could be that the board was told that you signed, and so they feel quite free in kicking you out now because you're obviously a liability. Remember. If you're not with them, you're against them."

"That appears to be the mentality that I'm up against, yes." She scrubbed her face. "It's a strange world we're living in."

"It is, indeed, but you are safe. You're here, and we intend on keeping you that way."

She smiled and said, "That would be nice."

"It would also be nice if you didn't try to run away just

before I got to you."

Her lips quirked. "I get that you won't believe me, but that part was not deliberate. I had no intention of running out on you."

"Sure it wasn't." He gave her an eye roll. "It's a little hard to believe you though, since it's happened twice now."

She winced. "And I ... I get that too, but really it wasn't deliberate. It's instinctual."

"Maybe your instincts could send you toward me and not away from me next time."

"I think I was. I think I was looking for you in the parking lot, knowing that you would be coming soon, but I hadn't realized ..." Then she stopped and added, "Honestly I don't know if I had that much cognitive thought at the time. I was starting to panic. Something was wrong, and I needed to get out of there, and I ... I just had that instinctive feeling that I trust."

He nodded. "I don't have a problem with that. Believe me. It's much better that you follow your instincts because obviously something or somebody was after you somehow. It would just be very nice if we didn't have any more repeats where I'm heading for you, only to find you've disappeared seconds before."

She smirked. "Or you could be a little faster."

He groaned. "Believe me. That's been brought up a time or twenty."

"Oh, come on. People can't possibly think you're responsible, do they?" She stared at him in horror.

"It's a little hard to explain to people that somebody I am supposed to be watching closely keeps getting away from me."

She winced. "Fine, I'll try hard."

"You'll try hard to what?" he asked, with amusement.

She sighed. "I'll try hard to not disappear on you."

"Oh, that would be great. That would be much appreciated."

She sighed. "You don't have to be so mocking."

He burst out laughing. "Hardly mocking," he replied gently, "but you do have to realize what this is doing to my reputation."

"I wasn't really thinking about that."

"No, I'm sure you weren't."

She laughed. "I'm certain your macho image can handle it."

He shrugged. "I'm not sure it can, actually."

She stared at him. "You won't get fired, will you?"

He shook his head. "No, I won't, but I certainly won't let you out of my sight again either."

She frowned. "It'll be a little hard to work with you hanging around all the damn time."

"Too bad," he said, with a grim smile, "because we're not having this happen again."

"Ah," she muttered and then nodded. "I guess that makes sense."

He sighed. "Hallelujah, you've finally seen the light."

"I don't know about that," she muttered, glaring at him, "but I can see that your ego has taken a hit."

He stared at her, his jaw slowly tightening up, as he asked, "Do you really think this is about my ego?" His voice was low and hard.

She glared at him. "Don't you try to intimidate me," she snapped. "I can do that with the best of them."

He stared at her. "Can you?"

"Absolutely," she declared.

"Then why don't you?"

She frowned at him and shrugged. "It's not my style. Just because I can do something doesn't mean I should."

"How about for the kidnappers, at least? How about you intimidate them so that they leave you alone."

"If I ever saw them, that might be possible. That's not really been something I've had an opportunity to do, has it?" He walked over to the coffeemaker, and she could see he was controlling his temper but not that successfully. "Look," she added. "I'm really not trying to argue with you."

"That's good." He put on a cup of coffee. "I can't imagine what it would be like if you were."

"Oh, don't start," she warned.

He burst out laughing. "Maybe I won't, but, wow, you can certainly push things."

"I'm not pushing anything," she muttered. "Just trying to stay alive … and to help people."

"That's what it's all really about though, isn't it?"

She looked over at him, lifting her head from her list, and nodded. "That's what it's always been about."

"But is that what this kidnapping and all this mess is about? The hospital seems to put paychecks over patient care, whereas you're all about patient care. The kidnapping stops you from being able to help people and may even scuff up your reputation, especially if they can make it sound like you're not stable—"

"They could do that," she admitted, "and, of course, I wouldn't be very happy if anybody listened, but it's possible."

He nodded. "And, if that were the case, you couldn't help anybody. How many patients have you had where there were confrontations, lots of anger, blame, or guilt, for example, where the patients couldn't be helped, and somebody thought that you should have been able to?"

She sank back on the couch and stared at him.

He nodded and asked, "That's what this is all about, isn't it?"

"I … I don't know." She continued staring at him. "I hadn't considered patients. That list is doctors, nurses, orderlies, kitchen staff, and anybody I had to write up because they weren't doing their job. I actually caught two staff members having sex in a patient's room one time." He stared, and her lips twitched. "Yeah, that was fun. What was I supposed to do? Just ignore it? Obviously not, so I had to write them up for it. The rules of conduct at the center are pretty strict."

"Would you have done any differently if you were running the place yourself?"

She pondered that, then shook her head. "No, not really. It was completely inappropriate. They were both on the clock at the time and in a room that a patient was waiting for, and, instead of looking after the patient, they were looking after themselves," she explained.

"Did your action cause much in the way of bad feelings?"

"Sure," she murmured, "but they didn't have a leg to stand on. Honestly I'm still not convinced that this has anything to do with anybody on staff there."

"If it isn't staff," he pointed out bluntly, "it's got to be patient oriented." She shook her head at that. He held up a hand. "What is the absolute worst scenario you've had to deal with in terms of patient care, where it didn't work out?"

"You mean, where I couldn't help somebody?"

"Sure," he agreed, "if you want to look at it that way,

yes."

She snorted. "That's easy. That would be the one that blew up in my face last year."

He sat down beside her, his gaze intense. "How do you figure that?"

She frowned at him. "You saw part of what happened, I guess, if not all of it."

"No, not all of it," he corrected. "I saw a lot, but I certainly didn't see exactly what happened. Was there any kind of follow-up? We haven't discussed that, and you didn't tell me anything about it."

"I didn't tell you because you didn't ask," she stated in frustration. "Yes, there was some pretty ugly follow-up."

"Like what?"

"The family was pretty clear in expressing how they felt about my efforts to help their beloved son," she replied bitterly. "There was absolutely no quarter given. They seemed to have no understanding of what he had done or what he was going through or what needed to be done for his care."

"Okay, I'm a little confused right now," Gray said. "In that attack on you six months ago, didn't he die? Either during the attack or shortly afterward?"

"No, he didn't die, but it burnt out his abilities, so he was essentially ..." She winced. "The last I knew he was completely nonverbal, in a coma of sorts, and not likely to change anytime soon."

"Have you seen him?"

"No, I haven't," she replied. "Not something I wanted to do."

"Is he still there?"

She looked at him and then shrugged. "He shouldn't be.

We're not that kind of facility."

"Would anybody have kept that information from you? Moved him there on the sly?"

"It's possible. I mean, people are doing all kinds of shit right now that I didn't see coming, so ... maybe. Did I know that they were? No. Would I have gone to see him if I did know he was there? No, I would have stayed away from him. And, if he's there, they ought to move him elsewhere again. He's taking a bed for someone we could help. He was there for analysis and testing before."

"Is he dangerous still?"

She pondered that for a moment. "Stefan would say everybody is dangerous, even when we think they aren't. My answer to that right now would be that I don't think he is a danger to anybody since he burnt out during our encounter."

"But you're not sure."

"No, of course I'm not sure," she replied crossly. "Every time we see more and more things that we shouldn't be seeing, craziness that shouldn't be happening, people with abilities who are well beyond what we ever thought possible. Every day in every way we're being challenged. I don't know whether it's just that more people with gifts are out there or if some sort of extra valve, I don't know, has been opened, so more gifted people are showing up than we ever noticed before. Whatever the mechanism, I've definitely noticed a lot more people with abilities showing up. Stefan would probably say it's because we opened the doors, and, having opened them, a lot more people are coming toward us, looking for help."

"Can you help them?"

"Most of the time I can help them," she stated. "And then you get somebody like Rodney, and there's just nothing to be done. At least nothing I could do."

"Why is that?"

"Because he's a sociopath, with a hell of a lot of energy abilities, and his entire bent was to hurt as many people as possible."

"Yet you didn't know that when you started treating him?"

She stared at him. "No, I certainly did not know that. Nobody could have known. That's just insane."

"Yeah, but it seems that what you deal with here are new levels of insanity." He grabbed her hands, then said, "You need to tell me exactly what happened afterward."

She stared at him. "Do I have to?" she asked, her voice soft. "It was incredibly painful."

"I know it was," he whispered. "I saw part of it while I was there because I was on duty, but I don't know what the aftermath was. Did the family threaten you?"

She gave him a half smile. "Only because the parents were in so much pain."

"That's fine," he muttered. "But what else did they do? How much of this is related to that?"

She shook her head. "None of it should be," she said, bewildered, "Why would it be?"

"Because now you're finally back working with patients," he noted. "This is the first time that you've been back, after everything that went wrong. So, if Rodney's family believed you're a danger to other patients and that you may have had something to do with what happened to their son, then it makes a twisted kind of sense."

"What? Stopping me from helping anybody else?"

"*Help* from your perspective, but that's probably not the language Rodney's family is using."

She felt everything inside her sinking, as she was forced to acknowledge that Gray could be onto something. "But even if that is the way they're thinking, this reaction is pretty extreme," she explained. "I mean, that's setting themselves up for a lifetime of trouble and a criminal record for themselves."

"Maybe they don't care. I mean, what was the fallout from their son's illness?"

She swallowed and shrugged. "I didn't stay in touch," she murmured. "I couldn't do that after—"

"I get that, and I don't have a problem with the fact that you didn't stay in touch," he replied. "There's only so much anybody can expect out of you."

She shook her head at that. "But you're making it seem as if I didn't do nearly enough."

"That's not my intent at all," he corrected. "That's absolutely *not* what I want you to get out of this. However, those parents may feel that you didn't do enough. Regardless, the fact of the matter is, we do need to follow up to confirm that they aren't involved in this."

"Follow up then," she said, hopping to her feet and walking over to the window. "I just hope there's nothing to find."

"I hope so too," he told her gently, "because that's the last thing we want. However, if there is anything to find, we must stop it."

She winced. "Okay. I'm sure you have Rodney's files. There was quite the case at the time."

"No charges were ever filed, right?"

"No, there weren't," she stated. "I didn't file against him. And I didn't do anything wrong. I mean, I tried to help a patient who attacked me and held me prisoner," she murmured. "He thought it was great fun. The fact that he could even do it terrified me, but the fact that he could do it as easily as he did ... terrified everybody else."

"Of course," Gray agreed. "What about other siblings?"

She stared at him and shrugged. "I don't know. I mean, I only ever spoke with the mother."

"What did she do for a living?"

"She was the CEO of some corporation or something like that," she shared, with a wave of her hand. "I didn't really get too many details. That's not anything I typically deal with."

"No, that's fine," Gray said.

She looked over at him, already on his phone, sending texts. "Do you really think this could be part of it?"

"It's been the biggest thing in your life. The one big issue that pretty well destroyed everything in your world."

She winced. "See? I worked really hard to get to a place where it hadn't destroyed anything, and I was finally getting back to my normal life." She sighed. "So, your phrasing isn't exactly what I want to hear."

"Maybe not, but let's not fool ourselves into thinking something is okay, when maybe it really isn't."

"Fine," she muttered. "You do your investigation."

"Now, from you, I'll need a list of patients we should look into. Anything that stands out."

"You mean, when something blew up with any of the other patients?"

He nodded.

"Does it happen? Sure. You get progress, and then you get patients who slide behind," she said. "We don't always get to know what causes the regression, whether it's you, the therapist, or family, or it's something else. I mean, there isn't a direct cause and effect that's clear-cut in cases like this. In some cases, the family is way too domineering, and the patient really needs to just be separated from them, so they can learn to grow and to have a life, However, most people, most families, aren't ready to hear that. And, in most cases, no way we can take away the family, even on a temporary basis, to show them that the patient just needs a bit of time apart from them."

"Is it just time away or is it a matter of cause and effect?"

"Sometimes there's an awful lot of abuse, though sometimes it's not abuse that you can see, like physical wounds. It's psychological abuse, and that can be so very damaging that we don't always see the effect, not until it's too late, and that's what happened to Rodney. His father was incredibly abusive, physically and mentally, to the mother. He was in jail at the time," she added, turning suddenly and looking at him. "That's right. He was in jail. He couldn't come to deal with any of his son's issues, and neither the mother nor the son wanted him there."

"*Huh.* That's another thing to sort out. I'm collecting information now, but I sure wish I'd known about this earlier."

"I didn't even think of it," she admitted, "but then I've made a practice of not thinking about it."

"Of course you have. Anything that's traumatic you try to put out of your mind."

"More than traumatic, since he almost succeeded, you know?"

Gray frowned at her. "Almost succeeded at what?"

She gave the briefest of smiles. "Almost succeeded in keeping me a prisoner in his own headspace."

He slowly lowered his phone and stared at her, rubbing

his face. "You're not joking, are you?"

"Oh, no, I'm not joking at all," she muttered. "He was incredibly strong, incredibly capable. That's how he subdued his victims."

"Victims?" he repeated.

"Yeah, he was actually committed to institutional care because he was a serial killer, but, of course, the doctors determined he wasn't fit to stand trial."

"I remember something about killing someone but *not* that he was a serial killer."

"Yes, he would capture them mentally, then have them do whatever he wanted, while he toyed with them physically, and they were completely incapable of getting free of him. I understood something was going on in his psyche, but I thought, in my naïveté, that I could meet him at a middle ground—in the hallway, so to speak, between life and death. That way I could talk to him and could see if I could convince him to come back to normal, come back to reality.

"Instead I found out that he was enjoying himself way too much. Once I went into his playground, he was the master, and I was the student because he'd spent a lifetime in there, learning to control people, learning to do what he wanted to do, instead of what other people wanted him to do. His mother was his victim as well, but I could never get her convinced to separate from him. So, of course, the more I tried to separate them, the more he fought to stay together with her because she was his lifeline in many ways. With her on his side, Rodney was pretty well invincible and got away with murder, time and time again," she explained.

"Jesus," Gray muttered.

"Yeah, Rodney was definitely somebody I didn't want to deal with long term, but I thought I could help him. Until I went in there and realized what was going on and found a psychic so strong, so skilled, and so happy in his little hideaway that he had no intention of ever coming out. I knew that, once he passed all the psych testing, he would be free and clear again."

"But he had killed several people," Gray stated, staring at her.

"Yes, but he wasn't convicted. Remember? He came here for testing, and I was pretty sure that he had the ability to influence several of the people on his medical team, and they were in the process of giving him a clean bill of health."

"Oh, Jesus," Gray muttered, now sitting down. "So you're saying he could control their minds?"

"In a way, yes, though I'm not sure I would go so far as to say *control* their minds. He certainly had the ability to control people without their knowledge. I mean, he grabbed a hold of me because I was fighting his release, and he didn't appreciate it."

"I wouldn't think he would," Gray agreed, frowning at her. "It seems strange that this is the first you've mentioned it."

She shrugged. "It's not a subject I like to talk about."

"No, and I get that," he murmured. He shook his head. "You know for sure he's burnt out, right?"

She stared at him. "You're bringing up thoughts that I don't ever want to even consider again. You know that, right? I thought he was gone."

"Are you sure he's not recovered in some way?"

"No, I'm not sure because I haven't been in his mind to see," she stated. "I don't dare. He knows my signature, so, as soon as I go in, he'll be all over me."

He opened his mouth, as if to ask questions, but didn't

say anything.

She smiled. "I'm glad you're not saying anything about that one."

"I need to though," he replied. "How am I supposed to ignore something so blatantly scary and question him without more information. Obviously I need to know more about what he can do and what he can't."

"What he can do is terrify even those of us who have spent a lifetime doing this," she murmured. "I don't even know how to explain to you how strong he is. Just know that somebody has the ability to snatch who you are as a soul, as a mind, as a consciousness, and keep you prisoner. And, for some people, quite possibly those who didn't have the experience I have, he could make them do things. And, in this case, I think his mom took care of him, without realizing to what extent he was pulling on her. His female victims followed his orders because the alternative was something they couldn't comprehend and didn't realize he was already doing to them."

"Wasn't there talk about cannibalism or something otherwise horrific?"

"You know, cannibalism is often used by people as a horror factor. It's the single most taboo thing imaginable, so, as soon as they do it, it gives them a sense of being all-powerful."

He nodded slowly. "I can kind of see that, though it doesn't make me feel any better."

"No, I'm sure it doesn't," she murmured. "Still, it doesn't change the fact that, if you get hung up on that word and that action, it actually gives Rodney more power."

Gray shuddered at that. "Can't say I want to even see the guy again."

"Did you see him at all?" she asked curiously.

"I was a part of an FBI team, hoping you would get answers. We were in the middle of an argument about what kind of care and what kind of treatment he would get, and how many answers he actually was willing to help out with. We were missing a lot of bodies at that time. But my shift was over, so I was in the process of disconnecting and handing off my shift when everything blew up."

"And that was one of the reasons I was going in there, wasn't it? I was trying to find the locations of his victims, you know, for the families."

He nodded. "Yet what happened to you was something so horrific that nobody really understood."

"No, they sure didn't. I did, but I couldn't do anything about it," she said calmly. "At least not at the time."

At that, he got up, sat on the couch with her, and asked, "What do you mean, at the time?"

"I don't know," she replied, without really saying anything.

He stared at her suspiciously. "You wouldn't try it again, would you?"

"With him? Not if I don't have to. Believe me. He's not someone I want to spend any time with. I would never want to share his headspace." He nodded but stared at her questioningly, and she smiled. "I don't have a death wish. You can count on that."

"Maybe, maybe not, but definitely something is off."

"Something's always off," she said gently. "Unfortunately that appears to be a fact of life in our world."

He pondered that, then shrugged. "I guess I keep coming up against new frontiers."

She laughed at the *Star Trek* reference. "We absolutely

do, and, for the most part, it's exciting. It's different. It's amazing. It goes well beyond the accepted capacity of our abilities as humans," she stated. "Only when you come up against somebody, like Rodney, do you realize how dangerous some of these people are."

"Go ahead."

She frowned, depressed about seeing how excited and energized he was.

He stared at her. "What's the matter?"

"You're filling me with dread," she said. "If my latest attack and all this mess does have anything to do with Rodney, it completely changes the game."

"In what way?"

"He had the ability to make people do things, and you don't have any idea how that can impact a facility like that. I also know that there's absolutely no way anybody else can deal with him. It'll have to be me."

He shook his head. "No way. You fought that demon enough. We'll handle it."

She snorted. "You really aren't hearing me, are you?"

He grimaced, then asked, "What's the worst thing that can happen?"

"He could make you shoot Grant, for example," she suggested. "You wouldn't have a bit of a say in it. Without a thought, you would pick up that gun, point it at your best friend, and pop him one, without a thought."

He slowly sagged against the couch and stared at her in horror. "Really?"

"Of all the things that I've ever said to you, you need to take heed of this one."

GRAY FOUND IT hard to believe, but the look on Cressy's face confirmed that she believed it entirely. And, if she believed it, he would have to be a complete fool to ignore it. He also knew that, once he told Grant what was going on, or what Gray suspected was going on, then Dr. Maddy was likely to get involved, and so would Stefan. Gray got up, noting that Cressy was almost in a dazed, blind, and numb state. Then he walked into the bedroom, closed the door, and phoned Grant.

When he explained what she'd just told him, Grant said, "Jesus, please, not that."

"I know. I mean, we've come at it from different angles from time to time, looking at doctors, looking at orderlies. Then I suggested to Cressy how this was all about patient care, so who would want to stop you from dealing with patients. She just laughed and said, *Nobody.* Then I had the audacity to ask who was the absolute worst-case patient she had ever had and what was the result. So she reminded me about Rodney, and we all remember how that had ended up."

"Yeah," Grant replied. "That's one of those cases that makes you think you'll never want to sleep ever again," he muttered.

"And again I missed a lot of it in progress. I came in at the end, finding Rodney beating her face, sitting on her, and she was out cold. I'd been around earlier, but I wasn't actually in Rodney's room at the time."

"And it wouldn't have mattered if you were because there wasn't a whole lot to see. Everything that happened, happened out on the ethers."

"God, I hate it when people say that because it makes me think it's a place I can actually go and access."

Grant laughed at that. "You can give that thought up for good because you can't. Or maybe not yet."

"Apparently. Still makes me wonder how Rodney ever got to be so strong."

"How did Cressy ever get so strong doing what she does? How did Stefan ever get so strong? How did Dr. Maddy get so strong? They all have the ability to do stuff that most of us can't even imagine, and then we come across people who can do it at will and don't want to be nice about it, and that's what we're up against with this Rodney guy. He's an asshole, always was. He likes to play mind games, and, if he thinks he can win at something like this, he'd be all over it."

"And now I have to wonder if that's what he's doing at the hospital right now," Gray said. "In a way it makes a sick kind of sense."

"It also means that he has healed and that he's out there, ready to cause all kinds of chaos."

"Is that possible? Then, of course, it is, as Cressy healed herself."

"I guess it's time I talked to Dr. Maddy and to Stefan," Grant suggested. "I'll get back to you soon." And, with that, Grant hung up.

Gray walked back out to the main part of the hotel room to find Cressy still sitting on the couch. "How about some fresh coffee?" he asked gently.

She looked up at him. "Maybe." She sounded like she was being led to the gallows.

"I don't want you dealing with him again," Gray stated. "You lost a big part of your life, and, even now, people are trying to damage your career, probably because of this guy." She just nodded and didn't say anything. "You could at least tell me what you're thinking."

"What's to think?" she asked, looking up at him. "He always had my number. I never quite understood that, but he always seemed to know what made me tick."

"Did you have an interest in him or something? … I don't know quite how to put it, but was there something between you two beforehand? Did you know him before all this in any way?"

She shook her head. "No, I'd never met him, never had anything to do with him, until he arrived there. There was a lot of secrecy about everything going on in his life, and I was asked to come take a look to see if anything could be done to help him. And, of course, in my world, there's typically something that can be done to help any patient."

"Was there for Rodney?"

"No, absolutely not," she declared, with a sad sigh. "Still, that didn't mean I was ready to give up. I did think we could try something, but I just had no idea at the time what that would be."

"Of course not." Gray winced. "In your world there's always something to try, isn't there?"

She smiled. "I was sure hoping there would be, and I was trying hard, you know? What can I say? Healing people is what I do, and I had never come across anybody like Rodney before." She wrapped her arms around her chest and sank back into the couch.

"He terrifies you, doesn't he?"

"He does," she agreed, with a nod. "And I have no problem at all saying that. If you took the worst nightmare of your life, put it on steroids, then make it a never-ending nightmare, that's what this guy is. And he loves it. Rodney absolutely loves the fact that he can terrify us."

"Terrify *you*," Gray corrected.

She looked over at him and smiled. "I get that you probably think you'll be completely immune, but I can tell you right now that you won't be." He hesitated, and she nodded vehemently. "Seriously, you need to let that one go."

"It's not that I'm trying to be better than you or anything else. I'm just looking for answers that will keep you away from him."

"You do realize that distance isn't a thing in something like this, right?"

At that, he froze. "Meaning?"

She winced. "Meaning that, if he wants to get at me, I don't have to be at the hospital or even on this continent. He can come at me from where he is right now."

"Ah, hell. I really didn't want to hear that."

"No, I'm sure you didn't," she muttered, "but that does appear to be where we're at right now."

"So, if he wanted to, he could reach out here and get you?" he asked.

"In theory, yes, though I'm hoping he doesn't know that. I'm hoping he hasn't got the strength for something like that. Before we panic and go down this road, you need to check and see if he's even cognizant and awake."

"Would it matter?"

She hesitated, then slowly shook her head. "In many ways, no. He could do what he wanted before, even in the much-depleted state he was in. In theory, he could be doing this from his place right now." She groaned. "I don't even know where he is. I did see a Rodney assigned to a room in the maximum security area, but it wasn't him."

"I've set Grant on that, and the team's working it too. So, it shouldn't be too long before we get answers."

She looked at him and gave him a half smile. "Yeah, but

now that you've brought it up, this recent craziness feels very much as if it could be Rodney."

"Yeah, but didn't you say something about signatures, about being able to recognize him?"

"Yeah, so remember that part about somebody potentially having the ability to sound like Stefan, to sound like the boss, sound like whomever? I'm wondering whether he also learned to mask his energy, or at least make it look less dominant, so that somebody looking and expecting to see a specific signature doesn't, so doesn't question it."

"I think I understand what you mean," Gray replied.

"Good, since I'm not completely sure that I do." When he frowned at her, she shrugged. "I'm not sure about any of this at the moment."

"I get it. So, let's just hole up here, and, as soon as we get answers, we'll take the next step."

"The next step is talking to him and sorting out what he's doing and how much he's aware of."

"Which is not a good answer for anybody," he murmured.

"It doesn't matter. It really doesn't matter," she muttered, staring at him. "Because, if it *is* him, he has to be stopped, no ifs, ands, or buts about it."

"Sure, but that doesn't mean it has to be you who does it."

She shook her head, giving him a sad smile. "I'm afraid it does."

"Why? What about Stefan and Dr. Maddy?"

Again she shook her head. "No, it's always been about me."

"Maybe this time it needs to be about somebody else," Gray declared, his tone harsh.

Cressy sighed. "No, that won't happen."

"Dammit, it has to happen," Gray snapped. "I can't have you going back into that scenario again."

She gave the tiniest hint of a smile. "I get that you think you're in control and that you think you have some idea of what's happening here, but honestly nobody really does. And, if this is what Rodney's doing, it'll have to be me who goes in there. I don't know anybody else who can."

"You told me that there are other people who have these skills."

"I can get help … and use you as a ground, for instance. I could use Stefan's help, but he can't go in there. It's not a case of opening a door and going in. It's a case of being let in. And, of all the people Rodney's dealt with before, if he will let in someone, it'll be me."

"Why? Why you?" Gray was beside himself in frustration.

"Because he wants to destroy me, and he can't do that, unless he opens the door and I walk into the room, into his playground, the playground where he spent all that time killing everybody."

RODNEY COULDN'T UNDERSTAND how humanity had survived, not when it was so low on the food chain. Sure, humanity thought it was doing just fine, but apparently it had no clue what was going on, and that just blew him away. What kind of a place was this that they could be taken in so easily? He knew that most people wouldn't understand what he was saying, and that was fine, but he did miss Cressy.

She had the ability to talk to him like nobody else ever had before. He knew that the two of them would have been perfect together, but she hadn't been interested. She'd only wanted to stop him from his games and his fun, and that wasn't something he was prepared to do. He had tried to teach her a lesson, and somehow things had gotten beyond crazy. Even now he was still hesitant about stepping out fully because he didn't know what had happened last time—or whether it would happen again.

If she'd planned on curtailing his activities, she'd succeeded in a big way, and it just made him angry. He'd gone dark for a long time, and it'd taken him forever to even get back out again, and now that he was back out, he was hesitant and cautious. He didn't want to be sucked into the vortex of nothingness, the way he had been before. He also didn't know if she'd done it to him, and, if she had, had she done it intentionally?

If she had, that was a different story. Nobody would be allowed to curtail his life like that, not if he was capable of stopping it. But the idea of meeting her again was compelling. She'd been such a light in his darkness, such hope that somebody was out there like him, someone he could talk to and be with. He didn't know if she understood just how important she was to him, to his plans, but, when things had blown up, he hadn't known what to do or who had been responsible.

He'd heard people say that Cressy had been badly injured from the whole thing too, and that had bothered him. But then he'd started to wonder if she'd had a part in it. Had she actually been the one who had done this to him? In that case, no punishment was strong enough. But he needed to know, and the only way to find out for sure was if she came back.

When he'd seen her in the hallways, he'd been so excited

that he'd struggled to maintain form and had lost it very quickly. His host at the time had been completely confused and had left, taking a few days off. But a few days away had turned into more than Rodney could handle, and, without his host close, it had been very hard for Rodney to get some kind of connection with someone else. Rodney needed a connection; he needed to know that he wasn't going crazy and that it had been Cressy, always Cressy, who could actually talk to him.

She'd been such a light, such a joy, and such a hope, … the only hope that he would ever get out of this place. He'd been working on the doctors to write him up in a much better light, to explain away his aberrant behavior. He had been working on the board as well. People weren't willing to listen to excuses. It's a good thing they didn't know about all his victims, but they did know about some.

Apparently that had been enough to stop people from finding any kind of sense of the world he was in and the things that he could do. He didn't understand that, except that it was all back to that fear again. So maybe it was a good thing that they were afraid. He didn't know.

He still had so many things to figure out, yet how? He needed Cressy. He'd never been as powerful as he had been when she was there, supposedly treating him. He laughed at that because he had treated her instead. He'd treated her to show her just what he could do, and, when she'd tried to escape from him, he'd proven what he could do. He was even more powerful with her, which had been such a heady experience. Yet somehow it had all come apart, though he still didn't understand how or why.

She shouldn't have had the ability to get away from him, but somehow she had. He thought he could do something about it this time, but he needed her back, and now he didn't know what was going on. Some of his energy had been erratic, as he had tried to get it back in control, but control was a hard thing to actually manage without her.

He thought he was stronger—at least he wanted to believe he was stronger—but maybe he was weaker and somehow something had broken inside. And, if that were true, he needed her more than ever. He wanted her back, where he could talk to her, where he could figure out if she really did have something to do with this.

He still didn't know what he would do about it because she was special, but he had to find a way to stop her from doing anything to hurt him. Once she understood how important she was to him, he was sure she would be easier to control. Yet, in the meantime, he couldn't do anything until she came to him.

At that, the doctor walked into his room, smiled at him, and asked, "How are you doing, Rodney?"

He smiled back. "Doing fine. I thought I saw Dr. Cressy here."

At that, the doctor asked, "Was somebody talking? I mean, I'm presuming you didn't see her. She didn't come in here, did she?"

Rodney hesitated, wondering what was the right answer, then shook his head.

At that, the doctor nodded with relief. "Good, she was only here for a few days, but she won't be back now."

"Why is that?" Rodney asked. Inside, he hated the fact that this guy was telling him that she wasn't coming back to him anymore.

"She didn't adjust well after her sabbatical, so you certainly don't have to worry about that."

"I would like to see her," Rodney said immediately.

"That won't happen," the doctor said, with a bright smile. "We have to look after all our patients, and she wasn't a good fit for this facility."

"She was great," Rodney declared, staring at the man, desperately trying to hold his hatred inside. "She's been the best person I've ever talked to."

The doctor frowned at him. "I didn't realize you felt so strongly about her."

"Absolutely I do. I know I've talked to my mother about it several times."

At that, the doctor nodded slowly. "Your mother has made it very clear that she would like to see your treatment with Dr. Cressy continue."

He nodded. "Absolutely, nobody else has had the same effect."

"Now that's not true," the doctor argued in a jovial manner. "Many of us have been working with you."

"And none of you are doing anything effective," Rodney snapped.

At that, the doctor stared at him.

Realizing his mistake, Rodney sighed. "I'm sorry. I was just so excited that she was back. So hearing your news is quite upsetting."

"I'm sorry to hear that, but we can't necessarily control all the patient-doctor interactions we have here. Just because you might want somebody in your corner, that doesn't mean we can make it happen."

Rodney stared at the doctor, hating that this man was trying to control what Cressy could do and could see and could be, when Rodney knew that she needed to be here with him. But absolutely nothing in the doctor's expression indicated that he would give in any way, and that just made Rodney all the angrier. He sat back in his hospital bed, then looked over at the doctor and said, "I'm awfully tired."

"Understood," the doctor noted, maintaining a bright smile. "We'll go over a few things first."

He glared at him. "I'm tired now."

The doctor hesitated, then wrote something down on his notes.

On a whim, Rodney reached over with his mind, grabbed ahold of the doctor, and helped him to write *Call Cressy, bring her back in.*

At that, the doctor got up slowly and announced, "I think I'll go make some phone calls." Then he quickly escaped.

Rodney didn't know if his mental nudge had done any good, but the fact that he even had the ability to do that much again had cheered him up immensely. He could start messing around with people here, although he didn't want to do too much in case they found out what he was up to. Not until he had Cressy. She was his answer for getting out of here. She was his answer for unlocking so much more power, for giving him the ability to do so much more. All he had to do was get her here.

CHAPTER 18

C RESSY OPENED HER eyes and stared around at the hotel room, trying to sort out where she was and why. When she heard voices off to the side, she turned her head to see Gray on the phone. As soon as he saw that she was awake, he disconnected the call, walked over, and sat down beside her on the couch.

"Hey. How are you doing?" he asked, picking up her hand.

She squeezed his fingers gently. "Better I think. I didn't realize I fell asleep."

He nodded. "Stressful days."

"Yeah, you're not kidding."

"I wasn't sure if I should just let you sleep here or get you into the bed."

"I won't be awake for too much longer. I'm pretty tired still."

"Yeah, but food first, then you can rest on your bed."

"If you say so," she murmured. She studied his face and then frowned. "What did you find out?"

He hesitated for a moment. "We found out some things. Did you know that Rodney's aunt is on the board of directors now?"

"Yes. I knew her from before. She was actually one of my biggest supporters."

"Any chance she's not a supporter anymore?"

She stared at him, then shrugged. "I mean, everything's all new now, so anything is possible. Still, I wouldn't have thought so. At the time, she was very understanding of the trouble Rodney was in, wanting to make sure I had the ability to go in and to get the information needed to help with the other cases."

He nodded. "I haven't talked to her."

"I haven't either. This is embarrassing, but I'd kind of blanked her out of my mind. I didn't see anything of her while I was back there."

"You didn't see her at all?"

She shook her head.

"Apparently she spends a good deal of time there. In addition to her duties on the board, she sees her nephew quite a bit."

"I'm sure she does," Cressy agreed, with a smile. "She's a very caring woman."

"That's good to know. I don't know if you realize it, but …"

Cressy closed her eyes and nodded, knowing what was coming. "I should have gotten it when you told me how she went in to see him all the time. He's there, isn't he?"

"Yes, he's in the maximum-security wing, but she's been trying to get him moved out in the general residences."

She winced at that. "That would be terribly dangerous."

"Right, but apparently nobody believes he's dangerous now."

"Of course not," she murmured. "People only want to see what's in front of them."

"Is that even fair?" he asked, looking at her gently. "Does anybody even know or understand what he can do?"

She closed her eyes, not even wanting to think about it, as it all flooded through her head, crowding out all rational thought. When she finally calmed down enough, she went through a systematic review of her few days at the center. The one thing that came to mind was a worrisome question. Why had she *not* known he was there? The answer was actually easier than ever to sort out—because she had kept her guard up.

She hadn't actually let herself open up to everybody. She had only opened up to the few people she'd seen and had worked with before, prior to this attack. Before things had blown up last year, she had been open, happy, and carefree at the center. She was certain that everything was under control and that no boogeymen were in her world. Finding out that she'd been so terribly wrong had been a horrible change, a horrible loss of innocence for her. So, when she'd returned to the center, all these months later, she'd been very locked down, very careful that she wasn't too open and that no predators were out there that she needed to be wary of.

It was a sad irony about the state of affairs in her world, yet something she felt she needed to do. And, with that, she had proceeded cautiously, not even aware that the very same monster who had attacked her before was actually on the premises. She had gone through some of the patient lists but hadn't gotten all the way through, and there hadn't been any alert for her either. Why was that? She pondered that for a long time. "Why would they not have told me that Rodney was there?" she asked Gray.

"I don't know. That's just another question to ask. Are you sure he's burned out?"

"There are abilities out there that we just don't understand and don't know everything about. Yet I would have bet my life that he couldn't have come back from that." Then she stopped and added, "Not if he was alone, at least."

"*Uh-oh*, I'm not liking that last bit at all. How could somebody possibly help him?"

She smiled. "I don't know. You're asking me questions that I can't give you an answer to, and I certainly can't give you the answers you want because I know nothing definitive on him. All I know is that he was absolutely burned out back then. Last I knew, he was comatose in a secure locked-down facility. He's clearly not in that facility anymore, if he's in ours, but, as long as he stays in maximum security, then, in theory, the rest of the place is secure as well."

"Would you ever treat him again?"

"Nope, not unless I had to," she replied cheerfully. "And, no, I don't feel guilty about it."

"I would hope not," Gray muttered.

"A lot of people think that we should be treating people like him, and I get that," she shared, "but it'll take somebody other than me. There's definitely trouble between us, so I can't take him on as another patient for myself."

"Are you telling me everything about that visit?"

"I don't know what you know and what you don't know," she said, looking over at him. "Was it fun? No. I think perhaps he saw me as an ally and was thrilled and excited to know that he could talk to me the way he could to everybody else in a normal way. Nobody else really understood what he was doing or understood what I was struggling to get away from, outside of Dr. Maddy and Stefan of course." She gave a wave of her hand. "Since then, many of us have come to understand what was going on, but, at the time, it happened so fast that I didn't really have any protection. And, if I go back in again, I still won't really have any protection because he's already got my number."

"So, you burned out over all this, and, if he burned out as well, would that have made him weaker?"

"No, absolutely not," she stated. "He could have gotten stronger, if he survived."

"Yeah, but you see? The lack of definitive details on so many points makes me very nervous."

"I get it, and don't worry. It doesn't make me feel much better either," she murmured.

"No, of course not. I'm sorry. I shouldn't keep bringing it up."

"If you don't, who will?" she asked. "So, you're sure he's there?"

He nodded. "Yes, I'm sure he's there."

"*Great*, so I'll have to go see him." He bolted to his feet, as she held up her hand. "There's no other way," she declared. "I still don't know if he's behind these current attacks, but I didn't think it was possible for Rodney to do this. So, if it's *not* possible, then we need to see if somebody else at that hospital is doing it. I don't know what to say, but I know it would be a lot easier to sort out if I were there on the spot."

"I would just as soon *not* have you anywhere close to that hospital."

"Right, but apparently other people don't want me there either," she murmured, "and I'm not even sure what to say to that."

Just then his phone rang. "Hey, Grant. What's up? Dr. Mendelsohn?" He looked over at her and nodded. "I don't know how she feels about that. She's not exactly a fan of the center at the moment." He explained a little bit about what she'd just shared, listening to Grant's feedback.

When Gray hung up the phone, she asked, "What about Dr. Mendelsohn?"

"He had a heart attack. He's alive, but he's in Emergency."

She stared at him. "That's not good. He's still a young man."

"But heart attacks do happen in young men too, right?"

"Yes, of course," she murmured. "Damn, that'll be a shock to the center."

"In what way?"

"He was one of the driving forces of change, like I was."

Then Gray asked, "So, any chance that somebody might have wanted him out of the way or even tried to kill him?"

"I don't like the way you think," she announced.

His lips twitched. "Yeah, well, if the world were different, I wouldn't have to think this way."

She sagged back onto the couch, frowning. "That's true enough," she muttered. "I would hate to think that whatever happened was brought on by something going on at the center, but I know there's been so much upset that maybe a heart attack isn't that far out of the equation. Did he put that much heart into the place? Absolutely," she declared. "He was like me, in that the place has been a very important part of his life."

"Yet you're using past tense."

"Do I have a job?" she asked, with a wry look.

"Don't they have to give you the job back?"

"Given the way they were trying to move me out of the place, I highly doubt it."

"I'm pretty sure the lawyers would have a heyday with that."

She shrugged. "Maybe, but I would have to give a damn

in order to let the lawyers go at it."

"Would you not fight it? It is your career."

"I know, but, as you said, if I fight it, then chances are very good they'll make my life hell in other ways too."

"You think they would destroy your reputation because of that?"

"They would sure try. They said as much already," she noted. "The question is, who is doing this and how much do they even care? And why would they do it when there are other ways to accomplish the same thing."

"Like?"

"I could be bought off, and they haven't even tried that."

"But would you take it?"

"I don't know. Believe me. I had to psych myself up to the fact that I was going back to that center, but I had stayed in touch with several of the doctors over the last six months."

"Was Dr. Mendelsohn one of them?"

"Yes, absolutely," she replied. "He's one of the few there who wanted patient care to be a priority, more than filling shareholder's pockets, although he tried to bridge the gap and keep everyone happy. I used to get frustrated with him when he sounded so wishy-washy, but his heart was definitely on the side of patient care."

"Of course, and, because of that, it made his life difficult too. Particularly with whatever happened in the meantime."

"I don't even know all that's happened. I heard some rumors but wasn't getting very far for answers, as if I were being deliberately kept out of the loop. Considering the kind of trouble I'd caused them, it kind of made sense."

"I don't know about *sense* in any of this, but it is kind of horrifying to hear just how much is going on in the background."

She shrugged. "It's politics, but every center fights it to a certain degree, I'm sure."

He shook his head. "Can't say I've ever seen anything like that at Dr. Maddy's place."

"But that's because she gets to control it," Cressy pointed out, with a wry look. "Remember that part. It might be a nice idea, but not sure I'm up for the work."

"Sure, and you know you also have to take a look at whether staying here is what's really good for your soul."

"Apparently it isn't." She stood and wandered around. "Is Dr. Mendelsohn at General Hospital?"

"He is. Do you want to go see him?"

She turned and nodded. "Yes, I do."

"Okay, let's go. We'll pick up a bite to eat afterward, then bring it back to eat here, and hopefully you can get some sleep."

"That would be good. I'm still not quite up to snuff apparently."

"No, and I don't want you going back to the center, not until we have some kind of security in place."

"Security to stop Rodney? You do know better, right?"

"I do know better," he admitted. "But humor me, okay? It's what I can do, so it's what I will do."

"Even though you know that there's absolutely no hope of stopping this man if he's half the person he was back then?"

"Maybe so, but I'm really hoping that among you, Stefan, and Dr. Maddy, there will be something completely different going on, and it won't be the same scenario as last time. And, as you keep telling me, you think he's completely burned out."

"I do think he's completely burned out, yes. The man I

saw, the man I was monitoring all these months—because believe me, I kept an eye on him—showed very little movement, very little cognitive activity of any kind. But anything is possible," she added.

"Right, hospital first then."

He got up, handed her a sweater, and shared, "It's starting to rain outside."

She put on the sweater, and together they walked out to his vehicle. When they got in the car, she looked around and said, "It's been kind of handy having you around to drive me here and there."

He laughed. "Happy to be of service."

"I mean it though," she said. "You've been looking after me very well, and I appreciate it."

"That's great, but gratitude is really not something I'm after."

"Doesn't matter whether you're after it or not," she replied, with spirit. "It's still better than the opposite."

At that, he burst out laughing. "Very true."

The trip to the hospital took a little longer, with the wet roads slowing traffic, plus the weird light of dusk obstructing drivers too.

Cressy chuckled. "I always think of this as the witching hour. Most people think of midnight, but this half-light is definitely the spooky time for me."

"Yeah, we don't need any witching hours or spooky times please," he replied, glancing at her.

"We may not need them," she agreed, "but that doesn't mean that you won't get them."

He sighed. "Tell me something. Will you always have weird stuff popping up in your life?"

"Probably. It's what I do." She looked at him apologetically. "It's just part of the deal. After seeing you struggle with it, I get why some guys may not want to hang around."

"Your abilities aren't really a problem for me at all. It's the part about having crazy psychotic serial killers after you that is giving me trouble."

"That makes sense. Believe me. I had to reevaluate what I wanted to do. But, in the end, I realized that I provide a valuable service, and it's something that not many people can do. So I just need a better way to screen those I can help from those I can't."

"Yeah, I agree with that completely," he stated. "I'm just not sure how one screens for crazy."

She smiled. "You know that we don't like to talk about them like that, right?"

"Sure, that's you, not me. I call a spade a spade, and, in this case, *crazy* gets to be called *crazy.*"

She shrugged. "I don't know. I've been working on some of that while I was on sabbatical, but I haven't had a chance to actually put it into play yet." He looked at her, frowning. She shrugged. "I mean, it was a sabbatical, but it wasn't. It was really a case of getting back my nerve and healing on all levels because I burned out really badly."

"Your senses?"

"Yes, my senses. It was quite an explosion and certainly devastating to my own abilities."

"Right," he muttered, then pulled into the hospital parking lot. Hopping out, he said, "Okay, here we are."

"Yep, hopefully I'll get in and see Dr. Mendelsohn."

"I often wonder if you can pull a trick like that, when you've got a badge or a medical license," he shared.

"If I had an operating license for this hospital, it would be a different story, but I don't, so no luck there."

He just nodded and didn't say anything. As they walked in, he identified himself and flashed his shield. The nurse nodded and noted that they were expected. Gray led the way, until they came to a private room. He pushed open the door, and she stepped inside.

Dr. Mendelsohn smiled at her. "Now here is somebody I'm really glad to see. Are you okay?"

"I'm fine." She walked over and reached for his hand. "How are you though?"

"I'm okay, but it's been a hell of a few days."

"Sorry, I didn't realize coming back would be quite so tumultuous or that they would try to get rid of me."

"And it shouldn't have been," Mendelsohn replied. "Everybody acknowledges the work that you do is very unique, and your success rate is phenomenal. But, once that board moved in, the trouble began."

"Speaking of board members"—Gray stepped forward— "Mrs. Arundale. How long has she been on the board?"

"A couple years now. … Why?"

"Was she instrumental in her nephew being at the center?"

He nodded. "He was moved to another facility, with higher security, and they had absolutely no problem with him. So after three months, she had him moved back." He looked over at Cressy apologetically. "I'm sorry that nobody told you about that."

"I didn't even find out until this morning," she told him. "It certainly would have been a shock if I had found out on my own."

"And with good reason. It was quite an ordeal for you. Believe me. Not very many of us are comfortable working with him, but he's been a completely different case now.

He's on heavy medications, and he's been no trouble."

She winced.

"I know," he said. "That's one of the reasons I was really happy you were coming back. I thought maybe you would be somebody to join forces with, so we could help our patients and not just drug them out. And, of course, everybody has a different methodology," he noted quickly, looking over at Gray, "so I'm not accusing anybody of anything illegal or inappropriate."

He nodded. "Believe me. I've already heard from her that she's all about patient care, and apparently the people running the place are all about profits."

"There was always a certain degree of that, but now it's become paramount, it seems."

"Any particular reason?" Gray asked him.

"I don't know. They would say that we're not making ends meet, but I don't understand why that would be, since we're way down on staffing numbers now, so they should be making a good profit just from that alone."

"Something's got to be going on," Cressy stated. "I mean, what other reason is there for cutting the budget so severely?"

"Money," Gray said. "It's almost always about money."

"Yeah, I know," she muttered. "It's still not something I want to think about."

"No, because you're all about the patients, but that doesn't mean anybody else is."

Dr. Mendelsohn nodded. "She's not alone there. A lot of us are all about the patients, but the center also has to be solvent. You can't have a facility like that running in the red. Both Cressy and I have put in our own personal money at various times, but typically to help bring in new programs and or specific things that we know will help the patients," he explained. "Most of the staff there are not into that. For many people, it's just a job. They come. They do their hours, they leave, and aren't at all prepared to put any of their hard-earned dollars back into it."

At that, Gray looked over at her, and she nodded. "We both have," she confirmed. "Sometimes it's necessary for radical therapies, extra group sessions, enrichment programs for a particular patient, or that sort of thing."

"It should never be necessary," Gray declared, staring at her. "I did see some of the financial statements that they published as part of their year-end reporting, and, to me, it didn't appear that they are in any kind of financial difficulty. There was an issue over some of the drugs though."

"Costing too much, which is pretty funny, considering they're the ones who have increased the drug use so much," Dr. Mendelsohn shared bitterly. "So they only have themselves to blame for that one."

"Don't they get subsidized?" Gray asked.

"Some things get subsidized," she confirmed. "Some of the drug companies give incentives to use their drugs at the exclusion of others," she added. "And that may sound horrible, but it happens all the time in the medical world."

He shook his head. "That shouldn't be allowed at all."

"Sure, it shouldn't be. But, hey, there are always incentives to push one drug over another, and believe me. Those incentives can be quite lucrative."

"Damn." Gray crossed his arms and leaned against a wall. He looked over at Dr. Mendelsohn. "So, was this heart attack a result of the stress at your job?"

"I think so," he replied. "Like Cressy, I'm wondering if it's time for a change. I've been there for fifteen years and loved every minute of it. Yet there comes a point in time when you just can't get along anymore."

"Has anything weird happened in the last few months, when Dr. Cresswell wasn't there?" Gray asked.

Mendelsohn shook his head. "Nothing weirder than what's already been going on," he said. "Budget cuts, people talking behind each other's backs, conversations that stop when you walk down a hallway. It's been very sad."

"What do you mean by conversations stopping?"

"The entire place has been split and divided by all this."

"When you say *all this* ..."

"The budgets. They've been taking votes on various things, and I've wondered if some of the doctors haven't been getting incentives to vote a specific way."

"*Great*, I wouldn't be at all surprised," Cressy replied in disgust.

"And again it shouldn't be allowed," Gray declared, staring at her.

"In a perfect world, it wouldn't be, and you would have a board and doctors who cared about patients above all," Cressy stated, "but that's just not the way it is. That reminds me of what a minister once told me, when I was surprised because he was growing marijuana in his greenhouse and having an affair with a church elder. He told me, *Everybody has this perception about how I'm supposed to act, but it's not fair because I should get to live my life the way I want to.* When I tried to explain to him that the perception was one that we all wanted to keep because it maintained our faith in the church and in religion, he told me that I was the one with the problem and that I should work on it."

At that, Dr. Mendelsohn laughed. "I hear you there, and, to a certain extent, that's true. Doctors are supposed to be there for patients, but many doctors are there for the paycheck, and it's just a job. They go home at the end of the day, as tired and as exhausted as the rest of us, and they just don't want to keep doing it at the same level that we do. Dr. Cresswell and I are very passionate about patient care, and it has worked well for us, up until now, but at present? Well, I don't ... I'm not sure my time there is of any value anymore."

"That's what I was thinking too," she added softly. "What we do and say doesn't have the same value as it did before."

"No, and the respect that you and I may have had in the past has waned. That flame has burned out for us."

"So, it's definitely time for a change in career," Gray noted.

"I don't know about *career* but definitely a change in *venue*," Dr. Mendelsohn clarified.

"Have you handed in your notice?" Gray asked.

Mendelsohn shook his head. "No, I'll take some time off after this and consider my options."

"Did you ever work with Rodney?" Gray asked suddenly.

"I've seen him a couple times, but he hasn't responded to any treatments, and he certainly hasn't responded to any of the doctors, not like he did with you, Cressy."

She nodded. "I may have to go see him."

Mendelsohn winced at that. "It probably would be a good idea if you did, but I have to tell you. He's not the same person."

"That's good," she said. "I'm not sure I can handle the same person."

"I know what you mean, but he is much easier now."

"Glad to hear that," she noted, and then she got up to leave. "I don't want to keep you, and you need to get some rest and think about what you want to do from here on out."

"Oh, I've been doing lots of thinking," he agreed, with a knowing smile. "I'm just not sure what the options are. I was thinking about another center my brother back east has been talking about. He's always wanted me to join him there."

She understood, but it was hard to see him leave. "Go then. You get to decide what you need to do for you," she stated firmly. "I hoped you would stay, but, if it's not something that we can make happen at this center, believe me. I understand."

"Will you stay?" Doc Mendelsohn asked her.

"I don't know. Again, like you, I've had other offers, but I'm just not sure that this is where I want to be anymore, not if I can't make the same kind of impact. If they'll hamstring me with a short budget, then ..." She just shrugged.

He nodded in understanding. "Let's be sure to stay in touch."

With that, she leaned over, kissed him gently on the cheek, and, within minutes, she and Gray were back outside.

GRAY'S PHONE RANG as they walked out to the vehicle. "Hey, Grant. What's up?"

"Just checking on a few things. Where are you guys?"

"We're just coming out of the hospital. One of the doctors that Cressy works with had a heart attack, so I brought her to visit him."

"Ah. And it's not related to the mess going on at the center?"

"Not that we can tell, no. Stress-related perhaps, unless

you have any kind of intel that suggests something else."

"Not at the moment, but there's not much I like about any of this."

"Why is that?"

"Because one of the newer members of the board was actually under investigation five years ago for money laundering."

"Money laundering?" he repeated, turning to look at her. "What happened with the investigation?"

"It basically came to a stop, as they couldn't get anywhere with it. No charges were ever filed, but he's been flagged on a kind of watch list."

"Interesting. When did he come onto the board?"

"About six months ago," Grant noted. "Just after Cressy left."

"She probably would have had a lot to say, if somebody like that came on the board."

"She probably didn't have much say on things like that," Grant reminded him.

He turned and asked her, "Did you ever have any say on board members?"

She shook her head. "No, not really. Once in a while, as a courtesy, they would pretend they were interested in our opinions, but nothing of substance, like choosing board members. Why?"

"Apparently one of the guys brought in just after you left has been under investigation in the past for money laundering."

She stared at him. "*Huh.* Considering the shenanigans going on right now, I don't even know if money laundering would be part of that. I mean, the budget cuts are hardly money laundering."

"No, but that sort of thing tends to go along with companies that take over places like this. They make acquisitions, then slim it right down to a lean machine, and then start running money through it."

"*Great*," she muttered. "I don't know how that works, but it sounds terrible. At this point, who knows what's going on."

Grant added, "Look. Take care of her because I don't really know what's coming here, but we'll start tightening the squeeze on the money laundering angle and see if we can make somebody uncomfortable."

"*Great*," Gray replied. "You guys get all the fun, and I'm stuck in woo-woo land."

Grant laughed. "Hey, woo-woo land is pretty freaking interesting. Just ensure the both of you stay alive."

"Yeah, that's just great," he muttered. Then he hung up, smiled at her, and said, "You know, if they'll do an investigation like that, it will blow the lid off everything there."

"Honestly that's what should happen," she said, drifting, "But ..." She shook her head. "I don't really know anything about that side of it."

"Why would you?" he muttered. "I think it's an interesting idea that all the changes potentially could have had this kind of a push behind them."

"Maybe," she muttered. "Personally I think budgets and health care shouldn't even be in the same sentence."

"Maybe not, but somebody has to pay the bills," he reminded her.

"I know, and it's never the people who have it. It always seems to be this constant squeeze on people without insurance, trying to find some way to make them pay."

"But reforms take a while, as you know."

"Yeah, you're not kidding," she agreed, as she yawned.

He looked at her and asked, "Ready to go home?"

"I don't know about home, but, yeah, I guess. We were supposed to pick up food, weren't we?"

"We talked about it. Are you hungry?"

"No, not really. Maybe in the morning I'll have more appetite."

"Will you get through the night without food?"

She pondered that, and then she sighed. "Probably not. Is there a health food bar around here anywhere, so I could get a green shake?" When he winced at that, she laughed. "Hey, it's just a pick-me-up, particularly when I don't have much appetite and am not getting good nutrition for one reason or another, that's all. Don't worry. I don't really consider it food either, but it has a place."

"Fine. Is there a place close to the center? Isn't that where you got them?"

"Yeah, there is," she confirmed. "Not that the center is anywhere I want to be right now."

"Nope, and it doesn't mean that we have to go there either. I was just thinking there must be a place to get them nearby, if you had them all the time."

She smiled. "You're right. There is."

With that, he followed her instructions and pulled up to the place. He walked inside with her, and she ordered a shake with as many greens as he thought he could stomach in a week. And then she really topped it, by ordering two of them. He looked at her and raised an eyebrow.

She nodded. "They're not that bad," she said. "And they're good for you, and right now we could both use the pick-me-up."

"Oh, I thought going home and getting some sleep

would be a good idea," he pointed out in a joking manner.

"That too," she muttered.

She paid for them, and, by the time they received their shakes and stepped outside, he was eyeing the frothy green thing with distrust. She chuckled. "I'm a doctor. Remember? Take your medicine and be smart about it."

"*Great*," he muttered, "but I can't say this is exactly a substitute for a steak."

"No, and, if I had the energy need for a steak, I would join you for one," she declared, "but I don't." And, with that, she sipped her shake several times and smiled. "It's actually very refreshing."

Her phone rang just then. She pulled it out and looked down at the screen, a bit surprised.

With a tone that held a hint of revulsion, Gray asked, "Who did you give that number to?"

"Keith," she replied, looking up at him. "Hey, Keith. What's up?"

"Hey," he replied, his tone worried. "Are you okay?"

"Yeah, sure I am. Why?"

"Because things are really crazy here."

"I know. I heard Dr. Mendelsohn had a heart attack."

"He did, but he had it after his session with a patient, and then Dr. Roybiss went down. Now Dr. Ann's not been feeling good either. She just left."

"That's not normal."

"We've got a skeleton crew on tonight," he shared. "I wanted to keep everybody locked up in Crazyville and put the whole place on lockdown, but management has said that's a no."

"What do you mean?" she asked, staring up at Gray. "What's going on?"

"A couple of the patients got out earlier today and had quite a brawl in the hallway. One of them got badly hurt and was taken to the hospital, and the other one has just been in a … I don't know. Maybe they drugged him or something, but he's just lying in the bed."

"Who is that?"

"The one who's injured is Sadie. She's only been here for a couple days, and I'm not exactly sure what happened. I did hear her saying something about she was just in the play-ground."

"Good God, is she back from the hospital?"

"Yeah, she came back about an hour ago, and Dr. Men-delsohn left about an hour before that."

"Was he involved in the altercation?"

"It was happening in the hallway, and he was one of the ones who happened to be there and helped separate them."

"Who was the other patient?"

"John. I don't know if you know him."

"No, I'm not sure I do," she said. "Do I need to come in?"

He snorted. "I don't even know if your keys work."

"Hey, I'm on that side of town anyway. Maybe I'll come take a look, especially if no doctor is on staff right now. I'm worried about Sadie."

"They did fix her up, but she's pretty upset, and she's just keening in her room."

"I'll come talk to her," she replied, making a sudden de-cision. "Be there in a little bit." She looked over at Gray, as she put her phone away.

"I DON'T THINK that's a good idea," Gray stated, for the

umpteenth time, as they pulled into the parking lot of the clinic.

"And I heard you loud and clear each time you said that," she replied. "Just a quick trip, in and out."

"You don't even know if your security card works. What if they don't let you in?"

"That will make it even faster then, won't it?" she said, with a bright smile. She led the way to the front door and using her key card, managed to get right in. "That answers that," she stated, as she held the door open for him. "I still have access."

"So, you still have a job, and you're still getting a paycheck," he noted, with a note of humor. "And, therefore, you feel like you need to do something."

She shrugged. "Sadie was one of those women I knew I could help. I'd actually contacted Stefan about her to see if we could do something to give her a hand in getting out of here."

"Why?"

"Because she's like me, like Stefan, like Dr. Maddy."

"Is she though?"

"Yes, absolutely she is."

He then asked, "Would somebody like that be a danger?"

"In her case, she's not."

Sensing something, he turned, looked around, and frowned. "It's awfully quiet."

"It's too quiet," she announced. She phoned Keith back. "Hey, where are you?"

"I'm down in the basement, sorting through laundry," he replied in disgust. "I don't think anybody put any laundry on, and the linens are low. We're trying to get the beddings changed, but, at this rate, good luck with that."

"Why are you changing beddings at this hour?"

"Because we didn't get done earlier," he noted, with a growl. "It's not my job either."

"No, I know," she stated. "I presume we've had accidents."

"After a day like today, several of them," he snapped. And then he groaned. "Not trying to snap at you. Where are you?"

"I just walked in the front door, and I'm heading down to Sadie's room."

"Good, she's a nice lady, and I'm not sure she should even be here."

"Maybe not. She could be one of the patients that I try to get moved."

"Yeah, I did hear somebody saying that one of the reasons they were upset with you was something about moving patients out who were paying bills."

"Yeah, but, if they don't belong here, they shouldn't be here," she protested.

"Oh, I agree with you. I was just reminded of the conversation I'd overheard."

"Do you remember who it was?"

"*Hmm*, I think it might have been Dr. Guidry, but you can't ask her right now because she went home sick. She was pretty stressed out and frustrated."

"Any idea why?"

"She got into it with the board today. I'm not sure what was going on with that either, but we had three board members doing a tour, and there was quite a confab over it all. I think she got the backlash."

"*Great.*" Cressy groaned. "That just adds to my not

wanting to stick around."

"I don't think anybody here cares. As long as they can keep the budgets down, they're happy."

"Yeah, I think you're right there," Cressy agreed. "Anyway I'm just coming up on Sadie's room. I'll talk to you in a bit." With that. she hung up and pointed the way to Sadie's room, for Gray's benefit.

"Why are we here?" he asked.

"Because Sadie was involved in quite a fight and had to go to the hospital today. I just want to confirm she's okay."

He watched as she approached the door, but, instead of opening it, she just leaned up against the wall and closed her eyes. "What are you doing?"

She held up a finger to her lips and whispered, "Just a minute."

He watched in amazement as her face calmed, and it seemed every expression possible just faded, giving her a slack look. He hated that. It made him think of some of the people lying in comas in these rooms. And then she opened her eyes, but something was off about that look on her face too. She turned and looked down the hallway and smiled. He stared at the hallway, wondering what she was seeing. Then her body slumped against the wall, and, damn, if it didn't look as if she had stepped out of it. He watched as this weird smoke headed down the hallway. He felt the hairs on the back of his neck stand up. "Jesus," he whispered.

Just as he saw more smoke in the hallway, he felt a pat on his shoulder, and then he realized he was holding her hand. When he dropped her hand, all of it disappeared. Immediately he picked up her hand and stared. "Good God."

Being in contact with her was letting him see things,

whether he wanted to or not. What he saw was an older woman, at least the form, somewhat of a form, in what seemed like a playground. She was doing cartwheels and laughing and running, and, when she saw Cressy's spirit, she raced up and gave her a big hug. The two women talked for a bit, and then her ghost-like figure returned to him and patted his cheek gently. Suddenly she was squeezing his fingers. He looked from his hand to her face to see the slack-jawed look now gone and the normal Cressy back again.

"Oh my God," he whispered. "I am not sure I want to know what you just did."

"Good." She smiled. "That's probably easier."

He whispered, his voice low, "Did you just leave your body and play with her in some kind of playground here? That is mad."

She laughed. "I didn't really play with her, but I was talking to her because this is her favorite playground."

"In the hallway?"

"It's not so much in the hallway, as she doesn't see the hallway. She sees open fields, blue skies, and sunshine. She sees what she would want for a playground. And she could leave this area for a real playground, but we are limited, or she is limited," Cressy corrected, "by the geographical location around her."

"And so that's what she's doing?"

"It is, and she's quite capable at doing it, which is one of the reasons why I was hoping we could get her some help."

"And yet," he noted, a thought coming to him, "with somebody like your Rodney guy around, who is so danger-ous, what are the chances that he could attack somebody like Sadie, who is innocent and open and just playing because she's happy, then using her energy or her body to cause hell for other people?"

"That's actually one of the reasons I came here," she admitted. "I need to ensure that Sadie was okay and to see who else was involved in the altercation and how she felt about it all."

"What did she have to say?"

"It was another patient, and she's okay, but she doesn't like that patient and wants to stay away from him."

"Great, but she probably couldn't identify the patient then."

"No, but she hasn't been here very long, which adds to the problem. Since she's new here, she doesn't know many names."

"But it would have been a patient that she would have seen somewhere along the lines of this wing?"

"Not according to Sadie," Cressy corrected, her tone turning soft and even more serious. "According to Sadie, it was somebody she's never seen before, and he wasn't very friendly. She doesn't like him, doesn't want anything to do with him, and asked me to keep him away."

"That's great. What now?"

"That's what I don't know. I don't know who it was."

"But you're afraid it was Rodney, aren't you?"

She hesitated, then winced. "I'm not sure who it was, but I'm starting to get an inkling of something."

"Yeah, you think so? What gave you that impression?"

"Because she said he was young. Very young."

He stared at her and shook his head. "But you don't have young patients here."

"I have one," she stated, her gaze steady on his face.

His eyebrows shot up. "What?"

"That's the trick. I'm not saying that it was him. It could also be somebody trying to make it look like him."

"Jesus, this is like man's worst nightmare."

"The problem is, we don't know who's involved."

"I can't have anything happen to that boy," Gray muttered, staring at her in shock. "That won't be allowed." And he raced toward Adam's room.

"Wait," she cried out urgently. But Gray wasn't listening, and, when he got to the door, he motioned at it. "Open it."

"Not yet," she said. "Stefan also put a guard on this room, so I need to check in with him first."

"Check in with him? What?" he snapped, glaring at her. "My job was to keep this boy safe and to find out what he knows about the family annihilator."

"I get that," she replied. "That's a large part of what we're doing here right now."

"I don't understand."

"No, but I'm afraid I'm starting to," she declared. She pulled out her phone and called Stefan. "Were there any changes to Adam's energy guard?" she asked.

"Yeah, a couple glitches earlier, and I figured it was when you were at the hospital," he replied. "Why?"

"One of the other patients had a meeting with somebody in the playground," she explained. "Sadie said it was a young patient."

"You think it was Adam?" Stefan asked in astonishment. "You also know that we see patients as younger in this form."

"I know, so I don't know whether it was Adam or if it was somebody else. But I'm outside Adam's door right now."

"Good. Go on in," Stefan said. "Let me know what kind of condition he's in. I've kept the guard up all day, the same as you have. However, as I mentioned, there were a couple glitches, and I just figured it's when you were recently attacked, and things shifted."

"Right, talk to you in a few minutes." And, with that, she hung up and nodded. "Let's go in and check."

She quickly unlocked the door and moved in. It was evening, nine o'clock, and, in theory, Adam should be asleep, but she didn't know how much care he'd had all day.

As she walked closer to the bed, Gray warned her, "Stop."

She froze, turned, and looked at him. "What?" she asked.

He motioned at the bed.

She stared through the darkness, her eyes finally adjusting, and then she said urgently, "Turn on the lights." He flicked on the lights, and she spun around, staring at the room. "Good God, where is he?"

The bed was empty, and so was the room. She immediately raced toward the front area, where the security station was, and told the single guard to put out the alarm that they were missing a patient, and it was the boy. He stared at her in shock and hit the alarm. Immediately the doors were locked and exits were sealed up. She turned to Gray. "You need to get backup in here, now."

He was already on the phone.

She faced the guard again. "Cameras, I need to see that hallway from Room 212," she stated.

"For what hour?" he asked.

"The last four hours," she replied. "At least let me see that, and we'll go from there."

He quickly brought up the video for the time frame she'd requested, and, with it playing at a much faster speed, they raced through the hours of tape, watching the cameras to see what happened. About an hour ago came a glitch in the system. He shared that they had a power outage, and it took a moment before it went to the backup generators.

"*Right.*" She stared at the footage, shaking her head. When there was absolutely nothing from that time forward, he asked her, "Now what?"

"It's that glitch," she snapped. "Goddammit. I need to see the maximum-security wing."

The guard winced and brought up the cameras on that hallway too. At the same time frame came the same glitch.

"Okay," she declared, "I'm going down there myself." She looked over at Gray, who was on the phone. She told the guard, "Tell him where I am, when he gets off the phone."

"Will do," he confirmed.

And, with that, she raced down to the max security wing. Behind her, Gray called out to her. And then she heard footsteps, as he ran behind her.

"Jesus," Gray snapped, "you're definitely not going down there alone."

"Maybe not," she agreed, "but some things are just not that simple." As she pulled into the wing, no security was around at all. "So much for security," she muttered.

"How much would you typically have at this time of night?"

"There should be somebody at that desk over there." She pointing to an obviously empty desk that had been empty for quite a while. "And a second one close by."

"But that's insane," he muttered.

"I know, absolutely insane." As she turned and headed back to face the door that hid the monster, she took a deep breath, then unlocked it and stepped inside. With Gray crowding in behind her, she turned on the lights to see Rodney staring at her, with a big fat smile.

"Hello, Dr Cresswell."

CHAPTER 19

"WHERE'S ADAM?" CRESSY asked Rodney urgently, Gray right at her side, frowning at the occupant in the bed.

"Don't know what you're talking about," Rodney replied, with that same smirk.

"Yes, you do, and you better tell me now."

"What if I don't?"

She stared at him, trying to figure out what her options were, while Gray frowned at her, clearly confused, wondering who she was speaking to. She understood his confusion.

Rodney looked at the man behind her. "Interesting that you brought somebody with you today."

"Yes, but we need Adam. Don't you hurt that little boy."

"Why would I hurt him? That boy is very special to me."

At that, she tilted her head and studied him. "Why?"

He grinned. "You really don't know anything, do you?"

"We're getting there, but we're still behind."

"Ah, and information is everything to you, isn't it?"

"Not necessarily, but it certainly helps."

"But that's because you don't really know who he is."

"Where is Adam?" she asked again.

At that, Gray looked at her. "Who brought Adam to this facility?" he asked Cressy.

She shrugged. "I didn't have anything to do with that."

But she held out her hand.

And Gray took it, startled at what he saw.

Cressy nodded at him, letting him know she understood what he was going through.

Gray stared at Rodney. "It wasn't your aunt by any chance, who brought Adam here, was it?" he asked.

"Maybe," he replied cheerfully. "I do like to have kids nearby. It makes me feel good."

"*Jesus,*" muttered Gray.

Cressy asked Rodney, "What did you do with him?"

"I didn't do anything with him," he protested. "I have no intention of hurting him. I just wanted to see you again. Just you."

She took a deep breath. "*Right.* So, to see me again, you had to go kidnap a little boy?"

"But not just any boy," he stated. "That's a very special boy. I'm really happy you guys brought me a playmate."

She stared at him. "What did you do to him?"

"I didn't do anything to him," he snapped. "I told you. I don't want to hurt him. He can be very useful for me."

"No, he doesn't need to be useful for you at all," she snapped back. "He needs a chance to live a life on his own."

"We all do," Rodney muttered. "Yet all of us don't get what we want."

"Says you," she replied, glaring at him. "I want Adam back, and I want him back now."

He shrugged. "As I said, I'm not trying to hurt him. I just need a little time with him."

And then she knew what he was doing. "Get out of his mind," she ordered. "Get out of his mind! You don't get to control him."

"What do you mean, *get to control him?*" he asked, still

smiling. "What makes you think that Adam and I didn't know each other from before?"

She stared at him in shock and turned to look at Gray. "You need to find out if that's true," she muttered, releasing Gray's hand so he was free to text and do whatever he needed to do.

"Search is already on," Gray replied. "We're trying to run down everybody in his known world. Particularly now that his aunt's calling the shots on the board."

"She's calling *some* of the shots," Rodney declared, "or, at least, she thinks she is."

At that, Cressy pinched the bridge of her nose. "You're controlling your aunt too, I suppose."

"Partially, at least when she can do things that are help-ful. Otherwise I leave it up to her because she's got a great brain anyway." Rodney chuckled. "There's only so much that she can do. I really need people more like you under my control. My aunt makes my life comfortable, but she can't get me out of here."

"No, not without a doctor's help," Cressy declared. "But what can Adam do?"

"Adam has the ability to do all kinds of things," Rodney replied. "And some of those abilities are very special."

She nodded. "That's what you really want, isn't it? You want to study him. You want to learn how he does what he does."

"I do," Rodney agreed. "I mean, being free of this place is one thing, but having the kind of abilities that Adam and I have? ... That's what makes our lives special," he said menacingly. "I don't want to lose that, but I do want to enhance it."

"So, you'll take over a boy's world, so that you can do

more damage?" she asked cautiously.

"Sure, why not?" Rodney asked. "Do you have any idea how much fun it is to play in this world, to know that people can't stop you, that nobody even understands what you do?"

"And you do? Understand it?"

"You're the one who spent all this time trying to make believe it's a happy place for the people here. Yet you don't even get anything out of it. I mean, they're even trying to squeeze you out of your job here," Rodney snapped, his anger bubbling in his tone. "I needed you to come back. I needed you back here for me."

"Who changed your medications?" she asked, and he just gave her a flat smile. "Goddammit, that was Mendelsohn," she noted, studying Rodney closely. "And then you put him in the hospital, with a heart attack."

"I had to make the place a little easier on me, didn't I?" Rodney explained, with a big fat smirk. "I needed to get you out of hiding, and, if that meant hurting Mendelsohn, then I was okay with it. Besides, he was getting a little flaky anyway, and that flakiness is dangerous. I don't understand why people can't handle this kind of stuff," he stated in frustration. "I mean, if I can handle it, why can't they?"

"Because you're taking over their system, and you're hurting them, and you're not trying to keep them alive. You're just trying to take from them. That wears them down. They're fighting to stay alive and don't understand what's going on in their world. It just becomes this battle that they don't have any power over."

"Exactly," he agreed. "Thanks for explaining that so clearly. It's too bad you brought this friend of yours though. I can see that you really care for him and that just means he'll be on my shit list."

At that, she froze. "Why?"

"You know why," he replied. "You're mine. You're the only person I can talk to this way at all, and nobody else can do anything about it. But you brought him here and that means that you care about him, which means that I hate him."

"No!" She turned to Gray, who was staring at the bed, perplexed. "That's not fair. He didn't do anything to you."

"I don't care if he did anything to me or not. He wants to do things to you that I won't allow," Rodney declared, glaring at her. "So here is a deal for you. He lives, but you have nothing more to do with him, and I get out of here."

She slowly smiled. "You do realize that getting out of here won't help much, right?"

"I figured that, once I'm out of here, you'll come up with some way to heal me. It's one thing to live like this, but I want my body back."

"That's why you want the boy?" she asked Rodney. When he hesitated, she shook her head. "Good God, you're actually wondering how you can transfer into his body, aren't you? That would put you back to being a twelve-year-old boy again."

"But with the brain of an adult," Rodney noted. "So I figured I was probably better off to do that, where I would live in his body, before I became an adult, and could actually take over and live the life I wanted, rather than trying to take over some of these people here, who are already kind of messed up," he explained. "I wasn't the easiest on them, when I was talking to some of them. So sorry about that."

She stared at him. "What the hell have you been up to in the six months that I've been gone?"

"All kinds of shit," he stated cheerfully. "You really

shouldn't have left me."

She stared at him, wondering how she couldn't have known this was going on.

"You *couldn't* have known," he confirmed. "And honestly it took me a long time to come back online." His mood shifted with mercurial speed, and he snapped at her. "I'm so blaming you for that, by the way."

"Oh, so now I'm to blame for that too?" she asked, staring at him in shock. "You have no idea what's going on."

"No, I don't. I want you to walk me out of here though."

At that, she took a deep breath. "Have you even looked at yourself?"

"You know I can't see myself. That was always one of the things I avoided doing."

"I get that," she said, "but I still need to know where Adam is."

"You won't know," he stated. "You won't know at all because I won't tell you."

"If you want me to get you out of here, then you have to tell me." He still hesitated. "What? Are you actually telling me that you can't find anybody else to use for your purposes?" she asked Rodney, taunting him.

"I can't use you," he admitted, "and that's a problem. I wanted to use you, but you're strong. And I'm not sure, but it seems that you're stronger than ever." He glared at her. "How is it that possible? After that blowup, I'm weaker but you're stronger?"

She shrugged. "It's energy karma. I wasn't trying to manipulate people all this time that you've been down, that we've been apart," she explained. "So it makes sense to me, but maybe not to you."

At that, he shook his head. "It doesn't matter. Get me out of here now." Then he got up from the bed and walked toward the door.

Smirking, she realized that he had no clue yet. She looked over at Gray. "Watch out."

He understood and held out a hand. As soon as she connected with him, he nodded. "I can see him," Gray confirmed.

"Yeah, and he's mad. He wants me to take him out of here."

Gray looked at her, startled.

She smiled. "He doesn't know."

"How is it that he doesn't know?" Gray asked in frustration. "He's here, making all kinds of demands and acting as if he's perfectly fine, perfectly normal. Yet nothing is further from the truth."

Beside her, Rodney cried out, "What is he talking about? What is he saying?"

"You can hear him, so you know perfectly well what he's saying."

"Yes, but it doesn't make any sense." Rodney stared at her.

"Then turn around and look at your body," she snapped.

"No, I won't."

"You need to. Then you'll understand the problem."

Slowly, ever-so-slowly Rodney turned and looked at the hospital bed, where his body—shriveled, shrunken, and comatose—was curled up in a fetal position. "No, no, no," he cried out. Then he raced for the door.

"Yes, yes, yes," she corrected. "After that session six months ago, you were given too many drugs, and you've been like this ever since. You're on life support. Your spirit may be free, but you have no physical movement. I can't even take you out of here," she shared. "This is where you're imprisoned."

Rodney stared at her.

She could tell that he was just starting to accept what his reality was, and then he lunged at her, his ghostly arms outstretched, trying to grab her neck. She immediately sidestepped him, releasing her grip on Gray's hand at the same time.

Rodney slammed into the machines that were keeping him alive. The electricity from his energy hit the machines, which then toppled, sparks flying from his contact with them and from the plug knocked out of the socket. Then came a set of sharp spurts, followed by one huge *pop*.

She stepped back in shock and looked over at Gray.

He stared at her and asked, "What the hell was that?"

She asked Gray, "Do you see him?"

"No, I don't. I don't see anything, except some smoke."

She walked over to where Rodney's body was still connected to the machines. She checked for a pulse, then shook her head at Gray. "He's gone."

"Dear God, how was that even possible?"

"I'll say the electricity that he disturbed caused some kind of a backfire, but we've got bigger problems."

"What's that?"

"He's after Adam. I don't know where Adam's gone to or who Rodney coerced to take the boy away, but Adam's missing."

He stared at her and asked, "It was Rodney?"

"It was him," she confirmed. "He was responsible for Dr. Mendelsohn's heart attack, but I'm not sure about everything else."

"Good God," Gray muttered. When his phone rang, he asked her, "Are you safe here?"

"I'm safe."

"I'll just be out in the hallway."

He stepped out of the room to answer the call, and she stared down at the body. She took several photographs and sent them to Stefan, but, as far as she could tell, absolutely no signs of life remained. She opened her senses and could confirm that his body was lifeless. A part of her felt remorse, and another part didn't even want to go there. Cressy left her body to join Sadie, who was still playing outside.

Sadie came running, a big smile on her face.

Cressy asked her, "Did you see little Adam?"

"Yes," and then she frowned again. She looked around nervously. "But that man took him."

"Did you see where they went?" Cressy asked.

She pointed. "Down the hallway."

"Right, okay. I'm trying to find him. If you see him, let me know."

Cressy returned to her body, then walked into the hallway and called out to Gray, "I'm heading down to the front hallway."

"I'm coming, but we don't know where Adam is. We're doing a full floor-to-floor search right now."

"Yeah, we need to do a bit more than that," she replied. "We need to do a heat-seeking search." She pulled out her phone and said, "Stefan."

I know. I hear you, Stefan replied. *Link with me.*

And, with that, she linked with him and could sense Dr. Maddy and several other people in the distant space in the background, but energy flowed through and around her. She said, "I need a direction."

Up, Stefan replied.

She immediately headed for the stairs.

Third floor, Stefan added.

"That's good, only one floor above where I am." She raced out onto the third floor.

There were no orderlies, no nurses; Cressy couldn't believe how slim the staffing was. "How far down?" Then she saw it herself.

A glow of energy came about halfway down the hall. She raced toward it and realized it was one of the lounges. She opened the door and stepped inside, then cried out because the balcony doors were also open. She raced outside and found the golden energy in the corner, with another energy around it. She stepped forward. "Keith?"

At that, Keith turned and looked at her, a big smile on his face. "There you go, Doctor. About time you got here." He held the boy in his arms.

Adam stared at her in terror, but he had a gag around his mouth, and his arms were tied. "Keith, could I have him back please?" she asked gently.

Keith looked down at the boy and frowned. "But I'm supposed to throw him off the balcony," he said in the calmest of voices.

"You were," she replied, "but the orders were changed."

He frowned at her and asked, "They were?"

"They were. Sorry to say, nobody told you about it."

He frowned. "I'm really tired of this place. I have to work overtime constantly, and I never get a break. They cut the pay, and they cut the hours, but they doubled the workload," he snapped.

"I know," she replied. "It's all right though. Now we'll see what we can do about getting you a better job."

He cheered up. "Hey, that would be great."

"But I really need you to put down Adam first. Maybe you'll want to check in with the person who gave you those orders and confirm that it's all okay."

He stared at her and then looked back down at the boy in his arms. "I guess I could. He is getting kind of heavy."

"I think you should give him to me. I'll hold on to him, while you check in."

"Okay, I can do that."

Keith handed Adam to her, whom she held close against her heart, and then quickly passed him off to Gray, who was right behind her. "Keith, sit down for a minute, and let me take a look at you."

"Why is that?" he asked.

"You're bleeding."

He stared at her, then looked down to see blood on his hands. He reached up to his head.

"What happened?" she asked, taking a step toward him.

"I don't know. I must have fallen and hit something, though I'm not usually that clumsy."

"I know," she replied. "It's okay. Don't worry about it. I'll take care of it, okay?"

He smiled at her and said, "Okay."

And, with that, he sat back down on the balcony, closed his eyes, and, almost as quickly as she'd arrived, Keith died right in front of her. She raced forward and checked for a pulse, but there wasn't any. She slowly stood, looked over at Adam, who had tears in his eyes, and she whispered, "You didn't have to kill him."

His eyes widened, and he stared at her.

"Let me take the gag off," Gray said, as he untied Adam's gag.

And Cressy asked, "It wasn't even on very hard, was it?"

"No, it wasn't." Gray stared down at Adam and asked her, "What's going on here?"

"Part of the reason Rodney wanted Adam is because Adam is very talented," she explained to Gray. Turning to Adam, she asked him, "You killed your own family, didn't you, Adam?"

His eyes widened again, and she nodded.

"Your dad? He was beating up you and your mom. Then one night you wanted him to stop so badly that you saw him in your head, being slashed by somebody who was very powerful—coming into the house, killing your family, and rescuing you. Didn't you?"

He silently stared at her in shock.

She nodded. "Later you realized it had happened exactly like your dream."

"How did you know?" he whispered, tears in his eyes. "I didn't mean to do it, and I didn't mean for Mommy to die too."

"I know you didn't." She crouched in front of him. "The thing is, when you're a dream stalker, like I am and like you are, you have to be careful that you don't actually hurt people."

He started to bawl in her arms.

She wrapped him up in her arms and just held him close.

In the meantime, Gray looked at her in shock and muttered, "Please no."

She shrugged. "All I can tell you is that something was happening that was terrifying, and he needed it to stop, and, just like me, when I create dreams or nightmares for people, he created a solution to his problem. That solution is what killed his family."

"Did he actually wield the knives?"

In her arms, Adam shook his head frantically. "No, no, no, I didn't. I didn't."

She held him close and nodded. "In his mind, he did. In his hand, he did not."

Gray closed his eyes, pinching the bridge of his nose. "*Jesus.*"

"I know. I know. Adam only wanted the abuse to stop."

"I didn't know it could happen," Adam whispered, bawling his eyes out. "I didn't know."

Gray looked at her, and she smiled, then hugged Adam gently. "I know that," she whispered. "I know you didn't mean it. I know you didn't even know you could do that. Unfortunately you're one of very few people who can."

GRAY DIDN'T EVEN know what to say. It was a very long night. Stefan had arrived to take charge of Adam, although Stefan didn't have a clue what would happen to the boy, and Stefan had a long talk with Grant about it. They still had a lot of ends to tie up, but it looked as if Rodney had been behind a lot of it, not realizing that his body was as damaged as it was and had needed even more energy, particularly in this case from his aunt, in order to keep functioning the way he was.

When they interviewed the aunt that evening, she had realized Rodney had quite a bit of psychic abilities and had wanted him here close by, so that she could monitor his progress. Plus it was so exciting to her to think that some-body with his physical damages could actually still be alive. But she was under the impression that Rodney's psychic abilities were so minor that he could basically communicate on another level because she kept hearing whispers in her head and wondered if it was him. But she couldn't talk to anybody about it because it was just a little too far out there.

Gray wanted to say a whole lot about it, but, like Grant, he stayed quiet.

As Gray walked out of the center afterward with Grant, he asked his boss, "Do you ever get to talk to anybody about this stuff?"

"When these cases come up, I reach out to Dr. Maddy and Stefan," he replied. "It's different for Drew, since he's married to Dr. Maddy and has immediate access to her and to her knowledge of all this. In your case, if you're lucky, you'll have total access to Cressy."

"Dear God, they must have had very lonely childhoods."

"They had *very* lonely childhoods, very abusive childhoods, and, only because of people like us, can they have somewhat normal lives now," Grant explained. "I know it's already too late for you, but I guess I should have warned you that, once you sign up for something like this, there really is no going back."

And, with that, Grant had led the way to the hotel, where Cressy slept.

Hours later, the guys were still sitting here and talking. Finally Grant said, "I need to head home and get back to my family."

Gray nodded. "Thanks for everything."

"Yeah, well, believe me. You'll need some help, when writing up this report."

Gray groaned at that. "I can't even imagine."

"No, I'm sure you can't." Grant chuckled.

"Wait. Then the little boy—Adam—how could he have

killed his family exactly like *the* annihilator?"

"Because his father had been watching it on the news," Grant said wearily. "And that boy just picked it up and, with such an imagination, it wasn't hard to get it close enough to have us wondering if it was the annihilator."

"But that also means that the annihilator is still out there."

"He is," Grant noted, "and that's unfortunate too because we still have to hunt him down. But there'll always be another annihilator. There'll always be another monster out there. All we can do is take it one day at a time and get them off the streets as soon as we can," he stated. "Then, when you get a chance, rejoice in being alive, healthy, and enjoy life itself." He nudged Gray toward the bedroom. "And remember to love her because, with these people, very little love has been in their lives, and they are as loyal as they come."

Long after his boss had gone, while standing in a hot shower, Gray wondered just what his friend meant and whether it was intended to be a warning about Cressy. When the bathroom door opened, he turned to stare through the streaming water, as she approached him.

"Hey," she said, as she stepped into the shower beside him, completely nude. She wrapped her arms around him and held him close.

He snatched her up into his arms and hugged her tight. "Dear God, all this stuff ..."

"I know. I'm sorry. It's kind of a lot for you to absorb."

He didn't even know what to say because *kind of a lot* said so much, yet absolutely nothing.

"Words are very inadequate when it comes to this," she murmured. "All I can tell you is that, as you come up against it more and more, it will make more sense, or at least you'll recognize some of it again."

He shook his head at that. "This was very disjointed, very confusing," he muttered. "And I ... I don't know that I'll come to terms with it, even in one thousand years." He dropped his head to rest on top of hers, wondering at this woman who was so completely comfortable in her own skin that she could just walk into a shower like that and hold him close—knowing that he was the one in pain, when he was the one assigned to help and protect her. Something was so open and so understanding in her gaze.

"I'm sorry," she began. "Some of this stuff? ... It's just too much, I know."

He didn't even have answers for her, but what he did have was a growing need between them, growing at a rate he could no longer ignore.

When she gently pressed against him, letting him know that she knew perfectly well what was happening, he smiled and asked, "Is this what you do after every bad session?"

"If I had a partner, I would be absolutely delighted to," she murmured, as she kissed him on his chin. "Don't tell me that you haven't figured out this is where we were heading."

"Thinking we might be heading in this direction is very different from knowing," he clarified, "and I don't appear to have your abilities to know this kind of stuff ahead of time. Otherwise I might have come prepared."

"I'm prepared," she replied. "In my business it's just smart to make sure things like that are always taken care of."

"Your business?"

"I just don't want any unpleasant surprises, when I'm dealing with so many patients."

"Right. ... As far as knowing that this is where we were heading? Well, I had an inkling this is where we were heading. Maybe I should rephrase that. I had a *hope* that this is where we were heading."

She looked up at him and tilted her head. "But I do understand if it's not for you."

He shook his head. "I don't understand anything, but what I do know is that I don't want to lose you. The whole thing through this whole deal was trying to keep you safe. And, even now, with all these shocks going on, the bottom line is still *keeping you safe*."

"I appreciate that," she murmured gently, as she kissed him again. "As you can see, I am very safe."

"But not because of me," he noted.

And she laughed. "Stick around. There'll be lots of opportunities for you to be a hero," she declared. "Particularly after what you've seen today."

He groaned. "I'm not sure my heart can handle much more of that."

"That's quite possibly why Dr. Mendelsohn is in the hospital," she murmured. "But you know? There's a good chance I can get Dr. Maddy to give him a shot of energy, and hopefully he'll be just fine."

"God, how many people were affected by this?"

"Lots," she muttered.

"You're thinking it was Keith? That he slashed your tires, that he put the bug in your back room, that he messed with the security cameras, caused the glitches? Oh my, that he knocked you in the head and stuffed you in a one of the big washing machines in the basement?"

"It was Keith."

"How did that work?"

"He was always very suggestible. He used to be a patient there, and he was so lost without that guidance and help. So, once he was cleared to go on day trips and such, he always wanted to just stay there. When he was discharged, he had real trouble adjusting, and, to help with the transition, he was hired to do some janitorial type work because it made him happy and secure to be in that environment."

"So, even though he said that he wanted to move and to be with you, would he have?"

"No, he lived with his elderly parents and worked there. He wouldn't have been able to leave," she said gently. "But I was interested in the list that he gave me of everybody else who he'd had interactions with."

"Who was on that list?"

"Among others, Rodney," she declared. "I had no understanding that Rodney had access to somebody like Keith. He shouldn't have been allowed that close, and that's the problem with a place like this. If they don't understand that they are putting janitors with patients, what with all their budget cuts, they are exposing both of them to harm. Then we get into the energy forces, which we really can't tell them about. Not understanding energy and the forces that these gifted people can actually put onto each other, it's a disaster waiting to happen.

"Keith was very susceptible to suggestion, and, once I realized Rodney was there, and he was on that list, then I knew that Keith was quite likely one of Rodney's pets. Sadly Keith died, but Adam lives and hopefully can be rehabilitated, guided in the right direction to use his gifts for good. So all's well that ends well."

"If you say so," Gray muttered. "I think I lost ten years of my life."

"That might be," she replied, her hands grabbing the bar of soap, as she gently smoothed it over his shoulders and then down to his groin.

He shuddered at her gentle ministrations. "You're playing with fire," he muttered.

"I hope so," she whispered. "The hot water won't last forever."

He burst out laughing, only to have the laughter die on his lips, once her hand slipped around his erection and slowly moved up and down in a motion that had him shuddering in place. "Oh my God," he muttered.

He slid his hands down and reached around to her buttocks, lifted her up against the shower wall, until she was almost head height, and kissed her gently at first, then with a fever that nothing seemed to assuage.

She pulled her head back ever so slightly and said, "We don't have to rush."

"Maybe you don't," he replied, "but I feel an outlet needing to happen, and then maybe all this will make sense."

"I don't know about making sense," she muttered, as she kissed him gently again and again, then started to wiggle against his erection, "but I'm all for an explosion." Then she grinned up at him. "Besides, I think you still owe me some food."

"Great, so you have an appetite for the soul and then what? Food for the stomach."

"Something like that, and, if we sleep together, I'll take that as soothing for my spirit."

He smiled and asked, "How about this?" Then he plunged inside, right to the hilt. She cried out, shuddering in place, and he whispered, "Are you okay? I'm so sorry. Did I hurt you?"

She opened her eyes, and they gleamed in the darkness. "*Shh*. I'm not only fine," she whispered, "I'm absolutely wonderful."

And then, surprising him, she started to ride. Slowly at first, while he widened his stance to hold her up in a better position, then faster and faster. By the time she collapsed into his arms, he had her pinned against the wall and drove in fast, with rapid movements, once, twice, three times, before his own body exploded as well.

When he could, he lifted his head and whispered, "You can come shower with me anytime."

She chuckled. "Good. I'm not planning on going anywhere for the next few days. How about you?"

"Not at all," he murmured. "Although I'm not sure about work."

"*Ugh*, work." She groaned. "I'm not sure about that either. But I do have a couple messages I need to check into."

"Of course we have an active investigation into the center."

"Right, so essentially we have all kinds of stuff to deal with."

"But that's not today's work."

"Nope, not today's," she agreed.

He helped her out of the shower, wrapped up her up in a towel, and, as she went to her phone, he added, "I did hear it ring earlier."

"I did too, but I ignored it." She checked her phone, hearing a message from Stefan's financial contact, saying that he'd found several members of the board all of a sudden wanted to sell their shares, getting rid of their connection to the hospital for good. He believed that something must be going on and wondered if the shares were likely to drop in value soon. He was of the opinion that they could probably pick up a voting majority at a reasonable price, if she was still interested.

She turned, looked at Gray, and gave him a bright smile. "What do you think? Should I take over the board?"

He laughed. "It's definitely where your heart is—or at

least where it was."

"It still is," she stated. "I hope you realize by now that the kind of work I do …"

"I get it," he interrupted, with a simplicity that surprised him. "Nobody else will really understand it except for people like us, but I'm all for it. So, if that's what you want to do, I think you should do it."

She grinned at him. "Good. If you want to order dinner, I'll call him back and tell him, *Hell yes.*"

"Will do." Then, instead of walking away, Gray walked toward her, picked her up, and twirled her around, then gave her a big kiss. "Hold that thought for after dinner."

She watched as he walked away. *Hold that thought* was one thing, but hold that thought with him in her life? Absolutely. She couldn't wait for whatever was coming, and, with joy in her heart, she quickly returned the call, anxious to speak to Stefan's money man.

And by the time she was done explaining all that had happened, he was laughing. "Okay, we'll give it a few days," he said, "but then I can move in for the kill."

"Good. Remember though, some money laundering charges may be coming up in the FBI investigation that could influence things too."

"In that case, the majority shares will be even cheaper. I'm pretty sure that, with any luck, you'll own majority shares yourself."

"That would be lovely," she said. "I would really like to have control over there and get patient care back to where it belongs."

"If need be, I'm happy to be a silent partner to help you make that happen," he offered. "I don't think patient care should be about dollars and cents."

"Oh, I'm really glad to hear that," she replied.

She ended the call, then walked into the kitchen to find Gray staring out the window. She murmured in his ear, "Seems it'll be something we can do."

He turned to her and smiled. "Does that mean you're staying here?"

"I am," she stated, then stared at him. "Are you?"

"Yes," he replied. "I was thinking so, if that's all right with you."

She opened her arms, grateful when they closed around him, as she laid her head on his chest. "I was kind of hoping you might want to stick around and see how things turned out."

His laughter rumbled under her cheek, and he whispered, "Sounds good to me. As long as you're up for a lifetime. Because I think it'll take me that long to figure out any of this."

She leaned backward and looked up at him. "A lifetime sounds perfect for me too." Her voice caught in the back of her throat. "You have no idea how much I've wondered if somebody was out there for me."

"There is," he declared gently. "I just didn't know how to find you."

"Guess what?" she said. "I'm found."

He laughed. "We both are."

He lowered his head and kissed her and promised her, "Forever."

She smiled and added, "On this plane and the next. Forever."

This concludes Book 24 of Psychic Visions: Insanity.
Read a sneak peek Soul Legacy: Psychic Visions, Book 25

Soul Legacy: Psychic Visions (Book #25)

Coming back home to work in the local hospital suits Dr. Cameron Wingford. Buying land from an old woman who'd needed the money cements his plans. Then the old woman's granddaughter returns home, and all the rumors begin— rumors that connect her to some weird event at the hospital every Halloween, an occurrence he had yet to experience, as he'd just moved there in November of last year.

Living on the fringe of society, Danica's strange family was an oddity that everyone in the community either mocked or avoided. She had never felt welcome, especially after being suspected of killing her own mother. She hated returning home. Hated everything about it—except for her grandmother, her last living relative. And now, her dying grandmother's request cannot be ignored. *Keep the property intact.* That meant approaching Dr. Cameron about the piece he'd bought, an act her grandmother regretted ... and an open wound to their legacy.

Open wounds bleed, and, as Danica finds out, this wound can only be healed in one specific way. Even then, a huge sacrifice is required ...

"TONIGHT IS A lovely quiet evening." Dr. Cameron Wingford beamed, as he glanced around the emergency room. This was his first Halloween at this hospital, and he'd expected more craziness than this. But it was a small town, so maybe they would dodge that particular bullet. "How odd for a Halloween night. No one's here."

"Sure, there is," the orderly said, nodding toward the big emergency room door.

Cameron turned to see a blood-covered woman standing on her own, with a shell-shocked look in her eyes.

Two nurses raced to her.

She held out her hands and then slowly, ever-so-slowly, like a cartoon, crumpled to her knees and then to the floor, before the nurses could catch her. Cameron raced to her side, checking for wounds. A moment later, puzzled, he sat back, frowning at his patient, then looked to his nurses, and shook his head. "She doesn't appear to have any open wounds. Let's move her to a bed and do a full workup."

They quickly laid her on a gurney and wheeled her into the next open cubicle. After transferring her to a bed, they did a full workup to see just what was going on.

The patient opened her eyes a few minutes later and stared up at him. She reached up a bloody hand, grabbed his lab coat, and whispered in a pained tone, "Help."

He gave her a reassuring smile. "It's all right. You're in the hospital now. Take it easy. We're trying to figure out what happened. You don't appear to have any injuries, but you're covered in blood."

"Not my blood," she whispered.

He knew that. He could see that. But where had the blood come from?

"My head hurts," she murmured.

"Right. It does appear to have some bruising, but I don't see any open wounds."

"Inside," she whispered. "My head's pounding inside."

"Where's the blood from?" he asked, trying to keep the urgency out of his tone. "Tell me who's injured."

"Accident," she whispered. "There was an accident. She's been hurt."

Cameron frowned and asked the nurse, "Where did she come from? Do we have any idea what kind of accident? Was she alone? Have the police been called?"

Behind him, the other nurse said, "I'll go find out," and she took off.

Cameron looked down at the young woman. "What's your name?"

"Daisy," she whispered. "Daisy. Danica. Daisy. Where's Danica?"

She kept repeating both names, so he tried asking again. "Is your name Daisy?"

She stared up at him. Her eyes grew wider and wider, and then a weird cry erupted from deep inside her throat, like a high-pitched whine. The unholy sound rattled his soul.

He immediately tried to calm her down, and then, without warning, the sound shut off immediately, and she collapsed back onto the bed, unconscious. He immediately ordered a CT scan to see just what was going on with her head, plus an X-ray to confirm any internal injuries they might have missed. The swelling on her head was his main concern. But he needed to know how bad it was and if she had any other injuries he couldn't see.

With her stabilized and barely conscious, he stepped back, as his patient was quickly wheeled out of the room. He looked over at a nurse, standing there, a notepad in her hand, frowning.

"What you find out?" he asked her.

"The police said they received a call of an injured woman covered in blood, walking on the street. They found her. She was alone and barely coherent and was calling out for Danica. They called an ambulance for her, but she disappeared into the trees somehow, and they've been looking for her since. They have no idea how she got here."

He looked for the hospital bed, rolled down to the end of the hallway, waiting for the elevator. "Do they have a name for her? We didn't find any ID on her."

At that, a security guard came in through the emergency double doors and said, "I followed the blood." He took a moment to shake his head. "There's quite a trail all the way back out the parking lot and across the road, before disappearing into the trees."

Cameron had that thought running through his mind, as he added, "So she may have walked here on her own." He stood here, staring down the hallway at the woman who'd now disappeared into the elevator. Something about her was familiar and yet distant. He couldn't quite explain it. Her cry had been unnerving, but the fact that she was completely coated in someone else's blood, with only a slight head wound? Well, that was an odd one for him. He glanced back over at the nurse to see her studying him oddly. "What's the matter?" he asked.

"I don't know," she said hesitantly. "When did you change your lab coat?"

"What do you mean?" He grabbed his coat by the front edges and gave it a shake. "I didn't change my lab coat."

She frowned, glanced at his lab coat again, and then dropped her gaze to the floor.

He looked at his lab coat and at the floor where she was staring and said, "I don't get it. What's wrong?"

"She grabbed your lab coat," the nurse said quietly, her gaze darting to his face and then away. "Remember that bloody hand?"

"I know," he bit off. "Of course I remember. What's that got to do with anything?"

"Your lab coat. … It's clean. As if she never touched it."

His eyebrows shot up, and he quickly took off the lab coat and checked it. He looked back at the nurse to see several other nurses and one of the orderlies walking toward him, all with the same look on their faces. "I didn't change my lab coat," he said in disbelief. "You saw me. I've been here the whole time."

She nodded. "I know, and that's the problem. It *was* bloody after she grabbed it. I don't know what happened. I don't know how it happened, but somehow all that blood … disappeared. And honestly … there ain't nothing good about that at all. Something spooky about that damn girl in the first place," she said, shaking her head. "But right now, that lab coat is seriously … *wrong*."

He laid his coat over the back of his chair, wondering just what was going on. Could they have been mistaken? Maybe the woman had only reached for him? No. He remembered the tug, as she'd grabbed on. He couldn't imagine that none of that blood had transferred. More than a little unnerved, he headed back to write up notes on the case and quickly phoned Radiology to ensure all was well with her scans.

The head of the department, in a testy voice, said, "I don't know what you're talking about. I haven't done any scans in the last hour. ... More like two hours."

"I sent a young woman up for a CT scan."

"Well, I haven't seen her yet." And hung up on him.

Cameron went to Radiology himself to see the CT results firsthand. Yet, when he got up there, he found the place empty. He wandered around and then went in search of the one orderly he'd seen take the stretcher here.

When he finally met up with him, the guy nodded and said, "I took her there, then was called away. Why? Is something wrong?"

"Yes, according to Radiology, they haven't seen her." At that, Cameron summoned security, and they did a sweep, clearing room by room, searching the small hospital. Thirty minutes later, when everybody reported back to Cameron, he had to admit one truth that he was still struggling to realize: *the woman was gone.*

There was no trace of her. A bed was found in the hallway, but no blood was on the sheets. So, if this had been her bed, there was no easy way to prove it. But Cameron couldn't stop staring at the clean sheets, remembering his lab coat ...

The same nurse who had commented on his lab coat spoke up in an eerie tone. "I tell you that girl's nothing but trouble. I don't know who she is, where she came from, but the last thing we need is a ghost around this place."

Startled, he turned and looked at her, and she nodded.

"I know you haven't been here long, Doc, but I've been here since time began, and it's because of incidents like this that I rarely work Halloween night. Something like this has happened before. Almost exactly like this."

Cameron shook his head. "What are you talking about?"

"It started quite a few years ago," she admitted in a low voice. "I would have to look up just how long ago. We had the same case of a young woman coming in, completely bloodstained, and she disappeared from the hospital. She had no visible wounds, also was covered in blood. She was sent for all the same tests, but she disappeared, and nobody ever saw her again."

At that, several of the other staff members spoke up.

"I heard about that."

"Yeah, I did too."

"Do you really think that's the same person. Or ghost rather?"

At the word *ghost*, silence fell around Cameron, as the staff all turned toward him, as if they expected him to have answers.

He was still wrapping his head around the fact that they were missing a patient. "I don't know what is going on now," Cameron said, his hands on his hips, "but I know I was treating a flesh-and-blood woman."

"Sure," the nurse said, looking at him pointedly. "A flesh-and-blood woman who didn't leave any bloodstains on your lab coat."

The other nurse looked at him and whispered, "So what the hell does that mean?"

Cameron had no answers. Who could? All he knew was that the young injured woman had asked for his help, and, before he could do much, she'd disappeared.

He had to find her.

Find Book 25 here!

To find out more visit Dale Mayer's website.

https://geni.us/DMSLegacy

Simon Says...: Kate Morgan (Book #1)

Welcome to a new thriller series from *USA Today* Best-Selling Author Dale Mayer. Set in Vancouver, BC, the team of Detective Kate Morgan and Simon St. Laurant, an unwilling psychic, marries all the elements of Dale's work that you've come to love, plus so much more.

Detective Kate Morgan, newly promoted to the Vancouver PD Homicide Department, stands for the victims in her world. She was once a victim herself, just as her mother had been a victim, and then her brother—an unsolved missing child's case—was yet another victim. She can't stand those who take advantage of others, and the worst ones are those who prey on the hopes of desperate people to line their own pockets.

So, when she finds a connection between more than a half-dozen cold cases to a current case, where a child's life hangs in the balance, Kate would make a deal with the devil himself to find the culprit and to save the child.

Simon St. Laurant's grandmother had the Sight and had warned him that, once he used it, he could never walk away. Until now, her caution had made it easy to avoid that first step. But, when nightmares of his own past are triggered, Simon can't stand back and watch child after child be abused. Not without offering his help to those chasing the monsters.

Even if it means dealing with the cranky and critical Detective Kate Morgan …

Find Simon Says… Hide here!
To find out more visit Dale Mayer's website.
https://geni.us/DMSSHideUniversal

Author's Note

Thank you for reading Insanity: Psychic Visions, Book 24! If you enjoyed the book, please take a moment and leave a short review.

Dear reader,

I love to hear from readers, and you can contact me at my website: www.dalemayer.com or at my Facebook author page. To be informed of new releases and special offers, sign up for my newsletter or follow me on BookBub. And if you are interested in joining Dale Mayer's Reader Group, here is the Facebook sign up page.
http://geni.us/DaleMayerFBGroup

Cheers,
Dale Mayer

About the Author

Dale Mayer is a *USA Today* best-selling author, best known for her SEALs military romances, her Psychic Visions series, and her Lovely Lethal Garden cozy series. Her contemporary romances are raw and full of passion and emotion (Broken But ... Mending, Hathaway House series). Her thrillers will keep you guessing (Kate Morgan, By Death series), and her romantic comedies will keep you giggling (*It's a Dog's Life*, a stand-alone novella; and the Broken Protocols series, starring Charming Marvin, the cat).

Dale honors the stories that come to her—and some of them are crazy, break all the rules and cross multiple genres!

To go with her fiction, she also writes nonfiction in many different fields, with books available on résumé writing, companion gardening, and the US mortgage system. All her books are available in print and ebook format.

Connect with Dale Mayer Online

Dale's Website – www.dalemayer.com
Twitter – @DaleMayer
Facebook Page – geni.us/DaleMayerFBFanPage
Facebook Group – geni.us/DaleMayerFBGroup
BookBub – geni.us/DaleMayerBookbub
Instagram – geni.us/DaleMayerInstagram
Goodreads – geni.us/DaleMayerGoodreads
Newsletter – geni.us/DaleNews

Also by Dale Mayer

Published Adult Books:

Shadow Recon
Magnus, Book 1
Rogan, Book 2
Egan, Book 3
Barret, Book 4
Whalen, Book 5
Nikolai, Book 6
Teegan, Book 7

Bullard's Battle
Ryland's Reach, Book 1
Cain's Cross, Book 2
Eton's Escape, Book 3
Garret's Gambit, Book 4
Kano's Keep, Book 5
Fallon's Flaw, Book 6
Quinn's Quest, Book 7
Bullard's Beauty, Book 8
Bullard's Best, Book 9
Bullard's Battle, Books 1–2
Bullard's Battle, Books 3–4

Bullard's Battle, Books 5–6
Bullard's Battle, Books 7–8

Terkel's Team
Damon's Deal, Book 1
Wade's War, Book 2
Gage's Goal, Book 3
Calum's Contact, Book 4
Rick's Road, Book 5
Scott's Summit, Book 6
Brody's Beast, Book 7
Terkel's Twist, Book 8
Terkel's Triumph, Book 9

Terk's Guardians
Radar, Book 1
Legend, Book 2
Bojan, Book 3
Langdon, Book 4

Kate Morgan
Simon Says… Hide, Book 1
Simon Says… Jump, Book 2
Simon Says… Ride, Book 3
Simon Says… Scream, Book 4
Simon Says… Run, Book 5
Simon Says… Walk, Book 6
Simon Says… Forgive, Book 7
Simon Says… Swim, Book 8

Hathaway House

The K9 Files

Lovely Lethal Gardens

Lovely Lethal Gardens, Books 7–8
Lovely Lethal Gardens, Books 9–10

Psychic Visions Series

Tuesday's Child
Hide 'n Go Seek
Maddy's Floor
Garden of Sorrow
Knock Knock...
Rare Find
Eyes to the Soul
Now You See Her
Shattered
Into the Abyss
Seeds of Malice
Eye of the Falcon
Itsy-Bitsy Spider
Unmasked
Deep Beneath
From the Ashes
Stroke of Death
Ice Maiden
Snap, Crackle...
What If...
Talking Bones
String of Tears
Inked Forever
Insanity
Soul Legacy

Biker Blues

Morgan: Biker Blues, Volume 1

Cash: Biker Blues, Volume 2

SEALs of Honor

Mason: SEALs of Honor, Book 1

Hawk: SEALs of Honor, Book 2

Dane: SEALs of Honor, Book 3

Swede: SEALs of Honor, Book 4

Shadow: SEALs of Honor, Book 5

Cooper: SEALs of Honor, Book 6

Markus: SEALs of Honor, Book 7

Evan: SEALs of Honor, Book 8

Mason's Wish: SEALs of Honor, Book 9

Chase: SEALs of Honor, Book 10

Brett: SEALs of Honor, Book 11

Devlin: SEALs of Honor, Book 12

Easton: SEALs of Honor, Book 13

Ryder: SEALs of Honor, Book 14

Macklin: SEALs of Honor, Book 15

Corey: SEALs of Honor, Book 16

Warrick: SEALs of Honor, Book 17

Tanner: SEALs of Honor, Book 18

Jackson: SEALs of Honor, Book 19

Kanen: SEALs of Honor, Book 20

Nelson: SEALs of Honor, Book 21

Taylor: SEALs of Honor, Book 22

Colton: SEALs of Honor, Book 23

Troy: SEALs of Honor, Book 24

Heroes for Hire

SEALs of Steel

The Mavericks

The Mavericks, Books 1–2

The Mavericks, Books 3–4

The Mavericks, Books 5–6

The Mavericks, Books 7–8

The Mavericks, Books 9–10

The Mavericks, Books 11–12

Standalone Novellas

It's a Dog's Life

Riana's Revenge

Second Chances

Published Young Adult Books:

Family Blood Ties Series

Vampire in Denial

Vampire in Distress

Vampire in Design

Vampire in Deceit

Vampire in Defiance

Vampire in Conflict

Vampire in Chaos

Vampire in Crisis

Vampire in Control

Vampire in Charge

Family Blood Ties Set 1–3

Family Blood Ties Set 1–5

Family Blood Ties Set 4–6

Family Blood Ties Set 7–9

Sian's Solution, A Family Blood Ties Series Prequel
Novelette

Design series
Dangerous Designs
Deadly Designs
Darkest Designs
Design Series Trilogy

Standalone
In Cassie's Corner
Gem Stone (a Gemma Stone Mystery)
Time Thieves

Published Non-Fiction Books:

Career Essentials
Career Essentials: The Résumé
Career Essentials: The Cover Letter
Career Essentials: The Interview
Career Essentials: 3 in 1

Printed in the USA
CPSIA information can be obtained
at www.ICGtesting.com
LVHW011926200124
769095LV00014B/512

9 781778 862878